sold
on a
monday

a novel

KRISTINA McMORRIS

Praise for *Sold on a Monday*

"In *Sold on a Monday*, Kristina McMorris has written a vivid and original story... McMorris brilliantly chronicles the way in which a moment's fateful choice can result in a lifetime of harrowing consequences. A masterpiece that poignantly echoes universal themes of loss and redemption, *Sold on a Monday* is both heartfelt and heartbreaking."

—Pam Jenoff, *New York Times* bestselling author of
The Orphan's Tale

"*Sold on a Monday* is a stunningly moving novel that takes on the Great Depression and one man's struggle with honor, ambition, and unimaginable sacrifice. Kristina McMorris has crafted a true page-turner that you won't want to miss."

—Laura Spinella, bestselling author of
Ghost Gifts and *Echo Moon*

"With her signature style, Kristina McMorris once again plucks a devastating heartstring... A real-life photograph stands as evidence to the heart of this novel: truth revealed, forgiveness found, and a story never to be forgotten."

—Sarah McCoy, *New York Times* and
international bestselling author of *Marilla
of Green Gables* and *The Baker's Daughter*

"McMorris shines in this poignant and compulsively readable novel about how one reporter's seemingly small mistake in judgment leads to utter catastrophe for children caught in the jaws of the Great Depression. Based upon a haunting historical photograph, and told with finesse and compassion, this story will linger long after the pages have all been turned."

—Stephanie Dray, *New York Times* bestselling author of
America's First Daughter and *My Dear Hamilton*

Also by Kristina McMorris

The Edge of Lost

The Pieces We Keep

Bridge of Scarlet Leaves

Letters from Home

sold
on a
monday

a novel

KRISTINA McMORRIS

sourcebooks
landmark

Published by Sourcebooks Landmark, an imprint of Sourcebooks, Inc.
P.O. Box 4410, Naperville, Illinois 60563-4410
(630) 961-3900
Fax: (630) 961-2168
sourcebooks.com

Library of Congress Cataloging-in-Publication Data

Names: McMorris, Kristina, author.
Title: Sold on a Monday / Kristina McMorris.
Description: Naperville, Illinois : Sourcebooks Landmark, [2018]
Identifiers: LCCN 2017061403 | (softcover : acid-free paper)
Classification: LCC PS3613.C585453 S65 2018 | DDC 813/.6--dc23 LC record
   available at https://lccn.loc.gov/2017061403

Printed and bound in the United States of America.
VP 15

For the children in the picture

"A thousand words will not leave so deep an impression as one deed."

—Henrik Ibsen

PROLOGUE

OUTSIDE THE GUARDED ENTRANCE, reporters circled like a pack of wolves. They wanted names and locations, any links to the Mob, every newsworthy detail for tomorrow's front page.

The irony wasn't lost on me.

In the hospital waiting area, on the same chair for hours, I raised my head when a doctor appeared. He spoke to a nurse in a hushed tone. His full mustache, peppered like his temples, vibrated with his words. My shoulders coiled into springs as I searched for a look, a suggestion of the worst. Tension heightened around me from others fearing the same. The sudden quiet was deafening. But then the doctor resumed his strides, his footfalls fading around the corner. Once more I sank into my seat.

The air reeked of disinfectant, bleach, and the cigarettes of nervous smokers. From the tiled floor came a shrill scrape, a chair being dragged in my direction. Tiny hairs rose on the back of my neck from more than the sound. Upon learning of my involvement, an officer had warned me a detective would soon be here to talk.

That man now sat down to face me.

"Good afternoon." He removed his brimmed hat, an act of casualness, and rested it on his lap. From his pin-striped suit and tidy haircut to his perfect white teeth, he was a recruitment poster for J. Edgar Hoover.

I didn't catch his name or the formalities of his introduction—my mind was muddled from waves of worry and lack of sleep. But I could guess what information he wanted. No different from the journalists amassing on the street, ever eager to pry. Hungry for answers I hadn't fully grasped.

If only I could escape—from this place and moment in time. How nice it would be to leap forward by a week, a month. The unseemly rumors would have long been buried, the puddles of blood mopped clean, the outcome of this day endured. I envisioned myself then in a dim corner of a café, being interviewed by a young reporter over coffee. His fresh-faced zeal would remind me of the person I once was, back when I first moved to the city, convinced that aspiration and success would crowd out the darkness of my past. The sense of not being worthy.

"What a relief," he would say, "that everything turned out fine."

For some, of course. Not all.

Then I heard "Can you tell me how it all started?" The reporter in my head blended with the detective before me. I wasn't entirely sure which of them had asked. And yet, as if through a lens, I suddenly viewed the past year with astounding clarity, saw the interwoven paths that had delivered each of us here. Every step a domino essential to knocking over the next.

With no small amount of regret, I nodded at him slowly, remembering as I replied.

"It started with a picture."

PART ONE

"Photography is the art of observation. It
has little to do with the things you see and
everything to do with the way you see them."

—Elliott Erwitt

CHAPTER 1

August 1931
Laurel Township, Pennsylvania

IT WAS THEIR EYES that first drew Ellis in.

Seated on the front porch of a weathered gray farmhouse, among the few homes lining the road surrounded by hayfields, two boys were pitching pebbles at a tin can. Ages six and eight at most, they wore no shoes or shirts. Only patched overalls exposing much of their fair skin tinted by grime and summer sun. The two had to be brothers. With their lean frames and scraggly copper hair, they looked like the same kid at different stages of life.

And then there were their eyes. From as far as twenty feet away, they grabbed hold of Ellis Reed. They were blue, like his own, but a shade so light they could have been cut from crystal. A striking find against the blandest of settings, as if they didn't quite belong.

Another drop of sweat slid from Ellis's fedora, down his neck, and into his starched collar. Even without his suit jacket, his whole shirt clung from the damn humidity. He moved closer to the house and raised his camera. Natural scenic shots were his usual hobby, but he adjusted the lens to bring the kids into focus. With them came a sign. A raw, wooden slat with jagged edges, it bowed slightly against the porch, as if reclining under the weight of the afternoon heat. The offer it bore, scrawled in chalk, didn't fully register until Ellis snapped the photo.

A breath caught in his throat.

He lowered the camera and reread the words.

Really, they shouldn't have shocked him. Not with so many folks still reeling since the market crashed in '29. Every day, children were being farmed out to relatives or dropped off at churches, orphanages, and the like, hoping to keep them warm and fed. But selling them—this added an even darker layer to dire times.

Were there other siblings being spared? Would the brothers be separated? Could they even read the sign? Ellis's mind whirled with questions, all lacking presumptions he would have once made.

Even, say, six years ago—at barely twenty and living in Allentown under his parents' roof—he might have been quicker to judge. But the streets of Philly had since taught him that few things make a person more desperate than the need to eat. Want proof? Sit back and watch the punches fly at just about any breadline when the last of the day's soup is ladled out.

"Whatcha got there, mister?" The older of the boys was pointing toward the small contraption in Ellis's hand.

"This? Just my camera."

Actually, that wasn't altogether true. It belonged to the *Philadelphia Examiner*. But given the situation, clarifying seemed unimportant.

The small kid whispered to the older one, who addressed Ellis again as if translating for his brother. "That your job? Makin' pictures?"

Fact was, Ellis's job of covering fluff for the Society page didn't amount to much else. Not exactly the hard-nosed reporting he'd envisioned for his career. A gopher could do the same work.

"For now."

The older boy nodded and tossed another pebble at the can. His kid brother chewed on his dry bottom lip with an air of innocence that matched his eyes. They showed no hint of knowing what life held in store. Probably a good thing.

While children who were adopted as babies were often raised as real family, it was no secret how kids acquired at older ages were valued. The girls as nannies, seamstresses, maids. The boys as farm and field hands, future workers at the factories and mines. Maybe, though, it wasn't too late for these two. At least, not with some help.

Ellis peered at the front windows of the house, searching for movement beyond the smudges. He strained to catch the clinking of pots or a whiff of boiling stew, any indication of a mother being home. But only the distant groan of a tractor and the earthy smell of farmland drifted in the air. And through it all came thoughts of reason.

What could he possibly do for these two? Convince their folks there had to be a better way? Contribute a whole dollar when he could scarcely afford his own rent?

Both brothers were staring at him, as if waiting for him to speak.

Ellis averted his attention from the sign. He scoured his brain for words with real meaning. In the end, he came up empty.

"You boys take care of yourselves."

At their silence, he reluctantly turned away. The plinking of rocks on the rusted can resumed and then faded as he retreated down the country road.

Fifty yards ahead, the Model T he'd originally salvaged from a junkyard waited with windows open. Its radiator was no longer hissing and steaming. Somehow its surroundings, too, had changed. The sprawling acres, the crooked fencing—only minutes ago Ellis had found them interesting enough to photograph for his personal collection. A decent way to pass time while his engine cooled from the August heat. Now they were mere backdrops to another tragedy beyond his control.

As soon as he reached his old clunker, he tossed the camera inside, a little harder than he should have, and retrieved his jug of water. He refilled the radiator and prepared the motor by adjusting the levers and turning the key. Back at the hood, he gripped the fender for leverage and gave the crank a hearty jerk. Thankfully, a second attempt revived the sedan.

Once behind the steering wheel, he chucked off his hat and started on his way, more anxious than ever to return to the city. In less than an hour, he'd be in a whole different world. Laurel Township would be a speck of a memory.

Spread over his heaped jacket beside him, his map flapped against air breezing through the car. Just this morning, that wrinkled page, penciled with notes and circled destinations, had guided him to his latest rousing assignment: a quilting exhibition by a ladies' auxiliary of the American Legion, headed by the sister of Philly's mayor. No doubt much of the needlework was impressive, but Ellis had grumbled with every click of the shutter. The fact that it was Sunday had further soured his mood, as he still needed to develop the photos and draft the article for his deadline tomorrow morning. So much for a day off. Yet now, humbled by that pair of boys, he felt ashamed of grousing over a job many would envy.

Though Ellis tried to push the kids from his mind, they circled back again and again as he rattled down the highway and out of Chester County. Still, not until he approached the *Examiner*'s building did he note the real reason they'd resonated so deeply.

If Ellis's brother had survived, he wondered, would they have looked just as similar? Would they both have been wanted?

CHAPTER 2

ARRIVING AT HER DESK, cloche hat still on and purse in hand, Lily cringed at what she had done.

Or had not done, rather.

On Friday afternoon, a labor reporter had been waiting for his photographs to dry, despite looking miserable from a cold. Lily's boss, Howard Trimble—an editor in chief who ran the paper with all the rigidity of a commander preparing for battle—had demanded to review the images first thing come Monday. Since the reporter would be away on a story then, Lily volunteered to help. *I'll turn in the photos*, she had promised. *You go home and rest.*

She wasn't one to make promises lightly, yet in the whirlwind of other tasks, she had forgotten. Now it was Monday morning—a quarter to eight. Fifteen minutes until the chief's regular arrival.

Lily tossed her handbag aside and hastened across the half-filled newsroom. Mumbled conversations traveled across the desks, each butted up against the next. In a regular changing of the guard, the *Examiner*'s daytime staff was edging out the remnants of the night crew.

Beside the elevator, she climbed the stairs—a faster route when ascending a single floor—and emerged in the composing room on the fourth level.

"Morning, Miss Palmer." A young, long-limbed fellow stood to her right with an armful of files. The name of the new hire escaped her.

She responded with a smile, only slowing when he pressed on.

"Supposed to be another sweltering week ahead."

"Apparently so."

"You do anything over the weekend?"

She had made the two-hour trek to northern Delaware as usual—to her real home. Not the ladies' boardinghouse nearby where she resided during the workweek. But the purpose of those trips, like so much else in her life, was not something she could share.

"I'm afraid I'm in a hurry at the moment, but enjoy your day." With another smile, she proceeded past him to reach the door in the corner. Fortunately unlocked, it led her into the pass-through. The sign on the second door—*Do not disturb*—was flipped backward, indicating that the darkroom was not in use and safe to enter.

Inside, a thin chain dangled from a light bulb overhead. She gave it a tug, illuminating the small, rectangular space with an eerie red glow. The air smelled of developing solutions that filled an assortment of trays, set among supplies on the counter lining a wall.

More than a dozen photographs hung from a wire that stretched the length of the room. Toward the end, just past shots of women proudly displaying quilts, Lily spotted the three pictures she had come for. Scenes from a steelworkers' union meeting.

She quickly retrieved an empty folder from the counter and unclipped the trio of photos. She had just finished storing them when a sight pulled her gaze. It was a simple picture of a tree—unless a person looked closer. The old oak stood in a field, alone, almost sad. Its branches reached forward as if longing for something unseen.

She surveyed the next image, of initials carved into a splintered fence.

K.T. + A.\

The last letter was unfinished, leaving strangers to imagine its intended shape. And more than that, its story. She moved on to another picture, then another. A discarded bottle cap pressed into a road. A single flower standing tall in a patch of dry weeds. From the way each photo conveyed a tale, she knew who had captured them.

Since starting as the chief's secretary the spring before last, Lily had stumbled upon Ellis Reed's personal photographs on two other occasions. Every image bore an intriguing perspective, a depth of detail that most would have missed.

Although few men in the business were willing to write for the women's pages, or settle for the pay, Ellis persisted with diligence. Like Lily, he had clearly been relegated to a job that bypassed his true talents. She never made mention of this, of course, as their periodic exchanges rarely surpassed basic cordialness...

The thought fell away as she turned.

Amid the red haze hung a photo of a sign. Two children on a porch were being offered for sale. Like cattle at market.

All at once, a tide of emotion rushed through her, unearthing old sediments she had worked to bury. The fear, the pain, the regrets. Nonetheless, she couldn't look away. In fact, even as moisture clouded her eyes, she pulled the picture from its clips for a closer view.

A flash of light jolted her.

The door had opened and immediately shut.

"Sorry!" a man called out. "It wasn't locked, and the sign's not flipped."

Lily recalled her mission. "Be right out!"

She collected herself, as best as she possibly could, and started for the door. As she reached for the knob, it occurred to her that Ellis's photograph remained in her hand.

A dark part of her wanted nothing more than to shred and burn the copy, along with the negative. But an internal voice supplied another idea. She could make something good out of the utterly horrible. She could bring children too easily forgotten to the foreground, a reminder that each of them mattered. A hard-won lesson from her past.

Without another glance, she added the picture to her folder and opened the door.

CHAPTER 3

THROUGH THE LUMPY MATTRESS, the bedsprings voiced a throaty creak.

Ellis tugged the pillow off his head and squinted against sunlight pouring through his window. He'd left it open to relieve the heat. City noises and the stench of fumes and sewage made for an unfortunate trade-off. He rolled toward his two-bell tin clock on the night table that doubled as a desk, blinking hard to clear his vision.

A quarter after ten. Fifteen minutes past deadline.

Shit. He must have shut off the alarm in his sleep. It was no wonder, what with the bickering couple upstairs keeping him awake half the night.

He clambered to rise, his sheet already pooled on the rough wooden floor, and cursed his urge to piss, requiring time he didn't have. In a few steps he reached the door—the lone benefit of an apartment the size of a broom closet—and joined the line for the bathroom, stretched halfway down the hall. Another downside of the nation's massive unemployment. Two years ago at this hour on a workday, hardly anyone but mothers, tots, and the elderly would have been home.

"Come on, already," he muttered. A scuttling mouse was the only one who budged.

In front of Ellis, a trio of middle-aged women ceased their conversation. Their pointed glares delivered a revelation: he had nothing on but his drawers.

"Jesus. Sorry." He reflexively covered himself. Though his average build had gained decent muscle through the years, in that moment, he reverted to the puny kid he'd been before puberty ran its course. A moderate stickball hitter with no hope of making the majors, a track runner whose confidence, and thus speed, always left him a few paces shy of a trophy.

On the upside, the need to relieve himself had subsided. Enough to wait anyhow. He hightailed it back to his flat, the women's gripes over his indecency and language echoing down the hall. At his washbasin, he splashed his head and body with day-old water, then threw on his laundered work clothes from the rope that halved the room. Shoving his article into his worn leather satchel, cradled like a football due to its missing handle, he dashed out the door. Someday he'd commute in style, not fretting over the price of gasoline. Until then, he'd sprint to catch the teeming trolley.

On board, passengers fanned themselves with folded newspapers or brims of their hats. Ellis noticed he'd forgotten not only his fedora, but also to tame his hair with tonic. The black waves were a short yet unruly bunch. Another reason to avoid a grand entrance today.

The rails squeaked and the bell clanged as the streetcar rolled on, slow enough to catch headlines shouted by paperboys.

"Lindberghs landing in Japan!"

"Young bandit slain, detective shot!"

"Runaway bride reunites with groom!"

Through the lingering haze—from mills and factories that

coughed and sputtered, straining to stay alive—City Hall came into view. Limestone and granite formed the majestic building. Atop its clock tower, a bronzed William Penn scowled over the unacceptable hour.

Ellis hopped off at his stop, barely avoiding a horse-drawn truck. He hustled down Market Street, weaving his way through pushcart peddlers and shoe shiners. He didn't slow until he'd entered the stony, five-story home of the *Examiner*. It was no *Evening Bulletin*, but with more than twenty years under its belt, it was still a respectable contender for nightly readership.

After a quick visit to the closest bathroom, Ellis boarded the elevator, joining two men from the proofing room. "Third floor," Ellis said.

The stooped lift operator completed his yawn before initiating the ascent, and the proofers rambled about dames they'd met the night before, a couple of shopgirls at Wanamaker's. The operator opened the door a foot above the third floor—more often it was a foot below, remarkably never level—inviting in the sharp scents of coffee and ink and a sea of cigarette smoke.

Ellis stepped down into the city room, the nerve center of the paper. In the middle of the desk-filled maze, editors of the four major departments were rigorously working in their seats. Thankfully, no sign of his direct boss, the managing editor, Lou Baylor. The stout man's bald head, often flushed from stress, made him easy to spot. Closer to deadline, he became a jittery ball of red.

Ellis slid right into the midmorning din. Rising chatter, from both the staff and portable radios, competed with trilling phones and clacking typewriters. Copy boys zipped about, everyone playing catch-up from the weekend. A perpetual race with no ultimate finish line.

A few strides from his desk, Ellis felt a tug on his elbow. He swung around to find Lily Palmer, a coffee mug in her grip.

"Goodness, Mr. Reed. Where have you been?"

"I…just… My alarm. It didn't ring."

The gal was a beauty, though not in the typical Jean Harlow way. She wore her auburn hair neatly pinned up. And her nose, slender like her lips, was dusted with light freckles. Today, though, he noticed her eyes the most. Not for their green-and-copper coloring but for their spark of urgency.

"Chief's been asking for you. You'd best get in there."

Ellis scanned the wall-mounted clocks spanning four time zones. The local hour read 10:42. Had word of his gaffe already gone all the way to Trimble?

At most papers of this size, the editor in chief would leave the managing editor to wade through the daily weeds. But as the oldest son of the retired founder, Howard Trimble rarely encountered an issue too minor to address, particularly when it warranted reproach.

Ellis dreaded one of those searing rants now. "Sure. Just need a minute to put my things—"

From the chief's office in the far corner came a bellow. "Can I get some coffee here, or do I gotta do *everything* myself? And where the hell's Reed?" Trimble's door was only half-open, but he could likely be heard all the way to the basement, where even the printing presses would be challenged to drown him out.

Lily sighed and arched a brow. "Shall we?"

Ellis nodded—as if given a choice.

Together, they made their way across the room, past lines of desks bookended by pillars of newsprint. In her low heels and straight black skirt, Lily walked without speaking. Ever graceful yet on the primmer side, she was never one to make idle conversation, though her silence now seemed daunting.

And then came the glance, an odd look. Maybe she knew something he didn't.

"What is it?"

"Mmm? Oh...nothing."

"Miss Palmer." Ellis stopped her a couple yards from the door, where she hesitated.

"You…look like you had a rough night is all."

He suddenly saw himself for the mess he'd become—face unshaven, mop unkempt, suit slapped together. Dapper as a hobo from an alley.

At least he had on more than his drawers. He shrugged a little. "Undercover story," he offered.

She smiled, the joke of it sadly obvious. Then her lips lowered as she turned for her boss's office. Ellis smoothed his hair, spiked and still damp, and followed her inside.

On the low file cabinet by the open window, the blades of a mechanical fan ticked with every rotation.

"It's about damn time," the chief barked from his seat. A tad round in the middle, he was rarely seen without a bow tie and spectacles on the edge of his nose. With eyebrows as thick as his beard, he resembled a kindhearted grandfather—until he opened his mouth.

Ellis perched on the visitor's chair. He propped his satchel against his shin, anchored for a tornado. As usual, the desk before him appeared to have been hit by exactly that. Letters, folders, scraps of notes. Memos, circulars, clippings. The mound was almost thick enough to bury a body.

A former writer's, for instance.

"Don't forget about your eleven o'clock," Lily was saying to the chief, handing off the mug. "Also, your wife phoned. She wants to know where you two are having dinner on Friday."

The chief halted midsip. "Christ. I forgot to make reservations."

"In that case, I'll tell Mrs. Trimble it's the Carriage House. They can seat you at seven." Lily didn't miss a thing. "I'll let the maître d' know it's your anniversary so they'll have flowers and something…special for the occasion."

The reference to alcohol was only lightly veiled, as it wasn't unusual to trade a generous tip for wine or champagne at even top-notch restaurants. For all its good intentions, Prohibition had swelled not only the public's desire to drink, but also corruption by mobsters now living the high life. A full week didn't pass without a headline about the likes of Max "Boo Boo" Hoff or Mickey Duffy or the Nig Rosen gang.

"Well then...good." The chief's tone actually bordered on pleasantness. But a moment later, he waved Lily away, and his hard gaze angled to Ellis.

"So," he said. "Reed."

Ellis straightened in his seat. "Yeah, Chief."

As Lily passed, her eyes seemed to say *Good luck*. Then she swung the door closed, rattling the glass pane, and the chief set down his coffee with a small splash. "Apparently, you've been taking some *interesting* pictures."

Thrown off, Ellis struggled with the implication. "Sir?"

"How 'bout you explain this." From a folder, the chief tossed a photograph onto the desk. It was of the boys on the porch, their gut-wrenching sign propped out front. The chief must have seen the other photos too. As the matter became clear, a weight dropped to the pit of Ellis's stomach.

"Chief, these were just... I had to kill time after the Auxiliary event. It was hot out there, and my engine..."

There was no reason to go on. Nothing was going to justify using a camera and film owned by the paper to take personal pictures, only to develop them with company supplies.

The chief leaned back and thrummed his fingers on the armrest of his chair, either contemplating or gearing up. It seemed best for Ellis to stay quiet.

"You've been working here...what, four years now?"

"Five."

A technicality. Ellis winced at the unwise correction, but then his own words sank in.

Five years wasn't eternity, though still a respectable chunk of time. After first toiling away in the morgue—an apt nickname for the windowless, dust-ridden archives room—fittingly followed by a stint of punching out obituaries, Ellis had pleaded for a promotion. *I'll cover anything*, he'd said. As timing would have it, one of the paper's two Society writers had just quit after getting hitched.

Ellis had pushed his male ego aside. The job was a bridge. Plus, it helped to know he'd be reporting directly to Mr. Baylor, who'd been picking up the slack since the Society editor left to care for her mother. Howard Trimble was never a bigger fan of efficiency than when it cinched the paper's purse.

That was two years ago. Despite subsequent requests for a shot at real news, Ellis was no higher in the chain. Mercifully, most assignments that required detailed descriptions of cake and chiffon belonged to his matronly Society colleague. But that still left Ellis with an endless series of gallery exhibitions and uppity galas, occasional celebrity sightings, and—his personal favorite— charitable fundraisers hosted by elites who ignored street beggars every day while strolling to shop at Gimbels.

If anyone deserved to gripe, it was Ellis.

He raised his chin, bolstered by pride. "That's right, it's been five years. And all the while, I've put in a hundred percent. Working near every weekend at any event I'm assigned. Never complained once. So, if you're hitting me with a reprimand, or want to can me over a few lousy pictures, you go right ahead."

Logic fought to rein him in; it was hardly a good time to be out of work, and Lord knew he'd never crawl back to his father for help paying the rent. But the hell with it.

There was no emotion in the chief's face. "You done?"

Ellis fended off any inkling of regret and issued a nod.

"Splendid." The man's tone remained level but taut. Like a wire that reverberated with every syllable. "'Cause the reason I'd called you in here was about writing a feature. A family profile to go with this photo of yours. If that isn't too much trouble."

The ticking fan seemed to suck all the air from the room.

Ellis forced a swallow and resisted the urge to loosen his

collar. Humility shrank him to the size of a jockey. Switching gears, he attempted to act natural. Deliberate. Less like a jackass.

"Sure thing, sir. Swell idea. I'll get right on it."

The chief said nothing.

Ellis jumped to his feet and grabbed his satchel, almost forgetting the photograph, and turned to leave before the offer was quashed. He barely made it through the door when a smile overtook his face. All the banal pieces and hollow events, the years of patience and fortitude—they'd finally proven worthwhile. Or could, rather.

Through the bedlam, he marched toward his desk, bridling his enthusiasm. No feature was guaranteed. The actual piece would still require approval. Everything about it had to be stellar. Strong quotes, pointed observations, all of it supported by facts. He was already planning his drive to the farmhouse when he reviewed the picture. The two brothers, helpless and scruffy, stared with their crystalline eyes.

Ellis's feet slowed as the scene came back.

The idea of interviewing those boys, or even their parents… Something about it felt wrong.

He tried to bat away the notion—reporters like Clayton Brauer wouldn't hesitate to charge after a good scoop—but the truth clung to Ellis: these weren't politicians or movie stars or anyone else who'd invited the spotlight, people fully prepared for widespread judgment. And that judgment could be loud and critical, to put it mildly, should an ugly truth belie the family's plight. Say, if the father was a drunk who'd gambled away the rent, or the mother had simply tired of her burdens. Depending on the story, the kids could suffer the most.

Ellis preferred not to take that chance. He just needed an alternate tack, free of harmful particulars. But he needed it soon. Wait too long and the chief's interest would wither, along with the offer.

Ellis checked the clock. There was still time before the chief's next appointment, though not much. Before second thoughts could take hold, he strode back to the corner office. He formed an appeal as he went, acutely aware of the risks.

The chief's attention had moved to a pile of paperwork. He spared the quickest of glances at Ellis, who eased in with a disclaimer. "You know, Chief, there's just one wrinkle. See, I'm not so sure this family would appreciate me bombarding them with questions." He got no further before a response flew back.

"Then jot down where the house is. I'll assign another writer."

"What? No. I didn't mean…"

A light knock sounded, and Lily poked her head in. "Sorry to interrupt, Chief, but the commissioner's here for your meeting."

The chief regarded his watch. "Yeah, yeah. Send him in."

She nodded and left the room.

Panic briskly climbed through Ellis. His big break was slipping away. "All I'm trying to say is that, well…this picture's about more than one family." Over his shoulder, he could see Lily and the commissioner closing in. He pushed onward, despite the chief's look of growing irritation. "After all, there's folks hurting everywhere. The bigger story is why this stuff's still happening. Other than the crash, that is."

During the lengthy beat that followed, Ellis clutched his satchel under his arm, the photo still in hand, waiting.

Finally, the chief shook his head, as if disapproving of his own judgment. "Fine. Write it up."

Ellis sighed, relief washing over him, but he knew better than to stay and celebrate. "Thanks, Chief. Thanks a million." He nearly backed into Lily, who'd just arrived with the commissioner. Ellis moved aside to allow them passage before returning to his desk.

Mind abuzz, he'd nearly forgotten about his Society piece. He retrieved the article and paired it with a quilting shot from the darkroom. After turning them in, luckily without backlash, he sank into his chair.

On a typewriter two desks over, Clayton Brauer's pointer fingers were engaged in rapid-fire hunt and peck. True to his ancestry, the guy had fair features and broad shoulders and the precision of a German machine. As always, a half-burned cigarette dangled from the corner of his mouth with a hint of smugness.

In the world of news, the vast majority of even hard-hitting stories went unsigned, a standard practice for any reputable paper. But thanks to flashy accounts of crime and corruption, the credit *By Clayton Brauer* had appeared in the *Examiner*—even making it onto Page One—more times than Ellis cared to tally.

Obviously, Ellis's feature wouldn't be a front-pager, but he was a hell of a lot closer to a coveted byline. More than that, to finally writing a story of import.

Ellis scrolled fresh copy paper into his Royal. Seeking inspiration, he again studied the photo. There were a variety of slants to consider. His fingers hovered over the keys, waiting for the words to come. Something provocative. Something newsworthy. Maybe even…creative.

CHAPTER 4

IN THE BOARDINGHOUSE the following week, while returning from the bath one evening, Lily had overheard her name.
Her ears tuned right in out of habit. Behind a partially opened
bedroom door, a couple of new tenants had been sizing her up.

She's a bit snooty, don't you think?

Oh, I don't know. Just seems too prim and proper to me.

If only they knew.

With a tendency to keep to herself, Lily could scarcely take
offense. She was no old biddy at twenty-two; her priorities were
just different from those of all the other young boarders. In the
evenings, they would moon over celebrity rumors, or the newest
talkies, or which boys they had eyes for at the last community
dance. Early on, some of the girls had invited her on outings,
yet she always declined. They learned not to waste their efforts.

Now, on a shaded bench at Franklin Square, she was starkly
reminded of where her own interests lay. All around, smitten
couples and cheerful families were prattling and strolling through
the lunch hour. She drew a breath and rubbed the oval locket

at the hollow of her neck. She envisioned Samuel's latest kiss goodbye, his sadness mirroring her own. *It won't be this way for much longer,* she'd told him, a phrase repeated so often she began to doubt her own promise.

The thought squelched her appetite.

She stuffed her lunch into her pail. Together with her book, she headed back toward the paper. Perspiration and humidity glued the stockings to her skin. Despite having time to spare, she cut through the city park. She was just passing the central fountain when honking and shouting broke out. A cabbie and an ice-truck driver were clashing over right of way. After a moment of gawking—their colorful language made them difficult to ignore—she spied a familiar figure seated at the base of a large maple.

Using a palm-size notebook, Ellis Reed appeared to be penciling and scratching out words in equal measure. Pages lay crumpled on the browning grass. Such doggedness made perfect sense to Lily, as she had acted much the same way in her proud days of working on the school bulletin.

All week, since learning of Ellis's opportunity, she had been tempted to inquire about his progress—his photo of the children still haunted her deeply—but his agitation had supplied the answer. It was clear the situation wasn't improving as he now wadded another page and threw it with force. Startled by the disruption, a lone mallard quacked and fluttered its wings before waddling off.

Ellis slumped against the tree, hands on his knees. His hat toppled to the ground, joining his pencil and pad, surrendered in defeat. Even his suspenders sagged heavily, bound to the dark trousers he wore with no jacket, his white sleeves unequally rolled.

Sensibility warned her not to involve herself—but far too late. She was, after all, largely responsible for his predicament. The least she could do was offer encouragement.

Nearing the tree, she navigated his rejected pages and corresponding demeanor. "You do realize," she said, nabbing his attention, "if you're looking to take out that poor duck, a shotgun would be considerably more effective."

His features relaxed as recognition dawned. He glanced toward the bird and murmured, "Only if it's made of gelatin."

She tilted her head, not following.

He appeared about to explain but shook his head. "Story for another time." A faint gleam shone in his eyes, blue as a robin's egg. After a beat of silence, he asked, "Would you… care to sit?"

Lily had no plans to stay long but felt odd looming over him as they spoke. When she agreed, he grabbed his strewn jacket and spread it out beside him. She eased herself down to sit properly in her skirt—oh, how she missed her girdle-free weekend wear—and set aside her belongings. Ellis was making a half-hearted attempt to straighten his black tie when his stomach growled, loud as a revving engine. Despite her best efforts, she couldn't hide her amusement.

"Guess I missed lunch," he said, a smidge embarrassed.

She reached into her pail and produced the last half of her sandwich. "Pastrami and Swiss on rye."

He hesitated only briefly before accepting. "Thanks." His smile delivered a pair of curved lines, like parentheses, to his cheeks. They brought to mind Samuel's dimples, which bore equal charm. Ellis's complexion even had a similar olive hue.

She returned to her purpose. "I take it things aren't going well with the article."

Ellis swallowed a mouthful of sandwich. He swiped crumbs from his lips with the back of his hand with an air of frustration. "I just don't see what the chief wants. Fine, he didn't like my first take. But I put everything I had into the next one. Spent almost a week poring over every blessed word."

Lily hadn't read either of his attempts, but she'd caught

cnough of the chief's responses to gather the gist. *As stale as week-old goddamn toast*, he'd so eloquently told Mr. Baylor, who had submitted Ellis's second version. It went without saying that the feature wouldn't survive a third strike.

"So, what was it about?" she asked.

"The last draft?"

She nodded, genuinely curious.

"Well…mainly it blasted the Smoot-Hawley Tariff."

Her confusion must have shown because he squared his shoulders to her before presenting his case. "Look, a bunch of DC lawmakers—they swore up and down that tariff was going to be great for all Americans. Plumb out of solutions? Tax 'em. Because that worked just swell for the Brits."

Lily wasn't opposed to his stance necessarily but failed to grasp the link. "And…the picture you took?"

"Don't you see? It's blatant proof of how wrong they were."

The correlation was a million miles from the personal chord the photograph had struck with her. When she failed to respond, Ellis's face dimmed, though he managed a weak smile. "I take it you're not a fan either."

She should have continued right on through the park. Her attempt to help was only worsening the matter. "I'm sure another idea will come," she said, a paltry offering. "Don't give up yet."

He looked almost puzzled. "Give up? On this? Not a chance."

She worried the implication had offended him, but just for an instant. He was merely resolved to reach his goal.

Perhaps for that reason she sensed she could prod—an act she normally avoided—to expose the raw relevance of that heart-rending image. Not for her, of course. For others.

"If I may ask, Mr. Reed, what does that picture really mean to you?"

His brow knotted. The question was unexpected.

"Because I would guess," she ventured, "that while you were

taking that photo, you weren't musing about some tariff or the lawmakers in DC. When you first saw those kids, what were you thinking?"

He opened his mouth, then promptly closed it, his answer reeled back in. She thought he would leave it at that or regroup with another economic stance. Rather, he gained a light rasp as he replied, "My younger brother. How he might've been."

Lily nodded, attempting to hide her surprise. It was clear his sibling had passed and, more tellingly, that Ellis was accustomed to keeping this part of his life tucked away. A relic in a dusty attic.

"I didn't realize it at first," he went on, "but that's what drew me over to that house. And then I saw the posted sign." He shook his head as if recalling its words. "Sure, I could've been appalled, wondering how a parent could do that. Sell them off like that. But I didn't feel that way."

"No?"

"As I drove off, I just kept thinking about those boys. They didn't ask for the bum score they're getting, but somehow they'll make do. Adults, we're all so busy griping about our tough breaks, and kids like them, their lives change in a split second and you hardly hear a peep. Not about the big things anyway."

Gaining conviction, he quickened his pace. "Even when life's downright lousy, most kids are still so resilient because…well, I guess 'cause they don't know any different. It's like they only realize how unfair their lives are if you tell them. And even then, all they need is the smallest amount of hope and they could do just about anything they set their minds to…" Voice trailing off, Ellis appeared to have said far more than he had intended.

Lily couldn't help but smile. There was such passion and honesty in his words. As with his photos, he had captured a perspective, a profound depth in details, that people often missed. A view that needed to be shared.

"I believe, Mr. Reed, you've found your story."

He narrowed his eyes. As he shifted his frame of reference,

his face lightened. His gradual smile was the infectious sort, lined with just enough warmth to unsettle her.

"Well," she said, "I'd best be off." She gathered her belongings as she got to her feet. When he politely started to rise, she urged him to remain seated. "After all, you have a lot of work to do."

"You are right about that." He laughed a bit. "I sure owe you one, Miss Palmer."

"Nonsense. It was my pleasure." With that, she left him to scribble and ponder.

True, she hadn't been forthcoming about her own reaction to the picture—about what had compelled her to pass it along to the chief, ushering the image toward publication. Perhaps at the root of her efforts, more than all else, was a yearning to feel less alone with choices she had once made.

Whatever the cause may have been, there was no reason to elaborate. She had said enough to help.

CHAPTER 5

THE VERDICT WAS IN. The article had been given the go-ahead, per Mr. Baylor. Ellis felt so light on his feet, it was a miracle he didn't drift up to the newsroom ceiling.

Yeah, it would have been nice to receive word from the chief himself, but Ellis wasn't about to nitpick. If all went well, he could soon be assigned to City News, making his way to the crime or political beat.

It wasn't such a stretch to believe, given the latest development: Ellis was now welcomed to submit similar photos, described as "human" with a "gut punch," along with—and here was the kicker—articles to accompany them.

Not losing time, he sat at his desk and leafed through his personal file of pictures.

Nothing there of use.

Other photos were stashed at his apartment, but all were more of the same. From here on out, he'd be scouring the streets and alleys, the docks and barnyards with an alert eye and a loaded camera never far from his grip.

"Hey, Reed!" hollered a political reporter known as Stick. The skinny guy with slightly bulging eyes was refilling his cup at the coffee station. He wasn't more than ten feet away, but his caffeine intake often made him as loud as a carney barker. "Just heard about your feature. Good for you!"

Several reporters suddenly glanced Ellis's way. In seconds, their interest cut back to their Tuesday leads and calls and fact-checking. But the moment still caused his pride to swell.

He limited his response to a simple thanks, not wanting to seem overeager.

"By the way," Stick said, "some of the fellas wanna try out a new joint for lunch over on Ludlow. Come if you're free."

"Sure. Why not?" More feigned nonchalance.

Stick gave a quick smile. Then he downed a gulp of coffee, probably his fifth cup of the morning, before jostling back to his desk.

Lunch outings were common bonding events among the core newspapermen. A year or so ago, Ellis happened to be at the same restaurant as a group of them and was asked to join. Eventually, out of their small talk arose standard wisecracks about Ellis being a "sob sister," a reference to female reporters, since most were relegated to sentimental assignments. Like the Society section. After a run of inside jokes he couldn't follow and tales from college days, which he'd never had, he'd slipped out with an excuse that was barely acknowledged.

But now, with a clear-cut invite, a respectable feature in the queue, things were taking a turn...

The thought was interrupted by a flash of burgundy. It was Lily's blouse, and Ellis perked up at the sight of her standing alone. A few desks down, she'd stalled to scrawl notes on a steno pad. If his luck today was any indication, he had every reason to be confident. Either way, he needed to act.

He strode on over while trying to look unrushed. She was about to step away.

"Miss Palmer."

"Mmm?" she replied, distracted.

He continued once she looked up from her notes. "I just wanted to tell you, in case you hadn't heard. My piece about the kids is scheduled to run Thursday."

"My, that's marvelous, Mr. Reed. Congratulations." She lit with enthusiasm, a good sign. One that would have cooled his simmering nerves if not for Clayton's typing at the nearest desk. The guy's precise rhythm perceptibly slowed as Ellis assembled his next words.

"Is there...something else?" Lily's voice, while still pleasant, gained a trace of impatience. No doubt the chief had already thrown her an endless list of tasks.

"Actually, there is." Though Ellis preferred not to highlight his Society duties, he dared to plunge in. "Tonight at the art museum, I'll be covering a new exhibit. Ancient collectibles from China. Should be quite a thing to see."

She gave a nod, waiting for his point.

No question, a woman like Lily deserved a proper courting—carriage rides, symphony seats, a dinner at the Ritz. None of which Ellis could afford. It was the main reason he'd tended to keep his distance. But after their exchange at the park—her going out of her way to help him, the surprising comfort of their talk, the way she'd blushed when he smiled at her—he figured he just might have a shot, even if the museum picked up the tab this one time.

"Anyway, they're hosting a reception for bigwigs and some press. There'll be food and music, the works. And I was wondering if you'd like to go. With me."

Lily's eyes widened a fraction. "Oh. Oh, I see."

The pause that followed could have lasted mere seconds but seemed interminable. Worrying he had misjudged the signs, Ellis tempered the invite.

"I know it's last minute, so don't fret if you need to pass. Just thought it was a way to say thanks, you know, for your help."

"Well, that's really not necessary." Lily hugged her notepad to her chest. Again, her cheeks held a pinkish hue, though in fairness, the afternoon heat could have been the cause. "And it's a pretty busy night for me, I'm afraid. But I do appreciate the thought."

"Maybe another time, then?"

From the handful of girls he'd dated during and since high school, he knew her next response would be telling. Her tone, above all, would clarify where she stood. But before she could answer, Mr. Baylor swooped in from the side. The hue of his bare head rivaled that of Lily's blouse.

"Reed, we gotta talk."

And with that, Lily was gone.

Ellis worked to suppress his irritation. It took a moment to regroup and center on the issue Mr. Baylor was relating. Something had happened...with a picture...of the kids...the negative.

Ellis's mind snapped to attention. "How's that?"

Mr. Baylor huffed. He didn't like to repeat himself. "I'm saying the damn thing's ruined."

"Ruined?"

"A new blockhead upstairs was cleaning an ink spill. Ended up knocking over some goddamn bleach. Your file's one of the casualties. Still got a copy of the article, but the print and negative are goners. We'll need a replacement."

Ellis stared at him, the impact of the situation taking shape. A tightness wound around his middle, a lasso of dread. "But, I-I haven't got one."

"Doesn't have to match exact. Just something close enough for the chief."

When Ellis stumbled across those kids, work had been the farthest thing from his mind. He hadn't even absorbed the words on the sign before clicking the shutter. Need extra images of a charity gala or any other event he'd covered over the past two years? He had mountains of them. But a photo of the two boys?

He'd taken just that one. How could he have guessed it would find its way to Howard Trimble?

As if on cue, the chief hollered from his office, beckoning Mr. Baylor, who raised a hand in acknowledgment. Turning back to Ellis, he added, "I'll need it by end of workday. Got that?" Then he headed off, not waiting for a response.

And thankfully so, because Ellis had no answers. In fact, he doubted he could scrounge up a voice.

A thick waft of smoke blew into his eyes, delivering a sting. Clayton was taking a break from his hunt-and-pecking to light a fresh cigarette. He picked a speck of tobacco from his bottom lip and lifted his square chin toward Ellis. "Don't sweat it, pal. Not the end of the world."

There was no sarcasm in his tone. But as he returned to his work, tucking his cigarette into place, his mouth gained its standard tilt. Or was it a smirk?

At this point, what did it matter?

Ellis marched back to his desk, battling an onset of panic. In the row of wall clocks, the second hands were relentlessly sprinting as if in a race. Local time was 11:08.

So much for his lunch plans.

He needed to knuckle down and stay calm. There was time to salvage this. He could plead with Mr. Baylor, ask him to run the article on its own.

Considering the chief's temperament, that was decidedly a last resort.

Ellis scoured for other solutions, yet all the while he knew he was skirting the most obvious one.

Although it was far from ideal, what better choice did he have?

⌒

Once again, there was no indication of a presence inside. The house looked still as stone.

Ellis stepped out of his parked car and onto the pebbled dirt. The hour-long drive had allowed for ample doubts and second-guessing. He'd had to remind himself of the message in his article, the hope and determination it could spark for folks in need.

Of course, it would be a lie to say he'd trekked to Laurel Township solely for the good of others. Raised in a home shadowed by a ghost, he learned early on that to be seen is to matter. But wasn't that what everyone wanted deep down? To know their lives actually made a difference? To leave their mark. To be remembered.

Now, though, with the sale sign nowhere to be seen, Ellis's concerns returned entirely to those boys. Only a few weeks had passed since his afternoon spent here. It had been safe to presume the brothers remained. Their farm road wasn't the type to draw traffic.

Ellis assured himself of this as he climbed the porch steps. A pair of one-dollar bills rustled in his trouser pocket. At his apartment, before fetching his car, he'd grabbed the cash out of his rent fund. He planned to offer the donation before taking the new photos. *A simple trade for a few pics*, he'd explain if the father was the prideful type. It could buy milk for the kids, some butter and bread. Even meat and potatoes for stew.

Holding on to that hope, Ellis swung open the screen door and knocked. Waited.

He knocked again, louder.

Still no answer.

That was when he spotted the wooden slat. It lay on a far corner of the porch, piled atop old firewood. He released the screen door, which rattled when it shut, and picked up the board. He flipped it over, cautious of the rough edges.

Around him, there were no marbles, no other toys or small shoes. No clues to say that the boys hadn't been pawned off to the highest bidder. Or, more likely, anyone who'd offered.

"They're gone."

Ellis turned, startled at first by the voice, then the message. At the base of the porch stood a girl, seven years old maybe, holding dandelions at her side. The overalls she wore, shirtless, covered the chest of her petite frame, but were well short of her bare feet and ankles.

He steeled himself. "You're talking about the two boys who live here?"

The girl nodded, bobbing her blond ponytail. "Rest of the family too. Ma says their pa got lucky, getting a mill job over in Bedford County, and right in the nick of time. Mr. Klausen's been threatenin' to... You know Mr. Klausen?"

Ellis shook his head.

The girl huffed to herself. "You ain't missed nothing there, that's for sure. Mr. Klausen owns a bunch of the houses 'round here and looks like a potato. You know, the bumpy kind with sprouts every which way. And when the rent's late, he turns mean *real* fast." Her emphatic expression said she'd seen the effect firsthand. From what Ellis gathered, so had the family of the boys who were no longer here.

"That's good news, then. About the job." He was relieved for the family. He truly was.

Granted, now knowing they were okay, he just wished he'd snapped a couple more shots when he had the chance.

"You want any?" she asked.

Ellis missed the reference.

"Only a penny a bundle. I made 'em myself. See?" She held out dandelions that looked to be twined in several groups of a dozen. Some drooped from the heat more than others. "A little water, and they perk right back up. I give you my word on that." She gave a solid nod to underscore her integrity on the matter.

Ellis honestly needed to hoard every cent he could, now more than ever. But he surveyed her thin cheeks and pink, rounded nose. Her eyes brimmed with such hope. As much as he tried, he couldn't refuse.

He shed a sigh. "Let me see what I got," he said and descended the stairs.

She grinned in anticipation as he fished through his trouser pocket and found three pennies. His first instinct was to surrender only one. But lessons ingrained from years of attending Sunday services with his mother—and his father too, though only in the physical sense—compelled him to be charitable. Just minutes ago, he was ready to give two full dollars to a family he didn't even know.

"Guess I'll take whatever this'll get me." When he placed the coins in the girl's hand, she gaped as if receiving a collection of rare jewels. Then she abruptly masked her exuberance with a steady, businesslike manner.

"That gets ya three bouquets." She handed him all but one of her slumped bundles.

Perfect, actually—for the funeral of his career.

"Thanks, mister." She kept her smile to a minimum, though the glint in her eyes betrayed her. Not waiting for him to change his mind, she wisely dashed off with pennies secure in her fist. In a blink, she crossed the road and started up the long dirt drive that led to another house.

A drop of sweat trailed down Ellis's cheek. The afternoon sun bore down on his back, his shoulders. Weight accumulated as much from the air as the pressure of the waning day.

Don't give up yet. Lily's words echoed back to him.

A downward glance, and he realized he was still holding the sign. He could always take a picture of the chalked words, include the house in the background. It wouldn't be nearly as powerful as the original image, but better than nothing.

He opened the car door, set the sign and flowers on the front seat, and retrieved the loaded camera from his satchel. Rising too fast, he banged his head on the ceiling. The vehicle creaked from the impact, and Ellis gritted his teeth through his cursing.

He was rubbing the sore spot under his felt hat when he glimpsed the girl, stopped at a large apple tree beside the house across the way. She was waving a smaller boy down from a branch, presumably with news of her big sale.

Despite the throbbing in Ellis's head, the makings of an idea came to him. They slid together like beads of sweat, like raindrops pooling on glass, forming an altered shape.

He had the sign and the setting. All he needed was a pair of boys. Maybe a brother was playing inside. Or a cousin, a friend.

If not, heck, the girl would do. With her boyish clothes and hair pulled back, who would notice? Only a few had actually seen the first photo, and likely none of them with a close eye. It wasn't a tactic Ellis preferred, but a reporter's success often depended on his ability to be resourceful.

Besides, if three pennies so easily raised the girl's spirits, maybe her parents would feel the same about two dollar bills. It would be no different from, say, paying models for a fancy advertisement in *Ladies' Home Journal*.

He checked his pocket watch. Half past twelve. No time to debate.

Leaving his car, he grabbed the sign and headed across the road.

CHAPTER 6

LILY SURVEYED THE NEWSROOM from her desk, ensuring discretion before lifting the receiver of her upright phone.

Ever since she declined Ellis's invite that morning, the notion of reconsidering had nagged at her. And why wouldn't it, given the meal scheduled at her boardinghouse? Every Tuesday without fail, supper featured steak and kidney pudding with extra onions, a favorite dish of no resident but her British landlady.

In all honesty, the appeal of an outing was less about the food than the company, as the rest of Lily's night would entail reading a book in the sparseness of her bedroom. Still, anything resembling a date wasn't an option with anyone but Samuel. The recollection of this made her miss him even more, spurring her to sneak in a quick call.

The female operator came on the line.

"Yes, hello," Lily replied. "I'd like to place a long-distance call, please."

"Could you speak up, ma'am?"

The commotion of the room buzzed about her, a steady rise

toward the daily deadline. Holding the neck of the phone, she brought the mouthpiece closer. "I said, I'd like to make a call."

"The number?"

Before the details could tumble out, a man appeared in Lily's periphery. She swiveled in her chair to find Clayton Brauer with a page in hand.

Lily's grip on the phone tightened, her chance to connect with Samuel vanishing.

"Ma'am?" the operator pressed.

A cigarette plumed at the corner of Clayton's mouth. He flicked her a nod in greeting. His eyes, light brown like his close-cropped hair, held the same self-assuredness woven into everything about him—from his broad stature and smooth voice to his snappy suits and polished wingtips.

"I'll ring back shortly, Operator. Thank you." Lily replaced the earpiece on the cradle as Clayton removed his cigarette and exhaled.

"Didn't mean to interrupt, Miss Palmer."

"Oh, no. It wasn't you." She pretended to search through paperwork on her desk. "I swore I had the number right here, but now I'm just not seeing it."

In the uneasy pause that followed, she imagined his reporter's gaze, inquisitive and doubtful, studying her every move. Yet when she looked up, his focus was aimed at the chief's closed door. Its glass pane provided a clear view of the meeting inside. Why was he being so snoopy?

"*Mr. Brauer?*" Her tone came out sharper than intended, a lingering effect of the interruption.

Not that it rattled him a whit. His gaze still on the door, he tilted his head. "Looks like old Schiller's packing up his ink," he mused.

"Retirement?" Thrown off, Lily turned toward the office. She strained her neck to see the exchange for herself. But the back of Mr. Schiller's shiny scalp, visible through his thin white hair, blocked the chief's face, revealing nothing. "Why do you think that?"

"Have you read his column lately?" Clayton faced her with an amused look. "All about travel, seeing the world. Safaris and deep-sea fishing. Schiller's definitely got the itch. I'd put money on it."

The range of topics alone wasn't unusual, as Mr. Schiller essentially ruled his own column, having worked at the *Examiner* since the paper began. In fact, with such seniority, he was rarely subjected to discussions with the chief, and certainly not in person.

Like now.

"Anyhow…here." Clayton set a paper on Lily's desk. "The sources the chief asked for." If he said anything more before walking away, Lily missed it. She was too consumed by the revelation, the possibilities congealing in her mind.

She slid open her bottom drawer. From beneath her supplies of pencils, stamps, and staples, she retrieved her forest-green folder. Its corners were bent, its edges tattered from years of storing the essays and columns she had crafted in school. She hadn't saved them all, only her level best.

When first arriving in the city, she had brought such foolish aspirations, all neatly tucked between those pages. A slew of interviews soon revealed her low odds, like the majority of other women, of becoming the next Nellie Bly. The daring adventures of the late columnist—from her record-breaking race around the world to her deliberate arrest for a report on jail conditions—were begrudgingly admired by even the staunchest of newsmen, but as a rare exception. By the time Lily had wandered into the *Examiner*, she wasn't ignorant enough to turn down a secretarial position. The reality of a regular wage had outweighed her pride.

If Clayton was right, however, a fresh opportunity loomed. And what better timing? She had just helped propel Ellis Reed's career. Perhaps, at last, she could make real headway with her own future plans. And in doing so, she could fulfill a long-held promise to more than just herself.

CHAPTER 7

THE GIRL BEAMED WITH DELIGHT when Ellis approached her farmhouse. It was similar to the other, with a porch and screen door, but with white paint under its dingy sheen. "You wanna buy *more*, mister?"

"Actually, I was hoping your father might be home." If around, the man of the house would want some say in any financial arrangement.

"He's gone," she said. The towheaded boy, barefoot and dressed in matching overalls, stood at her side.

"Off at work?"

"Nah. In heaven."

Her matter-of-fact tone told him it wasn't a recent occurrence, but still Ellis offered, "I'm real sorry to hear that."

The boy tugged on the girl's arm, as if skeptical about confiding in a stranger.

"Ah, don't fuss. This here's the fella who gave me the pennies." She exaggerated an eye roll, a message to say the kid was just too young to understand.

Ellis smiled. "I assume this is your little brother?"

"Little is right. Calvin here's only five."

"I *ain't* little." His round face drew into a pout, a plum becoming a prune.

"And I'm Ruby. Ruby Dillard. I'm eight and a half. Nearly nine."

Ellis's guess on her age had been fairly close, though a decade short if measuring on a precocious scale.

"Well, Ruby, you wouldn't have another brother around, would you?"

"Another?" She put her fists on her hips. "Heck no. I might not even keep this one." She fought a smile as Calvin's eyes, framed by thick lashes, sparked with defiance.

"Mamaaa!" He scampered into the house, their mother evidently inside. This provided a timely answer to Ellis's next question.

"Hey, mister, listen here." Ruby leaned forward and spoke in a stage whisper. "There's a lady at church—sounds like a dying cat when she sings—she calls Mama 'Geri,' like short for Geraldine, but Mama hates that."

"So…don't call her Geri."

Ruby nodded, an eyebrow raised, saying, *Trust me on this.*

Just then, her mother stepped out of the house. She was wiping her hands on the faded striped apron over her cotton housedress, Calvin peeking from behind. The sun highlighted her sandy-blond hair, loosely gathered in a bun.

"Can I help you?" Her tone was as even as her gaze.

"Mrs. Dillard, good afternoon. I'm with the *Philadelphia Examiner.* I apologize for troubling you in the middle of the day."

"We're not subscribing to nothing."

"No…no, that's not what I'm after."

"What, then?"

All right, skip to the deal. "The thing is, there's this article I've written for the paper. And I just need some photos of a few kids. It won't take more than—"

"Not interested. Ruby, come do your chores."

"But, Mama. Did you hear? I wanna be in the paper!"

"Young lady, I do not have the energy to repeat myself today." The woman indeed appeared tired as she coughed and batted away dust in the air, though she still looked capable of doing the same to her daughter's behind.

Ruby slumped her shoulders. As she trudged up the porch stairs, Ellis stepped closer. "Please, Mrs. Dillard. Before you make a final decision…" A few more seconds and these kids, like the previous two, would be gone. He scrambled to pull the curled bills from his pocket. "Rest assured, I can pay."

Ruby wheeled around. At the cash, her dainty jaw fell open and Calvin cocked his head, his eyes growing impossibly large. Geraldine wasn't taken in so easily, but neither was she turning away.

Noting his narrow opening, Ellis rushed to describe the photographs he required and the basics of the article. There would be no specific ties to her children. No names or other details beyond their township. The picture would simply represent the turmoil facing countless American families.

When Ellis finished, Geraldine crossed her arms. She studied him, evaluating, deciding. Her large, rounded eyes matched those of her children, but with a hooded quality underscored by dark circles, her ashen pallor suggesting a life drained of color. "I got laundry to hang out back. You can take your pictures till I'm done. Then the children got chores to do." Leaving it at that, she disappeared into the house.

Ellis wasn't sure how much time this gave him, but he guessed it wasn't much. Within minutes, he arranged the kids on the porch steps, side by side, and the sign in the foreground. The camera was ready for clicking.

Through the lens, he repeatedly captured their dirt-smudged faces, charming with their cupid lips and their ears that came to gentle points. Thanks to Ruby's coaxing, warmth increased in both their smiles, followed by their eyes.

Ellis was in the midst of snapping another picture—Ruby had just slung her arm around Calvin's shoulders—when Geraldine reemerged from the front door. Palm raised, she averted her face from the camera. "That's enough now. You got what you needed."

The session was over.

With safely a dozen good images on film, Ellis thanked the kids before Geraldine herded them inside. He met her at the steps and handed over the money, catching the subtle desperation in her face.

"I appreciate this, Mrs. Dillard. You've truly been a lifesaver."

She tendered a nod, but retreated without a word.

In the front window, lined with blue gingham curtains, Ruby suddenly appeared. As if taking the stage for a final bow, she waved, then slipped from view.

~

In no time, Ellis was back on the road.

Rumbling his way toward Philly, he pondered the new photos. The more miles he covered, the more his uncertainty stirred over the nature of the substitution. Though when he reached Center City, a dose of reality cut through his doubts. In front of Independence Hall, a group of browbeaten men milled about in suits and hats. Over their chests hung hand-painted boards.

WANTED: A DECENT JOB. KNOW 3 TRADES.

WILL TAKE ANY WORK. DO NOT WANT CHARITY.

FAMILY MAN. WAR VET. COLLEGE TRAINED. NEED A JOB.

Collectively, they sent a stark message to Ellis: lose sight of his goals, and he'd soon need a sign of his own. If ever questioned, he'd undoubtedly admit the truth. He had no intention of swindling anyone…and definitely not outright lying…

At the corner, he opened up the throttle of his Model T and swung onto Market. For once, he was grateful for the rattling of his godforsaken engine. Anything to drown out the whispers of his conscience.

CHAPTER 8

A WEEK HAD PASSED since the feature went to press, yet the letters and calls continued to roll in. Readers wanted to know about those poor, sweet children. As could be expected, there were those outraged by a mother's willingness to peddle her own flesh and blood, but the vast majority expressed sympathy for the family.

For proof, Lily needed only to glance at Ellis's desk. Among the latest donations were teddy bears, clothing, a ragged stuffed monkey, jarred preserves, pickled vegetables, and a rainbow quilt. Word had it a few letters even offered jobs and a small amount of cash. The whole lot, Lily had overheard, would be personally delivered by Ellis, citing the family's desire for privacy.

Such a preference wasn't a surprise, given the final photograph that went to press. A mishap with the original had apparently required him to provide images from a second roll of film. The chief had been dictating a memo to Lily that day, when Mr. Baylor interrupted with a folder of alternatives. Through the window of the chief's door, she had glimpsed Ellis watching the exchange from afar, looking too fidgety to sit. Once more, just as in the park, she'd had the urge to offer assurance. But who knew what her fickle boss would decide?

After a quick sift through the photos, the chief had latched on to the last in the stack: one with the mother on the porch, her hand splayed and face half turned away, with her children clinging to each other in the wake of that unsettling sign.

A display of hardships had gained a potent layer of shame.

Despite the photo's similar effect on Lily, she had managed to send Ellis a nod, relaying the chief's approval. He had brightened with a smile so wide and genuine that she found herself smiling back. Then the sound of her name in the chief's gruff voice had tugged her gaze from Ellis's, her mind back to her shorthand, and she was glad for it. She didn't need any more distractions in her life.

Never was that truer than today. In light of her imminent proposal, her show of diligence would be key. At the coffee station in the gradually filling city room, she was preparing the chief's cup in plenty of time for his morning arrival. But as she mentally rehearsed her speech, her hand jolted. A hot splash. She had overfilled the ceramic mug, the chief's favorite, almost dropping it onto the hard linoleum.

Focus, Lily.

She hurried to the lavatory to snatch a hand towel and went to work mopping up the puddle. She was still kneeling when greetings arose, young male reporters sounding anxious to impress.

The chief was here.

Twelve minutes early.

Lily groaned. She hadn't yet finished her routine of ensuring his mess of a desk was tidied, his coffee set out to cool—he preferred it black and tepid—and his ashtray emptied and placed at the ready.

"Miss Palmer!" he bellowed while entering his office, per his norm.

"Yes, sir. Be there in a jiff!" She scrambled across the room to reach her desk. This time, in lieu of a pencil and steno pad, she pulled out her precious green folder.

Once she'd confirmed Clayton's suspicions—Mr. Schiller was indeed retiring, though he had yet to make a formal announcement—she had spent every evening since, including bus rides to and from Delaware over the weekend, preparing. She had reviewed, retyped, and edited several of her past articles and had even composed new samples. While surely and regrettably not perfect, they were as ready as they would ever be.

"*Miss Palmer!*" The chief's impatience was climbing.

With a fortifying breath, she proceeded into his office. Morning sunlight streamed through the window, warming the room, but still she closed the door.

The chief's hat was balanced atop his suit jacket, which he had tossed over the visitor's chair. It was her duty to transfer the items to the coat stand in the corner. Instead, she stood and waited before his desk. The one she had neglected to tidy.

"Good morning, Chief."

Planted in his chair, he peered over the rims of his spectacles, looking more confused than perturbed. "Where's my coffee?"

The coffee. Oh murder. She had forgotten.

Yet she pressed on.

"Yes, before I get to that"—as if this had been her strategy all along, as if his cup of joe would be produced only after her demands were heard—"I was hoping we could speak privately. Before the business of the day picks up."

He began a search through documents on his desk but mumbled his agreement.

This was her moment.

"Sir, in light of Mr. Schiller's decision to retire, I'd like to submit an idea. After all, I presume you're going to need a new columnist by the end of next month."

"If you got someone in mind, jot his name down. Worry

about the coffee for now." He wagged a hand toward the door as though she required directional assistance—to a destination she could find backward in the pitch-black of night.

Behind her, a rise of muffled voices indicated the city room was coming to life. Soon, the daily whirlwind would ensue and any chance of a pointed discussion would fall away.

The chief looked up, his order ignored.

Lily applied her most persuasive smile. "I'm sorry to pester, Chief, but if you could take a minute to peek at a few writing samples, I'd be terribly grateful."

She wasn't the type to ask for much, and the chief knew this. She saw it in his eyes before he sighed. "Fine," he said and accepted the folder.

As he leafed through the pages, Lily had to resist fiddling with her locket. She recalled Ellis and his fidgeting, and wished he were there to reciprocate with a look of reassurance.

Then the chief bobbed his head. It was his usual sign of a satisfying read, but not a guarantee.

"Who wrote these?" He was still skimming.

A sudden lump formed in her throat. Submitting under a pen name might have been an option if the chief wasn't a stickler for facts. In his world, there were no near truths. She forced down a swallow. "I did."

He stopped reading. Slowly, he sat back in his chair. His thick brows were furrowed. "So, you're not happy with your job."

"Oh! Gosh, no, Chief. I mean, it's just fine." And it was, for the short term. "I thought I could write a column on the side, in addition to my normal duties." All of which she maintained without issue. If he didn't count today. She scrambled to remember her speech. "As you might recall, I was the editor of my high school bulletin. And several letters to editors I've written have appeared in various papers over the years."

He removed his glasses and rubbed the bridge of his nose. The mere act of deliberation prodded her to go on.

"I already have a list of possibilities, mind you. Most would offer a firsthand view of different walks of life. I'd even be willing to go undercover, to show what it's like to be a vaudevillian or a maid at a plush hotel. If you're interested, I could also—"

The chief flashed his palm. "Okay, I got it."

She nodded, fearing she had said too much, hoping she had said enough. "I can do this, Chief. I know I can."

He drew an audible breath, then let it out. "I've got no doubt." The subtle lightness in his tone caused her to smile. But when he replaced his spectacles and leaned forward, elbows on his desk, she braced herself. "Even so. Our readers expect a certain kind of column, Miss Palmer. They want someone who writes about life like...well, Ed Schiller."

The instant he finished, she forged ahead, prepared for this argument. "I know what you're saying, sir. However, this could actually help bridge the gap between our male and female readers in a variety of ways."

"How 'bout recipes?"

The peculiar question stalled her. "Pardon me?"

"Your folks over in Delaware. They own a deli, don't they? You must have some nice recipes you could share for the Sunday editions."

And then she understood. He was referring to the women's Food section. Right beside columns about fashion faux pas and party etiquette and how to become the perfect homemaker. They were the sorts of topics that a young Nellie Bly had been limited to cover at the *Pittsburgh Dispatch* before she left for better opportunities, better pay.

Goals aside, a nickel or dime a recipe wasn't worth the cost of Lily's dignity. At least not today.

The door rattled open and Clayton blew in. "Chief! Got the scoop on Duffy."

Tension in the room must have hung like a web because Clayton halted midstep and pulled the cigarette from his mouth. "Or...I can come back."

"Nah, nah. We're done," the chief said, to which Lily pinned on a tight smile of compliance. "You find out more?" he asked.

Clayton nodded, reminded of his purpose. "Murdered in his hotel room. At the Ambassador."

"Any suspects?"

The men scarcely took note of Lily stepping between them to retrieve her folder.

"Cops are questioning Hoff. Some of his henchmen too. But looks more like associates in the Irish Mob turned on him. Police are expecting thousands to show for the funeral. If you're on board, I could be off to Atlantic City in an hour."

Clayton emitted such enthusiasm that one would think Orville Wright had just revealed an aircraft that could soar to the moon and back.

Lily would leave them to their celebration.

She closed the door with more force than was prudent. Though who would notice? All of the city room was abuzz with the latest news. Philadelphia's very own Mickey Duffy, a bootlegger and numbers runner dubbed "Prohibition's Mr. Big," had officially been slain the night before. No wonder the chief had come in early.

In fact, his rejection of her pitch might largely have been a matter of poor timing. Perhaps she could revisit the proposal on a better day.

Oh, whom was she fooling? Approach him again, and she would receive the same answer. Push harder, and she would be lucky to maintain her current job.

Across the room, Ellis was busy speaking to Mr. Baylor in animated fashion, surely about another feature in the works. While the achievement of his first one had emboldened her with inspiration, it now caused her a sharp twist of envy.

Just then, Ellis glanced in her direction. Lily summoned her standard composure and continued on her way. After all, she had important tasks to see to. Like bringing warm coffee to her boss.

CHAPTER 9

NO ONE COULD HAVE PREDICTED how the article would spread. It was like a brush fire leaping from one paper to the next. First to Jersey, then Maryland, Rhode Island, and Illinois. Down to Texas, as far west as Wyoming. The dailies that had rerun Ellis's feature currently totaled nine. Ten if he included the original in the *Examiner*.

It was darkly intriguing, in a way. The sight of strangers in dire straits had become so commonplace that they were as good as invisible to most. But shine a spotlight on members of a single family—a pair of cute kids huddled together, a desperate mother shielding her face—and they became human. Folks who deserved compassion.

To be fair, Ellis had never intended to submit the picture of Geraldine. He hadn't realized Mr. Baylor had presented it to the chief until learning it was approved. Even now, well into October, the portrayal of the family still left Ellis unsettled.

In truth, everything about that photo did. The more compliments and success it garnered, the more deceptive he felt. So much had happened without planning and in such a short span. It was just two months ago when he'd managed to sell his big pitch to the chief.

Sometimes he wondered what else he'd sold on that Monday. His principles? His integrity?

At least readers' responses helped combat the guilt that gnawed at him. Kind letters continued to stream in, along with donations. Already he'd made three trips to the Dillards', leaving boxes of gifts on their porch late at night. He'd become a reverse thief, avoiding the awkwardness of directly handing them off, of having to explain how greatly the article's reach had widened. While the attention would thrill Ruby—maybe her brother too—clearly their mother would feel otherwise.

In any case, all Ellis could do was move forward. So far, it was working out reasonably well, both in pay and opportunity. For his last two pieces, he'd featured Siamese twins born in Philly who had defied medical odds, then a local actor once known from silent films, now frail and living in a shantytown dubbed Hooverville.

Such displays of a common humanity struck a note with readers. But it was Ellis's upcoming feature that made him particularly proud. The idea of highlighting coal miners in Pittston had come to him a week ago. As he rode a streetcar, the sight of a shoe shiner, pint-size and cheeks smeared with polish, jogged a memory.

Ellis had been about the same age, seven or eight, when he visited a mine near his childhood hometown of Hazleton. It marked one of the rare occasions when his father was stuck dragging him to work. As a machinery supervisor for the Huss Coal Company, his father was conferring with a drill operator when Ellis stumbled upon a pack of young boys eating lunch out of pails. From cap to boots, the kids were so dusted from coal that the whites of their eyes almost glowed.

His father's deep voice had shot from behind. Gruff as a roar, it had made Ellis literally jump. *I told you, stay in the truck.* The man was normally so stoic; it was the first time Ellis became truly aware of his father's solid, towering form.

Together they'd marched back to the truck, where his father took hold of the steering wheel. His hands shook with such anger that a belt whupping at home seemed a surety, punishment for wandering off. But the longer they drove, the calmer his father became. Finally, he said to Ellis: *Those mines are no place to fool around.* He looked as if he'd say more. Instead, he fell into the usual silence that accompanied their drives.

Ellis had known well enough to stay quiet, but his curious nature won out. *Pop, who were those kids?* His father's gaze had remained on the road, his answer grim and barely audible. *Breaker boys,* he'd said, a clear end to the conversation.

In time, Ellis learned more about the children, as young as six, used for sorting coal. Ten hours a day they'd labor over chutes and conveyor belts in a breaker, enduring cuts from slate and burns from acid. Losing fingers and limbs in the gears. Developing asthma and black lung. Some were even smothered by the coal itself.

Today, breaker boys were a thing of the past. Now there were machines that could do the job, but also laws regulating child labor. Laws that would never have been written, let alone enforced, without strong public support. How did that largely come about? Journalists.

The revelation had hit Ellis soon after that day at the mine. He was sipping a malt at the drugstore counter as his mother shopped for goods. A female customer was speaking to the owner, outraged over an article involving another breaker boy being maimed. She commended the "brave newsmen" for reporting such things—atrocities, she said—that the big coal companies wished would pass quiet as a whisper.

Typical of an only child, Ellis was always an avid reader. But from that day on, newspapers became his read of choice. When his mother attempted to sway him to the classics, worrying that local accounts of murders and corruption were inappropriate for a child, he took to sneaking articles under the covers after bedtime.

One day he, too, would become a brave newsman, he'd vowed. He would do the exact opposite of the lowly muckrakers that his father griped about—"vultures," he called them. In Jim Reed's world, a man of real value created something tangible and useful to society, practical items that could last. And that didn't include scandals and gossip in daily papers that amounted to "ink-stained kindling," worth a penny and discarded the next day. No, Ellis would do more than that. His stories would make folks sit up and listen. Impart knowledge that actually made a difference.

Nobody believed he'd see it through, however, this big dream of his. Except for his mother. In Allentown—where his family settled years ago, after his father was hired by Bethlehem Steel— you got your diploma, then you worked at a factory, producing cars or trucks, pounding metal for the navy. And forget about college. Those money-grubbing institutions were meant for pampered Rockefeller types who'd never known a real day's work. Or so it was said.

For a while, Ellis followed the crowd. He even dated on occasion until realizing it wasn't fair to the girls, whose singular goal was to land a husband and start a family. He couldn't risk being tied down for fear he'd never leave. Every week for more than a year, he just slung on his boots and gloves and ground away at a battery plant. But he did so merely to save up for his move to Philly and to buy engine parts for his junkyard find. To chase down the biggest stories, a reporter needed to get around.

His mother understood this, even when he quit his solid job at the plant to file newspapers for lower pay, only then to write drivel for the women's pages. He never had to explain to her how each step led closer to his goal.

His father, on the other hand, failed to share their outlook and had no qualms about saying so—which would make supper at their home tonight all the more gratifying.

Although Ellis had sent his mother clippings of his first three features, earning her praise over the phone, this would be the first time he'd see his parents since the pieces went to press. At long last, his father would have to admit that Ellis's career choices weren't foolish after all. He would see that his son's work held meaning, if at no other time than when Ellis shared his forthcoming feature about the mine.

It was just a matter of choosing the right moment.

~

"More pot roast, sweetheart?" his mother asked, seated to Ellis's right at the dinner table. Her chair was always the closest to the kitchen.

"I've had plenty. Thanks, Ma."

"How about some bread?" She reached for the crescents, heaped in a milk-glass bowl she'd owned since he was born. It was charmingly simple, yet purposeful and unchanging. Same as everything about his parents' two-story bungalow home. "Don't you dare say you're full," she warned, "or I'll have to point out again how thin you're getting."

Ellis's stomach was indeed running out of room—his weekly budget rarely allowed for a sizeable meal—but her smile was so encouraging he couldn't say no.

"Sure. Just one more." He swiped a roll, his third of the evening. The scent of warm bread always smelled like home.

When he took a bite, his mother sat a little taller in her floral housedress. Her blue eyes glimmered. They were a nice reminder of all the traits he'd inherited from her. Like the smile lines and rounded chin, the wavy black hair—hers invariably worn to her shoulders. She'd even passed down her medium build that ran slim through the hips.

Come to think of it, in his teenage years, a sturdier physique was the one way in which Ellis wished he'd taken after his father. Aside from the darker complexion they shared, reflecting their distant Portuguese roots, they bore little if any resemblance. Especially these days, with his father's brown hair turning thin and gray, his black-rimmed glasses now worn full time—the latter being a product of his wife's gentle but determined prodding.

"How about you, dear?" she asked her husband. "Another roll?" He was parked on Ellis's other side, at the head of the table, though it was easy to forget he was there.

"I'm all right." He waved off the basket, his hand calloused and fingernails stained faintly black. The same grease dotted his signature plaid shirt. He returned to the creamed corn on his plate.

The lull that followed didn't survive half a minute. Ellis's mother had long ago honed the art of filling the silence as one would potholes in a weathered road. She was a master of smoothing the tension with talk of radio shows, her knitting projects, health updates on the grandparents—her side living in Arizona for the sun, the others already passed—and the latest word on neighbors and friends, including those from Ellis's school days.

His ties to old pals in the area had faded over time, but he nodded along. And every so often a topic would interest his father enough to chime in.

There was a single subject they would never broach, of course, despite its presence in the empty seat facing Ellis.

At the thought, he could almost smell wafts of cinnamon apples spilling from their old home in Hazleton. He'd been sitting outside, poking at the cast on his arm, fresh from a bicycle tumble that day. Inside, his mother was baking a pie. He didn't realize the screams were hers—he'd never heard such sounds before—until she burst from the house with the swaddled baby, Ellis's father right behind. Her face was frantic with fear as they both climbed into the truck. Ellis must have been at least five.

Old enough to wait behind alone. Smart enough to save the pie from the oven, half of which he ate from the pan when hunger pangs set in.

That night, his mother had perched on his bed, her voice turned rough as sandpaper. *Sometimes babies just stop breathing, for no reason at all.* He remembered the tears on her cheeks and trying to comprehend how his brother had gone to live with the angels. He later awoke from his father's heavy footsteps, traveling here and there over the squeaky floorboards. It was a late-night habit he continued for years to come, as if he'd lost something that could never be found.

If his father had laughed even once since that day, or uttered a word about Henry's passing, Ellis couldn't say for sure. Though he'd guess the odds were no better than his mother ever baking another apple pie.

"Ellis?" she said, pulling his mind back. "Would you like some peach cobbler?"

He smiled at her. "I'd love some."

She was about to rise, leaving Ellis alone with his father. "Ma, hold on. You sit and relax. I can bring it out."

Naturally she protested, but they reached a compromise. While he carted the used dishes to the sink, she served up the coffee and dessert, and they all settled back in.

"I hope it doesn't have too much nutmeg," she said as Ellis and his father took their first bites. "I was trying out a new recipe from *Good Housekeeping*."

"It's perfect," Ellis insisted through a mouthful.

His father agreed. "Tastes fine, Myrna. Real good."

She smiled with more pride than relief. Then she resumed leading the chitchat that would fill the rest of their meal, and Ellis realized his chance was dwindling.

When they'd first sat at the table, she asked him how all was going at the paper. The general question called for a general answer. *Everything's swell*, he'd replied, certain she would eventually circle around and invite more detail. As of yet, that hadn't happened, but she did ask her husband now about a new machine at the steel plant where he served as a supervisor. His face even lightened as he described the efficiency and safety benefits of the purchase he'd been advocating for a year.

Ellis found the topic refreshing, for both his father's mood and the natural segue, since it tied in perfectly to the photo in his shirt pocket. He decided to finally bring it up himself, just as his father said, "How 'bout I check out your radiator before you go."

It was the type of phrase that cued a guest to pack up, signaling the visit had drawn to an end.

"Um, sure. I appreciate that."

In a single swig, his father finished off his coffee. But, as if reading Ellis's thoughts, his mother intervened. "Oh, there's still plenty of light out. No reason to hurry." She succeeded in swaying her husband as only she could. "Tell us, Ellis. What new story are you working on?"

He could have hugged her right then. Thrown her a parade. "I've got a new feature in tomorrow's paper, actually."

"Another? Already? And in the Sunday edition, at that." She brightened as she glanced across from her. "That's tremendous, isn't it, Jim?"

To answer, he gave his wife a mere nod, though his eyebrow lifted as if he couldn't help being impressed.

Encouraged, Ellis straightened in his seat. "See, I was trying to think of a subject to cover, and with a picture that could mean a lot to local folks. That's when I thought about the mines." If nothing else, he'd learned that Philadelphians loved reading about their own. "I brought it along to show you." He pulled out the photo and proudly slid it over.

"The two guys you see there, they grew up as breaker boys. And now they're operating machines that sort the coal for them. More efficient and safer too, like your new buy at the factory,

Pop. Can you imagine how many kids are alive and well today because of these mechanical sorters? On account of labor laws, too, thanks to the press not letting the problems go on as they had." He hadn't planned to insert the part about due credit; it just streamed out with the point of the article.

Yet something changed in the room. Ellis caught it in his father's manner, his gaze, now absent of any levity from seconds ago. Could his father have recognized the efforts to prove him wrong? To discount old doubts over his son's career, over notions of lowly muckrakers in the press? Or…was it something else?

His father always had a knack for spotting the strengths and weaknesses in any contraption. As a supervisor, he sought out the same in his workers. Maybe he alone could sense the fragment of deceit, like a faulty gear, in Ellis's tale of success.

Whatever the cause, even Ellis's mother appeared stumped by the wordless moment that was anything but quiet.

When his father came to his feet, his tone was raspy and low. "I better see about the car before it gets too late." With that, he headed for the entry and grabbed his toolbox from the closet.

Once he was gone, Ellis's mother pushed up a smile and handed back the picture. "Sounds like a wonderful article," she said. "We'll sure be excited to read it."

CHAPTER 10

OVER AND OVER AGAIN Lily had lied. It wasn't an ideal way to spend a Wednesday, but on four separate occasions, coworkers had asked if she was feeling well. She insisted she was doing just fine, which wasn't the least bit true. Not since yesterday evening, when she had secretly phoned from the boardinghouse. In a residence for unwed women with the highest moral caliber, such calls had to be made furtively. Informed of Samuel's condition, she began worrying herself sick.

I'll be on a bus first thing tomorrow, she'd contended. She was told not to come, that it wasn't necessary, that she was being ridiculous. After all, she would see him again on Friday. But that was still two days away. Days that would stretch out like years.

Thus, she strove to pass the hours as best she could. She busied herself with filing, phone calls, and dictation, reminding herself that to come and go as she pleased wasn't an option, not with a boss like Howard Trimble. Unless she hoped to be out of a job.

She even managed to refrain from phoning again about Samuel, save for once over her lunch hour. But now the chief had departed for a four o'clock meeting, gone for the remainder of the day. With a good portion of the city room cleared out, and the rest focused on tomorrow's deadline, Lily finally had sufficient privacy.

She summoned the operator on her desk phone and was connected to her family's deli. A shared line with their home above the store meant two chances to obtain an update. How could she possibly rest until she knew he was well?

Samuel was the center of her world, and of her heart. He was her first thought upon waking, her last before sleep.

He was her cherished four-year-old son.

A series of bleating rings ceased when her mother answered, and Lily cut in.

"How's he feeling?"

"Oh, honey. He's fine."

"His fever is gone, then."

"I told you, there's nothing to worry about." Her avoidance of the question caused Lily to clench the receiver.

"How hot is he?" At the pause, Lily demanded, "What's his temperature?"

A long, exasperated sigh. "A hundred and one."

"I'm coming home."

"But, Lily, you have work tomorrow. You'll have barely arrived before you have to turn right back around."

It was a valid point, given the two-hour bus ride each way. And the stops in their small town ran scarce in the evenings.

"Then I'll stay overnight."

"The first bus doesn't leave until eight in the morning. You know this."

"So I'll be a little late returning. The chief will have to understand."

"Now, that's just foolish."

Lily was already rising from her chair, ready to grab her handbag and set off straight for the bus depot. She would first leave a note for her boss, citing a vague family emergency.

"Lillian Harper." Her mother's tone shifted, firming on two words that instantly turned Lily into a child herself. "I understand you're concerned. But remember the last time you rushed back? All over a tummy ache. Even the doctor said it's not good for you to get riled up like this. And it's not good for Samuel either."

Logic said she was right. As was the doctor. Yet logic had nothing to do with the true reason behind Lily's fears over her son's well-being.

She was tempted to explain this at last. Her mother would understand, wouldn't she? After all, through the most trying of times, her support was a constant. Even when Lily's father, in an initial fit of devastation, had threatened to disown his only child. And who could fully blame him? Lily was supposed to be the "miracle baby" destined for greatness, a reward for ten taxing years of pregnancy attempts. At seventeen she had shown such promise, the first in the family line with plans to attend college, all of which she'd thrown away for a night with a boy she barely knew.

Mind you, that error became a blessing. Not only in the form of Samuel but also in the enduring love of her family, ultimately standing by her when so many others sneered. In fact, those looks of disgust had strengthened her with the will to part from her son every week. She had long ago learned to tolerate the judgment of her town, its size no larger than a thumbprint. She refused, however, to allow the same for Samuel, whose innocence provided but a temporary shield. Unlike the two poor boys in Ellis's first feature, he would never question whether he was wanted. Not if Lily had any say. By the time he was of school age, she would have enough funds for a fresh start in another city and an apartment of their own. She could even pass as a young widow now at twenty-two, eliminating the need to hide the most cherished piece of her life.

But until that time, she would worry—yes, far more than she

should. And though she had her reasons, she realized she would never speak them aloud. To her mother most of all.

"I can take you."

The man's voice startled Lily. She swung around to face Clayton Brauer, his hands resting in his trouser pockets.

"Pardon me?" She muted the mouthpiece against her chest. Her heartbeat quickened as she reviewed his comment.

"You need a lift, and my interview canceled." He raised a shoulder in his typical style, not bothering with a full shrug. "A car will get you there twice as fast. Then if you want to come back tonight, you'll make it in time for work."

"I'm afraid I'm...not sure what you might've heard—"

"Miss Palmer, if your son is sick, you ought to look in on him."

She froze, forgetting to breathe, until her mother's voice reminded Lily of the connected line. "Mother, I'll ring you back," she said and hung up the call.

As the top crime reporter at the *Examiner* for the past four years, Clayton had the chief's ear more than almost anyone on staff. The last thing Lily needed was her boss, along with her landlady, to learn she had been grossly untruthful, tracing all the way back to her job interview with Mr. Baylor, conducted on the chief's behalf.

Married? he'd asked.

No, sir.

Plans to change that anytime soon?

Oh, no. Definitely not.

He had looked at her, pleasantly surprised. *Good,* he'd said and jotted a note.

Why's that, may I ask?

The chief's last secretary, she got hired as a newlywed. Quit the day she found out she was with child. Chief decided there's less headache with no pesky family issues to worry about. Make sense?

In light of her goal, she had managed a nod. *None of those pesky issues here,* she assured him just to be safe, at which he smiled. The next thing she knew, she was being toured around the building, shown to a desk, and introduced to the chief, as well as to the publisher, a cantankerous man whose sightings were thankfully minimal. She even received a personal referral for a boardinghouse not far from the paper. In both settings, her acceptance and treatment as a virtuous young woman were undeniably refreshing, though never her main motives for keeping Samuel a secret.

She laughed now to convey amusement over Clayton's assumption, her pulse still hammering. "I think you've misunderstood, Mr. Brauer. It's my nephew I was checking on."

Clayton regarded his watch, her words like dust motes that had wafted right by. "I just need to see to something downstairs before the paper's put to bed. After that, we can head to Maryville if you're ready. All right with you?"

He knew—about her son, her hometown—even before the call, it seemed.

Then it came to her. Of course he would. A person didn't become a star reporter without picking up on the details, the subtle clues.

"How long have you…?"

"Not to worry, your secret's safe." With marked simplicity, he'd addressed two far more critical issues: Did anyone else know? Would he be telling the chief?

She nodded at him, thrown off but terribly grateful. Like the majority of the staff, Clayton resided in Philly. Delaware was hardly on his route home.

"I'll swing by when I'm done," he told her. "And listen, if you do decide to come back tonight, I'd be glad to drive and save you the return bus fare."

Although it would prevent the chief from throwing a conniption over her late arrival tomorrow, she was still reluctant to accept. "It's lovely of you to offer, but I wouldn't dream of making you wait around for me. You're already doing too much."

"The favor's not for you, Miss Palmer. Seeing as I'll be making the round-trip anyway, I'd much rather have someone to talk to other than myself."

She smiled, unable to argue, and Clayton flashed one of his grins before going on his way.

~

In fewer than two minutes, Lily was set to leave. The next fifteen were spent stealing glances at the wall clocks. She had pulled on her cloche, travel gloves, and dusty-rose sweater. She held her handbag, clasped and ready.

Deciding she would spare Clayton the extra steps, she wandered toward his desk and found it vacant. He was still completing his tasks.

She reminded herself to be patient, not to dwell on Samuel's fever, and happened to notice Ellis at his desk. Even from his profile, she detected a heavy expression as he stared at his typewriter, unseeing.

She suddenly reflected upon their encounter that morning. Two staff members had just questioned her about not looking well. When Ellis approached her desk, she'd insisted she was just fine before he could say a word. As it turned out, he had hoped to interest her in another outing after work, to a speakeasy called the Cove. A group from the *Examiner* often blew off steam there midweek. In hindsight, she had declined the invitation in a horribly rude manner.

Since their exchange at Franklin Square, she had made a concerted effort to maintain a comfortable distance, but over no wrongdoing of his certainly.

"Excuse me. Mr. Reed?"

He looked up at her, trance broken.

"Earlier today, I fear I treated you poorly. I hope you'll accept my apology."

The tension in his face loosened, enough for a partial smile. "I appreciate that. But it's not a problem."

She smiled back before he shifted his attention to his notebook. He seemed to be merely occupying himself.

Ellis's somberness couldn't have stemmed strictly from her behavior. There had to be something more.

"Is…anything else troubling you?"

He appeared to be contemplating whether to answer, deepening her concern.

In the background, a duet of typewriters clacked a jagged rhythm as a reporter wished another a good night. Yet Lily kept her focus on Ellis. While she didn't have time for a lengthy discussion, she likely had a bit.

She took a seat at the very next desk, purse on her lap, and caught the gratitude in his eyes.

"I got an offer," he replied before lowering his voice. "To work on City News."

A promotion. Lily was genuinely happy for him, lacking any of her prior shameful jealousy. "That's wonderful. You must be so proud." Then recalling his mood, she observed, "But you're not celebrating."

"It's the *New York Herald Tribune*."

"I'm sorry?"

"City editor called yesterday. Thought the *Trib* could use a reporter with some heart, he said. His wife has a friend just outside Philly and recommended my features. Still hard to believe."

Lily should have known this was coming. His articles, as much as his photographs, radiated with a care and sincerity that captivated readers. In the small world of news, a keen editor was bound to track Ellis down.

"Truth be told, Miss Palmer, that's why I asked you about going to the Cove. Guess I'm in need of some pretty good guidance again." He laughed under his breath, hinting at embarrassment for having to ask.

"So, you're still deciding?"

"Must be off my nut, right? It's a dream job for any journalist around."

Only at that moment did Lily realize how much she hoped that she, above all, was the cause of his reluctance. A silly notion, which she firmly pushed away.

"Then what's the trouble?"

He wet his lips, as if to ease the flow of words. "Thing is, when the chief assigned me that first feature, with the photo of the kids, I saw it as my big break. A chance to prove to everyone back at home that I could really do this."

"And now?"

"Now all these swell things are happening. But when I think about that picture..."

The actual issue becoming clear, Lily volunteered the rest: "You feel guilty. About making gains from their misfortune." It was an understandable response.

"No. I mean, there's that, of course. But it's...well..."

He connected with her eyes right then, and once more she sensed it. There was a truth he was guarding, an ardent secrecy she could relate to firsthand. Perhaps it involved the brother he had lost, his personal link to the photograph. She knew nothing more, outside of her own dark past evoked by the image.

"You can tell me," she assured him. "I promise, my lips are sealed." She could see again that he trusted her, despite having little reason to do so.

Wistfully, Ellis leaned toward her, his face just inches from hers. She caught the faint scent of soap on his skin, the warmth of his breath. She had no desire to pull away, feeling far more comfortable than she should. But as he went to speak, his attention caught on a sight behind her. Abruptly he drew his head back, and Lily just as soon discovered the reason.

"Don't mean to intrude," Clayton said to her. He held his

leather briefcase at his side, his fedora over his waist. "Just wanted to say I'm ready when you are."

Lily quickly gathered herself and rose. The way her nerves were skittering, one would think she'd been caught in an amorous act—which, of course, she had not.

"I can wait outside," Clayton added, "though we should probably hit the road soon."

With sweeping force, worries over Samuel flew back at Lily. How could she have forgotten, even for a minute?

"Yes. You're absolutely right." She angled in Ellis's direction, not quite making eye contact. "I'm sorry, Mr. Reed, but I do need to go."

"Nah. It's me who's sorry for keeping you." He delivered the words with a slight coolness as he straightened in his chair. "You already said you were busy tonight. I should've remembered."

The Cove. When he asked her to go, she had tossed out her stock excuse. Now she wanted desperately to correct his assumption—about her and Clayton as a couple—but there was no easy way to do so.

"Well then," she said. "I'll see you tomorrow." She pivoted toward Clayton, who held out his arm as if to make a show of it. She had progressed but a few steps when Ellis responded.

"Actually, that's pretty doubtful." His tone had gained density, a forthrightness that turned her head. "See, I've got a lot of packing to do. For the big move."

All Lily could do was stare at him as Clayton took the bait.

"Move, huh? Where to?"

"Got an offer from New York. From the *Herald Tribune*."

Ellis seemed to be waiting for a reaction—any reporter at the *Examiner* would be downright envious—but Clayton's mouth surprisingly slid into a grin. "Yeah? How about that." He even congratulated Ellis with a hearty handshake.

It took Lily a conscious effort to mirror their joy. She despised the acute sting of Ellis's choice. Though only a few hours away,

New York City—dubbed "the Big Town" for many a reason—entailed the start of another life. And leaving the rest behind.

Regardless, when the men's hands separated, she offered, "In that case, Mr. Reed, I wish you the best of luck." Then to Clayton: "We ought to get on the road, didn't you say?"

"After you," he replied, and she led him toward the exit, barring herself from looking back.

CHAPTER 11

IT WAS DIM OF ELLIS TO HESITATE. No reporter with an iota of sense would have turned down the famed *Herald Tribune*.

Sure, his decision would have been easier without the hindrance of his conscience. Lily had been right about the source of his guilt, of his success being built on the hardships of others, but that was only the half of it. The *Tribune* editor's raves, particularly about the photo of the Dillards, had reminded him of the truth. Or, rather, the lie.

He'd longed to tell this to someone, and not just anyone. To Lily Palmer. How the picture of those kids was meant to be a single rung on the rise of his career. How instead, although it shouldn't, that photograph suddenly felt like the whole ladder.

There was something about her that told him she'd understand, an underlying connection. At least he had thought so until Clayton's interjection made the situation all too clear. In that moment, reflexive pride had spurred Ellis to decide about the job. Once the words were out, he couldn't very well take them back. Even if he could, why should he? The move to New York was just what he needed. Before long, any memory of Lily and the Dillard kids would fade far into the distance.

Ellis told himself this as he geared up to phone the chief to make it official. He braced for a rant over a perceived show of disloyalty or ingratitude. While the man did mutter over the inconvenience, he ended up wishing Ellis well, even tinged with sincerity.

It couldn't have hurt that the actual Society editor was finally set to return in the coming weeks. Plus, a day rarely passed when a writer—aspiring or seasoned, man or woman—didn't swing by the *Examiner* on a hunt for an opening. As the saying went, only first-ranked reporters were irreplaceable—until they were replaced.

Ellis's father would reinforce as much with relish, if given the chance. That was precisely why Ellis prevented him the opportunity. After all, it was a time of celebration. When it came to sharing his news, he'd deliberately called during the workday to reach only his mother. *Oh, sweetheart, we're just so proud of you,* she'd said, bubbling with excitement. For an instant, he almost believed the plurality in her claim.

Within four days of accepting, he'd packed up his belongings—a minimal task if ever there was one—prepared his clunker for the drive, secured an unseen apartment in Brooklyn, and off he went.

Of course, one peek at his tenement would have quelled his mother's enthusiasm. For yet again, a single toilet accommodated an entire floor of renters, the walls were as thin as gauze, and tailed critters enjoyed occasional visits. But much improved over the last, his room had a real desk and chair, a bed mostly free of lumps and creaks, and a kitchenette with a sink that ran hot and cold water. Hell, a person could spin with arms spread wide and not risk scraping a single wall. And as a perk, with immigrants of all varieties as neighbors, if Ellis ever got the itch, he could take up just about any foreign language he pleased.

In truth, he could afford a better place. His starting salary was sixty bucks a week, a decent sum compared to his meager Society pay. But he planned to be smart, save up for a car engine before his old one petered out. Only then would he splurge a little—buy a new hat with a silk band maybe, or a snazzy gabardine suit. Items that would fit right in at the *Tribune*.

Like everything in New York, the paper was snappier in both speed and style. At least, it seemed that way the first afternoon he stepped into their fancy building and rode the elevator to reach the city room, a vast space teeming with smoke and intensity. Of all the Mondays to begin, he'd chosen a doozy. Al Capone had just been found guilty of tax evasion. Thomas Edison had gone to meet his maker. Thirty thousand Hitlerites had paraded through Germany. And, to top it off, while plowing through Manchuria, Japan was working to bar America from joining the League of Nations.

In short, Ellis's arrival didn't cause many ripples.

"Mr. Walker." He repeated himself for the third time, finally snagging the city editor's attention. A cluster of reporters had just dispersed from the man's desk in the center of the room, having confirmed their assignments for the day.

"What can I do for you?"

"Sir, I'm Ellis Reed." An expectant pause. But Stanley Walker simply checked his wristwatch while rising from his seat. His wiry frame stood a few inches below Ellis's height of five nine. His black hair held reddish tints and a light wave.

"You got a tip? Make it quick. On my way to a meeting." His light Texan drawl conflicted with his staccato pace.

"I... No... You hired me. Last week. To work here?"

A look of bewilderment crossed the man's clean-shaven face as he pulled on his navy suit jacket, which smelled of cigars. Around them, the familiar ticking of typewriters melded with radio chatter and layered conversations. "What's your name again?"

A prickling spread over Ellis's scalp from sudden fear that this had been a mix-up. "Reed. From the *Examiner*."

"In Pittsburgh?"

"Philly."

Mr. Walker snapped his fingers. "Right, right. The feature writer." He smiled, showing a flash of discolored teeth, then swiftly lowered his lips as if by habit. "Been one of those mornings. You understand."

"Completely." Ellis shook the man's hand with relief. "Again, sir, I appreciate the trouble you went to in finding me. You haven't made a mistake."

"I sure as hell hope not." Another tight smile rendered the remark difficult to read. Then he introduced Ellis to the assistant city editor, parked at the next desk, requesting he help Ellis settle in.

"I'd be obliged to," Percy Tate replied. Yet the moment his boss slipped out, Mr. Tate's attitude noticeably sharpened as he rattled off the basics—from the building layout and department heads to the standard tasks and daily schedule. His delivery was so brisk that Ellis missed half the details. He dared to ask for a repeat of a point and instantly saw his mistake in the man's hardened face. Everything about him—his eyes and nose, his build and demeanor—resembled a watchful owl. Just biding his time until he swooped in for the kill.

"Hey there, Mr. Tate," another man said, stepping in. His boyish face conflicted with his deep voice. "If that's the new guy, I can take it from here if you'd like."

Ellis had obviously failed to hide his befuddlement.

Mr. Tate tore away without hesitation.

"I'm Dutch." The fella offered Ellis a handshake, a genial though sly glint in his eyes. A heavy-lead pencil rested behind one ear, poking through his slicked, chestnut hair.

"And I'm…not sure what I did wrong."

"Ah, don't mind old purse face." He flicked his hand in Mr. Tate's direction. "Wasn't much better when I first got here."

Ellis managed a smile. "Thought it was something personal."

"Well, maybe a little," Dutch admitted. "A pal of his has been vying for a spot here for some time now. Could be sore about that. It'll pass."

Comprehending the issue, Ellis nodded. Not a great way to start off, but even more motivation to prove his worth.

"Now," Dutch said, "how's about a tour?"

~

Thanks to Dutch—Pete Vernon being his given name—Ellis quickly learned about navigating the labyrinth of floors, the late-night hours of a morning paper, and the key staffers to approach or avoid. As a married father of a toddler boy, with another babe on the way, Dutch kept his after-work mingling to a minimum. But he still slipped in a tour of Bleeck's, the speakeasy next door on Fortieth Street.

It was there that Mr. Walker regularly took his lunches, accompanied by a glass or two of scotch. Not that even the paper's higher-ups would object. Particularly since the *Tribune*'s owner was known to frequent the same joint in the evenings, putting away more than his share of Prohibition dew—apparently doing the same throughout the day in his large corner office. Fortunately for everyone, his wife was shrewd enough to handle many of the paper's business dealings. In fact, three years earlier, she could very well have been a driving force behind promoting Mr. Walker from the night staff.

According to Dutch, the visionary city editor had been tasked with infusing new life into the *Tribune*. Right off the bat, he replaced the deadweight of aristocratic progenies with a few veteran reporters, but mostly fresh, eager writers to pen stories of "women, wampum, and wrongdoing," as Mr. Walker liked to put it. In other words, he preferred spotlights on the feel and culture of the city to stale accounts of politics and economics.

It made sense then why Ellis had been recruited. Nevertheless, gaining his footing was more challenging than expected.

A few weeks in, and still adjusting to the paper's hours—often concluding well past midnight—he was at his desk one afternoon, about to drift off, when a portly reporter known as Dobbs smacked Ellis's shoulder with a scrolled-up page.

"Got a hot tip, but I'm jam-packed for the day. All yours if you want it."

Ellis scrambled to sit up and accepted with gratitude. So far, he'd largely been a legman, dispatched to gather serviceable quotes or supportive details for another reporter's stories. The rest of the time he served as a newsroom mutt, charged with a long list of menial tasks. The unwanted scraps.

This was his chance for more. Shedding the fuzziness of sleep, he strained to read Dobbs's notes about an elusive ship. The floating speakeasy, called the *Lucky Seagull*, had apparently been spotted on the outskirts of the harbor in the twilight hours. If located, it was just the kind of subject that could earn Ellis a byline.

Not *if*, he decided, but *when*.

～

Ellis spent the next three days investigating the ship's whereabouts. Each night, he trolled the chilly docks, a miserable task in November. Several dockhands confirmed rumors of such a vessel but had no other knowledge. Growing desperate, Ellis bypassed skepticism and paid far too much for a boat ride with a soused, smelly fisherman who swore to have spied the *Lucky Seagull* half a dozen times.

By dawn of the fourth day, Ellis had nothing to show for his efforts, save for a brutal head cold.

Though dreading to report back, he finally returned for the one o'clock news meeting. The group assembly was a daily occurrence around Mr. Walker's desk. Between coughs and sneezes, Ellis disclosed his lack of findings. He was halfway through when stifled laughs from the surrounding journalists made clear he'd been duped.

Once the gathering broke up, Dutch offered a sympathetic look. "Sorry about all that. If I'd heard, I would've warned you off." He gave a shrug. "On slow days around here, putting cubs on impossible assignments, it's like an initiation. Try not to take it hard."

"Sure. I get it." Ellis wiped his nose with a tissue and smiled to simulate his amusement.

After all the years he'd worked at the *Examiner*, it jarred him to be referred to as a cub. True, when it came down to it, his publishing success amounted to little more than a handful of features. Or really, some might say, to a single memorable photograph.

In fact, the truth of that blasted picture still lurked in the recesses of his mind. A new job in a new city, even in another state, had done nothing so far to wipe the Dillards from his memory. Through his long hours spent shivering on the docks, they'd seeped into his consciousness. He could still see them on that dingy porch, a backdrop to a borrowed sign. Like driftwood, they just kept floating back. The same went for thoughts of Lily Palmer.

A waste of time, he told himself. All of that was in the past.

Discounted by the likes of Mr. Tate, and perhaps now by Mr. Walker himself, he would charge forward with even more resolve.

And so, as the weeks rolled on, Ellis made feverish attempts to land a notable story. Always there was a reason for rejection: not enough meat, already well-covered territory, great theory but lacking ample evidence to take it to press.

In the meanwhile, he continued to justify his salary by covering basic city assignments, snatching a column inch here and there. Same as most, it was a duty at the paper that largely went unnoticed until marred by an error, like misspelling a star vaudevillian's name. Or reversing the ages of a mother and son who'd survived a house fire. Or in the caption of a photo, mistaking an ambassador's wife for his daughter.

Each instance earned Ellis a warning, the last two sterner than the first.

As a direct result, he became hyperdiligent when recording any information, confirming facts at least twice to prevent another blunder. This was precisely how he knew, without a doubt, that he'd correctly transcribed the time Dutch had given him for a council meeting at City Hall. Ellis was sent out to grab a comment from the mayor about a controversial zoning dispute. Yet he arrived to discover that the event had ended hours earlier and the mayor had left for a trip.

Straightaway, Ellis phoned Dutch, who apologized for the gaffe. Ellis therefore had no cause to prepare a defense when returning to the paper, where he was promptly beckoned to the city desk.

"Dutch told me about the mix-up," Mr. Walker stated. He was never one to yell, unlike old Howard Trimble, but a thread of frustration tugged at his drawl. "We needed the mayor's response to corroborate. Now we can't run the damn piece."

"Sir, I'll track him down. I'll get a quote by tomorrow—"

"Dutch'll handle it."

From the assistant city editor's desk, Mr. Tate shot Ellis his usual owlish glower.

Mr. Walker leaned back in his chair. He shook his head with a firm look. "Bottom line, Mr. Reed. This cannot happen again."

Equally stunned and bewildered, Ellis silently grappled for an explanation. But then he caught eyes with Dutch across the room. When the guy dropped his gaze, the situation gained clarity. He had pinned the blame on Ellis.

In any competitive business, let alone in New York, a man had to look out for himself. Especially in times like these. Ellis just never expected this from someone he considered a friend.

"I understand," he replied simply, in no position to argue.

All things considered, which of them would Mr. Walker have believed?

~

Four or five. No—six. Gently swirling the whiskey in his glass, Ellis tried to recall the number of shots he'd downed since planting himself in a corner booth at Hal's Hideaway. True to its name, the dim bar was nestled deep in an alley with a nondescript door, just blocks from Ellis's flat in Brooklyn. Entry required a special knock, which he'd gleaned from the janitor of his apartment building. The elderly man claimed to enjoy a nip of "rye gag" at Hal's on occasion.

On the low stage, a trio played the blues to a half-filled room, where a mix of tables and booths afforded decent privacy. But what Ellis favored most was that the place wasn't Bleeck's, a joint full of *Tribune* staffers who surely viewed him as a chump, thanks to that damn backstabbing Dutch. The guy actually had the guts to approach Ellis before day's end. Ellis had walked away, not hearing a word.

Folks in Allentown voiced warnings about his kind. The sneaky, greedy, double-crossing types. Ellis hadn't listened. And now here he was, on the brink of hightailing it home, washed up. A bum.

Lily was a smart one indeed. Given a choice between him and ace-in-the-hole Clayton Brauer, she'd picked the winner.

Ellis threw back his drink. No longer blazing fire down his throat, it melted away another layer of frustration. He'd need two more shots to dull the pangs of betrayal. Four, maybe, to drown out the sense of defeat.

Squinting toward a waitress—his vision had transformed her into twins—he waved to signal a refill. She nodded, then attended to other patrons. No rush on her part.

Ellis sank into his seat, eyelids growing heavy. He tried to lose himself in the notes of "Embraceable You," but voices behind him kept seeping over the high-back booth. The group's volume had been growing with every round of drinks.

With the state Ellis was in, he had half a mind to tell them to keep it down. But he was catching enough of their words—about a recent warehouse raid and a new member of their outfit—to know better. He'd be wise to turn a deaf ear, but the same nosiness that had doomed him to become a newspaperman compelled him to listen closer.

"We bloody need to do somethin'." The man spoke with a brogue, implying ties to the Irish Mob, a large faction in the borough. "We look like a bunch of dolts and killers, the lot of us. The boss is right. People see us as alley rats, and we'll never get the respect we deserve."

"Yeah, so? Whaddya have in mind?" This one's accent was clearly local.

"What, I gotta have all the answers?"

They were fretting over public perception, Ellis realized. Not an original concept, even in the underworld. Mobsters, at least the savvy ones, were businessmen, after all.

Ellis recalled an article. After the St. Valentine's Day Massacre, when Capone's men gifted the competition with a spray of bullets, the bootlegger's suave image suffered. Soon after, Capone himself began funding soup kitchens, as highlighted in the paper, to regain the public's favor.

An idea now formed in Ellis's head, a solution to more than a single dilemma. Sure, it came with a voice of reason, but it was tamped by a desperate desire to reverse his luck. More than that, a primitive urge to battle his way back. He envisioned himself as Jack Dempsey in the ninth round of a title fight. Pinned to the ropes. Refusing to go down.

Before Ellis could weigh the risks, he came to his feet.

At the next table, dizzy from standing too fast, he struggled to bring the men into focus. Two of the figures were seated together, their faces indiscernible. A third, with a scar on his jawline, stared straight at Ellis.

"What the bloody hell are *you* lookin' at?"

"I've got a proposal." Ellis aimed for assertive, trying not to sound shellacked. "A fairly easy way to solve your problem."

The brawnier of the seated pair jumped in. "Our problem, huh? So, you listening in on us? That it?"

Despite his mental haze, Ellis knew to skip to the point. "See, I'm a reporter at the *Herald Tribune*. And if you're looking to better your—"

"Take this eejit outside," the scarred Irishman ordered.

The guy who stood up topped Ellis by a good foot, plus a solid seventy pounds. As he gripped Ellis by the arm, tight as a tourniquet, the error in Ellis's judgment became strikingly apparent. But so did his need to blurt out the rest.

"I'm offering a trade that your boss is gonna love."

The hold on Ellis's arm remained, but the men were exchanging looks. He'd at least piqued their interest. But was it enough to save him from a one-way trip to the dump?

After a steely pause, a gleam entered the Irishman's eyes. "Take a seat."

CHAPTER 12

THE MARCH MORNING SKY filled Lily's window with an ominous gray, fitting for her rising angst. Two floors sat atop her parents' deli, with living quarters in the middle and both bedrooms on the third. Today, in her childhood room, even the familiar scents of pastrami and bread drifting through the vents brought little comfort. Nor did the sight of Samuel on the floor, drawing pictures of rockets and rabbits and family. If anything, his presence was compounding the issue.

"Mommy, look it!"

Lily twisted on her vanity stool, where she sat in her slip and robe, begrudgingly preparing for the day ahead. He was holding up another masterpiece, this one of the deli flanked by trees sprouting spring leaves. "Oh, baby, it's marvelous."

His toothy grin widened, his pale-green eyes and round face aglow. "I'm gonna show Gamma." He jumped up and rushed out of the room. His footsteps pattered down the hall and faded down the stairs.

While not the primary source of Lily's troubles, the fact that tonight would mark her first Saturday spent away from her son was hardly trivial. Already she spent so much time without him, mulling over what-ifs.

That wasn't to say she was immune to feeling silly over her worrying—like back in October, when she and Clayton arrived to find Samuel's fever subsided. To his credit, Clayton had expressed only delight, unfazed even by her son's refusal to engage with a stranger. Then again, her mother had dominated all, including her father's skeptical looks, while ushering Clayton inside for supper, her enthusiasm as clear as her will.

Hailing from a long line of bakers, Harriet Palmer was deceptively strong for her short form, topped by reddish-brown locks styled with nightly curlers. Together with her husband, the couple resembled the light and doughy rolls she baked every dawn, with the sweet demeanors to match.

Well, if one didn't count the expletives from Lily's father during radio broadcasts of Yankees games, which earned him routine visits to the confessional, or the piercing glares her mother reserved for opposition to matters she valued.

Clayton might have sensed the latter from the start, as he didn't hesitate in agreeing to stay for a meal. A month later, he accepted just as easily after driving Lily again on a Friday after work. It was a stop on his way to chasing down a lead, he claimed. Whether true or not, Lily couldn't resist saving herself an hour of travel time, for it meant seeing her darling Samuel run to her that much sooner. It meant another hour of his lively chatter and heartwarming giggles.

So it went, ashamedly with little protest on Lily's part—the benefits far outweighing any message she might be sending— until the drives to Maryville in Clayton's Chevy Coupe, followed by a family supper, became a regular occurrence unless a big story pulled him away.

By late winter, her lone bus rides to and from the city came to feel much longer for lack of conversation. She didn't always agree with Clayton's opinions. His stances, often to a maddening degree, were as black and white as the clippings of his articles. But as a seasoned reporter, on the crime beat at that, he had no shortage of intriguing tales or skillful questions—for Lily's parents, in particular—to prevent awkward lulls.

Over time, her father's defenses wholly thawed. It didn't hurt that Clayton was also Catholic and, though with German roots, "three generations American." He was swift to point this out, as if to sidestep any resentment related to the Great War. Not that anything could deter Lily's parents by then—or Samuel, who had grown equally comfortable from regular visits.

Besides, what wasn't there to like? Clayton Brauer had a respectful yet confident bearing and an upstanding career, key elements of a fine suitor. Most important, he showed no averseness to courting an unwed mother.

And yet, spring had arrived before Lily was forced to confront the standing of their relationship.

She had just walked Clayton to his car, parked in the crisp darkness outside the deli. Despite being aware she shouldn't bother, she scanned the town's main street for gossipy onlookers and found relief in the evening stillness. She thanked Clayton profusely, as she always did before his return to Philly. He replied by peering down into her eyes, and she recognized his intent before he leaned toward her. Given the ease that had developed between them, such an encounter was surely due. But once his lips pressed to hers, she reflexively drew away, an act that immediately smacked her with guilt.

"Clayton, I'm so sorry. I know you've been patient…"

A corner of his mouth lifted, and his thumb gently brushed her chin. "It's okay. I'm not going anywhere."

An expert at his craft, he had once again addressed her concerns in just a few words: that she could take all the time she needed, that he was a man she could count on.

He then climbed into his car but stopped short of closing the door. "There's an old pal I grew up with in Chicago—works at the *Sun* now. He's getting married next weekend at the Waldorf in Manhattan. If you're up for it, I'd sure love if you came along."

In the silence that followed, she realized she hadn't responded. She shook her head at herself and laughed. "Gosh, of course. I'd love to go."

He sent her another smile before starting the engine and driving away. Only then did it dawn on her that the wedding would interrupt her weekend routine. She considered changing her answer, though after their exchange that evening, paired with his ongoing generosity, how could she possibly?

Pondering this, she had ascended the staircase behind the deli counter. Up in the sitting room, her mother was knitting in her rocking chair by lamplight. The floral curtain on the window hung conspicuously open. Lily was in no mood to surmise what her mother had witnessed.

"Good night," Lily said quickly. She turned for the upper stairs, eagerly retreating toward the room she shared with Samuel. How she yearned for the peaceful sound of his rhythmic breaths.

"Dear, wait."

With great reluctance, Lily pivoted back. Her mother rested her knitting needles on the lap of her long skirt, an admonition in her sigh. "Lily, you mustn't forget. A man like Clayton doesn't happen along every day."

Here it came, an inevitable lecture on the horrors of permanent spinsterhood. Lily was suppressing a groan when her mother added, "You need to think of Samuel."

Lily just stared. How many times had she been told that she fussed too much over her son? True, in the beginning she had feared he would suffer from the void of an absent father. But no longer. He had a family who adored him. There was no denying that Samuel's life, while unconventional, was blessed more than many.

Before these thoughts could form words, however, her

mother held up her hand, a command to let her finish. "But you also need to think about *you*. Your father and I won't be around forever, and we simply dread the idea of you being alone." The heaviness and care in her voice were mirrored in her downturned eyes.

A parent's protectiveness, it seemed, was a beloved burden with no end.

Defenses lowering, Lily attempted to comfort her. "I appreciate your worry, but I'm not alone. I have our family. I have Samuel."

"And when he grows up? What then?"

He was so small and young, still so dependent. It shook Lily to imagine him off on his own adventures, perhaps half a world away.

"Mother, truly. I'll be fine."

"Yes, yes. You'll be fine," she said. "But will you be happy?"

~

The question had stalked Lily ever since. Even now, it loomed in every inch of her and Samuel's room, from the toy chest in the corner to their pair of narrow, quilt-laden beds. One of which would someday remain empty.

Shutting out the thought, she completed her french twist and applied red lipstick, preparing for her train to New York Pennsylvania Station, where Clayton would be waiting. So as not to encroach on her savings, he had arranged for her ticket and overnight stay at a place suitable for a lone female traveler. When Clayton made plans, he left little to chance.

At the closet, Lily stepped into her T-strap heels and fastened the gold buttons of her silken dress. With its jade hue and sweet-heart neckline, the garment was her only one elegant enough for a highbrow affair. She added her tweed coat and pinned on her green brimmed hat, each article bringing her closer to departure.

Just inside the entrance of the deli, she tucked her ivory gloves into her travel bag and knelt before Samuel. A smattering of customers blurred into the background. Lily forced a smile as she straightened the collar of her son's shirt, the misaligned buttons proof of having staunchly fastened them himself. "Now, be a good boy while I'm away. Promise?"

He nodded with such surety, growing ever more accustomed to making do without her. A pinch flared deep in her chest. But then he threw his arms around her neck and said, "I love you, Mommy."

"Oh, Samuel. I love you more." She savored the feel of his fine hair, auburn like hers, brushing against her cheek. He smelled of lavender soap and boyish sweat and bananas from his oatmeal. Tears pricking her eyes, she reminded herself that she would be gone for just a night. Tomorrow, an early train would loop her back to Maryville, where she would spend the afternoon with her son before catching the bus to Philly. Her mother thought it foolish not to travel directly back with Clayton, but Lily disagreed.

"Well then. I'd best be off." She kissed Samuel's sticky, dimpled cheek and broke out of his hug before she could reassess her plans.

On cue, Lily's father hollered from behind the counter, "Hey, Sammy! How about a gingersnap?"

Samuel scurried toward the cookie, a reliable distraction.

"Goodbye, sugar bug," Lily whispered. Travel bag in hand, she sent her father a grateful smile and slipped out the door.

Sugar bug. The origin of the nickname passed through her mind as she bused to the train depot. Years ago, on endless nights of colicky wailing, a dab of sugar on Samuel's tongue had delivered moments of reprieve until he wore himself out, along with Lily. And now part of her yearned for those bittersweet days. He would be turning five in June. It was all going too fast.

You need to think of Samuel, her mother had said. Once Lily was settled into her train car, she reevaluated the words. History had taught her to be wary when it came to men, including her own judgment in their regard. With Samuel to think of now, the stakes had never been higher.

The more she deliberated, weighing the idea of a future with Clayton, the clearer her path became. She rubbed her locket like a worry stone, a cherished picture of her son inside. By the time the train passed Trenton, her decision was made.

Still, to prevent wavering, she focused on the book she had packed. *Ten Days in a Mad-House*. It was Nellie Bly's firsthand report of committing herself to an asylum for a shocking exposé. Lily had read the account so many times one could easily question her own sanity. Rationale, perhaps, for what she was about to do.

After the reception, Clayton would escort her back to her hotel, and before parting ways, she would bring to an end what she never should have started.

~

The ceremony—aside from the stained glass, marble columns, and vaulted ceilings at St. Patrick's Cathedral—was fairly standard as marital masses went. It was the reception that boasted all the extravagance of New York high society. In the Waldorf Astoria, the grand ballroom swirled with a sea of tuxedos and formal gowns, of colognes and perfumes and haze from expensive tobacco. Conversations and laughter competed with the strings of an unseen quartet.

Save for the pretension, Lily couldn't refute it was an impressive affair. Six-arm candelabras flickered at the center of each round table. Spread over pressed white linens were identical displays of gold serving ware, crimson petals, and perfectly folded napkins. Gloved waiters served crystal flutes of champagne—the presence of two congressmen, as Clayton pointed out, apparently precluding the event from any legal hassles.

"May I?" Clayton slid Lily's chair out for her. By candlelight, in his white jacket and black bow tie, his hair slicked with pomade, he looked undeniably dashing.

She smiled politely and took her seat, joining the table of his New York press friends and their wives. With Clayton at her side, it occurred to her just how much like a couple they appeared, putting her ill at ease.

She welcomed the diversion of the bride's father giving a formal toast with a dose of wit, apt for an oil tycoon. He made only one playful jab about his son-in-law marrying up. Then the men at Lily's table plunged into their journalistic gabbing. Between drags on their cigarettes, they lobbed tales of wrathful editors, newsroom politics, and off-the-record scandals. They described run-ins with the infamous William Hearst and ribbed one another about which of their papers deserved the top spot.

Their wives also shared a common history, made clear by their gossip and updates on mutual friends. When the topic of their children finally emerged, Lily perked up at the chance to contribute. But then she recalled how any mention of Samuel would require an awkward explanation. Thus, she continued to nibble on her quail and sip her champagne, feigning intrigue over the words curling around her.

Not until later, as she rose to excuse herself to the powder room, did she feel the full effects of her drink, magnified by the warmth of the ballroom. Rarely one to indulge, she lingered in private to collect her bearings and remembered the ultimate mission of her evening.

Various women passed behind her as she stood before an ornate oval mirror. Once steadied by a few deep breaths, she started back for the reception. At the ballroom entrance awaited Clayton, their overcoats draping his arm.

"There you are." His tone was more anxious than relieved.

She sifted through her muddled thoughts, wondering just how long she had been in the ladies' room. "Are we leaving?"

"There's been a robbery. It's a jewelry store off Times Square.

A fatal shooting, maybe. Might even be Willie Sutton, escaped from the pen. That's the word we just got." He motioned to other newsmen collecting their belongings from the coat-check girls. When Lily was slow to react, he added, "Of course…if you want to stay, we can."

The distracted thrill in his eyes said he was already there, on the scene, formulating a story. Although she knew this was his job, his eagerness to race toward a dead body as if it weren't a real person who'd be mourned by loved ones made her cringe inside.

"No, that's fine," she said. "I have an early train. I should be calling it a night anyway."

"Ah, good. Then I'll just take you to your hotel first."

Her hotel—the location for a talk that obviously would have to wait.

He held her coat open for her. As she slid her arms in, she realized she still needed her purse. Had she left it in the lavatory? Or was it under her chair? Or perhaps…

"Lily?" Clayton was yards away when he discovered she hadn't followed. He returned with the impatience of a track star summoned back for a false start.

She dreaded to announce, "I still need to grab my handbag."

Now he looked as if his race had been canceled.

"You should go on. I can walk myself back."

He scanned her face. "Are you sure? Because I can wait." His willingness was there, despite his body already angling toward the exit.

"And miss the scoop? The chief would throw a fit. Really, you go. My hotel's only two blocks away."

He nodded with relief and smiled. "All right. You travel safely." He gave her a kiss on the cheek before hustling toward his friends already on their way out.

Suddenly it came to her: she had stored her valuables under her chair.

She didn't waste a second before weaving her way through the ballroom to reach her now-vacant table. There was her purse, just as suspected. Right then, someone repeatedly clinked a glass to quiet the guests, and the quartet halted within a measure.

Out of courtesy, Lily reclaimed her seat to wait out the toast. At the front of the room, the groom presented a speech directly to his bride, who stood daintily beside him. She blushed in a white gown that far surpassed the elegance of a typical wedding suit.

Lily didn't catch half of his words. She was far more captivated by the adoration in his voice, its raw vulnerability. He was surrendering not only his heart but his entire self. And his bride was no less willing, based on the connection of their gaze, so intimate that at one point Lily felt intrusive for watching.

Then the couple engaged in a kiss, publicly appropriate yet wholly tender, triggering an unexpected feeling in Lily. A romantic longing she had nearly forgotten existed, an ancient magnet pulling at her heart.

The room of guests applauded, the quartet resumed its playing, and champagne continued to flow.

Lily opened her handbag. Withdrawing her gloves, she revealed the envelope inside. It held a letter for Ellis Reed, regarding the children from his first feature. Forwarding address: *New York Herald Tribune*. She had planned to swing by the post office at Penn Station before boarding her morning train. It would be more efficient, she had concluded, to mail it in New York.

But now she had to wonder. Had there been another reason for bringing the missive along? She thought of her last discussion with Ellis, back at the *Examiner*, the unspoken trust, their faces mere inches apart. Once again she considered the words they had never shared. The misunderstanding, the cool parting. Perhaps her traveling here had been part of a greater purpose, one she had known unconsciously yet avoided seeing.

To deliver the letter in person.

CHAPTER 13

"IF YA WANNA FOLLOW ME, Mr. Reed." The platinum blond sounded all Bronx but looked pure Hollywood. She smiled coyly before swiveling in her red gown, a glittery number designed to accentuate the curves. The same applied to the brazen uniforms of the cigarette girls circling the room with their trays of goods.

As the hostess led the way across the checkered tiles, Ellis kept his gaze at a proper level. He was acutely aware of the couple trailing behind. Thankfully, from a glance over his shoulder, he found his mother looking upward in awe. Clutching her husband's elbow, she was gawking at the enormous crystal chandelier that threw gem-like sparkles over the candlelit supper club.

The Royal was a real oasis, aside from its entrance off an alley. It had peaked in popularity sometime in the early twenties, people said, but still drew a top-notch crowd. Ellis could understand why. It was nothing but class here, with silver domes over plates and waiters in black tails. Onstage, a colored band in white tuxedoes played snappy tunes with a piano, a bass, and an array of polished horns. Fitting for a Saturday night, the place teemed with glitzy dresses and Brooks Brothers suits, not unlike the one Ellis had donned. A navy gabardine three-piece with a silk tie and kerchief. He'd bought the spats just for tonight, aiming to look his best.

"Would this be to your liking, sir?" The blond gestured to one of the half-moon booths that ran the length of the wall, just as Ellis had requested. The majority of the regular tables and chairs were set in a U formation, cordoning an area for couples now dancing the Lindy Hop. A booth, thanks to partial dividers of long white curtains, lent more privacy and, Ellis hoped, a special touch for the occasion.

"This is great." He smiled and slid the gal a whole dollar tip before inviting his parents to sit first.

"Enjoy your evening," the hostess said before sauntering away.

Once settled in, Ellis removed his fedora, cream with a silk band, and rested it at his side. His father had done the same with his old brimmed hat.

"Like I was saying," Ellis told his parents, "I hear nothing but raves about the place. Fellas at the paper say it's got the best prime rib in town." As his father's favorite dish, the steak had been a key factor when Ellis made the reservation. "So, what do you think, Pop?"

The music melded with his father's mumbled reply.

"It's a lovely choice, sweetheart," his mother jumped in with a bright smile.

After weeks of her coaxing, the couple had finally made the trip to New York, a city Ellis had come to consider his home.

And to think, just four months ago, sulking at Hal's Hideaway over his editor's warning, Ellis had thought for certain he was on his way out. But with the help of far too much whiskey, he'd managed to make a deal with members of the Irish Mob. On the legitimate side, their boss owned a fur shop in Midtown. Ellis had suggested the guy run a charitable promotion: donating his proceeds from a weekend of sales to the Children's Aid Society. A newsworthy story Ellis could pitch.

Just like that, a batch of furs fell off a truck and floated down a river—according to the insurance filing anyhow—and boom! Money was raised for the kiddies. In exchange, Ellis received a solid tip about a congressman who had the gall to skim off veterans' benefits. Cautiously separated by a week, both stories found a cozy spot in the *Tribune*.

Then came a bonus.

Compliments of his Irish contact, Ellis received a list of several other crooked politicians, with sufficient clues to their shady deeds. Incredibly, this one required no return favor. Since the fingered officials were in the pockets of Russian, Jewish, and Italian mobsters—in other words, not the Irish ones— exposing their dirt was repayment enough. Ellis never directly tied the lawmakers to the underworld, as he had no desire to take a dive into the Hudson quite yet, but inadvertently it was a win-win.

In a nutshell, he'd taken his lumps and come back swinging. Jack Dempsey would have been proud.

Still, not pushing his luck, Ellis had expanded his network to the less daunting of society. For an extra buck here and there, switchboard operators and hotel bellboys shared juicier scoops than just about anyone. Not to mention local firemen. Close observers of their territories, and with loads of downtime in the firehouse, they readily shelled out tidbits for free.

Before long, Ellis's biggest challenge became writing pieces fast enough. He'd reported on everything from graft in city licensing and racketeering in the housing industry to a senator's simultaneous upkeep of three mistresses.

An impressive feat, that one.

In truth, Ellis's articles lately had been heavier on flash than substance, but sometimes you had to fill the gaps until the next big break. Just last week, for instance, a widow was hoping to identify the murderer of her husband, a notorious rumrunner from Queens, and Ellis had covered the séance. They couldn't all be worthy of a byline—although, incredibly, he'd already earned two. Neither of them had graced Page One, where so far his articles had appeared unsigned, but all were now money in the bank—quite literally, thanks to some finely aged scotch.

He'd presented the bottle as a Christmas gift, a risky dent in his savings, while daring to ask the *Tribune*'s owner for a raise. He'd aimed for eighty bucks a week, hoping for seventy. But after several shared highballs in the middle of the day, they somehow landed at eight-five.

The best part? Ellis finally felt like an official "man of Park Row," and tonight his parents would share the same view. At least, that was the plan.

"You sure you don't want something more…festive?" he asked, referencing their goblets of water. "Maybe some sherry to go with your dinner, Ma."

The waiter stood like a sentry at attention. Any drink was game after he'd pocketed Ellis's early tip with all the slickness of a politician.

"The night's on me," Ellis reminded his mother.

Looking tempted, she glanced at the last of Ellis's gin martini, served in a teacup—as were all libations here as a precaution for a raid. But before she could decide, her husband answered for them both.

"We'll stick with water." His eyes, bare of glasses tonight, were unwavering. His openness to an occasional nip at home apparently didn't extend to public settings.

Ellis's mother smiled and nodded at the server.

"Very well, then." He angled toward Ellis. "And for you, sir. Would you care for a refill while you peruse the menu? A double perhaps." No doubt he detected the need for one as a way to reduce the tension that had spiked since he'd presented the leather-bound menus. Specifically after Ellis's father confirmed that the listed prices were in dollars.

"That'd be splendid."

The waiter dashed off. Part of Ellis wanted to join him. He had to remind himself that his father was far outside his realm of comfort. That much was evident from how he kept tugging at his collar, fighting his tie like a noose.

You ever see me in that getup, means there's been a funeral, he'd replied when asked by Ellis, as a kid, why he never wore suits like passersby on the street. *If I ain't paying my respects, I'll be the one in the box.*

The fact he was now wearing the one suit he owned, simple and black and solely on Ellis's account, was a gesture not to be missed.

"I gotta say," Ellis offered up, "you both sure look swell tonight." He gestured with his teacup. "And that brooch looks beautiful on you, Ma."

Beaming with pride, she patted the silver stemmed rose. "Thank you, Ellis."

At his new flat in the Bronx, before they'd all walked to dinner, he'd pinned the gift to the plum cardigan layered over her matching dress. All the while, his father had moved stoically around the place—not a mansion by any stretch, but finally an apartment Ellis wasn't embarrassed to show. He'd rushed to furnish it just days before their visit, despite their predictable decline to stay overnight.

His father was now surveying the club with the same unreadable gaze. "You eat like this all the time?"

To appease the man's frugalness, Ellis was about to say no. But why lie? He'd proudly earned the money, one paycheck at a time.

"Once a week or so, I guess."

"So you've already saved up for a new engine, huh?" There was no subtlety to the doubt in his tone.

"Actually," Ellis said, "I've been wanting to tell you. I changed my mind on that."

Confusion tightened his father's features as he waited for an explanation.

"Just figured it was time to stop wasting dough on the old clunker and start fresh. Maybe get a new Ford Roadster. Buy it straight off the line." This would mean no more mechanical help from his father, surely a relief to them both.

"A roadster," his mother said, concerned. "Those are awfully speedy, aren't they?"

"Not to fret, Ma. I won't do anything foolish."

His father huffed. It was a brief sound but sharp with condescension. Then he dropped his attention to his menu, scrutinizing the prices. Judging.

And right then it became painfully clear: since the start of their evening, he'd been doing nothing else.

Ellis simmered with frustration, yet he willed it not to rise. The night could still end up pleasant enough. Particularly with more gin.

He downed the rest of his cocktail, ready for that double. "So," he said, picking up his menu. "What have we got here?"

In his periphery, he glimpsed a nearby cigarette girl who was scanning the club, waiting for buyers to signal their interest. Although neither parent was a smoker, Ellis had known his father to enjoy a rare cigar with pals from the plant.

Perhaps some puffs could mellow his mood. They certainly couldn't hurt.

"Hey, miss!" Ellis raised his hand, his voice lost to the tide of conversations and notes of a sax. He was about to try again when his father muttered something indiscernible, but loud enough to convey derision.

Ellis turned to face him, just as his mother spoke in a firm hush. "Jim. Please." As in, not here. Not tonight.

His father hedged before closing his mouth. He returned to

the menu, his solid jaw twitching as if struggling to contain his words. None of them good. Undoubtedly all for Ellis.

"You got something to say, Pop?"

His father's eyes snapped up, then quickly narrowed. He'd plainly caught the challenge in Ellis's question.

His mother broke in lightly. "Let's just decide on our meals, shall we?"

Ellis didn't stray from his father's hardening gaze. And why should he? He'd grown tired of remaining quiet, of backing down. The only time he wasn't invisible, he was doing something wrong.

"Well, go on. I'm a man now. I can take it."

His father shook his head, another dark laugh. "That's what you think you are, huh? A man. Because you've figured out how to burn through your money?"

Ellis's mother touched her husband's arm, but he pulled back and swept a glower over Ellis. "Look at you, parading around in your fancy suits and hats. Your new apartment. You pass around bucks like penny candy, trying to be some big shot."

Ellis's simmer was turning to a boil. He didn't deserve any of this, particularly from a guy who barely knew Ellis at all. Had hardly ever bothered. Back in Philly, he used to worry that his initial success from the picture of the Dillards had flagged his father's suspicions. Now a revelation dawned.

Fists on his knees, Ellis leaned forward. "You know what? I was trying to treat you and Ma here to a nice night on the town. If this is all making you jealous, it's not my fault." He caught his mother's faint gasp.

His father stared at him. "What'd you say?"

"That's right. Because I'm actually making something of my life." Once his words flew out, there was no pulling them in. The implied comparison hung in the air as his father sank back in his seat. His mother watched, hand held to her mouth.

After a long moment, his father nodded heavily, as if

conceding. That single gesture stung Ellis with shame. And yet, the feeling was dulled by an odd rush of relief. A hope of finally achieving some sort of understanding.

"Maybe you're right about that," his father said. Then his voice turned cold. "'Cause I obviously failed if this is how my only son turned out."

The ending was a punch to the chest. Having let down his guard, Ellis felt the knuckling of each and every syllable—but not just for himself. For a brother who'd long been written off as if he'd never existed.

"You mean the only son who lived."

"*That's enough*," his mother cut in.

In that instant, the world ceased beyond their booth. They had become a trio of statues, limbs unmoving, barely breathing. All Ellis could hear was the thundering of his own pulse.

Slowly, as if coming to, his father picked up his hat. He stood from the table, eyes distant, almost foggy. With an expression still carved from stone, he started toward the exit.

Ellis's mother came to her feet, preparing to follow.

"Ma…" Ellis didn't know what to say. Regardless of who was right or wrong, better or worse, he despised the idea of hurting her. "I'm sorry."

She turned to him, her face sullen, and patted his shoulder. "I know, sweetheart. I know," she said and kissed him on the cheek.

As Ellis watched her trail after his father, the waiter swooped in with a full teacup. A tad too late.

Maybe right on time.

"Will it be a table for one, sir?" The look on his face indicated he'd witnessed the couple's hasty departure.

"I suppose…" Ellis was still trying to absorb all that had happened.

"I'd be happy to take your entrée order if you're ready. Or I could give you more time to decide." When Ellis didn't respond, the waiter took the latter for an answer. But in the midst of stepping away, he paused. "Of course, sir, if you're open to a change of plans, I do have a suggestion that might be of interest. Something to end the evening on, perhaps, a higher note."

Ellis couldn't imagine anything improving this cruddy night of his. But then, he was in no rush to head home, where the quiet would inevitably force him to dwell on his family and his father and their ugly sparring of words. "Such as?"

Rather than elaborate, the waiter signaled to the blond hostess, who smiled knowingly before coming his way.

CHAPTER 14

LILY WOULD TYPICALLY SHY AWAY from entering a place like this on her own, and at such a late hour in an unfamiliar town. Vital to her search, however, Jack Bleeck's was the preferred haunt of the *Herald Tribune*. At least according to a grandfatherly bellman at the Waldorf Astoria, who had lit with pride over his extensive knowledge of the city.

Hopefully, the bartender at Bleeck's could say for certain.

"Sure, I know Ellis. Comes in all the time." His answer, over the din of the crowd, fluttered Lily's hopes until he added, "No sign of him tonight, though." But then he told her to wait there, that some scribes from the *Trib* were hunkered down in their usual corner and might have a clue to Ellis's whereabouts.

The bartender guessed well. At the paper, one of the reporters had apparently overhead Ellis's plan to take his folks to a spot called the Royal. No other details, but it was enough.

Lily bid her thanks and, with little thought, hurried to hail a cab. She was compelled by the sense of running down a lead. Or, if being honest, by the prospect of seeing Ellis.

In the weeks following his abrupt move to New York, her mind had often wandered as she worked at her desk. She would imagine herself on some corner in Philly, or eating lunch at Franklin Square, where their paths would cross in a vision cut short by the chief's bellowing of her name. A few times, she even came close to phoning the *Tribune* to alert Ellis when a letter arrived about one of his old features. But the excuse would have been shamefully transparent, she feared, dooming their conversation to an awkward end. Plus, as the months went by, there was Clayton to consider.

Yet here she was now, in the neighborhood as it were, impulse trampling logic. It was a tendency of hers that historically led to trouble. Still, she succeeded in barring the thought until the doorman of the Royal, stationed atop the alleyway stairs, permitted her entry and shut the door, sealing her in. It was then that she observed the guests at the end of the sconce-lit hallway. In the coat-check area they were arriving or leaving as couples.

And it occurred to her: What if Ellis had brought a date? This was assuming he had even made plans here tonight. What a ridiculous gamble.

Lily gripped her purse, debating on turning back. But then she recalled the letter. She had come this far already. What could a glimpse possibly hurt?

Retaining her coat, she proceeded through the entrance framed in burgundy velvet drapes. The main hall held an elegant world of diners, waiters, and candlelight. It resembled the wedding reception in that way, but with less stuffiness and livelier music.

"Good evening, miss." A shapely blond woman in a glittery dress stepped out from behind her black podium. "You meeting someone?"

"Yes. Well…possibly. I'm looking for an old friend. I've been told he was here. Or might be, rather."

The woman appeared dubious. In a place like this, celebrity patrons surely drew nosy fans. "I'd have to check with the table first. Make sure it's not a problem."

"Of course." Lily should have been more specific. "I normally wouldn't intrude, but I'm only in town for the night, and I was really hoping to at least—"

"What's the name?" The hostess was already gazing down at the reservation book.

"Reed. First name: Ellis."

"Ah, sure." The woman looked up, her tone promising. But then she shook her head regretfully. "I'm afraid his dinner guests wrapped up early, and Mr. Reed had another engagement."

He was gone. It took Lily a moment to grasp this, to accept the finality of her efforts.

She glanced at the bustling supper club. If only she could have come sooner, or knew where he went next. She regarded the hostess. "Mr. Reed didn't happen to say…" Oh goodness, she was being irrational now. "Never mind. Thank you all the same." She managed a partial smile before treading toward the draped entry.

Really, the outcome was a blessing. Come morning, she would be back on a train, common sense restored. Any memories of some youthful romantic yearning would soon dissolve into the practicality of her life.

"Wait a sec."

Lily slowed. She turned to find the hostess closing in with a gauging look. "Just promise me you aren't some old steady aiming to spy on the guy."

Lily was puzzled at first, then adamant. "No. Definitely not. Just a friend."

The woman gently smiled, her lips red and glossy. She tipped her head. "Then follow me."

~

In a blink, Lily became a mouse in a maze. She scampered behind the hostess, winding through the kitchen, where cooks were stirring and frying and plating food for frenzied waiters. A mixture of spices rode the air scented with boiling carrots and sizzling steaks.

"Through here," she said when Lily paused, questioning the destination. "A shortcut."

To what, Lily had no inkling. But she hazarded to follow her guide into the storage room. Behind stacked barrels marked as flour waited a narrow staircase. Apprehensive, Lily trailed down the steps. A single light bulb hung overhead.

At the base stood a metal wall. The woman knocked and waved at a small hole, and magically the barrier slid open. A brawny Italian allowed them passage. Lily had just edged past him when a swirl of voices caught her ear.

The hostess held open a black curtain, split down the middle. "Welcome to Oz."

Lily crept onto the astounding scene. Suited men and dolled-up women were sidled up to tables of cards, craps, and roulette. They held cocktail glasses and cigarettes on long black filters. Smoke rose from the corners of their mouths.

From reports of raids in the paper, Lily had learned a great deal about backroom gaming halls. She had just never envisioned stepping into one herself.

"You all right from here?" the hostess asked.

Lily intended to voice her thanks, but might have only nodded before the curtain dropped, leaving her on her own. She had to remind herself why she had come.

As she ventured through the room, dealers in bow ties and vests conducted the festivities. Cheers and laughter flowed in waves. Phones sat on a table near a wall chalked with betting odds. To the side, a bartender prepared drinks at his post.

While flapper fashions had largely disappeared from the street, viewed as too garish since the market crashed, rolled stockings and fringed dresses cut above the knee still flourished in this underground haven. Lily could have passed as a schoolmarm in comparison, yet that didn't stop several men from leering.

It was difficult to imagine the Ellis she knew attracted to such a place.

Ironically, this was her last thought before she registered his familiar features. His hat at a jaunty angle, he stood at the head of a craps table, where he downed a swig of liquor. A waitress swooped in to relieve him of his glass as the surrounding players submitted their bets.

Ellis tucked a cigar stub into his mouth and scooped up the dice. From the corner of the table, a stylish woman called something to Ellis, prompting him to hold the dice out for her. She blew on his hand for luck, seductively enough to make Lily blush.

At last he rolled.

"Snake eyes!" declared the dealer. The crowd collectively groaned, and a cane-like stick was used to rake all the cash into a mound.

Lily had sacrificed so much, devoted such effort, to save every penny she earned. Her teeth clenched at the display of sheer flagrancy and waste.

Ellis lifted his gaze, passing right over her before cutting it back. He removed his cigar and stared as if doubting his own vision—who knew how many drinks he had consumed? Then a smile crossed his face, his delight undeniable. She had clearly become the only other person in the room.

And yet, this moment bore no resemblance to the reunions she had pictured.

He strode the full distance to where she stood, as she made no effort to meet him.

"Lily! How did... What are you doing here?" His blue eyes brightened, emanating with shades of the sincerity and warmth she actually remembered.

She worked to align her thoughts. "I was in town and heard you were here." She was on the verge of opening her purse. She could simply hand over the letter. It was her primary reason for finding him, after all. But now…now there was more she wished to know.

"Is there a quieter place we could talk?"

He smiled wider, not catching the clip of her tone. "I'll get my coat."

~

The apartment building sat only three blocks away. On another day, with any other fellow, Lily would never have agreed to such an intimate setting. But Ellis was as eager to show her his new home as she was to gauge him further. She wanted to know just how far he had strayed from the man she knew. Or suspected she had known.

On account of the sprinkling rain, they had walked briskly from the Royal, providing little chance to speak until they arrived.

"I haven't done much to the place yet," he warned her, opening the door of his flat on the third floor. "Just moved in a couple weeks ago and been too busy to really jazz it up."

She brushed raindrops from her hat and shoulders before following him inside, where he illuminated a standing lamp with a tug of its chain. After closing the door, he set his hat beside the phone on a small entry table. "Could I take your coat?"

"I'll keep it on. Thank you." She had no sense yet of how long she would stay.

He removed his own overcoat, doffing his suit jacket at the same time—a struggle due to the liquor, she guessed. "I know it's not the best of neighborhoods," he went on. "But it's got a real kitchen and bedroom. Even its own bathroom and toilet and…" His sentence broke off. "Too many details," he muttered.

While he stored the garments on a coat tree, Lily stepped toward the sitting room. The beige walls smelled faintly of new paint. An oriental rug lay below a sizable brown davenport and maple-wood coffee table. On a square stand in the corner was an RCA radio, sleek with its arched body of polished wood. Although no single item blared with extravagance, the residence as a whole seemed somewhat lavish for a relatively new reporter, considering the steep prices of the city.

Ellis came closer. His necktie was loose and casual.

She pinned on a smile. "You've done awfully well for yourself."

He smiled back, tinged with uncertainty. After a brief lull, he asked, "How about a drink?"

She nodded. "Water, please."

"Drink of the night," he said under his breath.

She tilted her head, not understanding.

"Water it is," he confirmed lightly and retreated into the kitchen.

Lily padded across the rug and set her gloves and handbag on the coffee table. On the wall to her right, picture frames of various sizes created a collage of sorts. No—more of a shrine, it seemed upon closer inspection. For highlighted at the top, hung at eye level, were two articles featuring Ellis's byline. A slew of unsigned but sizeable clippings, presumably also by him, took up the second and third tiers.

She skimmed the topics: salacious affairs, a scandalous divorce, a séance for a mobster's widow. The others, mostly of political corruption, at least possessed more merit than sensationalism. But of them all, not a single piece resembled the deeper human stories he had once prided himself on writing. The stories that had made Ellis different.

"You didn't tell me," he said, arriving with two glasses. "What brought you to New York?"

She accepted the water, turning away from the wall. "A wedding."

He went still. "You…got married?"

She realized how it could have sounded. "No. Not me. A friend of Clayton's."

Ellis's shoulders relaxed, but just as swiftly an air of tension returned. He clinked his glass on hers. "Cheers," he said, which Lily echoed.

As she drank her water, Ellis swallowed a gulp of amber liquid, its potency obvious from its scent. Evidently he hadn't had his fill. Unlike her sips of champagne earlier, nothing about his behavior tonight indicated a rare occurrence.

He gestured toward the davenport. "Want to sit?"

She politely agreed but assumed the far end. He followed suit by taking the opposite side and set his glass atop his knee. Streetlamps threw slices of light through the partially open blinds of the room's lone window. Down below, motorcars rumbled in passing.

Lily thought to bring up the letter then, her excuse for seeking him out.

"So," he said, "where *is* that beau of yours?"

She had to reconcile the reference. Her instinct then was to correct his assumption. But for now, she had no idea where she and Clayton stood. And honestly, after observing Ellis at the Royal, she felt no obligation to explain.

"There was a robbery during the reception. Near Times Square. He rushed off to cover it."

Ellis looked incredulous despite his heavy-lidded eyes. "And he left you there?"

The question took her aback. "I… Well, yes, but…I told him he should."

After a moment, Ellis nodded. "Okay."

The single word in and of itself was just fine. His tone, however, rang of disapproval.

"It was a big story," she contended. "Some were saying it might have been Willie Sutton. Maybe a fatal shooting too."

She expected a glint in Ellis's eyes, maybe envy from missing out—what journalist wouldn't be interested?

But he just raised his glass for another swig, his mouth hinting at a smirk. "Suppose it makes sense. After all, that's typical Clayton Brauer, right?"

She suddenly felt defensive on Clayton's behalf. And for herself. She resented the inference that when it came to courting, she would let herself be tossed aside—something she had vowed to never do again. Still, she strove to remain casual. "Oh? And how is that exactly?"

Ellis appeared surprised by the need to clarify. "C'mon, you know his type."

She waited for the answer.

Finally, he leaned toward her, as if divulging a secretive insight. "Need help from the guy? Better yell 'fire.' Yell 'murder' and he'll grab a pen." Ellis chuckled while reclining into the cushions and swirled his drink.

Whether or not truth underlay his remarks—in fact, gratingly, she knew it did—Lily wasn't nearly as entertained. "But you're wrong about him. I go to Maryville every weekend to…help with my parents' deli." She barely caught herself. "And he's repeatedly gone out of his way to drive me there, wanting nothing in return."

"Wow. Nothing, huh? That's…impressive." It might have been just another wisecrack, an attempt to be clever, but there was an edge in his humor tonight that didn't sit well.

Then she considered the source, the hypocrisy on full display.

"I'd be careful if I were you, Mr. Reed," she said with a thin smile, "judging other reporters for what they'll do to get ahead."

At her less-than-playful jab, Ellis's humor receded. He turned tentative, deciphering. "Meaning…?"

She shrugged. "Meaning, no topic appears out-of-bounds for your shot at a byline these days. Unless I'm missing something on this self-congratulatory wall of yours."

He threw a glance toward the frames and straightened a little. His drink was no longer moving. "Nothing wrong with being proud. I worked hard for those."

"And by 'those,' I presume you're referring to all the meaningful stories 'with heart' you were hired to cover."

"What I'm writing," he told her, "is important."

"Oh, I can see that—with such titillating pieces on mistresses and mobsters. Although…after tonight, I can safely surmise how and where you're getting your biggest scoops."

That one touched a nerve. It was plain on Ellis's face and in the curtain of silence that dropped between them.

She had gone too far. She knew this. The question was why. In reality, they were no more than distant friends, good acquaintances even. After months apart, how did she feel the right, the need, to state her disapproval?

He stared at her, unflinching. Given his current condition, it was up to her to promote a truce.

"I'm sorry for that. Truly. I shouldn't have—"

"No. Go on."

She stalled at his coolness.

"I'm sure as a secretary at the *Examiner*, you've got all kinds of *great* career advice."

Lily just sat there, stunned. Though he couldn't have foreseen their full impact—or perhaps somehow he did—his words pierced holes straight through her pride.

Her mind told her to march out, or lash back at minimum, but the whole exchange left her short on will. Her lone thought was that coming here had been a grave mistake.

Slowly, she set her glass on the table and gathered her gloves and purse. On her feet, she pulled out the envelope she had come all this way to deliver. Now she simply wanted it out of her possession, her duty fulfilled.

"This is for you." She placed the sealed letter beside her glass, eliminating any chance for their fingers to touch.

Ellis's features were softening. Awareness, maybe even regret, was setting in. But she refused to meet his eyes.

"It's about the children in your first feature," she said, regaining her defenses, her clarity. "If you even remember who they are."

There was so much more she could say, about what she had learned of that photo. About the damning secret he harbored. About how pictures, like people, so often were not as they appeared.

Instead, before Ellis could speak, she walked out the door.

CHAPTER 15

REPLAY THE CONVERSATION a dozen different ways, and the conclusion was the same: he'd been a righteous jackass.

After Lily's departure, Ellis had caught a glimpse of that reality before he dozed into oblivion. The following morning, nausea and the pounding in his skull had made thinking of any kind damn near impossible. But as the day had waned and the fog of his memories cleared, he couldn't escape the shame from his barbs.

Sure, he'd been soused. And yeah, he'd been primed for battle after the row with his father, an exchange steeped in too many layers to process just yet. But mostly, he'd been riled by the mirror in Lily's words, reflections of himself he'd dodged for months.

Now he couldn't shake them. On a drizzly Monday afternoon, impelled by the letter she'd delivered, he dug from his desk other reminders of his deed. The city room buzzed around him as he finally opened the small mound of posts. They'd continued to trickle in even after he first started at the *Tribune*, forwarded from the various papers that had picked up his feature. Each expressed sympathy for the family. Several envelopes held a buck or two.

Before she left, Lily had questioned if he actually remembered the kids. As if he could forget. He'd just shoved them into the deepest caverns of his mind, an attempt to keep his sanity. Their faces, dual symbols of his guilt, had haunted him like ghosts, even in New York. Among kids on the street, in Central Park, at Times Square, he'd see Ruby smiling, laughing, toting a bundle of flowers. He'd see Calvin climbing a tree or hiding in the folds of a mother's skirt. And the truth behind the photo wasn't the only cause. What needled him more, as Lily noted long ago, was how the family's hardships had boosted his career. The higher he rose, the uglier that fact became. By busying himself with reports of corruption and scandals, he'd done his best to forget.

"Did your friend find you?"

Ellis was so immersed in his thoughts it took him a moment to realize the question was for him, and even longer to trace it to the man standing at his desk.

"Your lady friend," Dutch clarified. "She was asking around at Bleeck's. I'd heard you talking about hitting the Royal with your folks. Figured you'd want me to pass it along."

Ellis narrowed his eyes, the series of events clicking together. At the same time, he was grasping the idea of speaking with Dutch at all. "Yeah. She did."

"Oh. Good."

In the background, someone launched a paper plane and a phone rang. A reporter yelled for a copy boy.

Dutch adjusted the pencil behind his ear. He lingered until awkwardness strained the air. When he edged away, Ellis failed to add anything more.

What would be fitting to say? The last they'd spoken was months ago. Soon after the City Hall blunder, Dutch had made two attempts at a flimsy apology.

All right, fine. In hindsight, they might have been genuine. The pressure of a new baby, combining a lack of sleep and desperation to keep his job, had led to "a gutless choice," Dutch had said. Evidently, when Mr. Walker had assumed Ellis was at fault, Dutch didn't voice a correction. He'd later offered to make it right, but the opportunity was long passed by then. Ellis had simply dismissed him icily, and they'd avoided each other ever since.

In reality, perhaps the guy wasn't so bad. Even decent, well-meaning people could make poor choices under pressure. Just look at Ellis. He at least owed Dutch a word of gratitude now for directing Lily his way. Granted, in light of the outcome, it was like thanking a nurse for a dose of cod liver oil: just because it was needed didn't make it pleasant going down.

For the time being, his priority was Lily.

He reached across his mound of mail and retrieved his phone. Keeping the earpiece on the cradle, he scrounged for the right words. His own apology couldn't sound flimsy.

That was assuming he even got that far before she hung up or was pulled away by the chief. Ellis could send a letter instead, wire a telegram. Both of which, however, could wind up in a waste bin or returned weeks from now unread.

Right then, the city editor was passing the aisle of desks, hat and coat on. He was scooting out for lunch.

Ellis made a decision.

"Mr. Walker," he called out. The man turned with reluctance, looking impatient for his afternoon refreshment. When he approached, Ellis cut to the request. "I was wondering, sir, if there's any chance I could head home. Back to Philly. For a personal matter."

Intrigue flickered in Mr. Walker's eyes, but he wasn't the type to snoop unless the subject was worthy of print. "You're wanting tomorrow off?"

Ellis had simply meant over the next few days. But yeah. Why not? Until he settled all with Lily, any attempt to work would be a bust. "It'd be a real help."

"Gone just a day, then." Not a suggestion, but a limit. A large portion of the man's duties, magnified by the tough economy, was ensuring that those on his staff were earning their pay.

"Yes, sir."

"So long as you don't forget, I want a new pitch by Thursday."

"Sure thing. I'm working on it."

"That what this is all about?" Mr. Walker gestured to the letters splayed over the desk.

Ellis now wished he'd opened them in private. "It's just some reader mail. About an old feature in the *Examiner*."

Mr. Walker nodded. "The kids with the sign."

An impressive guess. Though Ellis shouldn't have been surprised. The success of that feature had been chiefly responsible for catching the editor's eye. And when it came to notable stories, the man's memory was an archive.

Mr. Walker peeked at his watch. "Well, I'm off to lunch." He continued on his way, but he just as soon halted and wagged a finger. "It's not a bad idea."

"Sir?"

"There are plenty of readers who'd want to know more. If you're already traveling thereabouts, how about a follow-up on the family?"

Another piece on the Dillards...

The mere suggestion turned Ellis's stomach as Mr. Walker ran with the thought. "Were the kids kept, sold, given away? Are they better or worse off? If the story's got meat, it might be worthy of a Page One pitch."

How the hell do you follow up on something that never happened? Ellis yearned to say, but replied evenly, "I'll look into it."

A quick nod and Mr. Walker strode onward, leaving Ellis to subdue a rising sense of dread.

In more than one way, his past was muscling back to the surface.

~

The plan changed en route.

On the drive from New York, having pulled out at first light, Ellis was over halfway to Philly when he chose to reverse stops. If he waited until Lily's lunch break to arrive at the *Examiner*, she'd likely have a moment to spare, ideally in private. And that meant Laurel Township would come first.

The decision about a sequel piece was even easier to make. Despite the instinct to cover his tracks, one article based on a falsehood was more than enough. He wouldn't be writing a second. The point of this trip, on the contrary, was to bring closure to the issue. Now he knew how. A single act would finally affirm that the journey had been worth the risks.

At last, Ellis steered onto the short dirt drive flecked with pebbles, ending at the Dillards' home. Except for the leaden midmorning sky, the scene matched the image in his memory. The farmhouse with its covered porch. A film of dirt over its white paint. An apple tree set against rolling fields of hay.

Once parked, he stepped out of his car and patted the chest of his suit. The thick feel of the envelope, stuffed in his inside pocket, confirmed the gift was there. To the seven dollars accrued from his drawer of mail, he'd added twenty-three of his own. He'd be pretty strapped until next payday, but it was the least he could do. If the family had treasured two measly bucks, this would be a gold mine.

He only wished he'd done it sooner.

On the porch, he opened the screen door and rapped with his knuckles. When he received no answer, he knocked harder.

Still nothing.

Unlike the donations he'd delivered before, he wasn't about to leave thirty smackers on the Dillards' front steps.

After a third knock, he removed his hat to peer through the

window. The narrow space between the blue gingham curtains limited his view.

From behind came the groan of an engine. He turned around, hopeful, only to discover a man driving a truck toward the house.

Ellis descended the stairs, anxious to make clear he wasn't a shifty lurker. He gave a friendly wave as the vehicle rolled to a stop.

"Can I help ya, neighbor?" the grizzled man called from his open window, the motor running. The side of his black truck featured stenciled white lettering: *U.S. MAIL.*

"I'm looking for Geraldine Dillard. Any idea where I might find her?"

"Mmm, wish I could tell ya." The man scratched his beard. "But Mrs. Dillard never registered a forwarding address."

"You're saying…she moved?" Ellis gazed back at the house, stunned by the news. "When?"

"Tough to say exactly. Once the kids were gone, she scarcely came out. All's I know is a few months back, landlord told me to send the bills his way till there's another renter."

Ellis struggled with the explanation that implied a mother's grief, punctuated by a single phrase: *The kids were gone.*

His thoughts flashed back to his brother. A swaddled bundle hurried out of the house and swept away. Buried in a small plot at a cemetery surrounded by trees and flowers.

Ellis met the man's eyes. "What happened to them…the kids?"

"Well, now, I didn't see nothing firsthand."

"But you know something."

The postman tossed a glance over his shoulder, as if assessing the area before disclosing town gossip. "Only thing I heard is from Walter Gale—ol' Walt works down at the train depot. Handyman and such. Even helps out as a cabbie when the need calls. Walt says some fancy banker took the train in. Brought along a picture in the paper, one of this here house, and paid for a ride straight over. Left with the little ones the very same day."

Relief swept through Ellis, having initially assumed the worst, but the feeling promptly vanished. "So, they've both been adopted."

"Adopted? No, no. Not from what I gather," the postman said. And right then, the notion of what was coming, the twisted reality of what Ellis had caused, struck with the force of a barreling train, even before the man finished. "Them kids were outright sold."

PART TWO

"There is nothing to fear except the persistent refusal to find out the truth."

—DOROTHY THOMPSON

CHAPTER 16

THE DRIVER SAT PARKED along the street, his features shadowed in a shabby black car. Lily caught a glimpse from the deli's front counter as shoppers dwindled at last. It was almost closing time on Saturday, the busiest day of the week, with customers stocking up for Sunday meals.

"Dear, would you mind?" Lily's mother handed her a nickel and two pennies.

"Mr. Wilson?"

"Who else?"

Once again, the longtime patron had shuffled away with his weekly goods—always salami and provolone—and left his change.

Lily sprinted out the door, not bothering to remove her apron. Specks of rain dotted her arms, left bare by her short-sleeved cotton blouse. The early-evening air carried an electric scent. She caught up with Mr. Wilson a few doors down, outside Mel's Haberdashery, where he thanked her with a bashful smile.

On her way back, she brushed her hair from her eyes, the rest pinned up for her deli work. She was about to pass the old, black Model T when the driver opened his door and stepped out.

"Lily, wait."

She froze.

It was Ellis Reed.

He pulled off his hat and held the brim awkwardly with both hands. "I'm sorry to just show up like this."

Her teeth clenched, as did her stomach. A week had come and gone since their bitter parting in New York, yet the lashes from his words now turned fresh and raw.

She had been absurd to ever discount Clayton for the man standing before her. Having realized this, and with Clayton busy all week at the paper, she had postponed firming her stance on the courtship front. Aside from this: she would never again let emotion squander sensibility, even at the risk of winding up alone.

"What do you want?"

"To apologize, for my behavior that night. For the cruddy stuff I said. I'd planned to say this days ago, but...some things happened..." His gaze rose to hers, and the marked sincerity in his eyes couldn't be overlooked. Nor could his effort.

"The drive from Brooklyn," she realized, "must be three hours."

He gave a small shrug. "A letter wouldn't have been enough."

She related to the concept, more than he could possibly fathom, but she maintained her guard.

"That's why I'm here," he went on. "To tell you in person."

Before she could temper a response, a pair of ladies—the town librarian and the organist from church—pardoned themselves for interrupting the conversation to pass through, abruptly reminding Lily of their surroundings.

Somehow Ellis, surely without help from Clayton, had been able to find her. Here, in Maryville. How much else did he or others know?

She moved closer before asking, "How did you know where I'd be?"

He gestured his hat in the deli's direction. "You mentioned coming here every weekend. To help out your folks."

"Oh, yes. I forgot." The connection eased her a bit, yet her worlds still needed to remain separate. At least for those unworthy of her trust. "Well, I accept your apology, Mr. Reed, and I appreciate all the trouble you've gone to. Now, I'm afraid you'll have to excuse me."

She started to leave, but he spoke again. "You were right, by the way. About the stories I've written. The things I did to get ahead..."

When his voice trailed off, she finished for him. "Like the children," she said, "in the *second* picture." She wanted to hear him say it. But he stared at her, baffled by her knowledge. "I know the kids weren't the same, Ellis."

His face turned heavy with regret, far more than expected.

Still, she returned to her purpose, aware of other townsfolk on the street. "Why don't we talk more another time? Maybe when you're back in Philly. Right now, I do need to help close up the store."

"Of course," he said quietly. His suit was wrinkled, his jaw unshaven. He looked as if he'd not slept in days. Their last encounter, while ill fated, couldn't alone have been the cause.

"Mommy," a small voice called.

Lily spun around. "Yes?"

Only then did she wince. Samuel—her precious secret—stood at the deli entrance with half a cookie in his hand. His shirt was marked with flour from baking with his grandmother. "Can I eat it? It's extra and broke. But Gamma says I gotta ask."

Behind Lily, astonishment was undoubtedly rolling over Ellis's face.

"Mommy, pleeease?"

She nodded with little thought. In that moment, he could have asked for a box full of nails and she would have agreed.

Samuel burst into a grin. He disappeared inside before Lily collected her resolve, her reasoning, and turned to Ellis. "You have to understand," she insisted. "The chief never would've hired me. And the boardinghouse certainly wouldn't have been an option if anyone there knew."

Ellis's expression indeed held surprise, but with merciful subtlety, absent of judgment. He glanced back toward the deli. "He's a good-looking boy, your son."

She hugged her arms to her chest, more than the rain delivering a chill. She was starkly aware of the upper hand she had just surrendered, which perhaps was never rightly hers. "Thank you."

Silence billowed between them until he asked, "How long have you known, about the kids in the photo?"

"A while." It wasn't her intention to be vague. "I kept wondering what troubled you about them, after you came to me. Eventually, I looked closer at the picture that went to press."

"But you didn't tell anyone," he guessed.

She shook her head that she hadn't. "You wrote a good article. It deserved to be read." Perhaps unconsciously she'd had another reason: her own experience from compromises made to get by.

She noted her hypocrisy now, judging him as she had—his role in their spat aside. "It's all in the past anyway. No reason for you to dwell upon what's done."

At that, he angled his head away and again kneaded the brim of his hat. There was more to the story.

"Ellis? What is it?"

Dread, like a vine, wound through her, even before he answered. When he did, each word, each imagined scene, sowed further devastation from what had come to pass.

A vacant house.

A mailman's tale.

A ripple of consequences from the click of a shutter.

Digesting it all, Lily watched a puddle forming on the street. The sky darkened and rainfall thickened. There were too many thoughts and feelings to process all at once.

She looked back at Ellis and couldn't tell if the mist in his eyes was from weather or emotion, though she suspected it was both.

They would sort this out—they had to. But not out here, not in the rain.

"Come inside," she said, unsure if he heard her until he closed the car door to follow.

～

Tension hovered over the table as the family ate supper with minimal conversation. It didn't help that Lily and Ellis, though toweled off and mostly dry, still resembled mutts from an alley. Even Samuel's drawings of family and cakes and sunbursts, taped to the room's powder-blue walls, failed to lighten the mood.

Lily's mother had asked Ellis to stay for supper. Based on her tone, however, the invitation was a mere courtesy. If Lily had any doubt, she needed but peek at either end of the table, where her parents exuded as much suspicion as displeasure. The fact that Ellis was seated across from Lily and Samuel, in the chair often reserved for Clayton, made the core issue even more glaring.

To Ellis's credit, he upheld an amicable front in spite of his quandary.

Foraging for conversation, Lily informed him that her mother had hand-painted the little bunnies on the ceramic meat-loaf dish, rabbits being Samuel's favorite animal. Ellis was quick to compliment Lily's mother, on both the dish and the meat loaf. For this, he received the briefest of thanks.

Lily's efforts to engage her father fared no better, as small talk about baseball only led to his questioning of Ellis. "You a Yankees fan?" His challenging tone didn't make clear the correct response was yes.

Lily stiffened when Ellis paused from eating. "I'm afraid I've been too busy lately to follow the games much. But I understand they've got a strong lineup this year." The diplomacy of his reply, though impressively quick, indicated that if he cheered for any team, it wasn't the Yankees. Her father's scowl said this didn't get past his sensor.

Before Lily could intervene, Ellis swiftly turned to Samuel: "So, you're a fan of rabbits, huh?"

Samuel kept his gaze low, ever averse to strangers, using his spoon to push through his mound of mashed potatoes.

Lily gently prodded, "Be polite and answer Mr. Reed."

Samuel rendered a stiff nod.

Lily met Ellis's eyes, sneaking him a wordless apology—inviting him inside wasn't meant to compound his troubles—but he came back with a warm smile. Paired with a small shake of his head, he told her not to worry. And so, supper plodded along in the all-too-cozy space. The sounds of drizzling rain and periodic thunder provided their only reprieve until Samuel stifled a giggle.

Lily cut a glance toward her son before tracing his focus across the table, landing on the long-eared rabbit fashioned from a linen napkin. Like a puppeteer, Ellis sent the animal hopping to the bowl of glazed carrots, where it wiggled its nose. Samuel laughed again, and the intensity in the room gave ever so slightly. Even Lily's parents couldn't hide their surprise, their grandson's joy reliably infectious.

Samuel's interest had just begun to fade when Ellis said, "How about a turtle?"

This time Samuel nodded with vigor, and Ellis went to work. He folded and tucked and tugged until the rabbit had transformed into the shelled creature. The turtle crawled along the table's edge, garnering more giggles, before Samuel asked for a bird. Ellis gladly obliged, appearing to almost forget his burden.

Lily slipped away to serve pieces of her homemade rhubarb

pie, which Ellis praised though barely had the chance to eat. He was too busy filling half a dozen other requests. Even one by Lily's father—at Samuel's urging.

By the end of the meal, neither of Lily's parents had fully relinquished their guardedness, but they did fulfill their roles as proper hosts. Her mother even offered accommodations for the night on account of the weather.

"Thank you," Ellis replied, "but really, I've already imposed too much."

Lily's mother tsked. "No sense leaving till it's safe. Lillian, fetch the spare sheets." The implied instruction was to make up the sofa.

For more than one reason the extended stay unsettled Lily. There was no practicality, however, in sending a tired driver out into a storm at night.

~

Every minute slogged into the next, stretching endlessly toward dawn. The pounding rain had gradually let up. In the bed beside Lily's, the quilt over Samuel's chest rose and fell with each breath. She inhaled his faint boyish scent, envious of his ability to rest.

In the dimness, she counted the stripes on the wallpaper of white and marigold, a relaxing habit since childhood. But tonight, not even warm milk would deliver her to sleep.

Just then, she caught a noise. She raised her head from the pillow and listened. Another creak suggested movement on the floor below. Her parents never ones to stir this late, she surmised that Ellis's mind, like her own, was spinning over two children not meant to be sold.

How could Ellis—or she, for that matter—ever find peace until they knew more?

An idea came to her. It would mean shaving a few hours

off her weekend with Samuel, but there was no better option. She had to tell Ellis, and now. If he were to leave by dawn, she would miss him altogether.

With quiet care, she slid out of bed, tied on her robe, and made her way down the stairs. In the sitting room, Ellis stood at the window, the curtains half-open. Moonlight softened his features as he stared into the night. Though he still wore his trousers, his suspenders hung loose down his thighs. Only a sleeveless undershirt covered his torso, the muscles of his arms and chest defined by shadows.

Lily suddenly worried over the unseemly meeting. She was dressed in little more than a nightgown. Not even slippers covered her bare feet. She took a step back, causing a floorboard to creak.

Ellis turned. "Did I wake you?" His voice was soft and raspy, threaded with concern.

She shook her head.

It would be silly to retreat now.

She moved just close enough to be heard well in a hush. "Tomorrow, I think we should go to the Dillards' old area. To Laurel Township."

"Lily." Already there was an objection in his tone. Maybe he had considered it before. But he needed to hear her out.

"This train worker—the cabbie—he saw it all happen. He might know more: about where the kids went, why their mother did what she did. You said yourself she didn't seem the type to do such a thing."

"Lily," he said again, "I appreciate the suggestion, and I definitely plan to dig around. You don't need to get involved, though. That's not the reason I told you. You didn't do this. I did."

"You're wrong." As he shifted to fully face her, Lily forced down the emotion, the guilt that had been mounting all evening. "I gave the chief your first picture. I found it in the darkroom.

When I saw it, as a mother… Well, it hit home." She opted to simplify, not up for delving needlessly into her and Samuel's past.

Ellis's brow lifted, an expression of finally grasping a missing piece. For a second, Lily wondered if he might resent her for instigating this terrible mess.

Instead, he answered, "It's still not your fault. I'm sure you were only trying to help."

"Fine. Then let me keep doing that now. I need to, Ellis. Please."

Graciously, he didn't ask why. He just considered her words, then let out a breath. "So, we'll go together."

Her burden lessened a fraction, for at least they had a plan. When they traded smiles, the space between them became far too quiet, too close. And yet, Lily hesitated to leave.

Spread over the sofa, the sheets remained smooth and unused. A restless night lay ahead for them both.

After all, discoveries awaited. Surely nothing of the worst sort. "You do know we're likely worrying over nothing, what with a wealthy banker willing to raise the children. We could very well find out that everything turned out for the best."

"Absolutely," Ellis said. "We could."

Together they almost sounded convinced.

CHAPTER 17

MORNING ARRIVED IN A BLINK. Wafts of coffee and baking bread seeped through the bleariness. For a moment, Ellis was back in his parents' home, waking to the scent of his mother's rolls.

Since their disastrous outing a week prior, he hadn't reached out to his folks. It wasn't for lack of courage; he just didn't know what to say. Other than act like it never happened, or apologize and shoulder the blame. Either route was standard when dealing with his father. But honestly, Ellis was just too tired to slap another bandage over the festering reality of the man's disapproval.

Besides, how could he ask for any level of respect until the mystery of the Dillards was put to rest?

A pair of small eyes peeked from the hallway, drawing Ellis back to his actual surroundings. "Heya, Samuel," he whispered, not wanting to wake anyone, and got a wave in return.

The kid had been a surprise, no question about it. But so much more about Lily became clear. Ellis had long ago seen how smart and skilled she was at her job. Now he had a sense of her bravery too.

Sitting up, he stretched his back. After years of the rickety bed in Philly, a cushioned sofa was pretty darn comfortable, though it had still taken half the night to catch some shut-eye. "Any idea of the time?"

Samuel shook his head.

Through an opening in the curtains, light from the overcast sky gave only a hint to the hour. Ellis's pocket watch was stored in his suit jacket, slung over the rocking chair by the window. As he rose to retrieve it, Samuel approached. He presented a linen napkin tied into a wad, causing Ellis to cock his head.

"It's a snail," the boy explained proudly.

"Oh yeah. I see it. A real swell one too."

A smile, lined with perfect baby teeth, bloomed on Samuel's face. Then he scurried off, and the memory of another boy—Ruby's brother—swung back at Ellis. The round face and large eyes, the thick lashes. The vision of Calvin fueled Ellis for the day's mission.

In a flash, he threw on the rest of his clothes. Down the hall, he was surprised to find the family around the dining room table, already dressed and finishing breakfast. He assumed their low voices were intended to keep from disturbing their unplanned guest. But when he said "Good morning," the discussion snapped off.

Lily returned the greeting, as did her mother, who brought him a plate of biscuits and fried ham. Ellis took a seat, not quite hungry after his full supper the night before. He dove in regardless. He was halfway done when Lily's father spoke to him over the rim of his coffee mug.

"Family's headed to mass soon. You attend mass on Sundays?"

Ellis swallowed a bite of bread, aware he was again being scrutinized. This time, he didn't bother to get creative. "I was actually raised Protestant, sir, but I did grow up going to church."

Silence gripped the room, confirming the man's stance.

Lily interjected, "We really should set off soon, Mr. Reed...if we're going to make a stop for work on the way back to Philly."

Rising from the table, Ellis thanked the family, his cue to pack up undeniably welcome.

⁓

The majority of the drive passed without conversation. Not that Ellis minded. Lily, up early with her son, dozed through even the car's rattling. With sun rays reaching through the clouds and warming her face, she couldn't have looked more peaceful. It was the first time he'd seen her hair worn down over her shoulders—by daylight anyhow. In ladies' trousers and a casual shirt beneath her coat, with barely a touch of makeup, she really was a natural looker.

It took a concerted effort to keep his eyes on the road.

At last they entered Chester County. They were closing in on the train depot closest to Laurel Township when jostling from a small pothole stirred Lily.

"This is it," he told her. The station sat at the end of a road. He pulled over to park. Fields and gravel surrounded much of the area, with distant storefronts glimpsed over a hill.

Lily reclaimed her handbag from her side, shaking off the dust of sleep. A look of determination sharpened her eyes, and Ellis refocused on the goal.

"Let's find some answers," she said. When he nodded, they opened their doors.

⁓

Inside the train depot, flyers pinned to a corkboard fluttered from the door closing behind Lily and Ellis. The waiting room held four long benches, only one of them occupied. An older gentleman in a beige, plaid suit balanced a suitcase on his lap. His eyelids drooped on his gaunt face.

Ellis led the way to the ticket booth. The clerk, a bespectacled middle-aged woman, stood hunched over a book. She lifted her gaze to Ellis, appearing somewhat irked by the disturbance to her reading. "Where to?"

"Good morning, ma'am. I was hoping to find a man who works here. Mr. Gaines, I believe?"

"Gale," she corrected.

"Mr. Gale—that's the one." Ellis was accustomed to imprinting names directly to memory, a vital skill at the paper, but the postman's details had been clouded by circumstance. "Do you know if he's around?"

The clerk appeared suspicious.

Lily chimed in brightly. "We just have a personal matter we hope Mr. Gale could help us with. I promise we won't take up much of his time."

The woman answered flatly, "Walt's not scheduled on Sundays." Then she sniffed and added, "But he does usually swing through to check in."

"That's great to hear," Ellis said.

"That's *no* guarantee."

Ellis understood, but it was better than nothing. Pressing for the man's home address would clearly prove fruitless. "Any clue when he might be by?"

The clerk sighed, bordering on a huff. "Next few hours maybe. I'm not Walt's keeper."

Lily replied, "That's most helpful. We'll gladly wait where we'll be out of your hair."

There was no need for Ellis to concur. The clerk's attention had already dropped to her book.

Ellis and Lily receded to the closest bench, where he took a seat. She chose to stand, gripping her purse, her gaze diverted to her side of the room. Her sparse answers to his attempts at basic conversation made clear a wedge remained between them. She had come for a single reason.

Church bells rang in the distance as Ellis hung his fedora on his knee. He was mindlessly tapping the brim when Lily murmured something to herself, then marched back to the clerk. When she returned, her steps and speech were hurried. "The clerk thinks a wedding just let out. I figure the town pastor is bound to know about the goings-on in the community. If I can catch him, maybe he'll be willing to share. Shall we meet here after?"

It made sense, about the pastor as well as to split up. They could cover more ground. "I'll be waiting," he barely said before she flew out the door.

Over the next hour, impatience growing, Ellis endured the snores of the gentleman on the next bench, remarkably still seated upright. A train passed through without stopping before a teenage girl entered to purchase a ticket. She boarded the next train, as did a couple leaving for their honeymoon. The groom elatedly announced this to the clerk, prompting a muttering of condolences.

Each swing of the entry door caused Ellis to straighten, only to sink back into his bench, until a tall, lanky man arrived in a flat cap and unbuttoned jacket. He ambled toward the ticket booth, all knees and elbows. In greeting, the clerk's mouth stretched into something resembling a smile. But it just as soon flattened when, in discussion, she pointed Ellis's way.

Ellis scrambled to his feet. "Mr. Gale?"

The man continued over with an inquisitive look. A lump of chewing tobacco bulged from his bottom lip. "Call me Walt."

"Ellis." They traded a handshake.

"What can I do for ya?"

Thankfully, Walt took no convincing at all to step outside and speak in private.

CHAPTER 18

A HINT OF WHITE SMOKE greeted Lily as she neared an open door inside the modest-size building, roughly a mile's walk from the train depot.

Not smoke, she realized. Chalk dust. At the blackboard, before several rows of wooden desks, a young, freckle-faced boy in a sweater vest and woolen knickers pounded two chalkboard erasers together, creating a fresh cloud. He sneezed twice in quick succession.

"Bless you," said a woman in the corner. Seated at the teacher's desk, she was the only other person in the room. She had short, black hair and a face as full as her figure, set off with high cheekbones. A Spanish-like skin tone gave her a touch of exoticness. "Now, keep at it, Oliver. I prefer not to be here all afternoon."

"Yes, ma'am," he mumbled, white dust on his cheeks.

The two-room schoolhouse was on the back side of a church, where it doubled as a Sunday school. The cordial pastor, freshly assigned to the area, had directed Lily here for possible insight into the situation.

"Pardon me. Mrs. Stanton?" Lily said upon entering.

The teacher twisted in her seat, her ample bosom stretching her blouse. "May I help you?"

"I certainly hope so. Pastor Ron sent me your way."

Mrs. Stanton brightened. "This is regarding the blanket drive?" she ventured. Without turning, she declared, "I don't hear any erasers, Oliver."

The boy resumed cleaning with another whack, and Mrs. Stanton waited for Lily to go on. Due to the topic, Lily moved closer before explaining. "Pastor Ron mentioned you might be able to shed some light on a matter. One involving a former student of yours."

Mrs. Stanton looked intrigued, though still cheery. "And which child would that be? I've taught quite a few."

Lily smiled kindly. "I'm sure you have." Conscious of the boy's presence, she lowered her voice. "Her name is Ruby Dillard."

Mrs. Stanton's mood changed, doused like a flame. After a beat, she gave her throat a quick clearing. "Oliver, that's enough for today."

The boy perked up for only an instant before he abandoned the erasers and sprinted for the door.

"And don't forget!" Mrs. Stanton called out, halting him. "Next time you choose to *lick* a classmate, what should you expect?"

He sighed. "The paddle."

She motioned her thick chin toward the door. "Off you go."

The boy's infraction played out in Lily's mind, an amusing scenario that vanished when Mrs. Stanton leaned forward, elbows on her desk. "Has something awful happened, with the man who took those sweet children?"

"To be honest, Mrs. Stanton, that's precisely what I'm trying to find out."

The teacher's brow creased. "I don't understand. You're not a child worker?"

"No, I'm…" How could Lily describe herself in the simplest form? "I'm a friend of a reporter who recently connected with the family."

"I see," Mrs. Stanton said. "The reporter."

Unable to gauge the woman's tone, Lily hurried to inject a note of compassion on Ellis's behalf. "That same friend last visited the Dillards in the fall, when he delivered another batch of donations for the family. So, you can imagine his surprise when he stopped by last week and discovered the news."

"Yes, well. The situation was a surprise to many of us." More graveness than resentment echoed in Mrs. Stanton's words, encouraging Lily to press on.

"Would you know where the children are now?"

Mrs. Stanton shook her head, a solemn motion. Then her gaze drifted to the middle of the room, perhaps visualizing Ruby at her desk.

"Do you have any idea why they were…given up?" A milder term for it. "I'd have thought the donations would've made such a thing avoidable."

Her eyes still distant, Mrs. Stanton spoke as if thinking aloud. "I would've offered to help out with Ruby—her brother too—if only I'd known of her condition earlier."

Lily blinked at this. "Condition?" The word sent her mind spinning.

Was this the reason Geraldine had given away her daughter? Had she viewed a wealthy banker as a solution, ensuring better medical care for a sick child?

But then, why send her son off too? Why take the money in exchange?

"Are you saying Ruby was ill?" Lily asked. "Mrs. Stanton?"

The teacher broke from her thoughts. "Oh, no, not the girl," she said, causing but a flash of relief. "I was referring to Mrs. Dillard."

CHAPTER 19

SCENTS OF DIESEL AND FARMLAND intensified as the afternoon sun elbowed its way through the clouds. Its filtered rays cast shadows across the railroad tracks. On the side of the train depot, Ellis had found a quiet spot of shade to stand and talk.

"Now, like I said," Walter Gale reiterated, "I only caught what I could see and hear from my motorcar."

"Completely understand," Ellis assured him. He wished he could jot details on the notepad in his pocket, but given the subject matter, Walt didn't feel comfortable going on record of any kind. It didn't matter that Ellis, as the author of the related article, was just following up now for personal knowledge.

"So, what can I tell ya?" Walt hitched his hands on the denim trousers that hung a bit loose and short on his thin frame.

"At the Dillards' house that day, do you remember there being a sign? The one that was in the paper."

"About them kids for sale?" Walt thought hard, using his tongue to adjust the tobacco under his lower lip.

Ellis feared that leaving the jagged board behind had somehow led to this.

Walt's prominent Adam's apple shifted before he replied, "Don't recall so." Then he dropped his chin toward Ellis. "But you wanna know something interesting about that sign? The folks down the road...the Joneses? They posted one just like it before they up and moved."

Heat, like a current, zipped down Ellis's spine. He braced for the damning conclusion.

"Gave Mrs. Dillard the idea, I'd gander." Walt shrugged. "At any rate, that man did hand over a hefty pile of green for the two little ones. That I did see clear as day."

A mix of relief and shame continued to burn within Ellis as he aimed to focus. "Got anything else you could tell me about him?"

"Oh, I'd say he was...six feet or so. Average build. Mustache and glasses. Wore a hat, so can't say about the hair."

Ellis nodded along, despite the common description. If he were sketching a wanted criminal, half the men in the country would qualify for the lineup. "Anything more?"

"He was fairly soft-spoken. Seemed nice enough...as bankers go." Walt's derision over the occupation wasn't rare these days. But for Ellis, the detail might prove a benefit. It was the same tidbit the postman had passed along.

"Did the man specifically mention working at a bank? Or is that just a guess?"

Another casual shrug, though this time with a look of pride. "I worked at Penn Station, over in Pittsburgh, long enough to tell. Watched passengers come and go. That fella? Had a silk suit and fancy, polished shoes. Those were my first clues. When he first paid me to wait, I saw his bills were in neat order. All ones, twos, fives, and what have you. 'Accountant or banker?' I asked. 'Banker,' he says. He looked right confused, but didn't take the time to ask how I knew, like most people do. Just went on to handle his business about the kids."

His business. The two words sliced through Ellis, razor sharp. Blades of his own making. He had to remind himself that he wasn't the only one involved.

"Did Mrs. Dillard... Was she upset at all?"

Walt spat his dark saliva onto the road. "Hard to say. Didn't show it much. But for folks around here, during these times, they grow used to not having a whole lotta choices."

"What about the kids? How'd they behave through all of it?"

"After hugging their mama? The boy took some cajoling to get in the car. He was confused some. But once we were on the road, he got pretty darn excited about taking a real train ride. Asked lots of questions."

"And the girl?"

"Heard her sniffling during the drive. Otherwise, didn't make a peep from what I recall."

Ellis fought to block out the scene, not wanting to imagine that little girl's spirit broken into pieces. "You didn't hear where they were headed, did you?"

Walt shook his head. "Afraid that's everything I know." He wiped some spittle from his lip and glanced at his watch. "Well, if that does it, I'd better get a move on. Got errands to run before supper."

Ellis dreaded releasing his sole witness, but it seemed the man had shared all he could. "Thank you, Walt. I appreciate your help."

After a handshake, Walt strode over to a dusty car parked across the road. He climbed inside and started the engine.

Ellis was still well short of a sensible explanation. He hoped Lily was having luck gathering more clues.

"Come to think of it!" Walt suddenly hollered, his window down. "You might ask Blanche, inside there, about tickets sold—the last week of October. She's likely to know where that train of theirs went."

Ellis glanced back at the depot, connecting the name to the clerk. "You remember the exact week?" he yelled back, not meaning to sound incredulous. Fortunately Walt didn't appear to view it as a challenge.

"Wedding anniversary's on the twenty-eighth. With the fare from that banker, bought the missus a jar of cold cream she'd been hankering for. Well, good luck to ya!"

Ellis raised a hand in gratitude.

With a final spit, Walter Gale drove away.

CHAPTER 20

THE SIGN ON THE FRONT DOOR of the house hung a bit crook-
edly, but its message, printed in block letters, was abundantly clear.

UNLESS EMERGENCY
DO NOT DISTURB DR. BERKINS
ON WEEKENDS

Lily paused a mere moment before knocking. She had come
too far, in every way, not to see this through. It had taken
another half mile of walking to reach the town doctor. Akin
to her family's deli, his home doubled as an office. It was a
one-level house, painted rust red with white shutters. A woven
welcome mat appeared well worn from use.

She knocked again.

Rising warmth from the sun, absorbed by her coat, caused her
lower back to perspire. Her palms slickened around her purse
handle as she observed the area. Another house stood to the right
and one to the left, a half acre between each, yet she could hear

only the soft chirping of birds. Perhaps the weather had lured the neighborhood out for a spring picnic.

Then footfalls echoed from inside. Shoes on a hardwood floor.

Lily straightened, assembling her greeting.

The door opened to a man who looked to be in his midsixties. He had a slender frame and a pleated forehead, and held a linen napkin in his grip. "Yes?"

"Dr. Berkins? Hello, my name's Lillian Palmer. I apologize for bothering you on a Sunday."

"Feverish?"

"Pardon?"

"Your face, it looks flushed. Other symptoms?"

Thrown off, she had to reset her thoughts. Classical piano music, with light static, played in the background. "No, sir. I'm here about a personal issue."

He released a heavy breath, acknowledging the nonemergency. Nonetheless, he stepped aside. "Come in, then."

Appreciative, she nodded. After he shut the door behind her, she followed his slightly hunched form into a room just off the entry. There he clicked on a lamp, set upon a rolltop desk against the wall, before shuffling over to a window to close the curtains. A brass chandelier glowed over a doctor's table in the center of the space, and a china closet displayed medicine bottles and other supplies, more evidence of a converted dining room. Fittingly, the air smelled oddly of chicken soup and antiseptic.

"I'll be finishing my dinner in the kitchen while you remove your undergarments," he said. "When you're ready, open the sliding doors over here."

It finally hit Lily how her *personal issue* had been interpreted. She wouldn't be surprised if her flushed cheeks were now beet red. "But…Doctor—"

He flicked his wrinkled hand. "Nothing to be ashamed of." His tone dragged, having clearly spent decades comforting modest women with the very same words.

"Truly, though. I'm not here about an illness. I mean, that is why I came. Just not about mine."

He tossed aside his napkin and crossed his arms, signaling her with a weary nod. Another familiar tale.

"If I may, I'd like to ask you about Geraldine Dillard." Lily paused, allowing the name to register.

Dr. Berkins said nothing. Yet he knew her. More than that, he knew something about her. That much was plain in the set of his jaw, the firming of his lips.

"Please understand, I normally wouldn't intrude upon another person's privacy. But Ruby's teacher, Mrs. Stanton, shared that Mrs. Dillard had a 'condition.' I was hoping you could tell me more. You see, I have concerns about her children for good reason."

The doctor's arms were still folded, but he appeared curious about Lily's motives. A predictable reaction. Reporters and physicians had this much in common: at their core, they were solvers of puzzles and riddles.

"Go on," he said, hence Lily gladly did.

In essence, she repeated what she had told Mrs. Stanton, stressing how much it would mean to learn the true factors behind the fate of the children. To know that their outcome was the best one possible.

The doctor seemed unmoved. When he responded, his manner was professional and measured. "I have a policy, you understand, of not revealing patients' records. Particularly to those who have no ties as kin."

Why had she expected otherwise? She was a stranger off the street, not even from their community, asking for a person's intimate information.

She was running out of ideas—and time. The drive to Philadelphia still lay ahead.

"That being said," he continued, "these are unique circumstances."

Stunned for a moment, Lily neglected to answer. She simply watched him bend beside his desk and finger through the low file cabinet.

"I gather she had suspicions for a while, of it being tuberculosis," he said. "When she came to me in the fall, she was coughing a fair amount of blood. Soon after, without the children to care for…" He pulled out a folder and skimmed his notes. "Indeed, I recommended she consider the Dearborn Sanitarium, over in Bucks County. There are nicer places, of course, but it's an acceptable facility for those of limited means."

Lily vaguely noticed the classical tune had ended. The soft static from the needle on the inner record had become the sole sound in the house.

She pushed herself to ask, "How long do you think she has left?"

"*Had*, I would say, sadly. I estimated no more than…two months. Three at best."

She recalled the woman in the picture, fingers splayed, half turned away. Same as the chief, most readers had viewed the pose as one of shame. They had no idea they were seeing a mother whose stunted life would not include the young boy and girl huddled before her.

Lily's heart sank, weighted by the unfairness of it all.

Now she understood—not just why Geraldine had given up her children, but why she would take money in return. Care at a sanitarium would not be free.

These were the thoughts that persisted in Lily's mind as she soon walked toward the depot. In fact, she startled when she glanced up and stood a stone's throw from her destination.

"Lily," Ellis called to her. He had been leaning against his car, waiting. He stepped toward her looking eager to confer. But his expression quickly dimmed, undoubtedly mirroring hers, as she prepared to share the news.

CHAPTER 21

THREE DAYS AFTER RETURNING from Laurel Township, Ellis was still dwelling on the official word he got from Lily. She'd taken it upon herself to phone the sanitarium, said she couldn't fully rest until knowing for certain. The director only confirmed what the doctor suspected.

Geraldine Dillard had passed away.

In hindsight, Ellis recognized the clues. The dark circles under her hooded eyes. The weariness and ashen skin. The coughing.

Her look of desperation when he'd handed her those two crumpled dollars took on new meaning. He hated more than ever to think of how he'd benefitted from her being in that photo. His one consolation was the donations the article had gained for the family—and now, a seemingly better home than an orphanage for the kids.

That wasn't enough, though, to let Ellis rest. His mind remained jumbled and his writing blocked, his nightmares preventing any decent rest. The favorable description of the banker should have given him a sense of peace, but didn't.

Millstone—that was the man's name. Ellis had learned it from the ticket clerk. Walt the cabbie had been spot-on about asking her for details, although she didn't exactly celebrate the request. Her initial curt response had wavered only after Ellis offered a small fee—a tactic proven reliable with more than switchboard operators and hotel bellboys. A little skimming through the late-October travel logs, and there it was on the twenty-fifth of the month. Reserved under Alfred J. Millstone were three first-class tickets. The man had even splurged on a private train car.

Destination: Long Beach, California.

Two thousand miles away. It was about as far as a person could get from rural Pennsylvania without leaving the country. With its endless sunshine and Hollywood glamour, the name evoked visions of palm trees and white sandy beaches. But Ellis still worried.

"Reed?"

In the newsroom, a circle of eyes cut his way. At the center stood Mr. Walker, staring with arms crossed.

"Yes, sir?"

"I said, any updates or new ideas?"

"I'm, um, still working on some. Hope to share more soon."

The editor sighed, just like he had at every one o'clock meeting over the past week, when Ellis gave variants of the same answer. Then, as usual, he moved on to another reporter in the group—this time an energetic new hire with more story pitches than a flapper had tassels—and Ellis returned to his thoughts.

He didn't realize the meeting had broken up until Dutch appeared before him. "You okay?"

"Yeah...doing fine."

Dutch was obviously unconvinced. But without another word, he flipped his notepad closed and started toward his desk. It was then that an idea struck Ellis, a combination of elements colliding.

He was far from eager to ask. After their strained history,

requesting a favor straight out of the gate wasn't ideal. But given Dutch's former job at the *San Francisco Chronicle*, Ellis had to chance it. He owed that much to Geraldine.

"Dutch, hold on."

A mix of surprise and caution played over Dutch's face as Ellis treaded over, suddenly unprepared. A common theme in his life these days.

"Listen, Dutch. I know you and I… It might be too much to ask. We haven't talked in a while."

"What are you after?" This was the perfect opportunity for the guy to hear him out, then to tell him to stick it.

"You still got contacts in California?"

"A few."

"Thing is, I'm trying to track someone down. A banker from Long Beach. Name's Alfred Millstone."

Dutch didn't react. A bad sign.

But then, as if realizing there wasn't more to the request, he snatched the pencil from behind his ear. "Millstone, huh?"

"That's right. Alfred J."

Dutch scribbled in his notepad.

Ellis was about to thank him, but Dutch seemed to head it off, a faint smile in his eyes. "I'll make some calls," he said.

Simple as that. It was the start of amends long overdue.

~

Hunched over his typewriter, Ellis corralled his focus. No chatting or trips to the coffeepot. No making or taking calls. Within an hour, he managed to scrape together a basic piece about a current battle between Democrat and Republican lawmakers over a bill to legalize beer. He was tempted to suggest they break out barrels of the stuff at their next session; they might get along well enough to finally get something done.

The article wasn't a showstopper, but it would do until Ellis's verve for the job returned. All around him, juicy headlines were waiting to be nabbed. Just this week, the City Trust Company case had been tossed out of court, letting sizable crooks off the hook. Meanwhile, down on West Forty-Seventh, two couples had been booked for counterfeiting banknotes after stuffing $2,500 worth in their mattresses. Then there was the Presidential primary, with Franklin D. Roosevelt taking the lead.

Unfortunately, none of that felt as important as it should.

"Here he is, ma'am." A copy boy had guided a visitor over and promptly sped off.

Ellis had to do a double take. "Ma. What are you doing here?"

"I thought it would be nice…to surprise you."

Ellis was as befuddled as she appeared to be, though for different reasons. Clutching her pocketbook with gloved hands, she was absorbing the churning of activities and voices and noise that Ellis barely registered anymore. In a simple yellow dress and a cream cardigan, she was a canary caught in a storm.

He rose to greet her, but then braced himself. "Did Pop bring you?"

"He's at the plant. He'll be working late, repairing a machine. I took the train."

Ellis tried to mask his relief. He wondered if his father had any inkling of her excursion. She rarely traveled alone.

"Well, it's good to see you."

"I would've called ahead, but…I was just hoping we could talk over coffee."

Her strategy became clear. She suspected Ellis would delay a planned confrontation if given the chance. And she was right.

He regarded his editor's desk at the center of the city room. Mr. Walker was out for an early lunch, a luxury not meant for everyone. Yeah, reporters could come and go as needed, so long as they were pulling their weight. And lately, Ellis was slacking. What was more, any of his scoops with real teeth—for pieces that mattered—were becoming a vague memory.

Simply put, it wasn't a wise time to sneak off for a social visit. But still. This was his mother.

"Sure thing," he told her. "Lead the way."

~

At a café on Thirty-Ninth, they ordered coffee and crullers. The place was only half full, eliminating the need to yell to be heard. Ellis expected her to ease in with small talk—about neighbors or train travelers or tasty recipes she'd recently discovered. Instead, she got straight to the point.

"Ellis, I came here today because there's something you need to know. Regardless of how it might seem, your father is genuinely proud of you."

Oh boy.

"Ma, look. I appreciate you coming all this way, really. But it's pretty dang obvious how Pop feels—"

"I am *not* finished."

The last time he'd heard her speak so firmly, he must have been in high school. His muttered cursing over doing chores had earned him a scolding and a bar of Ivory to the mouth. He could still taste the suds if he really thought about it.

"Sorry. I'm listening."

She nodded and clasped her now-bare hands on the table. "Back when your father worked at the coal mines, there were accidents on occasion. Far too often, they involved children. And yes," she said, "I know that you were inspired by the reporters who wanted to help. But, sweetheart, not all of them were in it for a noble cause. There were some, your father said, who would pay miners, or even the police, for tips about terrible accidents. They'd arrive even before the poor families had been given the news."

At that moment, their chirpy waitress returned. Ellis and his mother fell into an awkward silence as the girl unloaded their order from her tray. "Enjoy," she said and bounded away, a stark contrast to the mood of the table.

Ellis waited patiently as his mother sipped her coffee. Wherever was this leading?

When she set down her cup, she held it with both hands as if needing to steady herself. "One day, your father was called in for an emergency. He had to help pull out another breaker boy who'd gotten caught in the gears. It took more than an hour." Sadness glossed her eyes, her voice turning hoarse, and it went without saying: the kid never made it home.

Ellis could still see those boys in his mind, blackened by dust, their eyes shocks of white. He recalled the tension in the truck after leaving the mine, his father fuming over Ellis wandering off. *Those mines are no place to fool around*, he'd scolded Ellis that day.

"In the end," she went on, "your father carried the child out. As he laid him down, a reporter was right there taking pictures. The flashbulb snapped, and so did your father. He punched the man over and over until miners pulled him off. Days later, the reporter threatened to sue Huss Coal…"

The rest faded off, but Ellis waited to hear more.

She took a breath. "The company chose to settle. As part of the deal, the reporter demanded that your father publicly apologize. It took everything in him, but he did it."

Ellis struggled to imagine the words *I'm sorry* coming out of Jim Reed's mouth. It was far easier to figure out what had occurred next. "That's when we moved to Allentown. And Pop started at the steel plant."

She nodded, and Ellis sat back, the chain of his life formed by links he never knew existed.

"Sweetheart," she said, reaching across the table to pat his hand. "I know your father hasn't always been the easiest. But I thought if you knew more, you'd understand. Deep down, he's truly proud of what you've accomplished. He just has trouble separating his past from the work you do."

Outside the window, people were streaming in both directions. They crisscrossed on the street, strangers in passing, each on their own journeys. Just like Ellis and his father.

No doubt his mother's theory would be nice to accept, if not for its crucial flaw: his father's coolness began long before Ellis's career would have posed any issue.

All the same, Ellis offered a smile. "Thanks, Ma. I'll keep it in mind."

~

After seeing his mother off at Penn Station and racing back to the paper, Ellis was relieved to find Mr. Walker still out. Unfortunately, the same couldn't be said of his assistant, Mr. Tate, who bore all the smugness of a truancy officer.

"You're back," Dutch said, stepping up to Ellis's desk. "Got something for ya."

Mr. Tate was peering at Ellis, then at the clock.

"Reed, you listening?" Dutch pressed.

"Sorry." Ellis shifted his attention, and recalled Dutch's task. "What've you got?"

"I heard from an old pal who moved to the *Los Angeles Times*. Turns out he was familiar with this Millstone character. Said he remembered a story they ran about him a few years back."

"What kind of story?"

Dutch's expression, the tension in it, told Ellis the news wasn't good.

"What? Banker fraud, corruption charges?"

"Nothing like that," Dutch said. "It involved a kid."

CHAPTER 22

AT HER DESK, LILY REREAD the article for the third time, gripped by the latest report. According to the *New York Times*, the child had been abducted right out of his room in the family's home, just over an hour north in Hopewell.

For Lily, the boy's status as the son of aviation hero Charles Lindbergh was inconsequential. Save as a reminder: no amount of money, fame, or success made a parent entirely immune from suffering the unthinkable.

Every day this week, on her walk to and from the *Examiner*, she had anxiously anticipated paperboys shouting, *Lindbergh baby returned! Home safe and sound!* But the investigation was dwindling. Cold trails and blind leads were reducing the family's meager hopes, now reliant on negotiations with the kidnappers.

One more child added to Lily's prayers.

While her own son was never far from her worries, now neither were Ruby and Calvin. She wondered if they had known their mother was ill. Had she shielded the truth for fear they would refuse to leave her? Did they assume she just didn't want them? If only they could have heard her true feelings straight from her...

The thought drew Lily back to the *Times* article. Aided by memories of Ellis's old features, the human aspect of them, a revelation formed. While she couldn't erase her own past, any more than she could ensure a good life for the Dillard children, maybe she could help, even in a small way, with the reunion of another family.

The chief was in his office alone. Now was the time to speak up.

Over the growing activity in the newsroom, Lily gave his door two cursory knocks before letting herself in.

"Chief?"

"Yeah, yeah. Lunch with my wife's nephew. I got it." Rising from his chair, he crushed out a cigarette in his ashtray. "I swear to Jesus, if this kid shows up late again—and I mean by two damn minutes—I'm walking out."

Punctuality ranked only a hair below his penchant for accountability and, yes, truth.

As he unrolled his sleeves and refastened the buttons, Lily maintained her purpose. "Sir, after reading an article today, I was thinking about the Lindbergh case."

"You and everybody else on the planet."

"Yes...but, you see, the newspapers keep focusing on the hard facts of the case: the suspects and gangs they've ruled out, the searches through houses and ocean liners. Of all the quotes I've seen, from the police and Mr. Lindbergh, these are the predominant topics."

"Miss Palmer, your point."

"What about *Mrs.* Lindbergh?"

"What of her?"

"Perhaps an in-depth interview in the *Examiner* could help. She could talk about her son's favorite foods and games and lullabies. We could include personal photos of their family, together and happy. A reminder that this is a real child, not just a bargaining chip for a ransom."

The chief barked a laugh as he pulled on his suit jacket. "Tell that to the kidnappers."

"That's *exactly* what we should do." Her boldness erased his smile. She eased herself back. "At the end of the day, these criminals are still people. If Mrs. Lindbergh directly appealed to them, to speak of the terror she and her husband are going through, it might prevent the child from being harmed. At the very least, readers might pay keener attention to potential clues right around them."

"And let me guess. You're just the one to land that interview."

When Lily hedged, as she honestly hadn't contemplated that far, he shook his head wearily. He thought she was being strategic, pouncing on the opportunity of a tragedy.

"I promise, sir, this isn't about me."

That wasn't to say she had abandoned her writing aspirations. The fact that upon retiring, Mr. Schiller had been replaced by yet another sports columnist, of all things, continued to irk her, but that didn't pertain to the issue at hand.

The chief waved her off as he put on his hat. "Mrs. Lindbergh's probably been asked plenty and turned 'em down. What makes you think she'd even want the spotlight at a time like this?" His tone made the question rhetorical. He figured his secretary, the non-reporter, had no valid grounds for the suggestion.

Except she wasn't speaking as a reporter. Nor as a secretary.

"Because as a mother I'd want to be heard."

She caught herself only after the words were out. By then, the chief was checking his watch, the statement brushed off as hypothetical, and he strode out the door.

The answer to her pitch lay starkly in his absence.

～

Lily's subsequent mood wouldn't make her the most charming of company today. But since Clayton so rarely asked her out to lunch, as they largely separated their work and social interactions, she didn't feel right about canceling.

"You sure you're okay?" he asked once they had boarded the elevator.

She knew better than to say a negative word about her boss before leaving the building, but several strangers in front of them were busy with their chatter. She confided quietly: "It's the Lindbergh baby. I just thought…"

"Ah. Of course," he said, bewildering her.

"Of course?"

How would he know?

More important, why was he smiling?

He shook his head at her. "Like your mother keeps saying, you worry too much."

He thought she was fearful about Samuel, of him disappearing in a similar way. But that wasn't it. Not at this moment. Even so, the patronizing nature of Clayton's words stung like salt in a recurring wound. She'd endured all the condescension she needed for one day.

"I was referring," she corrected, "to an article in today's *Times*." Her tone came out a bit strong, but not enough to disturb the conversing strangers as the door opened on the second floor, where a rewrite man boarded.

Clayton studied her, clearly struggling to identify the problem. "So…you're upset about what the police said. How they won't work with Lindbergh's so-called underworld emissaries?"

Naturally he had read the same article. Perusing the big morning dailies was expected.

"I suppose." It was simpler to agree at this point.

"Well, I hope you can see why. Those crooks wouldn't be helping out for nothing. There'd be favors to repay. Classic case of the ends not justifying the means."

Lily's mouth went slack. If Samuel were at risk of being harmed, she would stop at nothing to protect him. "And if the child were yours? Would those principles still take priority?"

Several passengers glanced toward Lily. The sudden quiet—from Clayton too—shot heat up her neck. She stared straight ahead, the tension brewing, until the door opened.

"First floor," the lift operator announced.

Lily followed the group out, anxious for the open air. In the entry, Clayton gently tugged on her arm, guiding her to a stop.

"Lily. If something else is bothering you, anything at all, you can tell me. I hope you know that."

After a second, she raised her eyes. From the sincerity in his face, the kindness in him, a tide of guilt crested over her. He didn't deserve such a venting.

"I'm sorry, Clayton. I don't mean to be irritable." There was too much to explain, too many confidences to break. "It's just been one of those mornings."

His mouth steeped into his usual smile. "Working for the chief? I'd say that applies to almost every morning."

She found herself smiling back as he planted a kiss on her forehead, a loving gesture that melted away the remnants of her frustration. "I'd bet a nice lunch at the Renaissance would help."

Aware they were alone in the lobby, she followed an impulse to lean toward him. *Or this*, she thought and kissed him on the lips. When she drew back, the surprise in his eyes—from a reporter not easily taken off guard—filled her with satisfaction. "Now, shall we go?"

His reaction was morphing into delight. "To anywhere you'd like."

"The Renaissance will do." She warmly hooked his elbow, and together, they continued toward the exit. After stepping aside for a few people to enter, they joined the bustling of Market Street. The scent of roasting nuts from a vendor cart provided mild reprieve from wafts of city odors as she and Clayton wound their way toward the restaurant.

Glad to redeem their date, she asked about his newest leads, always guaranteed to launch him into conversation. And though she was listening, a thought pulsed in a corner of her mind. A tiny but persistent sliver.

One of the strangers back at the *Examiner*, coming through the door...there was something familiar. Those features... Lily knew them...

A block from the restaurant, she stopped. "Oh my God." She visualized the scene again, verifying.

"Lily?" Clayton's voice sounded distant, hollow. "What's wrong?"

She looked at him, grappling for an answer. "I-I have to go back. I just realized."

"What is it?"

There was no time to explain. "Go on in. I'll catch up with you." As she rushed off toward the *Examiner*, the world's noises dropped away. There was only the thudding of her heart, her heels slapping pavement, and her hopes repeated like a prayer.

"Please," she whispered. "Please still be there."

CHAPTER 23

ACCORDING TO DUTCH'S PAL at the *Los Angeles Times*, Alfred Millstone had appeared in the papers here and there over the years. As vice president of the American Trust Company in Long Beach, the mentions would be expected. All of them were trivial except for one: a funeral announcement.

Two years ago, the Millstones' only child perished in a car wreck. According to reports, no sign of foul play. Then recently, over in New Jersey, the president of Century Alliance Bank took a trip off a bridge—as many a man had since Black Tuesday—and Mr. Millstone had crossed the country to fill the opening.

It now made sense to Ellis. Ruby and Calvin were part of the couple's attempt to heal, to move on. Start fresh.

In a much smaller way, this was what Ellis, too, had hoped to do by coming here today.

The building was a typical two-story bank in Hoboken, with a tailor shop to one side and a barber's to the other. To arrive before closing, Ellis had to slip out of the *Tribune* early, this time steering clear of Mr. Tate. After his mother's visit and the news from Dutch, his chances of productivity were shot. And the drive to Century Alliance, just across the Hudson, had been too much to resist.

Inside, framed photographs of the branch's pooh-bahs hung on a wall beside the entrance. Ellis's heart stalled a beat at the engraving beneath the top portrait:

ALFRED J. MILLSTONE, PRESIDENT

The man was much like the cabbie had described. He had kind eyes behind horn-rimmed glasses, a gently sloped nose that led to a blunt end, and a thick mustache, dark and tidy like his hair. Not the sort of person you'd imagine trading a stack of dollar bills for two barefoot kids on a farm.

Ellis turned to scan the room, seeking the real-life version of the banker among the smattering of faces. A security guard, stocky as a bulldog, cleared his throat while eyeing Ellis. A message. Snoopiness was no more welcome here than behind a peep tent at a carnival.

"Afternoon," Ellis said. "I just came in to see—"

The guard pointed sharply toward the tellers' stations. Another hint taken.

Ellis joined the shortest line, behind three bank patrons, and observed the area with more subtlety. Offices for management appeared to be up the stairs. He'd head there to find out, but the guard was still watching.

Soon enough, it was his turn with a clerk, a young woman who, unlike the guard, seemed rather ecstatic to be working in a place stocked with a hefty portion of the city's cash. "Good afternoon, sir. How may I be of service?"

"I'd like to speak with Mr. Millstone, if I could."

A hitch in her smile. "Oh? Is there a problem?"

"Not at all. I was considering opening an account. With a substantial deposit."

"Ah, that's grand. One moment, please." She stepped away to confer with an older woman, caught in passing with an armful of files. The teller returned with a semi-frown. "Unfortunately, Mr. Millstone is tied up in meetings for the rest of the day. However, our manager would be happy to assist you. If you'll wait here, I'll let him know—"

"Actually," Ellis broke in with a smile, "I'd prefer to come back. Mr. Millstone was referred by a trusted friend, you see."

She assured him that she understood, and Ellis retreated to his car, where he camped out like a PI. He'd parked just half a block down, ensuring a clear view of the entrance across the street.

When working for the Society page, every so often he'd been tasked with following a celebrity to nab an intriguing picture. A chore he'd despised. Sure, not enough to deter him from later tracking a senator and his harem of mistresses. But this here was different. This wasn't for his career; it was personal. He needed to know for peace of mind—for Geraldine—that the man who'd taken the kids was as good and upstanding as one would hope.

The bank had been closed for nearly twenty minutes, the sun sliding low in the sky, before a mustached man stepped out of the doors. Ellis sat up. In a charcoal-gray suit and a matching hat, Alfred Millstone adjusted his grip on a cane that appeared more for style than necessity.

Ellis exited his car, prepared with any number of questions: directions to City Hall, recommendations for a show or restaurant. As a reporter, he was never short on queries. He was in the midst of crossing the street when a taxi pulled up to the banker, as if scheduled with no need to be hailed.

A truck blasted a honk. Ellis stumbled back a step, barely missing the vehicle, its cursing driver determined not to swerve.

Welcome to Jersey.

Mr. Millstone had just shut the cab door, about to leave.

Ellis could always come back another day, but a new plan came to him. One that could lead to far greater assurances.

Before he could weigh the decision, he hightailed it to his car and rushed to follow.

At a discreet distance, he trailed the taxi to a neighborhood roughly three miles from the bank. A string of impressive Victorian homes lined the north side of the street with intermittent trees. The south side hosted a small park.

When the cab stopped, Ellis pulled over and turned off his engine.

Mr. Millstone soon climbed out. He tipped his hat to the driver and trekked up the short rise of stairs and into the house. The paint was mint green, the trim and porch stark white. Two chimneys topped the steeped roofs, and an intricate gable added more charm. By all appearances, the outcome looked pretty decent for the kids.

Assuming they were there. Ellis hadn't yet verified that fact. But one peek through the window could end the mystery—his worries, too, if he saw them doing well. Perhaps a meeting with Mr. Millstone wouldn't be needed after all.

The thought was enough to propel Ellis.

He got out of his car just as a paperboy bicycled past, tossing rolled editions to front doors. The kid drew from his shoulder bag like an expert archer handling a quiver. When a woman walking her pup disappeared around the corner, leaving the street vacant, Ellis ascended the steps. On the porch, a wire basket of empty glass bottles awaited a dairyman's delivery.

Ellis looked cautiously through a narrow gap in the lace curtains. In a parlor room on a large Persian rug, a young girl sat before a floor-model radio. She wore a sailor dress, black Mary Janes, and a red bow in her hair. No ponytail or overalls. But it was her. Ruby Dillard. Bright and clean as a new penny.

On an antique love seat, a slender woman in a fashionable day dress held an open book on her lap. Contentment curved her lips, seemingly more from watching the girl than from listening to the radio. In the background, a white-manteled fireplace and

Tiffany lamps adorned the room. The whole scene befitted a cover of the *Saturday Evening Post*.

Through the window came the soft sound of laughter. A young boy's giggles.

Calvin.

Relief drifted through Ellis, his spirits lifting, until a light creak shot from behind.

He swung around to find the front door opened. Alfred Millstone was reaching for the evening paper, the startle clear on his face.

"Mr. Millstone. Good evening." Ellis felt just as jarred, but also embarrassed by his audacious plan to lurk. What the hell had he been thinking?

"Who–who are you?" the man stammered.

Ellis needed an explanation fast.

Then he thought: Why not tell the truth? This was indeed the person who'd relieved Geraldine of her burden. He might want to know that she'd passed, that he'd done a good thing, in case he had doubts.

"Sir, I'm Ellis Reed…with the *Herald Tribune*." Ellis held out his hand in greeting.

Mr. Millstone turned markedly stern. "A reporter?" He made no move to accept the handshake. "What is it you want?"

There was irony here—that a newspaper was welcome at the home, while a newsman plainly was not. He and Ellis's father could well be instant pals.

But then what did Ellis expect? After all the bank runs following the market crash, a double hit-job on folks' savings, reporters hadn't portrayed banks, or their executives, in the best light.

"You answer me now, or I'll phone the police." Mr. Millstone's high forehead shone with a slight flush, triggering Ellis's gut to intervene.

It told him to leave well enough alone, that there was no good reason to press on. Hadn't he disrupted enough lives already?

He could simply toss out an excuse for his presence and be on his way.

"Sir, I'm…working on a piece. For the paper. A profile."

The man's eyes tightened behind his glasses. "On?"

"Well…you, Mr. Millstone."

What sounded like a western, with horses' hoofbeats and *yippee ki-yay*s, projected from the radio. Its burst of gunshots reverberated through the silence on the porch.

Ellis needed to elaborate to prevent a police summons that could end in a similar way. "As I'm sure you know, after Black Tuesday, trust in the banking community's been set back a bit. A personal profile on prominent bankers like yourself could help remedy the situation by rebuilding relationships with your customers."

Obviously, Mr. Millstone wasn't going to agree—a good thing. Ellis just needed to provide an easy out. "If you'd rather not, that's certainly fine. We could—"

"When?"

Ellis blinked. *Shit.*

"I presume you have a deadline in the near future."

Ellis mentally scrambled, mustering a look of gratitude. "How's tomorrow?"

Mr. Millstone's demeanor lightened the smallest amount. "Fine. Two o'clock." Then he stressed with a pointer finger, "At the bank."

"Yes, of course. I look forward to it."

A quick sniff, and Mr. Millstone bid good night. Then, as if suddenly recalling his purpose for coming out, he snatched up his evening paper and shut the door.

Ellis exhaled in a quiet rush. "Well done, dimwit," he muttered to himself.

When he turned for the steps, he noted the window. The view of the parlor, along with the children, was gone. Someone had drawn the drapes.

~

The phone was ringing as Ellis approached his apartment. He unlocked it and rushed inside to pick up the handset on the entry table. He'd barely said hello when a woman answered.

"Ellis? Oh, thank heavens you're there."

He hesitated, pleasantly surprised by the voice. "Lily...yeah. I just walked in."

"I've been calling and calling—at work, then your apartment—but I couldn't reach you."

At her urgency, he brought the mouthpiece closer. "What's happened? Are you all right?"

"She came to the *Examiner* to find you. I barely caught up to her, just leaving the building. There's more you need to hear, but she wants to tell you herself."

"Wait a sec. You've got to back up." None of it was making sense. "Who is...*she*?"

Now Lily was the one who hesitated. After a breath over the line, she replied.

"Geraldine Dillard."

CHAPTER 24

A PASSING GLANCE shouldn't have been enough to recognize her. After all, the only picture Lily had seen of Geraldine was grainy and gray from the press, half of her face obscured.

Lily wondered later what had sparked the revelation. Was it a hunch? Gut instinct, intuition? More likely, it was plain wishful thinking. No doubt, all week, she had been seeking Geraldine's face among strangers in passing. She was too invested at that point, she supposed, to accept the finality of their findings.

In the end, those findings were wrong. At least those that had been relayed by the sanitarium's director. There was no greater proof than the reemergence of Geraldine, lured to the *Examiner* by Lily's inquiry on Ellis's behalf. But with Ellis gone to New York, Lily welcomed Geraldine to speak in confidence, yearning to help.

And so, in the privacy of the darkroom—the location a true mark of coming full circle—Lily listened to her story and agreed. Ellis, too, needed to hear it straight from the source.

As Geraldine waited at a nearby diner, Lily juggled her

work tasks with desperate attempts to reach Ellis. In the midst of her fourth try, Clayton appeared at her desk, back from lunch—*their* lunch—and her stomach dropped. She had completely forgotten.

Her face must have conveyed her horror because the apology was just forming on her lips when he leaned toward her and smiled.

"Done it myself. It happens. We'll blame the chief." He assumed that pressing duties for her boss had looped her back to the paper. "Anyway, I ran into some pals from the *Bulletin*, so it worked out fine. We'll catch dinner soon?"

"My goodness, *yes*. Thank you for understanding, Clayton."

After a wink, he went about his job. His sheer kindness over the slipup made her feel even worse.

Only the ringing in her ear reminded her of the receiver in her grip.

Another unanswered call.

Hours later, not giving up, she rang from her boardinghouse. She had brought Geraldine with her, having promised to summon Ellis.

Admittedly, visions of him rolling craps and swigging liquor in some gaming hall had flitted through her mind until at last he answered the phone, his voice stunned but clear.

She gave him few details.

He didn't need them to decide.

"Tell me where you are," he said.

~

It was a little after eight when the rattling of a car engine again drew Lily toward the foyer. The evening was slipping away.

Geraldine's bus ride back to the sanitarium, in Bensalem Township, would leave at 9:32. Out of pride, despite the drive taking well over a half hour, she declined to stay until morning. Lily would have pressed the issue if the boardinghouse didn't frown upon overnight guests. She was already pushing her limits.

The landlady, Miss Westin, had retired upstairs for the evening, same as the only other tenants in the brownstone who hadn't ventured out to a movie palace or a vaudeville show. Lily had properly alerted Miss Westin that a second friend would be paying a visit—just without specifying gender. The prim British woman would have insisted upon chaperoning.

That certainty now sent Lily racing again to the heavy oak door to prevent a ring of the bell. Beneath a glowing streetlamp, there was Ellis, striding up to the entry. She tempered her volume despite her eagerness. "Come inside," she said, and closed the door behind them. His concern and confusion, evident in his blue eyes, had surely amassed over the length of the drive.

Aware of the most glaring discrepancy, she didn't wait for the question. "When I phoned the sanitarium, they did tell me Geraldine had passed."

"It was a mix-up, then."

"That's what I thought too. But she'd simply asked them for privacy when she first arrived there. She was hoping to live out her final days without attention from anyone. Particularly the press."

He shrugged his brows, acknowledging the sensibility in it. Then those features drew together. "How ill is she now?"

He wanted to be prepared. But it was best to see for himself.

"She's in the den."

Ellis removed his hat, gearing up, and Lily led him onward. Dark panels of wood covered the floor and walls, lending the brownstone a gothic feel in the evenings. Tonight even more so, given its widowed guest risen from the grave.

Past the narrow staircase and a small phone table, they entered the den. The scent of lemon polish mingled with that of the aged books that lined two walls of shelves, each stretched to the twelve-foot ceiling. The painting of a cobblestone village flickered above the fireplace.

Geraldine sat upon one of two matching upholstered chairs, staring into the flames. Still in her overcoat, she fingered a button on her long skirt.

"Mrs. Dillard?" Ellis said. When she turned and nodded, he edged forward with eyes narrowed, absorbing the state of her condition. "I didn't... They said that..."

He faltered for obvious reason. In the amber firelight, aside from her tired eyes and stragglers of her brown hair loosened from her bun, she showed no resemblance to a woman on her deathbed. In fact, given her healthful appearance, any claims of a grave illness seemed part of an elaborate conspiracy.

Lily chimed in to explain. "Her doctor was mistaken. It wasn't tuberculosis."

Ellis continued to stare at Geraldine. "When did you find out?"

Geraldine's hands, weathered but strong, went still as she thought. "Must've been a month after leaving for Dearborn."

"The sanitarium," Ellis murmured, reconciling the name.

"The director there did some X-rays for me, and some other tests. We call her Doc Summers, even though she ain't an official doctor. It's on account of *her* that my lungs were finally treated for the right infection. Now that I'm well, she's even let me stay on to give a hand with other patients."

Lily tried to brighten, an offering of support. "I'm sure they're grateful to have you."

Geraldine smiled but with a solemn undercurrent. "It's been good for me too. Helps to have a purpose, with my husband gone...and now the kids."

Tough as an ox, her husband wasn't sick a day in his life, she had told Lily, until he stepped on a rusted nail. He died of lockjaw a week later, leaving a desperate widow to take in sewing and laundry to scrape by with two children.

Lily glanced at Ellis, his face dimming with remorse.

"Why don't we sit down," she encouraged him. He gave a half-hearted nod, likely questioning if he was prepared to hear more, but he followed.

As Lily settled into the chair beside Geraldine, Ellis perched on the tufted settee across from them. Hat upon his lap, he ventured, "Miss Palmer said you wanted to speak with me?"

"I do," Geraldine said, but with a look of warning. "I don't want none of this in the paper. You hear?"

"Not a chance. You have my word."

She studied his face. Appearing satisfied, she sat back stiffly and began. "I told that man the kids weren't for sale. No matter what he saw in that picture. But he persisted all the same. Put fifty whole dollars on my porch…though I barely noticed at the time." She shook her head—at either the banker's stubbornness or the fact she had missed such a thing.

"I was having more bad days than good 'round then, and just that morning, I'd coughed enough blood to give me a real scare. I was just so tired all the time, and it was only getting worse. And I thought…maybe this was the Lord's doin', sending this person to us right then." Geraldine's eyes glimmered with moisture. When she dropped her gaze to her worn black shoes, Lily recognized a fear in her, an expectation of being judged.

"He just had so many reasons," she went on, "how he and his wife could give the kids a good life. Better than I ever could, sick or not. But they had to stay together—Ruby and Cal. That's what I told him. I made him swear."

The room went quiet for a stretch, save for the crackling of firewood. Ellis noticeably swallowed, and Lily realized then how much her own throat had constricted, in spite of already knowing the story.

Geraldine gained sudden conviction. "You gotta know. I'd sooner die than spend *one cent* of that man's money." She looked at Ellis, almost daring him to challenge her.

"I believe you," he stressed.

"As do I." Lily's voice verged on a whisper.

Slowly Geraldine nodded, the tension around her mouth relaxing.

Perhaps not feeling a need to, she made no mention of the old mason jar she had described to Lily: a transparent display of those cursed dollar bills. Each one surely a reminder of a mother's shame, no matter the reasoning behind her choice.

Instead, she kept her composure and proceeded with intent. "Now, Mr. Reed," she said, "when Miss Palmer called, she told Doc Summers you were hunting down what happened to me and my children. Finding out about their new parents and such."

"Yes. That's right."

"Well, when you do, when you know more, I want you to tell me. And don't you worry, I'm not looking to steal 'em back. They're to stay right where they are, and they're not to hear about any of this. I just need to know firsthand that they're safe."

Ellis proffered a heavy smile. "I understand."

Lily was dumbfounded. She had been certain that the point of Geraldine's visit was to acquire Ellis's help, to combine forces to reunite her family.

Then Ellis added gently, "And I can tell you already, Mrs. Dillard. From everything I've seen, they're being well cared for, just like you hoped."

Lily scrambled to absorb his words, his claim that sounded literal. "You actually saw them."

Why would he withhold such important news? Was there something he wasn't saying?

"It just happened today," he said quickly, as if sensing her worry. "I tracked them down over in New Jersey."

Geraldine looked almost panicked. "They were going to California. Where it'd be sunny and warm. That's what the man said."

Ellis raised a hand to calm her. "It was the truth. He and his wife were living in Long Beach, or thereabouts. Then he got a job at another bank—a big promotion in Jersey—and they moved into a real nice house there."

The sudden relief sweeping over Geraldine was palpable. An internal dam, clearly bound by every fiber of her strength, had splintered, sending a rush of tears to her eyes. "So, the kids... they're doing all right?"

"I wasn't able to talk to them," Ellis said, "but from a distance, Ruby looked happy enough and healthy."

"And Cal? He was there with her?"

"He was. He was even laughing. At some radio program...a western, I think."

Geraldine brightened, her son's giggles clearly echoing in her ear. Though not a minute later, that glow faded. It had to be bittersweet, the knowledge that someone else could so easily bring her son joy. That such a sound would become a mere memory for Geraldine.

Which was why Lily couldn't let that happen.

"Mrs. Dillard, it's not too late. We can fix this together, I'm sure we can."

Geraldine swiped at her eyes and straightened in her chair. Fervently, she shook her head. "There's nothing that needs fixin'. Life is just how it should be."

"But...if you do want them back—"

"Knowing they're happy and healthy is all I need."

"Well, yes, I understand that. But—"

"I've said my piece."

Lily wanted to protest further but refrained. It was painfully clear there was no swaying Geraldine.

At least, not tonight.

～

They walked to his car in silence, Lily and Ellis together. Streetlamps and the white glow of a three-quarter moon threw shadows over the pavement. She could have said goodbye from the boardinghouse, sent him off at the front door, but there was more she needed to tell him.

As though he expected as much, he waited beside his car door with hat held low.

"Those children should be with their mother. Now that she's well again, it's unfair to keep them apart. You must know in your heart she doesn't actually want to live without them."

"Lily, listen…" While spoken softly, there was dissension in his words.

"Yes, I know. The Millstones have prominence and a fancy home and in all likelihood mean well. Still, you heard Geraldine. She's working as a caregiver now. She'd find a way to manage."

"I'm sure she would." His agreement sounded genuine. "Unfortunately…it's just not that simple."

"She's their mother. It is that simple. What could possibly be more important?"

He released a sigh, as if dreading to voice the answer. "I feel for them, Lily. Trust me, I do. But even if Geraldine demanded them back, I can't imagine the Millstones handing them over without a fight. They'd have almost everything on their side, including a top-notch lawyer. I'm familiar with enough cases to know that no reasonable judge is going to return the kids to a poor widow." He added with reluctance, "Especially one who sold them."

"They weren't really for sale, though. You *know* that."

He went quiet, and she worried she had seemed accusatory. That wasn't her intention. She was only stressing his full knowledge of the situation.

But then he rubbed the back of his neck, thinking things over. Perhaps sifting through options.

"Ellis, there must be something we can do."

He raised a shoulder, meeting her eyes. "If I thought it would help, heck, I'd pay the legal fees myself. But to take this on, any lawyer worth his salt would have to believe there's even a remote chance of winning."

"So, we'll build a stronger case."

This caused him to smile, and she noted how naive she appeared.

Maybe in some ways she was, because she absolutely had to believe a solution existed, that the powerful bond inherent between a mother and child could surmount any obstacle separating them. And yet, Lily had also learned how the support of another person, even unexpectedly, could prove far more vital.

Geraldine needed their help, more than she knew. Ellis couldn't deny this fact once given a glimpse through Lily's perspective.

"If I deserved a second chance," she told him, "so does Geraldine."

He tilted his head, just a fraction, but his attention was fully captured.

For the first time to anyone but family, she would tell her story. Not all of it, mind you. But enough.

"The summer before my senior year," she began, "I was staying at the shore with a friend and her family. And I met a boy. He was charming and handsome, and the way he'd look at me...I thought for certain it was love. Of course, I discovered how foolish I'd been when he stepped out with another girl. But it was too late by then...to reverse what I'd done."

She let the implication dangle, unwilling to recount the evenings of sweet whispers and strolls on the beach, of chills and hand-holding and kisses that led to more.

"I was young and terrified. I knew the scandal it could bring my family...and the baby. So, I agreed to give him up." The reference to Samuel needed no clarification. Ellis's nod made clear he understood, inviting her to go on.

"It was the most logical decision in the world. I even wrote a letter for him to read one day, explaining it all." No message could have been harder to draft, yet she had persisted for everyone's benefit. "Then he was born, and I took one look at this beautiful, perfect child that was actually part of me, and I couldn't do it. The papers were already signed, but I begged and pleaded anyway. If my father hadn't stood up for me, and for Samuel, the adoption agency would have taken him. And I'd have made the biggest mistake of my life."

In the darkness, Lily could still see the scenes playing out. They were silent images, like a Chaplin picture projected on a screen. As they blurred and faded, she dragged her gaze back to Ellis, her sudden dread of judgment akin to Geraldine's.

Thus, the acceptance she found—in the depth of his eyes, in his whole bearing—meant more than he could have imagined. "So, you understand now?"

He affirmed as much by the tenderness of his smile. "I do."

A sense that he was coming around buoyed her hopes. "The Dillards belong together, Ellis."

"And...to make that happen, they'll need help," he finished.

"Precisely."

In that way, they were no different from a family like the Lindberghs, she realized. Only, for Geraldine, there was no bloodhound team of officers and agents working day and night. No hefty savings to offer as a reward or to entice a trade. No prominent name to incite national headlines. All she had was Lily and Ellis and the truth of what was just.

If at all within their power, how could they not try?

CHAPTER 25

"MR. REED, A MOMENT." Mr. Walker's thin drawl didn't do much to soften his ominous tone.

Like the rest of the group, Dutch was breaking from the daily news meeting, but he paused to flash his clenched teeth at Ellis. The gesture surely meant *Hang in there, buddy*—though it felt more like *Pal, you're in for it.*

Probably because that was just what Ellis was telling himself.

When Mr. Walker had skipped over him while asking for updates around the circle, Ellis was relieved at first, as he still had no big project in the works. Not one for the public anyway. But then he'd caught a smirk from Mr. Tate, indicating that bypassing Ellis wasn't an oversight.

"Follow me." Mr. Walker now led Ellis through the standard chitter of the city room and into the privacy of the meeting room. The space was limited to a plain, rectangular table surrounded by well-worn chairs. Every wall was left bare, save for a single working clock. Aside from paper and ink, it was the greatest necessity in the business.

As Mr. Walker closed the door, Ellis peeked at the time. Half past one. Despite last night's drive to and from Philly, he wasn't weary enough to forget his two o'clock with Mr. Millstone. For any chance of making it, he had to leave soon. A prospect that wasn't looking good, based on Mr. Walker's folded arms, his jutted jaw. Add a gun belt and a silver star to the man's suit, and he could pass as a southern lawman reaching his diplomatic limit.

Ellis prompted, "Is something wrong, sir?"

"I was planning to ask you the same. Because for the life of me, I can't fathom where your head's been lately."

Ellis doubted that was true. Mr. Walker appeared to have a very clear idea about which body cavity Ellis had been using to store that particular part. But since cracking a joke in that regard wasn't going to help, he merely listened.

"Early on, I did have some reservations about bringing you on board. But then you found your stride. Broke some solid stories." Mr. Walker paused then, and Ellis wanted to cut to the end as much as he dreaded it. "If you have some notion, however, that a couple of bylines means you can sit back on your haunches—especially at *your* level of salary—you're going to be gravely disappointed."

The nature of Ellis's generous raise had always carried a backroom-handshake feel. Apparently the paper's accountant wasn't the only other staff member aware of the specifics.

"I assure you, sir, I don't think that at all. In fact," Ellis reminded him, "I volunteered just yesterday to write up a piece about the beer bill." After everything that had happened since, it was hard to believe that only a day had passed.

"Ah, yes. The mystery piece."

Ellis puzzled over the description.

"You know...a mystery. When logic tells us something should be there, but for some reason it never appears."

"But, sir. If you recall, I punched out that piece in plenty of time for deadline." Ellis had actually finished it before his mother surprised him with a visit, had even gotten approval right after.

"Okay. Then who'd you leave it with?"

Ellis hated to assign blame, but he remembered clear as rain. Before departing early for the bank, he'd gathered his belongings, and on his way out, he handed his pages off to...

Except...he hadn't. The damn things were still in his satchel.

"Christ." He ran a hand over his eyes.

"Well then. Assuming you're not trying to claim the Almighty is responsible, sounds like we settled that issue."

Ellis pointed toward the door. "I've got that article right at my desk. I can grab it right this second."

"It's done," Mr. Walker said. "I had Hagen write it up. You were nowhere to be found. An increasingly recurrent theme, it seems."

The article wasn't urgent. Reassigning it, specifically to the eager rookie with a billion ideas, was a bold flag of frustration.

Ellis lamented the flub, but not nearly as much as being viewed as a shirker. "I'm sorry, Mr. Walker. I do value my job, honest. Like I mentioned before, I just had some personal matters that needed my attention."

"So do we all, Mr. Reed. And if that warranted perpetual free passes, we wouldn't have a paper. Besides, we're in the news business here. I don't have to explain to you the importance of perception."

Nope, he really didn't. Misperceptions were just what had led Ellis into the current mess with Lily and Geraldine and Alfred Millstone.

The thought pulled Ellis's eyes toward the clock, his editor's lecture droning on until the room broke jaggedly into silence.

Mr. Walker's gaze turned steely. "You have somewhere else to be right now?"

Ellis could still postpone the appointment. Given how it came about, though, he doubted he'd get another shot. And a one-on-one meeting could reveal just enough details to help those kids.

"Across the river," he hazarded. "For an interview."

Mr. Walker considered this, and Ellis feared an inquiry over specifics. Instead, the editor cast him an unreadable look before opening the door. "Then I suggest you get going."

~

Those parting words normally would have scratched at Ellis's mind. He would have reviewed them for intent, for a sign of finality. A message that he needn't bother to return. But all he could think of now, as he drove toward Century Alliance, was that every resident on Manhattan Island had ventured out for an afternoon drive, enticed by the moderate spring weather.

Within seconds of pulling up to the bank, he was parked and sprinting toward the entrance. A drop of sweat slid from his hat.

"No running," the guard inside growled, slowing Ellis to a brisk walk.

He maintained his pace up the stairs, glad nobody stopped to question him, and introduced himself to the lone secretary stationed outside three executive offices. She had a graying helmet of hair and wore a blouse with a puffy bow below her chin. On the door closest to her desk, the frosted-glass pane was marked *Alfred Millstone.*

The woman made a show of peering over her bifocals at the oversize wall clock—he was twenty minutes late, according to its Roman numerals—before she perused a scheduling book. Ellis remembered her. Via the teller downstairs, she was the one who'd declined his prior request to meet with Mr. Millstone. Now it was sorely evident she might turn him away again, on principle alone.

He was about to explain himself when she rose from her chair. "This way."

Gratefully, Ellis followed her into the neighboring office. There, Mr. Millstone sat at a mahogany desk that neatly displayed a pencil holder, prism paperweight, files, and more. He was packing tobacco into a sleek wooden pipe—not his first time that day, based on the smell that blended with the scents of ledger ink and old East Coast money.

"Mr. Millstone." Ellis extended his hand, which the man accepted this time, even rising from his wingback chair.

"I was beginning to wonder if I'd see you again."

"I apologize, sir." Ellis was doing so much of that lately that one would think he was trying to set a record. "Before I could go, my editor needed me for some pressing items."

"Well, bosses can be troublesome that way, can't they?" The reply held a hint of levity as Mr. Millstone nodded at his secretary, who yielded a partial smile before closing the door. "Please, sit down." He indicated a visitor's chair facing his desk, and they both settled in. "The truth of it is, Mr. Reed, I owe you an apology as well."

Ellis paused while pulling his notepad and pencil from his coat pocket. He hadn't anticipated this bit. "How so?"

"A good number of people are still enduring rough times, as you know. When you're a banker, and a stranger comes knocking, it can make you a little nervous."

"I imagine so." Ellis gave a reassuring smile, and Mr. Millstone's eyes warmed behind his glasses. Then he lit his pipe, stoking the tobacco with a series of puffs as Ellis waited.

"So," the man said, snuffing out the match, "what can I tell you today?"

How about an update on the kids you bought in Pennsylvania?

Ellis stored the thought. As with cracking any big story, he'd work his way in gradually.

"Well, for the profile, Mr. Millstone—"

"Alfred will do."

"Alfred." Not a shock. Bigwigs often figured a personable

exchange meant a more favorable article. "To start off, I was hoping to hear a little about your job here as president."

"Sounds innocent enough."

The choice of words was a bit curious, all things considered. But as soon as Ellis opened his notepad, Alfred launched into a description of his daily tasks, followed by a list of his overarching duties. He presented himself as a genial gentleman, just as the cabbie had said, though with a spark of passion over his occupation. So much so, he took only momentary breaks, solely to stoke his pipe, while delving into the importance of banking in the community, stressing the necessity of efforts to help honest, hardworking citizens succeed.

Ellis had to scribble to keep up. When he flipped to a fourth page, Alfred stopped and shook his head. "By golly, I did ramble on, didn't I?"

He'd probably gone for a solid fifteen minutes, but now wasn't the time for him to go quiet.

"It's refreshing, actually. With a person of your stature, it can be hard to pry out more than a sentence or two for a quote. Unless it's election time."

Alfred laughed a little. He returned to his pipe, its sweet, woodsy scent filling the room, and Ellis glanced down at his notepad.

"Let's see now," he said as if referring to prepared questions. As if details of Alfred's life weren't already embedded in his brain. "I've heard you hail from the West Coast. Is that right?"

"Yes. That's correct."

"California, was it?"

"You've done your homework."

Ellis smiled. "Requirement of the trade."

Alfred nodded, amused. "It was the Los Angeles area."

The answer wasn't terribly specific, but truthful. Ellis didn't push on that one. "I'm sad to say I've never been west of Ohio. That's gotta be quite a change, from one coast to the other."

"It certainly is."

"Something in particular bring you out this way?"

Alfred took another puff, blew it out. "Family reasons more than anything." When he didn't elaborate, Ellis had to nudge.

"Family, huh?"

"My wife and I had long talked about living closer to relatives in New York. When the position opened up here at Century Alliance, I finally had the opportunity to make that happen."

"That's dandy." Ellis jotted a note, neither of them mentioning his predecessor's grim end. "And how's the rest of your family been with that? As far as adjusting to the move."

Alfred gave a small shrug. "You know how kids are."

In a friendly manner, Ellis displayed his left hand, bare of a wedding band. "You'll have to enlighten me."

Alfred hummed in acknowledgment and leaned back in his chair. "As parents, I suppose we can't help but worry...about new schools, new friends. We want to protect them. Keep them safe from the world, from anything that could possibly hurt them...from what we can't see coming..." His voice gained a distant quality, same for his eyes.

After a moment, Ellis wondered if he should speak, cutting short Alfred's evident drift into the past. But then the man continued. "In the end, of course, they're the ones who adapt and persevere without batting an eye. We can learn a lot from our youth." He looked straight at Ellis. "Don't you agree?"

Ellis nodded before the sentiment rang with familiarity. In essence, it echoed his own article that had accompanied the Dillards' picture.

Had Alfred, too, done his homework?

"Mr. Reed, I'm going to be honest with you." Alfred suddenly lowered his volume, followed by his pipe. "And this is off the record." He shot a glance toward the door, as if confirming its closure.

Ellis tucked his pencil in his notepad, his neck muscles tensing. "It's off."

How much did the man know? How much was he willing to share?

"A bank in New Jersey," Alfred said, "would *not* have been my first choice." He confided this in all seriousness, though he trailed it with a smile.

From the release of tension, Ellis couldn't help but smile back.

There was no mention of a fatal car accident, nor of how Ruby and Calvin had joined the Millstones. There was also nothing, as best as Ellis could tell, in Alfred's manner that merited alarm.

"Sometimes," Alfred added lightly, "we have to make sacrifices for the ones we love. You understand."

Ellis thought of Geraldine. What she'd chosen to give up, purely for the benefit of her children, was a prime example. "I do, sir."

A knock came then, announcing the secretary's return. In the doorway, she held a brimmed hat and overcoat. "Mr. Millstone, it's time you departed for the station." A suitcase and cane was posted outside the door.

"That late already." He sighed and returned to Ellis. "Business trip to Chicago. I'm afraid we'll have to wrap up for today."

"No problem at all. I think I got everything I needed."

"Excellent. Well, I'll be back on Sunday. Feel free to ring me if you have any other questions."

"I will, sir." They both stood to shake hands, and Ellis thought to slip in a disclaimer. "Naturally, it will be up to my editor when, or even if, to run the piece, but I'll certainly keep you updated."

Alfred smiled. "I do hope so."

~

Ellis had conjured the profile idea solely as an excuse to assess the banker. Now he was actually tempted to pitch the thing to Mr.

Walker. No matter how horribly inconvenient, the reality was that Alfred seemed to be as nice a fella as they came.

Something Geraldine might have pegged from the start.

Clearly she wasn't the type to hand off her kids to just any stranger, even a wealthy, dapper one. She'd chosen them a good home in every way, it appeared. With Ruby and Calvin settled in after all these months, perhaps they were genuinely happy where they were.

And really, wasn't that the most important thing? That they had the best life possible? Harsh as it sounded, it wouldn't take a bookie to calculate the odds of which future held the most promise. Geraldine no longer even had a home of her own. Her only requests were to know her children were all right, and that the arrangement be left alone. In going further, wouldn't Ellis and Lily be overstepping largely for the sake of their own consciences?

After all, the sanitarium director had gone so far as to declare Geraldine deceased to protect her from unwanted attention. A court battle would inevitably lead to a swarm of reporters, photographers, and readers outspoken with their opinions. And when it was all over—when the kids and Geraldine and the Millstones had all been dragged through the legal and public muck—the judgment would most likely be the same.

Ellis dreaded to admit any of this to Lily, of course. Based on her experience with Samuel, he understood why she wouldn't want to hear it. But the fact remained that similar dilemmas could have different solutions. And, as Ellis could vouch for, a common bloodline didn't guarantee a thriving, loving family.

Maybe Geraldine was right.

Maybe life was just how it should be.

CHAPTER 26

WITHOUT A DOUBT, the situation was not how it should be. This Alfred Millstone fellow could hang the moon, and Lily's stance wouldn't budge.

"Lily, at least consider it." These were Ellis's words on the phone, but his tone said *Woman, you're being stubborn.*

It was as if he could see her at her work desk, shaking her head at his reasoning.

"Lily?" he pressed.

Over the afternoon noise of the newsroom, she answered, "All right, I'll consider it."

And she would. For two full seconds, she reviewed his summary of the meeting he'd just had with Alfred Millstone, and still she disagreed.

"Listen, I gotta scoot," he said. "My editor will have my hide if I don't get a story going. Just promise you won't do anything rash. Not without talking to me first."

"Yes. Fine."

He sighed over the line, as if reluctant to leave someone who claimed to simply be admiring the view—from the ledge of a building.

"I promise," she said. This was the truth, in the literal respect. She had no plans to do anything she deemed rash.

Only…necessary.

~

The trip there and back would take half a day at most. Lily would catch the earliest train to New York so as to return in plenty of time for supper.

"I give you my word on that, sugar bug." She knelt before Samuel, still in his pajamas, inside the deli's entrance. Through the windows, the waking sky colored his pouting cheeks with a soft orange glow.

"But, you said we'd do a picnic."

At the counter, Lily's mother was readying the register for the shop's opening in an hour. Her father's whistling drifted from the back kitchen.

"And we will soon, Samuel. I swear it." Lily brushed a powdery brown smudge from his cheek, remnants of his breakfast cocoa. He jerked back a little, his eyes down. "Please understand. I truly hate being away from you. But there are two other children out there, and they don't get to be with their mommy at all. I want to try to fix that."

Samuel's gaze remained on his loafers, both polished by himself. It was one more skill he had learned from her parents, a small milestone conquered in her absence.

The thought would normally have baited her to stay, but she couldn't ignore the countless milestones Geraldine stood to miss.

"Come now, give Mommy a hug goodbye." She opened her arms to him. "I need to catch my train so I can hurry right back."

He glanced up at last, but pinched his mouth in frustration and rushed off through the deli.

"Samuel," she called out, his sprint continuing up the stairs.

Lily's mother stepped out from behind the counter. "Not to fret. He'll be all right."

Rising to meet her, Lily insisted, "You know I'd never cut into our time together if it weren't important."

"I know that, dear."

Clayton had been occupied for the weekend, leaving Lily more time to ponder during her bus ride to Maryville. Once settled in, she had divulged a portion to her mother in confidence, but only the basics, not wishing to violate Geraldine's privacy.

Granted, some would say she was about to do just that.

"I'll be back soon," she said and kissed her mother on the cheek.

"Have a safe trip." Her mother offered a strained smile. She was either weary from waking or dubious over Lily's plans. Before Lily could determine which, she grabbed her handbag from the floor and left for the station.

~

It was just after eleven when Lily arrived on Maple Street. She had walked from the depot in Hoboken, saving money on a taxicab. The round-trip train fare was costly enough.

She referred once more to the address inscribed on a scrap of paper—secretaries were as skilled as anyone at locating such details—and stopped at the designated home. It was light green with white trim and as perfect as a dollhouse.

Too perfect, she decided.

At the park across the street, children reveled in the rare freedoms afforded by a temperate Saturday morning. The chorus of their giggles, a reminder of Samuel awaiting her return, sent Lily straight up the steps to reach the front door.

After pocketing the address and her traveling gloves, she knocked.

Birds chirped from trees that dotted the area, and a rattling car passed on the street. The possibility of the driver being Ellis—which certainly it was not—caused her palms to perspire. And what for? He wasn't her father or her boss, and certainly not her beau. She didn't require his approval to come here. Still, guilt niggled at her.

She pushed it away as she rang the doorbell. A direct appeal to Mrs. Millstone was the answer. She was a fellow mother who understood the loss of a child. With her husband away on business, Mrs. Millstone would be free to meet Lily alone.

Unless she, too, had traveled for the weekend.

Lily clutched her purse, clinging to her hopes. She reached out in a final attempt to ring the bell. Before she made contact, the door opened. A young housekeeper stood in greeting. In a black dress and white apron, she wore her hair pinned up tight.

"Sorry to keep ya waitin', ma'am." Her lilting accent pegged her as an Irish immigrant. Fittingly, her pale skin held freckles more pronounced than Lily's. "I was knee-deep in the wash and was slow to hear the door."

"That's quite all right. I'm just delighted somebody's home." Lily smiled in partial relief. Even if the lady of the house wasn't in, the housekeeper would likely know her whereabouts.

The girl smiled timidly in return. She couldn't have been more than sixteen. "Is there something I can help ya with?"

"There is, in fact. I've come to see Mrs. Millstone."

"Is she…expectin' ya, ma'am?" Her tone said she doubted that was the case, as the girl would have been alerted to prepare for company.

"She's not," Lily affirmed, "but it really is an important matter. You see, I'm an old work colleague of Mr. Reed. I believe he was here recently." At the girl's uncertain look, Lily added, "He's a reporter, from the *New York Herald Tribune*, and came to speak with Mr. Millstone."

"Ah, I see," the girl said. "And you're with the paper too, are ya?"

"I am. Well…the *Philadelphia Examiner*, that is." The girl's eyes brightened, impressed by this, but Lily remained steadfast. "Is Mrs. Millstone available to speak?"

"I'd be glad to check. If you'll wait here a minute."

Lily nodded and soon discovered the estimate wasn't an exaggeration. After less than a minute of disappearing inside, the housekeeper returned. "The missus would be pleased to receive ya. Do come in."

In the foyer, the girl offered to take her coat, but Lily politely declined. Given the purpose of her visit, it seemed too casual, too friendly. Moreover, depending on how the conversation went, she might not be welcome for long.

Following the girl over the white marble floor, Lily surveyed the wide, sweeping staircase, the chandelier overhead. The air held an almost sweet, powdery scent. Though Ellis hadn't been past the front door, he was right about the residence.

But Lily wasn't here to admire the decor.

Rather, to block out visions of the children running about, unencumbered by the vastness of space, she trained her focus on a darker thought. She considered the disparity of fortunes between bankers and too many of their patrons, those with little choice but to live in shantytowns or to beg on the street.

Or, God help them, to sell their own children.

When the housekeeper entered the parlor, a woman gracefully rose from a claw-footed love seat, ready for a greeting. She appeared to be in her midthirties. In a cream silk blouse and a black A-line skirt, she wore her dark-blond hair sleek around her face, with soft pink touches on her lips and cheeks. A string of pearls looped her neck.

"Ma'am, may I present…" The girl suddenly winced. She had neglected to ask for Lily's name.

"Mrs. Millstone," Lily kindly jumped in, "I hope it's all right to introduce myself. I'm Lillian Palmer. I appreciate you agreeing to meet with me."

"Call me Sylvia." She smiled and invited Lily to sit in the ornate chair across from her, its striped upholstery boasting a satiny shimmer. As Lily obliged and set her purse down, Sylvia signaled to the housekeeper. "Claire, some tea for our guest."

With a grateful glance at Lily, Claire scurried over to the service cart parked next to the upright piano. As she filled a blue-and-white colonial teacup, a match to the one on the end table beside Sylvia, Lily noticed the framed photos on the fireplace mantel. From a distance, she could best make out the details of a portrait in the center. Indeed it was Ruby, cleaned and cared for just as Ellis had described.

"That's my daughter," Sylvia pointed out. "She's lovely, isn't she?" The prideful glow in her face caused Lily's throat to tighten, adding a rasp to her reply.

"She is."

"Technically she's ten, but going on twenty according to her teacher. Always so much going on in that head of hers."

Lily was thankful for Claire's delivery of the tea just then.

"Oh, Claire, that reminds me," Sylvia said. "Please tell my sweet girl she needs to practice the piano once more before supper if she wants tapioca tonight. And don't you dare let her say she'll simply go without." Sylvia rolled her eyes in jest and told Lily, "It's her favorite dessert, so there's no getting that one past me."

Claire politely bowed her head and pivoted to leave. Her footfalls continued through the foyer and up the stairs.

"To be perfectly honest," Sylvia said conspiratorially, "as a young girl, I was terrible about practicing. Now wish I'd been more diligent." She brought her cup and saucer to her lap. "Come to think of it, that might not have helped. I was truly awful. Sadly, I never had the natural ability that my daughter does."

An image of Ruby, seated at the piano, materialized in Lily's mind. The lessons, and certainly the piano itself, weren't luxuries Geraldine could afford anytime soon.

Sylvia took a sip of her tea. "I'd gladly ask her to come down and play for you, but this is her special reading time. Once her nose is in a book, I'd have to pry it out. I hope you don't mind."

Lily shook her head, attempting to shed thoughts of Ruby's happiness here, wanting even more to discard the undeniable sense of liking Sylvia.

Assuming her husband was similar, no wonder Ellis felt conflicted.

"I'm much the same," Lily managed. "When it comes to reading."

"Yes, well, there are worse vices a person could have." Sylvia smiled and took another sip. "Do you have children as well?"

Lily had to think before answering. Everything about their exchange had left her feeling unprepared. "One. A son."

"Oh, that's lovely." With a look of wonder, Sylvia rested her cup on her saucer. "Of course, I know boys can be a handful at times, with all that energy bound up in their little bodies. But what father doesn't secretly want a small version of himself running about? I'm sure your husband is as proud as a peacock."

Lily smiled before drowning the truth with Earl Grey. It could have used cream and a sugar cube, but she gulped it down.

"Now," Sylvia said, "what else could I tell you about our family? I imagine there are some specifics you need for the article."

Lily's grip tightened around her drink. Whatever Claire had passed along about Lily's employment or her ties to Ellis, her purpose had been misconstrued.

The sound of footsteps down the stairs preceded Claire's return to the foyer, but there was no reason to call her in here to sort out the correction.

Lily set her cup and saucer aside. The plan to come right out with the issue had been far easier in her head. "I'm actually here today to speak about Geraldine Dillard," she began.

A small crinkle formed upon Sylvia's nose. "I'm sorry… I'm not familiar with her." There was nothing insincere in the woman's manner, nor was there any hint of uncertainty.

Was it possible she had never learned of the name? Had her husband not bothered to ask for such a significant detail?

Lily didn't want to insult Sylvia by duplicating her maternal title, but there was no other way to say it. "Mrs. Millstone, Geraldine is the mother of the two children you're caring for."

Sylvia smiled once again, this time with a tinge of sympathy. "I'm afraid you're mistaken. We have only one daughter. She's the one I was telling you about."

A seed of impatience was sprouting within Lily, hastened by confusion. "Yes, I understand there's just one girl. But I'm referring to her brother, Calvin. He's the boy, along with Ruby, that your husband purchased in Pennsylvania."

Adopted. Lily realized she had bypassed the more mindful term when a shroud of silence dropped over the room. Sylvia's lips lowered at this, and her eyes darkened. But not from offense, it seemed. There was a struggle for comprehension. It was like watching the grayest of clouds encroaching on the horizon, a transformation that Lily could actually feel as her own puzzlement inched toward dread.

Had Alfred Millstone procured the children on his own accord and not shared the circumstances with his wife? How would he have explained Ruby being added to their charge?

Perhaps as a lone urchin he had found in an alley. Or an orphan inherited from a relative who had passed. In any event, why would Alfred deceive her?

A sudden crashing noise jolted Lily. A cup and saucer— Sylvia's—had tumbled to the floor and shattered. An amber puddle spread over marble.

"Are ya all right, ma'am?" It was Claire, hurrying into the room. A broken piece crunched beneath her shoe as she attended to Sylvia, whose face had gone pale.

"I…I must…lie down."

"Certainly, ma'am. Let me help." Claire guided her upward and escorted her toward the foyer. In tandem, they plodded up the staircase and out of view.

Lily was scouring the encounter for rationale when her gaze circled back to the mantel. Slowly, she came to her feet and closed in on the photographs. Beside the center image of Ruby was one of her hugging a doll, and another of her in a garden. The next was a formal portrait of the family—with one thing missing from them all.

Or more aptly, one *person*.

The revelation slid up Lily's spine, an icy finger, launching a shiver through her veins, and a halting question through her mind.

Where in heaven's name was Calvin?

PART THREE

"There is not a trick, there is not a swindle, there is not a vice which does not live by secrecy."

—JOSEPH PULITZER

CHAPTER 27

THE PHONE RANG on Saturday afternoon.

In his apartment, Ellis was throwing together a sandwich, a ball game airing on the RCA. Unlike his buddies back home, he was never a die-hard baseball fan, but he'd always be a Pennsylvanian. When the Phillies played, you listened. Especially on days like this, when they were beating the blasted Dodgers. Four to two, top of the sixth.

Another ring.

Ellis made his way from the kitchen, licking a dab of mustard from his thumb, and realized the caller had to be his mother. He took an extra moment to reach for the handset.

When he sent her off at the station, he'd agreed to visit soon for supper. *Soon* being a conveniently vague term. But now, since his father was surely tuned in to the game, something he and Ellis used to do together—meaning they'd listen in the same room—his mother had two hours of free time to mull. And call.

It was time for Ellis to do his part, to smooth over the cracks in their family's foundation, to continue on as they had for decades.

He picked up the phone.

Only it wasn't her.

"Ellis," Lily said, "I need to talk to you."

For a split second, he was happy to hear her voice. But then he registered the greeting. Whatever came next wasn't going to be good.

~

For the remainder of the weekend, Ellis racked his memory. He reviewed and reevaluated details he had accepted as fact. Though he'd never actually seen Calvin through the window, he knew he'd heard the boy's laughter...

Unless it was part of the radio show.

But during the interview at the bank, Alfred had spoken of *kids*, in the plural.

Or was he referencing children in general? He never did mention that he had a boy and a girl—or any specifics about them at all.

Still, Ellis refused to believe the worst. When Lily phoned from her parents' home, just returned from the Millstones', he'd combed her story for a sensible explanation.

Maybe an illness had caused Sylvia to grow faint, and a fever jumbled her words. Maybe she just meant Calvin didn't live there now, as he was off at some prestigious boarding school. With sons of the wealthy, who knew how young they started them out?

Whatever the case, Ellis convinced Lily to wait on telling Geraldine. No reason to sound an alarm until they learned more. Lily had agreed on the condition that he would act quickly.

He hadn't planned to do otherwise. His own apprehension was churning, a slow but relentless motion, as if roasting over a spit.

The best option was to confront the one person, aside from Alfred, bound to know the truth.

~

Amid the Monday morning bustle, it wouldn't be difficult to follow a person unseen. Even in Hoboken.

Ellis counted on that now as he trailed Sylvia and Ruby from their house. Hand in hand, both looked properly suited for the day. A flared dress and angled hat for Sylvia, a school uniform and yellow hair bow for Ruby.

But no sign of Calvin.

The walk lasted around ten minutes, ending at an imposing brick school. Sylvia bent to straighten Ruby's collar before releasing her into the stream of children, most arriving on their own. Other escorts bore the looks of young nannies.

Only after Ruby stepped through the doors did Sylvia turn to reverse her path. Ellis maintained his distance across the street. He ventured to guess she'd be back in the afternoon to accompany Ruby home.

To talk to the girl one-on-one, he'd have to pick his moment.

A playground abutted the west side of the school. As long as the weather held up—the merging patches of clouds could go either way—an outdoor recess was sure to be on the schedule.

And so he would wait.

Apartment buildings strewn through the area were interspersed with the usual stores. At the barbershop, he bought a copy of the *Tribune*—ironically, the only paper they sold—and parked himself on a bench. From the cobbler shop behind him, wafts of leather and shoe polish escaped with each swing of the door.

He perused articles to pass the time. The bolded headlines and coveted bylines further reminded him of the daily news meeting that loomed ahead.

Finally, a burst of high pitched voices grabbed his attention.

Students were pouring out of the school, set free to skip and pounce. They fanned out over the playground.

Ellis abandoned his paper on the bench. As he made his way across the street, he sifted through the young faces as if panning for an elusive nugget of gold. But even a closer scan—over their swinging and sliding, their battles in hopscotch—failed to produce Ruby.

Then he saw it.

The yellow hair ribbon.

Off by herself, on the side edge of the grounds, Ruby was milling beneath an apple tree. It wasn't nearly as full or sturdy as the one beside her farmhouse, where its branches easily supported her brother and his dangling, but maybe she still found comfort in the similarities it held.

From behind the tree, Ellis walked up casually, hands in his pockets. It had been too long for her to remember him. He didn't want to scare her away.

"Enjoying the quiet over here?"

Ruby looked up from the leaf in her hand. She shrugged.

"Don't want to play with the other kids, huh?"

She glanced toward her classmates, the shrieking and hollering like a cauldron of glee, and Ellis expected another shrug.

"Not allowed," she replied.

Evidently, it was a quarantine of sorts. Swapping overalls for a uniform must not have tamed the spitfire of a girl he recalled, and honestly, he was glad to hear it. "You've been causing some trouble, then," he said lightly.

"Got a stain on my sweater. From the teeter-totter." She pointed toward the seesaw that kids were launching up and down with gusto. "Happened weeks ago, but still can't go on the thing." Focusing back on the leaf, she tore off pieces and flicked them aside. Not in a musing way. More of a rigid act steeped in irritation.

Ellis noted the lone, matronly teacher on recess duty. She was surveying the playground as a warden would a prison yard. It took no effort to imagine her enforcing such a ridiculous penalty. He'd try his best to stay out of her eyeshot.

"Whatcha doing here anyway?" Ruby asked. "You come to take pictures?"

It took him a second to process the connection. Impressed, Ellis smiled at her. "I didn't think you'd remember me."

"Why's that?"

"Just that it's been a while." About eight months, incredibly. "And we only met that once... Well, twice, I suppose."

"Saw you from my window lots of times, bringing boxes to our porch. Food and things."

Another cause for surprise. Each time, he'd parked at the end of the drive, headlights diverted from their windows. Under the veil of night, he thought he'd been sly. "You knew it was me all along?"

She picked up a fresh leaf and resumed her tearing, a little gentler now. "I'd hear that motor of yours. Sounded like it was hurtin' something fierce."

"Yeah. It was." Ellis laughed to himself. "Still is."

Her cheeks warmed, and a smile he recognized curved her small lips. "I liked the pickled beets you left. The pears too. Could've done without the chickpeas."

"Didn't care for the taste?"

"Oh, I liked 'em going down just fine. It's the *after* that was the problem. And I don't mean from me, if that's what you're thinkin'." She pointed emphatically. "Sharing a bed was no picnic when Cal tooted up a storm. That stink could've knocked out a bear."

Ellis couldn't help but laugh again. "That bad, huh?"

"You wouldn't think something so big could come out of a person that small, and not just from chickpeas. This other time, my brother took on a dare to..." She stopped there, and her gaze lowered to the ground, her joy vanishing with her words.

"What?" Ellis pressed gently. "What'd your brother do?"

She shook her head, adamant. "I don't got—have—a brother."

Ellis peered at her, stunned by the lie. The girl had obviously been coached. He was suddenly as eager as he was fearful to probe further. Bracing himself, he lowered to a squat and met her at eye level. "You know, you first asked me why I came. Well, it's actually about Calvin. If you have any idea where he went, I was hoping you'd tell me."

She curled her bottom lip. Her reluctance was clear, yet Ellis couldn't let up.

"The thing is, I swore I'd make sure he's okay. And I'm trying to keep that promise. But I'm not sure I can without your help."

Studying his face, she considered his plea. Quietly she answered, "He's with Mama."

Ellis cocked his head before he distinguished the reference. "You mean Mrs. Millstone? The mother you live with now."

"No," she told him. "My old mama."

Now he was truly perplexed. "You're saying your mama— Geraldine—*kept* Calvin."

After a moment, Ruby issued a nod.

The claim made no sense. It didn't line up with accounts from the cabbie and the train clerk, even Geraldine herself.

"That sure is interesting to hear. See, I was told that you and Calvin rode the train with Mr. Millstone. All the way to California. Then you moved here, to Jersey, with Mrs. Millstone too."

Ruby nodded again.

At the boardinghouse, maybe Ellis had given Geraldine enough details to locate the children on her own. Over the past week, had she reconsidered her stance? Had she managed to take her son back?

Just then, past Ruby's shoulder, Ellis saw the teacher starting in his direction. Time was running out. "And what happened next?"

"After school one day," Ruby said, "I got a letter from Mama. I was so excited 'cause I thought she was finally better and it was time to go home. To our farm home."

So, the girl knew her mother was sick, maybe all along.

"What'd the letter say?"

"That she loved me very much…but…but he could only afford to look after one of us." Ruby's voice thinned, and tears welled in her eyes. "Since I'm older, Calvin needed her more. That's why she'd come to fetch him."

The bell rang.

Recess was over.

Desperate for a delay, Ellis wished he could comfort her. "Honey, I've got to know. Did you ever *see* your mom? When she came to get Calvin."

Ruby shook her head. "It'd be too hard for her. To say goodbye again."

"But how do you know? Did someone—"

"Sir, may I help you?"

Ellis met the teacher's grimness with an instant smile. "Morning, ma'am." Grudgingly he rose. "I was just happening by. As a friend of the family, thought I'd say hello."

The woman looked to Ruby. "Is that so?" A strained pause, then the child nodded. Thankfully. "All the same, these are school hours. In the future, your visits would be best kept to the family's personal time."

"Right. I'll definitely do that."

The teacher pivoted sharply on her heels. She flicked her hand toward the other children, all funneling into the school. "Back inside, Victoria!"

Ruby shot Ellis a final glance before following the order, leaving him astounded once more. The girl was now being called Victoria.

She'd been stripped not only of her family, but even of her name.

$\sim$

The minute Ellis returned to the paper, he phoned the sanitarium. The director, now aware of Ellis, put Geraldine on the line.

Calmly, Ellis asked about a letter to Ruby. No details of its content or other mentions of Ruby's story, nor of the girl's renaming.

Just as he'd feared, Geraldine was at a loss. Ellis sloughed off the letter as an apparent misunderstanding. And her request that followed—asking him to peek in on the kids every so often—further confirmed his suspicions.

Geraldine had never come for her son.

Lily was right to be concerned. Either the couple had given Calvin away or something grave had happened while Ruby was off at school. The latter could explain Sylvia's reaction.

But no. Ellis refused to accept that scenario. As a reporter, he prided himself on detecting the truth. Something in Alfred's manner, when they chatted about kids, would have raised an alarm in Ellis.

Or had his view been skewed by a desire to see only what he wanted?

"Dutch," he called out. The guy was wandering by with notepad in hand. Seeing Ellis, he strode right over.

"Hey, you missed today's meeting. Thought you might be out sick."

Ellis didn't feel in the best of health, but it wasn't from a cold.

He skipped past that issue for a vital one. "Your pal in LA—I think you said he was going to send the clips he'd found for me. You mind following up when you have a sec?"

Dutch bit out a laugh. "See that pile there?" He gestured to the mail layered haphazardly on Ellis's desk. "Might go through it every so often. Here…" From a quick sift through the stack, Dutch handed over a small manila envelope. "I dropped it off for you last week."

"Guess that's what I get for giving my secretary time off." Ellis made the joke not just to keep things light with Dutch, which it did, but also to subdue his own fear. Its slow burn was heating to a blaze. He felt it even before sliding out the clippings as Dutch strolled away, before flipping to the obituary about the

Millstones' late daughter, before staring at her portrait featuring a familiar sailor dress, a ribbon tied in her hair.

Victoria Agnes Millstone, the caption read.

Ellis had easily figured the Millstones were aiming to fill a void. He just hadn't envisioned their daughter being literally replaced by Ruby, looks and all. Even without the same ribbon and dress, the two virtually could have passed as twins.

Every unnerving aspect had just been magnified tenfold.

Though dreading to share the news—how would he ever explain this?—Ellis slid his phone closer. He was still processing it all as he rang the operator, who put him through to Lily's line at the *Examiner*. But it was the chief who picked up. He seemed even more rattled than Ellis.

"Took the day off," he grumbled, explaining Lily's absence, and hung up before Ellis could ask anything more.

A day off? The chief didn't say she was out sick.

After her trip to Jersey, she must have extended her weekend to make up for lost time with her son. Ellis debated on waiting, not wanting to intrude, but for Calvin's sake—and Ruby's—he had to make the call.

To connect to the Palmers, he requested their deli. The phone rang only once before the reply came without greeting. "Dr. Mannis?"

"No…Lily, it's me."

"Ellis?" She sounded on the brink of tears.

In that instant, any other thought in his head, including his reason for calling, evaporated like mist. "Lily, what is it? What's happened?"

Her voice trembled as she answered over the line. "Something's wrong with Samuel."

CHAPTER 28

LILY FOUGHT BACK THE ECHOES of her conscience.

This is all your doing. You did this to him.

From the chair beside Samuel's bed, she peeled away the folded washrag. Heat radiating from his forehead had nearly dried the fabric. His cheeks were red as rose petals, his eyelids puffy and sealed. She dipped and wrung the cloth, for the hundredth time over the past day, in the porcelain basin on the night table.

Your son is going to die. All because of you.

She wanted to scream, to shake Samuel's bare shoulders until he stirred. She longed to go back and erase the curse she had caused. But all she could do was place the cooled rag across his damp hairline.

On Saturday, she had returned from New Jersey in the late afternoon and immediately phoned Ellis about Sylvia. She had barely finished when her mother beckoned her downstairs to assist with the weekend rush. Samuel chose to stay in their room. Normally, he would have followed her to the deli, a pup at her heels. He relished any opportunity to help. But he was clearly still cross over the postponement of their picnic.

"It's good for him," Lily's mother had assured her and handed over a hunk of Gouda to be wrapped for a customer. "Children need to learn. Plans change. That's life."

"You listen to your mother," Lily's father said in passing, behind the counter. "It's easier that way. Believe me." He added a wink.

Even if Lily disagreed, it had become harder to dispute parenting choices when weekdays required entrusting her son to their guidance. Plus, Samuel's behavior that night—stubbornly silent, poking at his supper—only reinforced her mother's point. Lily chose to step up before her parents could intervene, a reflection of maternal strength as much as her mood. Dwelling on Calvin had heightened her nerves.

"Samuel, your grandmother and I worked hard to make this meal. Now, eat your supper."

"I'm not hungry," he mumbled. He was slouched in his seat, his gaze fixed on his fork.

Lily's father reliably jumped in. "Aw, c'mon, Sammy. A clean plate or no dessert. Without you, I'll have to gobble up the whole chocolate cake myself."

"I'm *not* hungry." His obstinate tone pushed Lily to the edge.

"Samuel Ray. I'll remind you, there are a lot of people out there who'd be grateful for that food."

And that was the truth. Every Friday night since Lily's childhood, folks with pockets as empty as their bellies had gathered at the back door of the deli, where her father doled out leftover cheese, scraps of meat, and rolls gone stale. All of which he had undoubtedly hoarded with purpose.

"If you're not going to sit up and behave yourself, you can go straight to bed."

When Samuel slinked off without a fuss, Lily ignored her sense that something was off. Later, after the dishes were cleaned and dried, she went to him for a talk. She planned to reiterate the lesson but with a warmer approach. How could she blame him for lamenting the loss of their special date?

By then, he had cocooned himself in his bedding, and his breaths were heavy from sleep. "The boy must be growing," her father reasoned the next morning. It was the most obvious explanation for Samuel's rare grudge and lengthy doze.

Her father insisted they not wake him, even to trade goodbyes. Joining the owner of the local general store, Lily's father periodically traveled to county and state fairs, this one an overnight trip, to purchase meat and other goods at bulk price.

Lily had agreed with her father and let Samuel sleep well past breakfast.

But as the hours dragged on, inching closer to her own departure, she pulled back the bedcovers and found Samuel's hair soaked with sweat. A touch to his face nearly scorched her hand. This wasn't a simple passing cold. Yes, she was always quick to worry, but she knew this was different.

And her mother appeared to know it too, despite her calm reporting of a nurse's instructions over the phone. Today, same as yesterday, they were to watch and wait. The closest hospital was overcrowded and thirty miles away, and his ailment could pass with rest and an aspirin.

Maybe the nurse was right. She had to be. Even though Samuel had never before been this hot and for this length of time.

If only Dr. Mannis, the town doctor, could assure Lily it wasn't a case of the flu or rubella or typhoid. Or any other merciless illness that killed children every day. His wife promised he would call the minute he returned from fishing. It took every ounce of Lily's strength not to rail over the man's negligence— this was Monday, for Pete's sake!

Declaring him an enemy wasn't going to help. But what would?

She scoured her mind as she held her son's hand. It burned like heated coal, yet she held it to her cheek. *Please, God, please don't take him*, she prayed, excruciatingly aware she had given up that right...

A knock broke through the thought. Her mother stood at the bedroom door, eyes red-rimmed in the afternoon light. She had shuttered the deli early. Neither of them had slept the night.

"Dear, your friends are here to help." There was no trace of an opinion in her voice, only desperate hope.

This, from Lily's mother, marked the scariest moment yet.

From the hall, Ellis entered the room. He greeted Lily and said, "You remember Mrs. Dillard..."

Lily expected a story to follow. Not for Geraldine to join them next.

A spate of confusion shot through Lily. "What...are you doing here?"

"Just came to lend a hand." Geraldine stepped toward Samuel in an observant manner as Ellis expounded.

"Since your doctor's been out, I called Dearborn. The director said she'd come help. I stopped to get her on the way, but two of her patients had..." He didn't finish, the reason evident. "She just couldn't leave. Geraldine, though, offered to come instead."

"He's burning up all right." Geraldine was holding her inner wrist to Samuel's temple. "How high's it been?" Beneath her open coat, a full white apron suggested work as a caregiver. But how much experience did she really have?

Lily hesitated to reply. "A hundred and three. For two full days."

"Any rash?"

Lily shook her head.

"Been vomiting? The runs?"

"No."

"That's good. Still need to keep water in him."

"But he won't swallow," Lily insisted. Not to quarrel, but because their attempts had been maddeningly futile.

Geraldine turned to Lily's mother. "Got an ice block?"

"Several. Down in the deli."

"We'll need a bunch of tiny chips. We can tuck 'em in his cheek."

Ellis volunteered, "I'll fill up a bowl." He hurried off toward the stairs.

"Now, let's work on cooling him down. Have we tried a bath yet?"

Lily's mother again answered dutifully, an oddity from a woman accustomed to captaining her household. "We asked the nurse about an ice bath. She said to hold off unless he had a seizure."

"Lukewarm is better, and no reason to wait."

"Lukewarm?" Lily said, trying to shut out a vision of her son convulsing. A possibility that had been scaring her to no end.

"That's right."

"But…won't that heat him up even more?"

Geraldine raised her palms. "Sounded crazy to me too. But over and over, Doc Summers has shown me it works best. If the water's too cold, it causes the shakes and that fever could bounce back even worse."

"Still, though," Lily said, "the nurse on the phone—"

"Miss Palmer, if you want your little boy to get better, you need to trust me. I promise I can help."

Lily broke from Geraldine's gaze to behold her son. He was suddenly so small and frail, defenseless as a newborn. She glanced at her mother, in search of guidance, wishing her father were here.

Even so, no matter their views, Samuel had only one mother. In the end, it was up to Lily to make the choice.

"I'll run the water," she said.

～

The next hour passed like years, and mere seconds.

Samuel's temperature gradually lowered to match the bath water and the redness of his skin receded, lightening to the color of peaches. Relief streamed through the home as Ellis carried the boy, dried and swathed in a towel, back to his room. For Lily, that feeling became a tide when Ellis beamed while laying her son down, saying, "Hey, you rascal. Welcome back."

Samuel's eyes had opened.

Lily rushed to kneel at his bedside. He appeared to seek clarity as she stroked his cheek.

"Mommy," he said groggily.

"Hi, sugar bug. We sure have missed you."

Puzzlement crossed his sweet face. "Where'd...I go?"

Lily could barely contain the elation bursting inside of her. Based on the wide smiles around the room, she wasn't the only one.

She kissed his forehead, his button nose. She held his hand, now savoring the normalcy of its feel.

At last, giving her mother a chance to ogle, Lily rose to move aside. Halfway up, her mind went dizzy and her vision grayed. A grip on her arm, her waist—from Ellis—kept her from falling.

"I've got you," he assured her as the haze thinned.

"She hasn't had a thing to eat or drink in days," her mother said.

"I'll be fine." Lily's balance was returning.

"Mr. Reed, would you take her to the kitchen, please? There's plenty of food to be had." Heading off an objection from Lily, she said, "Window's open in there. You could use the fresh air, Lillian." The captain had officially reassumed her role. "We'll keep close tabs on Samuel."

It went without saying that his temperature could rise again, the very reason they hadn't drained the tub. But Lily's mother was also helping now by slipping ice chips into his mouth.

Everything would be all right.

Because of Geraldine.

"Thank you," Lily said to her, the two words ridiculously inept. Geraldine smiled all the same and settled on the chair beside the bed. Humming a lullaby to Samuel—"Daisy Bell," from the sound of it—she wrung out the cloth in a bowl of fresh water.

The notes soothed Lily just enough to back away, and she followed Ellis to the kitchen, where he went to the counter and sifted through the bread box. He spoke kindly without turning. "Pastrami and Swiss on rye, I'm guessing."

Yes. It was her favorite. But she couldn't find her voice.

All the relief that had shoved out her fears had suddenly drained away, leaving her empty, barren of strength. She slid downward against the paneled wall until seated on the linoleum. The sounds of cupboard doors opening and closing, of drawers sliding out and in, came to a halt. Ellis's voice was distant, not registering, until he lowered to sit beside her.

"Your son's gonna be okay, Lily. He is." When he gently clasped her hand, tears surged through the shell of her, filling every cavity, pooling behind her eyes. And riding those tears was the shame of her past.

A shame she couldn't hold in for another day, another minute.

"I once told you how scared I was…when I was pregnant with Samuel. I didn't tell you everything."

Expression unchanging, not judging, Ellis nodded for her to go on.

"At first I prayed it wasn't true, that my body was just off-kilter. Then I prayed that I could keep hiding it from my parents. And when that was nearly impossible…" The ending stalled in her throat, yet she forced it out. "I wanted God to take my mistake away. That's what it was to me. A mistake. At the drugstore, I overheard the pharmacist giving a woman medicine after a miscarriage, and I thought, *It happens all the time. From accidents and falls, or for no reason at all.*" Lily's voice gained a shake, as did her hand. Ellis held on tighter.

"Late one night, my parents were asleep. It was here in this house. I was in my nightgown at the top of the stairs, looking down." Even then, it had pained her to think of how long and hard her parents had waited for a child of their own, the endless hoping, the heartbreaks. "All it would take was one big step. Just one, and it could all be over. But when I stood there, gathering the courage, I felt Samuel kick. Maybe it was just a fluttering. But I finally understood that this baby was real. A real child was growing inside of me."

She shook her head at the memory, at her stupidity for not comprehending such a thing from the start. For not seeing that there would still be consequences. "Now every time Samuel comes down with even the smallest of colds, I'm beside myself. I'm terrified God's going to answer those prayers and punish me for what I did."

"*Almost* did," Ellis corrected, and Lily lifted her gaze. "But you didn't."

"Yes, I know…but if Samuel hadn't moved right then, I could have lost him for good."

"But you didn't," he repeated. "You didn't take that step."

"Ellis, you're not hearing me." She drew her hand away, partially out of frustration, though mostly out of feeling unworthy of such effortless compassion.

A lengthy quiet stretched between them before Ellis spoke again. "You know I'm no Catholic, Lily. Truth is, I don't remember the last time I stepped foot in a church. I just think… you've spent all these years worrying and waiting for the worst. But if you ask me, He answered that prayer of yours already… when you were on those stairs and felt your son kick."

Lily's urge to counter him ceased, his unexpected words sinking in.

Since Samuel's birth, her fears had grown and spread like weeds, choking out the roots of motherhood joys. To be worried was to be a parent. But to accept Ellis's view was to choose life over guilt. It would mean recognizing a sign that perhaps she should have seen all along.

Lily didn't realize her tears had broken free until Ellis used his thumb to wipe them away. The weight of her burden seemed to lessen with the shedding of each drop.

He started to sit back, perhaps readying to stand. Without planning, she kept his palm from leaving her cheek. And he stayed. He looked at her, as if right into her. A lifetime had passed since they had been this close, their mouths just inches apart.

A moment later, his lips were on hers. She couldn't say who had leaned in first. The heat and blending of their breaths consumed her senses.

Then his hand trailed the length of her neck. He slid his other hand through her hair, and a tingling covered her arms, her sides. The kiss deepened. Her heart pounded. She moved her fingers over his shirt, settling on his chest. His muscles tensed from her touch. He was strong yet tender as he drew her closer. There were more breaths, more yearning.

Until a voice.

"Lillian."

She froze. The world around them, which had fallen away, instantly reappeared. The recognition of her mother's presence hit like a slap.

Lily and Ellis separated and scrambled to their feet. They became teenagers caught in the coatroom at a school dance.

"Your son is asking for soup."

Ellis averted his eyes, appearing as flushed as Lily felt.

"Soup?" she stammered. "My, that's a good sign."

"It is," her mother said. A pointed pause. "Soon enough, I'd say Geraldine can be on her way."

And by "Geraldine," she meant Ellis. Her tone made this clear—not reproachfully, but as a needed reminder after an emotional trial. There was Samuel to think of. And Ruby and Calvin.

And Clayton.

"You're right," Lily decided. "It wouldn't make sense to keep her."

CHAPTER 29

ON THE DRIVE HOME, Ellis should have been paying attention. But Lily Palmer dominated his thoughts. Their kiss replayed over and over like a nickelodeon picture on a loop—regardless of her cooler send-off. Whereas Geraldine received an earnest hug, Ellis got an appreciative handshake. A reassertion of where they stood. It was a hard pill to swallow, as he could still feel the softness of her hair and skin, her lips. And that was nothing to say of the strength and beauty he saw in her while she cared for her son.

No surprise, then, that it took him a hefty chunk of the ride to notice Geraldine's reserve. She'd trained her eyes on the evening sky past the windshield. Her hands were clasped on her lap.

"You were pretty amazing back there," he said, breaking the quiet.

"Well…there wasn't much to it, really."

"I think the Palmers would disagree. Doc Summers too, I'd bet."

"Just doin' what she showed me. She's a fine teacher."

"I'm sure. Though it's obvious you're a natural for this kind of work too."

A bath and ice chips alone weren't the revelation. It was her balance of confidence and care, her ability to incite trust in folks grappling with their greatest fears.

"I suppose," she said. "Course, choices are often clearer when it's not about your own kin."

Once the words were out, they clung to the air. The dual message, seemingly unintended, turned her away.

Ellis was mining for a response when he heard her murmur, "I wonder sometimes if they'll forget who I am…"

A crushing thought. There was no need to identify *they*.

"God, no, Geraldine. They couldn't. They won't."

She didn't answer, and he realized that nothing said in this moment would change a damn thing. Hence, silence reigned for the remainder of the drive, with Ellis at the wheel and Geraldine facing her window. If not for discreet swipes of her eyes, no one would guess she was crying.

By the time they reached Dearborn, Ellis couldn't deny the truth: Geraldine Dillard wanted her kids back. More than practical reasons, though, kept her from demanding such a thing. It was shame. He saw that now, more than ever, after Lily's story in the kitchen. In different ways, both mothers believed that losing their children was the atonement they deserved.

And both of them were wrong.

He decided right then to have another meeting with Alfred. A bold one. The man would hear Ellis out, the whole account, and consider the options. If he wanted to keep the issue out of the courts and papers, he'd start by disclosing Calvin's real whereabouts and the facts behind Ruby's letter.

Sometimes we have to make sacrifices for the ones we love. Alfred's comment floated back. The potential extent of those sacrifices haunted Ellis now, and long into the night.

In the morning, at the paper, Ellis had to shelve the notion.

He'd arrived early to make up for yesterday's absence, as well as for leeway. After the news meeting, he would jet out for a surprise visit to the bank. Until then, hunkered down at his desk, doing his best to stave off thoughts of Lily, he'd type more trite details about the city proposal to rename a local library.

No Pulitzer Prize here. But unless he wanted a daily spot in a breadline, producing something was better than nothing.

"Mr. Reed, a word." Mr. Walker's voice carried easily over the morning quiet.

Ellis steeled himself for another chiding. On his way to the city desk, he gladly paused to let a copy boy speed by, then trudged up to the editor.

"Got an interesting call this morning." Mr. Walker let the remark hang there, as if baiting a reader to turn the page. "Came from the president of Century Alliance Bank, a gentleman named Alfred Millstone."

Ellis aimed for stoic. "Oh yeah?"

"Said you'd approached him about a profile piece. Highlighting the redeeming traits of bankers today and some such crud." Mr. Walker leaned back in his chair, fingers steepled across his middle. "He wants me to kill it. Asked that you not contact his family again."

His family. Not just Alfred. Clearly the couple had compared notes. Had they talked to Ruby too?

"What'd you tell him?"

"That it wouldn't be a problem, since I wasn't aware of any profile assignment to begin with."

Dandy. The chances that Alfred's secretary, much less the bank guard, would let Ellis through the door had just dropped to nil.

But first to salvage his job.

"Mr. Walker, if you'll hear me out—"

"Fact of the matter is, you've been so scattered lately, it didn't occur to me till I hung up what you've really been up to."

Ellis's explanation shriveled in his throat. He swallowed it down. "Sir?"

"I assume you've been snooping around the Millstones, hunting down a lead. I can see why you'd be quiet about it, given their ties to Giovanni Trevino. But with everything I hear...just be careful, Mr. Reed."

Right then, a known press agent caught the attention of Mr. Walker, who invited him over for a new discussion.

Ellis's thoughts were whirling, but he couldn't show it. He simply stepped out of the way while trying to decipher the warning. The name Trevino was a shadow on the outer edge of his mind. Dark and familiar, no specifics.

As he turned around, he spied Dutch arriving. The guy was hitting the coffee station even before his desk, signaling a rough night of sleep. Ellis met him there.

"Dutch, got a question."

"Uh-huh." Dutch was sniffing the pot to determine the freshness of the brew.

"Giovanni Trevino. That name mean anything to you?"

"Sure...right..." Dutch was still distracted, now pouring a cupful. Ellis waited for him to finish. It was important to be clear. "What've you heard?"

"Rum-running, I think. Owns a few supper clubs, gambling halls... Some say he's tied to the Black Hand."

The shadow suddenly took shape. "Are we talking about *Max* Trevino?"

"Max. Yeah. Same guy."

Ellis didn't know a whole lot about the man, outside of him belonging to the Mafia. But he definitely knew about the Black Hand, a group known for extortion of small businesses throughout New York. The members were Italian. Unforgiving. Brutal.

"Why do you ask?"

Against a sudden weight of dread, Ellis forced a shrug. "Just curious."

~

The Tuesday traffic was cooperating. Ellis's first good omen of the day.

Of course, if he were smart, he'd turn his car around, let all this Millstone business go. But he couldn't. In light of the Mob links, his concerns over the kids had doubled. Even Alfred's trip to Chicago, a hub for organized crime, gained new context.

Time to return to the source—not Alfred, but Ruby. It was still early enough to catch her morning recess, if he hurried.

He was crossing into Jersey when he sensed a car following behind. A black Packard. It trailed his every turn, like a tin can strung to the bumper, all the way to Hoboken. Across from the school, Ellis pulled over and the Packard rolled right past.

A relief, if not for the driver. His pockmarked cheeks, common scars from smallpox, distinguished a man like him in a crowd. Ellis had seen him before, but where?

Then again, after Mr. Walker's heeding, maybe paranoia was kicking in.

There was no time to sort it out. The kids were already on the playground, squealing and flailing under the spring sun.

Ellis climbed out of his car. Just as he'd hoped, Ruby was lingering alone by the apple tree. The matronly teacher was again focused on her more active charges. Still being cautious, Ellis started in Ruby's direction.

With a few yards to go, he caught her gaze. Apprehension flitted across her face, but she put a finger to her lips. She waved him to the back side of the tree, where he squatted to her level, obscured from the teacher's view.

"I'm not supposed to talk to you no more," Ruby said in an urgent hush. "I kept hoping you'd come back, though. There's things I gotta tell ya."

"About Calvin?" It was Ellis's first thought.

She crinkled her chin, confused, and shook her head. But the intensity that returned to her eyes suggested a scenario just as troubling.

"Honey, are *you* doing all right?"

Her silence held long enough to provide an answer, and he regretted not asking the question last time, right from the top.

"If I can, Ruby, I absolutely want to help you too."

The corners of her lips rose a little, and Ellis realized it might be less from his offer than his use of her name. Ruby, not Victoria.

"Then I need a favor," she whispered. "I gotta get a message to my mama, 'cause I've given it heaps of thought. See, Claire— that's our housekeeper—she's teaching me to sew. She's gonna show me how to knit and crochet too. And I already learned about doing laundry and fryin' up food. So, Mama needs to know I'm ready to earn my keep. That way, it won't cost her nothin' to have me, and we could all be together again."

The plea squeezed Ellis's chest. A vise around his lungs.

He had come here about the letter, to find out if it held other clues and when it had arrived. Could she pass the note along? Had she overheard anything at the house?

But now, face-to-face with her, he found himself at a crossroads. Samuel's sickness had exhibited the resiliency of children, sure. But also their vulnerabilities, their reliance on those who care in order to survive.

Ruby waited for his reply.

He had to decide how much to share. Beyond that, just how far he was willing to go.

A shrill whistle cut in. It came from a chisel-faced man standing beside the teacher. A cop. He must have been passing on his beat. Or hell, maybe the Packard driver had sent him over.

"You!" the cop yelled. "Stay right there!"

The command was definitely for Ellis. Yeah, he might have been trespassing, but he could explain himself if given a chance.

Unfortunately, the man's aggressive strides, paired with the billy club in his clutches, made clear a diplomatic chat wasn't in the cards.

"I'll come back when I can," Ellis told Ruby. Her expression reflected his alarm, but there was no time to say more, only to take off in a sprint.

"Halt!"

Ellis aimed to reach his car. Halfway into the street, he noted that cranking his old engine wouldn't be an option for a fast getaway. He'd have to lose the guy through the city blocks.

"I said halt!"

A glance backward confirmed that the officer was right on his heels. Then a honk blared and a car swerved. Ellis stumbled, narrowly avoiding a collision. As he scrambled to his feet, a tug to his collar whipped him around, causing his elbow to strike something hard.

The cop's face.

Christ.

Quicker than a blink, Ellis was flattened to the ground. Both arms were yanked behind him. His cheek scraped against the pavement, hard.

"Stay down," the cop ordered, his bony knee in Ellis's back. "You're under arrest, you damn fool."

CHAPTER 30

LILY HADN'T WANTED TO LEAVE HIM. From a mere change of perspective, however, she had gained a profound sense of comfort that Samuel would be safe. That, as his mother, she could protect her child without a perpetual fear of the worst.

Geraldine Dillard deserved no less. If only Lily could find a way to help.

"Miss Palmer!" The chief's hollering tugged her mind back to the newsroom.

She rose from her chair, grabbing her steno pad and pencil, just as Clayton caught her eye. From his typewriter, he shot her a wink, reminding her of their date this afternoon, and returned to his draft.

He had invited her to lunch when he checked on her earlier, concerned over her absence the previous day. She made but brief mention of Samuel's fever—not wanting to dwell, she had reasoned to herself.

In truth, after the kiss she'd shared with Ellis—a reckless mistake, the culmination of an emotional day—her feelings were jumbled enough. Adding sympathy from Clayton would only tangle them more, creating knots impossible to undo.

The chief shouted again, and Lily resisted plugging her ears while entering his office.

Planted at his desk, he peered over his spectacles. "Shut the door. Take a seat."

"Yes, Chief." She complied without question, as the letters and memos he dictated to her were occasionally confidential.

"Miss Palmer," he said then, "I assume you know how I feel about honesty." It was a daunting start if ever there was one. The greater cause apprehension, though, was the shifting of his bearded jaw.

"I do."

"Good. 'Cause I've got a question about your need for time off yesterday. The excuse you gave was pretty vague. And now I think I know why."

Lily held her pencil and pad snugly on her lap. In the wake of her maternal fretting and sleeplessness, she should have been resigned to any turn of events. Particularly the inevitable. After two years of working for the chief, this confrontation was just that.

Still, she shrank inside from his disapproving tone.

"There's a woman just called. Wanted to confirm that a Lillian Palmer worked here at the *Examiner*. Evidently, you two became acquainted while you were pinning down some sort of…interview."

Lily blinked. It took her a moment to jump from Samuel to Sylvia, and the implication that Lily would peddle lies for her own vanity.

"Chief, I assure you," she said, "I never specified that I was—"

He held up a stubby pointer finger, halting her defense. After all, he hadn't reached his question yet. Very possibly a variant of *How fast can you pack up your desk?*

"I notice you've been distracted, not acting yourself. And I'm well aware of your bigger ambitions. So, I'm asking you now, Miss Palmer." At last, here it came. "Are you actively seeking employment elsewhere as a writer?"

Employment elsewhere?

As a writer?

Baffled, she had to backtrack through the links of his rationale. "Sir...no. I wasn't...no."

"You certain about that?"

She replied more fervently. "I'm positive. I was helping out a friend, and it was a simple misunderstanding. Nothing more."

As she held the chief's gaze, the skepticism seeped from his face. He sat back in his chair. His relief reflected hers, the causes decidedly different.

"Well, all right," he said with a hint of embarrassment. No one in the news business liked to be wrong. "Back to work, then." He flicked his hand toward the door and promptly returned to his articles. The issue was settled, and that was that.

Except it wasn't.

Lily found she couldn't move. She was tired—physically too, yes—but mostly she was weary from guarding her past, from being afraid. Above all, she was done with feeling ashamed of the proudest accomplishment of her life.

The chief looked up. "There something else?"

"Yes. There is."

His evident value of her secretarial skills, while reassuring, didn't allow her blanket impunity, but she charged on, a confession long overdue.

"The reason I was gone yesterday, sir, is because Samuel was sick. Samuel," she said, "is my four-year-old son."

The chief remained expressionless. Only his eyes betrayed his surprise.

"I should have spoken of him from the start," she admitted, "but I needed this job...and a place to live, which Miss Westin surely wouldn't allow if she knew. You see, that's why he lives with my parents in Maryville, where I visit every weekend. But I'm saving up so when Samuel's of school age, we can live in the city, the two of us together."

She almost continued but held off. The fact she didn't proclaim herself a widow established the nature of her situation, divorce being nearly as scandalous as a mother never wedded. Yet somehow, through the awkward tension, the potential consequences bearing down, Lily found herself sitting up straighter, even as the chief came back with a level reply.

"Will he be running around here while you work?"

The query was so unexpected she had to think. "No, Chief."

"Around the boardinghouse?"

"No. Of course not."

"Then I don't see the problem."

And with that, the chief's focus dropped from Lily to his work pile.

The utter simplicity of the exchange left her almost confused, a smidge dizzy, and feeling altogether foolish.

Could it have always been that easy? Or was it the product of her job dedication over time? Perhaps it was her show of strength while volunteering the truth on her own accord.

She settled on a combination of them all as she made her way toward the door. Each step became lighter than the last, until she reached for the knob.

The safest choice was to take her leave, but an idea was emerging. Not in pieces. Rather like a photograph being developed, an image coming forth, already complete. And it entailed far more than her *bigger ambitions*.

Empowered by a fresh injection of moxie, she pivoted to face him. "Chief, one thing more," she said, and he begrudgingly glanced up. "It's regarding a potential new column for the paper..."

"Ah, Jesus," he murmured, though not in a way that told her to stop.

"A column," she said, "about single parenting. The realities of it, the struggles, the highlights. Not just for women. For men too." Her enthusiasm grew as she spoke. Like her previous vision for a column, this would still be an adventurous endeavor, but with deeper meaning for people like Geraldine.

"There are likely just as many mothers widowed from the Great War as fathers whose wives were lost to childbirth, or other terrible tragedies. I can tell you firsthand, they don't need advice about how to prepare the perfect dinner by five, or about the latest fashion trends. What they need is understanding. To know they're not alone. They need to hear—"

"I got it, I got it." The chief heaved a sigh that sent gray specks drifting from his ashtray. Again his beard twitched, but he didn't say no. Yet.

He thrummed his fingers on his desk. She knew the concept was progressive, but just maybe it was the type of risk Nellie Bly would have applauded.

At last the chief answered. "I suppose I…might be able to squeeze something in."

He was agreeing.

To her idea.

For her own column.

Lily could barely contain her smile.

"On two conditions," he stressed, stunting her joy. "It doesn't interfere with your regular duties. And second, you don't *dare* make all those dead parents out to be martyrs."

She would agree to both, of course, though the oddity of the latter caused her to hedge.

The chief added with reluctance, "My father drank away near every cent we had before putting himself in the grave. We made out just fine, me and my brothers, but only on account of my mother. We clear on that?"

Lily was stricken by the personal nature of the admission. Even more so, she was astounded by the connections to be made.

For now, she managed to reply, "Completely. Thank you, Chief."
He simply nodded and resumed his work.

～

Today, no challenge in life could temper Lily's thrill, for this
reason: If she could accomplish one seemingly insurmountable
task, why not others?

As an added boost, a story broke in the paper. On a recent
radio broadcast, Mrs. Lindbergh had made a personal appeal
about her kidnapped son, including how to care for him and
what baby foods he most enjoyed—right in line with Lily's
suggestion that the chief had waved off. But that didn't matter
now. The broadcast had led to a tip about a suspicious, child-
less couple who'd just stocked up on those exact food items.
Authorities were optimistic.

How wondrous would it be if both families wound up reunited?

On her lunch date with Clayton, after celebrating news about
her column, she would speak to him about the Dillards. He
was, after all, an ace reporter. It was time to seek his advice—in
confidence, of course. She would have to trust that his strict
views on right and wrong, on good and bad, wouldn't prevent
him from doing all he could to help.

She later told herself this as they settled into a cushioned
booth at Geoffrey's. The restaurant was on the top floor of a
twelve-story building, affording an impressive view of City Hall
and William Penn standing tall in bronze. With damask linens
and single roses in etched, crystal vases, the restaurant was even
lovelier than the Renaissance.

The thought of their forgotten date still caused Lily twists
of guilt.

But all of that faded, along with their surroundings the clinking of ice and tinkering of china, the chattering among diners in
their daytime finery—at the announcement of a job offer.

Only it wasn't Lily's.

"My, Clayton," she said. "The national desk." The waiter had only just stepped away after taking their orders. "That's marvelous."

Clayton brightened. "It's the *Chicago Tribune*," he said, throwing her off further.

"Chicago?"

"You know I grew up there," he reminded her, "and how I've always wanted to go back."

"Yes. Certainly. I remember." She hadn't known he meant so soon.

"That's why I've been gone so many weekends lately. With my parents down in southern Illinois now, I needed to go back on my own, to check out areas to live in. Make sure it really made sense." His expression took a turn, growing serious. "Lily, I want you and Samuel to come."

"To...Chicago?" She repeated the name again as if it were an alien planet, and Clayton laughed a little at her confusion. Or maybe from a touch of his own nerves, she noted, as he pulled a shiny gold ring from his suit pocket.

"Sweetheart, I want you to marry me." After the briefest pause, he added with conviction, "And I want to care for Samuel as my own son."

Lily took in a light gasp. The proposal alone was enough to stun her. The consideration given to her child only multiplied that effect as he continued. "You'd never have to work again. You could be home with him every day, all day. No more buses, no waiting to see him on the weekends. We could be a real family."

From the row of tall windows, light glinted on the diamond at the center of the band, perfect and round and lovely. In its reflection she envisioned the life he was offering. She saw a home of their very own and a future full of promise.

"I know it's a bit of a surprise, but a good one I hope." His tone matched the rising worry in his soft-brown eyes, exposing a vulnerable side of him she had never seen. Moved by this, and so much more, Lily hastened to respond.

"It's incredible, Clayton. All of it." As a smile spread over her lips, his did the same but at an angle she recognized. The kind brimming with an assuredness that made others feel safe.

"If I'd had my way," he said, "I would've preferred to ask you at a nice, long candlelit dinner. Not a lunch hour like this. But I'm supposed to give notice to the chief today, and of course I had to come to you first."

The scenes in her head, easily formed as hypotheticals, fell away at his last remark. "You've accepted the job already?"

"Well…yes."

In the quiet beat that followed, he reached across the table and placed his hand over hers. "I know it might seem fast. But I've thought it all through."

She didn't doubt him there. He wouldn't have asked without thinking of everything. "I'm sure you have, but…"

"Lily." The sincerity in his voice, from just her name, stopped her. "I love you. And I want to do this for us."

Us.

That was how he thought of them. With all the benefits the move and promotion would add to their lives, why wouldn't he have nabbed the offer? He would have been foolish not to. Just as she, too, would be foolish not to accept his.

Wouldn't she?

Teetering on a choice, toes on the edge of a cliff, she smiled.

~

The rest of the day passed in a blur of phone calls, memos, and internal questions with no easy answers. Patches of absentmind-edness slowed Lily's productivity and left her working late to assure her tasks were done with diligence. She couldn't risk erring today of all days. She could ruin her chance to actually write her own column, the shot of a lifetime. One she would have to abandon if she accepted Clayton's proposal.

If.

She had asked him for a little time, saying she had to be cautious with a child to think about. He said he understood, even insisted she keep the ring in the meanwhile. In agreement, she tucked it with care into a coin pocket of her purse, and they left it at that.

It hadn't seemed right to share news of her own job opportunity. After all, if they were to marry, the point would be moot. As it ought to be already. Honestly, what was the great debate? To be torn by the prospect of a column, which could wither faster than it bloomed, would be as selfish as it was silly.

Clayton was smart and charming and kind. And he loved her. She was far too protective of her heart to say she loved him in turn, but she cared for him deeply. That much she knew. She also knew she would be safe with Clayton, as would her son. There would be no more critical looks or whispers to endure. No more discomfort during chats on marriage and parenting. No more chances of ending up the fool with another man—like Ellis. The emotional pull she felt around Ellis Reed was enough to warn her off.

The list of no mores continued throughout Lily's trek to the boardinghouse. There, her room of solitude waited—without Samuel, without anyone. The way it would remain for at least another year if she stayed on her current path.

The bleakness of that vision was so engrossing that she didn't sense another presence until footsteps registered from behind. A dim city haze further veiled the shadowed figure.

Lily hugged her purse to her body. Clayton's ring would be a thief's lucky find. She increased her speed. But like echoes in a cave, the footfalls kept pace with her own. Not stopping, barely slowing, she threw a glance over her shoulder. The head lamps of a passing car threw beams at her eyes. Dots of light floated in the air.

Someone was definitely following.

CHAPTER 31

ELLIS WAS BOOKED at the Hudson County jail. It smelled exactly as he would have guessed. An aromatic brew of stale booze, mold, and piss. The bowls of slop they served didn't rate much better.

For assaulting an officer and resisting arrest, his bail was set at fifty bucks. A slight problem, given the sum of eight dollars in his wallet. He was permitted one phone call—and he wasted it. His bank in Manhattan had frozen his account, and no amount of pleading, even with the manager, garnered more than "We'll gladly look into that, sir."

A favor paid to Alfred, no doubt. Banking had to be like any other business in that way. Members looked out for their own. Or maybe the man's underworld ties played a factor. It would certainly explain the guard's unwillingness to grant him another call, answering "Later" in a gruff baritone to each of Ellis's requests.

On the upside, he had ample time to choose which person to ring. A whole workday, in fact. It was evening, and he was still stuck in this narrow cage with nothing but a thin, stained mattress on a cot. A good portion of the neighboring cells would surely be occupied by dawn. The drunkards were steadily rolling in.

Rants from one of them competed now with keys clanking as the barrel-chested guard paused at Ellis's cell. "Let's go," he said, unlocking the door.

Ellis scrambled from his bed.

Eager for that second call, he considered various folks as he was escorted down the corridor and through two sets of locked doors. He ruled out Dutch, given the late hour and funds required. The guy had his own family to worry about—same as Lily, naturally the first person who'd rushed to mind. Mr. Walker was an even easier no. Maybe one of the reporters Ellis had traded small favors with in the past, at various papers around town, would be worth a try. If he could reach them.

At the end of a hallway, the guard pointed with his stick. "In there."

Ellis was directed into a room with no phone. Just two chairs divided by a table, and a man in a dark suit who stood facing a barred window. The setup, likely reserved for legal chats, suggested that somehow a lawyer had come calling, until the guy turned.

Alfred.

"Sit," the guard ordered.

Dread swirled as Ellis rounded the table and took a seat. He should have expected this.

Alfred dismissed the guard to stand post outside the door and settled into the other chair. Left in privacy, he gestured toward Ellis's face with the fedora in his hand. "It appears you've had a rough day."

Ellis resisted touching his cheek. It still stung from the meeting with pavement. "I've had better."

"No question you have." Alfred set aside his hat that carried the scent of pipe tobacco. He laced his fingers so casually you'd think they were sharing after-dinner bourbons. "I must admit, when I asked an officer to patrol the school area, I imagined only a warning would come of it, if anything at all."

There it was. The cop's arrival on the scene hadn't been a coincidence.

This also meant that Alfred had waited all these hours to make an appearance.

"Guess I'm an overachiever."

"Apparently so." Alfred's smile lifted the edges of his mustache. In contrast to their last encounter, the man's pleasantries now made Ellis wary. "Mr. Reed, I'm here because I'd like to clear up some confusion. But first, I'd like to thank you."

"Thank me…"

"I believe we got off on the wrong foot. As I'm sure you're aware, your female colleague's recent visit was rather upsetting to my wife. And your intentions appeared even more question-able after I contacted your editor. All of that, however, was before I spoke with Victoria."

Unless the Millstones had acquired a spiritualist, he was referring to Ruby. But Ellis refrained from pointing this out. Antagonizing Alfred would only hinder the bail situation, let alone an inquiry about Calvin. "How's that?"

"Once I learned who you were—that you were responsible for her picture in the paper—I realized I actually owed you my gratitude. Indirectly, you helped me and my wife through a very dark time."

There was no reason to prod. It had become apparent that Alfred was the type who operated with planning and purpose. What that purpose was, Ellis hadn't figured out yet.

"My wife and I married rather late in life, you understand. So, we felt extremely fortunate when Sylvia gave birth to our daughter. For ten years, Victoria was our absolute pride and joy, and then…she was gone."

"In the accident," Ellis volunteered, not unkindly.

"Yes. I suppose you've read about that." Behind his horn-rimmed glasses, Alfred's eyes lowered a bit. "On a winding road, with so much rain, the car just slid right off. It couldn't have been prevented, but Sylvia still blamed herself. Officers hammering her with questions didn't help. Reporters too." There was resentment in his voice, though seemingly not directed at Ellis.

"After the funeral, she spent nearly a month in bed. It took several more before she left the house at all. Gradually, she improved, even journeying out with old friends on occasion. Then one day, the maid was airing out our daughter's room. While dusting the shelves, she broke a figurine. Victoria's favorite glass fairy. Sylvia became hysterical. When the maid phoned, I rushed straight home, but the damage was done. Sylvia's blue mood returned, even deeper than before. She rarely ate or slept, and her health rapidly declined. As her husband, I felt so helpless to save her, I felt as if—" He stopped suddenly. Bringing his fist to his mouth, he coughed once and cleared his throat.

Ellis withheld any response as Alfred reset himself before going on.

"The doctors agreed she belonged in an asylum. She could receive proper treatment there, they said. The arrangements were finally being made when Sylvia stumbled upon that newspaper. I'd left it folded on my night table. I had barely skimmed the pages myself. If I'd seen the photo, I definitely would've noticed the girl's striking resemblance to our daughter."

"So you replaced her." At this point, Ellis couldn't hide his irritation. This wasn't a goldfish they were talking about. Flush one down the john, and pick up another.

"I realize it might seem...unconventional. I had reservations myself. But Sylvia was so hopeful. She was entirely convinced it was a sign, a gift straight from heaven. In the end, there was no decision to be made. I set off to Pennsylvania to bring the girl into our family, one who plainly needed us as much as we needed her."

Ellis winced at the account, or more aptly at what was missing. Because there wasn't just a girl. There was also a boy. At the thought, Geraldine's words swung back—the stipulation she'd required—and the scene came together.

"You had to take her brother, though, or there was no deal."

Alfred looked surprised, almost impressed. "That was the agreement, yes…which I respectfully honored. And now, Mr. Reed, I ask that you do the same for me." He leaned forward, geniality fading. "After all that I've shared, with everything considered, I trust you'll see how a second article about the children would only cause unnecessary harm."

And therein lay the goal of this heart-to-heart.

Admittedly, the presumption was sound—Mr. Walker had once proposed an article precisely in that vein—yet it was still mistaken.

"Listen," Ellis said. "I've got no interest in writing a story about the kids. Or your family." He knew he'd just relinquished the threat that could have served as leverage. But being on the level seemed the wisest route.

Alfred peered intently through his lenses. "What is it you want, then?"

"I need to know the boy is safe, for personal reasons."

Ellis waited, not adding what he'd been told by Ruby. If he'd learned anything from his job, it was that truths tended to float to the surface when, after a little stirring, you simply let a person talk.

But right then, the door to the room opened. A drunkard's profanities projected from the hall as the baritone guard delivered a chair to Alfred's side, an act explained when Sylvia walked into the room. She jolted when the door shut behind the guard, and Alfred stood up.

"Darling, I told you to stay in the waiting area." His worries were almost as evident as his wife's unease about her surroundings.

"I have a right to be here," she said, straightening with purse in hand.

"Yes, dear, but I've already handled this. There isn't going to be any article to trouble yourself over. He only wants to know about the children, to verify their well-being."

This didn't sway her from claiming a spot at the table.

"That's all I'm after," Ellis affirmed, but still she eyed him, unconvinced.

"Then why all the sneaky behavior? Why not just come out and ask?"

Alfred sat back down, a flush mottling his skin.

The question briefly stumped Ellis. Then he recalled the guilt and secrecy that had plagued his involvement from the start. The lies at its core were like the jaws of a trap, still biting down, the slow bleed going on, draining the good in his life, and the lives of others, until he pried that trap free.

With the truth.

"There's more to the story, is why." Surely to his detriment, he professed, "The picture wasn't real...that is, the *picture* was real, but the sign wasn't theirs. I put it there myself." Not a day would go by when he wouldn't regret that choice. "The point being, Geraldine had no intention of selling her kids."

Sylvia stiffened. The tendons in her neck went tight as wires. "You're wrong. Because she did just that. Isn't that right, Alfred?"

Ellis charged on. "She was sick back then. The diagnosis was wrong, but she didn't know yet. She thought she was incurable. Mr. Millstone, you saw her yourself. By the time you were there, she couldn't have looked well."

Alfred's mouth parted. He struggled to answer, and his gaze retreated to his hat.

Sylvia burst out, "This is preposterous! That woman made her choice." Visibly trembling, she curled her fingers as if readying to claw, to swipe in defense of what was hers. But then she glanced at the purse in her clutches and seemed to steady from a thought.

"We've already been more than understanding. When that *mother* conveniently wanted her son back, we agreed without a hassle." While saying this, Sylvia produced a folded paper from her handbag and slid it toward Ellis. "See for yourself."

The letter.

Guarded with suspicion, he flattened the note, bare of an envelope.

My dearest Ruby, it began.

The script was unrefined, peppered with misspellings, but legible enough to decipher.

Ellis's mind flashed on an image of Geraldine penning the letter. The message matched Ruby's summary, of choosing one child over the other, of apologizing for not saying goodbye in person. It was heartrending. Cruel.

And he knew without a doubt...

"Geraldine didn't write this," he said. "And she doesn't have her son."

Alfred's eyes flickered toward Sylvia, an indiscernible look.

All along, Ellis had refused to imagine the worst. Now it was unavoidable. Still, before the couple could argue or walk out, he needed to play it smart.

"Mr. and Mrs. Millstone, I know you understand the grief of losing a child. The horrendous tragedy of it, the unfairness. Victoria was obviously a special little girl. Not being a parent myself, I can't fathom the pain you went through from the accident. What I do know is that you have an opportunity here, a chance to reunite a mother with her children. Please," he said, "help me do that. Tell me what happened to Calvin."

In the midst of his appeal, Sylvia's demeanor had gone slack. There was a glossiness in her eyes, a distance to her stare.

"Mrs. Millstone?"

Alfred abruptly came to his feet. "Darling, it's best we go." He put a hand on her shoulder. As her awareness returned, her attention landed on Ellis.

"Come now," Alfred said. "Sylvia?"

She shook her head.

"Darling, really. I think it's best—"

"No," she said flatly.

Alfred lingered in place. Ellis could see him weighing the alternative of dragging her out, creating a scene that would summon the guard. Grudgingly he lowered back into his chair.

What was he afraid she'd say?

Ellis bit down, anxious for Sylvia to speak.

"I first need you to swear, Mr. Reed, that there'll be no more questions, no more poking around. And that you'll stay away from all of us for good, so we can go about our lives just as before."

Before. As in, before Ellis's funds were blocked and he was tossed in a cell? Or before the children were stripped from their real mother?

He replied in all honesty, "Afraid I can't guarantee that." Sylvia's fingers curled again before he elaborated. "Not with a court date that'll require me to explain why I was at the school. The judge will want to hear about my ties to your family. I bet there'll be a slew of questions, too, that I won't know how to answer." In sum, it was better if she filled him in on the details now.

Sylvia mulled this over and quickly arrived at a decision. "I'll see to it that the charges are dropped," she said.

"And if I don't want them to be?" The challenge had just left Ellis's mouth when he recalled the brutality of her husband's shady connections. He braced himself but didn't back down. "I figure it's one way to get some answers of my own."

A hint of panic crossed her face, a mental scramble in a test of wills. "If you feel that's absolutely necessary, then…then I'd suggest you prepare to face another charge."

"Oh? What for?"

She lifted her chin and her features hardened. "An inappropriate relationship," she stated. "With our daughter."

Alfred's eyes widened, yet he remained silent. He was simply a passenger on a runaway coach, set to plow through Ellis's life.

Hands balling into fists, Ellis seethed at what Sylvia was suggesting. Every disgusting bit of it. Being in a jailhouse was the only thing keeping his voice level. "No judge'll buy that. Not without a shred of proof."

"I'm sure you're right," she conceded. "But what of your boss? Or your friends and readers? It's remarkable, really, what people take to be truth simply because they saw it in the paper. Isn't that so?"

His admission of the photo had, within minutes, backfired in the harshest of ways.

How many writers from competing papers would jump on that story? Maybe even from the *Tribune*? He could see the highlights now: reporter stages a picture of two poor kids, trails them across state lines, fakes an assignment to get closer to the girl, gets arrested after being ordered to stay away.

It had sources. It had scandal. And all of it was true. Even without a false accusation of indecency, his reputation and credibility would be shot.

As would any chance of Geraldine seeing her children.

Ellis fought an onslaught of nausea while steering back to his mission. He asked, slow and firm, "What…happened…to Calvin?"

Alfred, too, was looking at Sylvia, awaiting an answer.

"I see you need time to think things over," she said to Ellis. "I trust you'll let us know when you decide."

A surge of anger sprang Ellis to his feet, and Alfred scrambled to rise with a defensive arm across his wife. A silent standoff.

"Everything okay in here?" the guard asked, suddenly in the room. His question was clearly meant for the Millstones.

Ellis had no other option. With effort, he eased himself back. Not only for his own sake, but for Ruby and Calvin. This wasn't the way to uncover the truth, or to help either kid.

"We're fine," Alfred answered for them all. He dropped his hand to gather his hat. "It's time to go, Sylvia."

Without further protest, she rose from the table, her face eerily unreadable. The couple exited the room, leaving Ellis to stare at two empty chairs. His pulse throbbed at his temples.

"Party's over. Back to your cell." The guard's command didn't register at first. When it did, Ellis mindlessly stepped forward until a single thought grabbed hold.

"I need to get outta here."

"Won't be tonight."

Ellis looked at him. "Why?"

"Bail clerk's gone. Have to wait till morning."

Was that the Millstones' plan, a flexing of muscle? A whole night behind bars just might encourage cooperation.

"At least let me have a second call." A half plea, half demand. "Please."

The guard waffled through a long blink.

It was just as possible that the cops were teaching Ellis a lesson for smacking their fellow pal in blue. If so, he hated to imagine what other ways they might take revenge if he stayed here much longer.

The guard huffed. "Make it fast."

Ellis nodded with vigor, and his mind swam. There had to be someone around with enough money or pull, or both, to spring him loose. A new level of desperation produced two possibilities: the first was the Irish mobster who'd traded tips that once saved Ellis's career, and the second…was Ellis's father. Soliciting help from either one would come at a price.

Sadly, it wasn't an easy choice.

CHAPTER 32

TWO BLOCKS FROM THE BOARDINGHOUSE, Lily's heart pounded like a tribal drum, a portentous beat in her ears. She was well accustomed to walking the city streets on her own, even at night. But anytime she became too comfortable, a report on the wire about a mugging, or worse, would revive her diligence. As a mother, she couldn't afford to ignore a feeling that something wasn't right. And that intuition now sent a chill over her skin.

She hurried around the last corner. Footsteps in the dimness further quickened in her wake. On the verge of breaking into a run, she dared a second look back, and someone called out. "Wait! If ya please!"

The voice, being female, was largely disarming, but it still took a second or two for Lily's feet to slow.

"Miss Palmer..." The lilt of the woman's tone was young and familiar. Hat pulled low, she approached slightly short of breath. "It's only me...Claire."

"Claire?" The girl's face was pale with freckles. Out of context, and without the sight of her red hair, the Millstones' house-keeper hadn't immediately connected with Lily's memory.

"I didn't mean to startle ya, ma'am. I was waitin' outside the newspaper building in hopes of seeing ya come out. From across the street, I couldn't be sure 'twas you."

Lily smiled with relief and patted her chest. "It's quite all right."

"I woulda phoned instead, but when I tried this mornin', the gentleman said you were far too busy to take calls."

The chief.

And the woman he had spoken with was Claire. Not Sylvia, as Lily had presumed.

"So you traveled all this way?"

"It was a day I'd planned to go visit with me sister. But she agreed. This had to be done, she said."

Voices cut through the evening air, and Claire's head snapped toward them. A jovial-looking couple were nattering on while crossing the street.

Returning to Lily, Claire clutched her coat collar under her neck. "Is there a place we can speak, the two of us?" Her wariness over meeting in the open pointed to an unfortunate conclusion: Lily's sense of foreboding was warranted after all.

"Come with me."

~

In the house, supper had already been served to the tenants, the dining table cleared. Lily had scarcely touched her veal at lunch, ordered by Clayton on her behalf—his proposal had stifled her decisiveness over even the menu—but food remained the least of her concerns.

Particularly now, observing Claire.

Taking a seat in the den, the girl worried a loose seam on her skirt, her hands aged beyond her years, her coat still fastened. She resembled Geraldine just then, softened by lamplight, perched on the same chair.

"Could I get you some tea?" Lily asked.

"No, thank you, ma'am. I really shan't stay long."

Lily nodded. She closed the door, dulling the sounds of boarders in the parlor. Their high-pitched giggles dwarfed the symphonic notes crackling from a gramophone.

Across from Claire, Lily lowered onto the settee. Ellis's spot. How she wished he were here now.

Claire fiddled more intensely with her seam. "On the bus, I thought of how to say it all. Now it's slipped away, it has."

Lily pushed up a smile. "Just begin wherever you'd like." She attempted to bar any notions of what might be coming, along with regrets of not thinking to approach Claire first. Of course, finding the opportunity would have been a challenge unto itself.

"It's the boy."

"Calvin…"

"When the missus hired me on, around year's end, they'd only just moved to the house. 'Twasn't but a month, and she'd had her fill. All the lad's crying and carrying-on. His sister tried to explain he was just missin' their mam and their old home. But this only agitated the missus more. I did my best to calm the poor boy, to keep him from actin' out. And Mr. Millstone would thank me for helping his wife. 'She's still so fragile,' he'd say…" Claire's story trailed off as her features gathered in a pleading look. "I didn't want to be part of it, Miss Palmer, but I needed the extra money."

"Part of it?" Lily breathed, but the housekeeper continued.

"She was in need of surgery, my sister was. And if I said no to the missus, I feared she'd sack me straightaway."

"Claire," Lily interjected, "*what* did Mrs. Millstone pay you to do?"

Hesitant to a maddening degree, Claire dropped her gaze to

the floor. Her voice lowered to a near whisper. "The missus told Calvin of plans for the day. Said I'd be takin' him to a special winter zoo, with his sister off to school. Even packed a wee suitcase for the boy. To be ready if we made a night of it, she told him. As we rode the bus together, he started askin' after the animals. 'Twas the most I'd ever seen the child smile." Claire's lips lifted at the memory, though just as soon fell with the quivering of her chin. Tears filled her eyes. "The lad trusted me, and I betrayed him. The staff at the children's home, they had to pry his hands from my arms."

The vision caused a squeezing of Lily's heart. Indeed, there were far grimmer scenarios. But for Lily, there was little relief to be found in a child's pain of feeling wholly unwanted, cast out not just once, but twice. "Is Calvin there now? At the orphanage?"

"Couldn't say, ma'am. I went back first chance I had, to see if he was all right. But the director there, he warned me to steer clear, he did. Said the boy needed a more pleasing disposition if a fine set of parents were ever willin' to give him a home, and I'd only ruin his chances. If I coulda taken him in myself, I would have. I'd take in the poor lass, too, if I had the means."

The reference to Ruby was almost as alarming.

Lily leaned forward in her chair. "I need you to be candid with me, Claire. Is his sister safe in that house?"

Claire's shoulders hunched and her chin pulled in, a mouse backed into a corner. She was unaccustomed surely to stating her opinion. Not one bearing such importance.

"Please," Lily said. "If you care for those children as much as you say, you have to tell me what you know."

A wave of giggles drifted in from the parlor. The contrast of emotions a single room apart—perhaps even greater in a house one state away—was woefully striking.

Claire slowly raised her eyes, though only halfway. "All was peaceful for a spell, without Calvin there. Yet after time, the missus only worsened."

"Worsened...how?"

"More and more, 'tis as if her daughter never died. Any reminder often upsets her...if the lass insists she doesn't like marmalade or ribbons in her hair or playing the piano. And if she damages anything that belonged to their other daughter—a dress, even a book—it can mean standing in a corner for hours, or writing pages and pages of the same sentence, apologizin'."

Ellis had mentioned something once. About Ruby being kept from the playground for staining her clothing...

But Lily had greater concerns now as she reflected upon another handwritten page. She had her suspicions but yearned to know for certain. "I understand that Ruby received a letter from her mother, right after Calvin was taken away. Sylvia wrote it herself. Didn't she?" The question being largely rhetorical, Lily hadn't expected the spilling of Claire's tears, the straining of her voice.

"The words were from the missus...but the writin' was mine." Droplets clung to Claire's chin as she finally met Lily's gaze. "Oh, Miss Palmer, I'm so very sorry. I didn't want to do any of it."

Lily's compassion shifted to this poor, young girl, strapped with a load of guilt from impossible choices. Deserving of forgiveness. Lily reached out and squeezed Claire's hand. "This is my doing much more than yours. I assure you, I'll do all I can to make it right."

Though with a tinge of confusion, Claire gained an air of hope. She wiped her tears with her coat sleeve. "Are ya goin' to fetch the boy, then? You *must* think of him first."

Before Lily could form an answer, Claire added, "I know plenty who've grown up in children's homes much the same. They can be fine enough for the good 'n' quiet type. But for those who don't settle easily...the tales aren't ones I'd care to repeat."

In other words, Lily needed to investigate in a hurry. After the passage of at least two months, Calvin could be in dire need of rescue from a place that could leave scars of every sort.

Assuming he was still there.

CHAPTER 33

ONE LOOK AT HIS FATHER'S SCOWL, and Ellis saw the mistake in his choice. Accepting help from an Irish mobster would have had fewer repercussions than what now lay in store.

The fact that it was past ten at night—a blatant violation of his father's early-to-bed, early-to-rise regimen—was cause for a foul mood. His need to shell out fifty whole smackers was the greater issue.

Amazingly the sergeant hadn't inflated the price for a release outside of the clerk's hours. But then, Ellis's father had spent decades as a supervisor. He knew how to reason with people, to speak their language and find solutions. Unless you were Ellis.

At the front desk of the police station that connected to the jail, his father jammed a folded page into his coat pocket. Tangible proof, at last, of his son's many failings. This much was clear by the way he shook his head at nothing in particular, even after Ellis thanked him again.

"It's done," his father said.

No other greeting. No questions about a court date. No asking what had happened.

Did the man even care?

Ellis followed him out of the station, a flashback to their trudge from the principal's office. Back in junior high school, Ellis's rebellious period was brief and virtually harmless. Pranks like rubber cementing a teacher's chair—Mr. Cullen objectively deserved far worse—had succeeded in capturing his father's attention. Just not long enough to make the gags worth the trouble.

The difference now was that Ellis wasn't a kid, and recognition of this sort was the last thing he wanted. Why couldn't his father see that?

Why couldn't he see Ellis as anything but an inconvenience?

"Like I said on the phone, Pop, I'll pay you back soon. All right?"

In the glow of the gas lamp, his father was descending the concrete stairs, several steps ahead. "You're the one with all the dough."

A cheap shot, given the circumstances.

"I told you, I just gotta straighten it out with the bank."

"Yeah. So you say."

Ellis slowed at the base of the stairs, still on edge from the Millstones. He didn't need this too. "What's that supposed to mean?"

His father continued toward his truck, ignoring him. The concept was nothing new, but this time Ellis refused to let it slide. "You think I'm lying?"

At the lack of an answer, Ellis stopped cold. Yeah, he'd screwed up with the picture of the kids. But now he was struggling to do the right thing. His life was imploding because of it, and his own father didn't give a damn. "Well, *do you*?"

It had to be the most he'd ever raised his voice to the man, but he didn't regret it. Not even when his father swung back around, the surprise in his eyes snapping to anger. "You've made it clear what you think of my opinions."

A grudge from the supper club. Granted, accusing his father of jealousy was an ugly claim, one with little substance. Jim Reed was the prideful type, never envious. But Ellis, feeling knocked to the floor, had scraped for any ammo within reach.

Evidently, his father was still carting around that bullet.

Recognizing this, Ellis tried to tamp his emotions. "Pop, I'm sorry. The things I said to you last time… I didn't mean 'em. Can't you understand? I just wanted to show you how well I'd done. Let you see what I've accomplished."

"Oh, I understand plenty." His father hitched his hands on the hips of his trousers. "And I've got enough smarts to know that if you keep up with all these fancy ambitions of yours, you'll be in Leavenworth next. Or maybe that's what you want. Anything for a headline. Ain't that the business?"

Why wouldn't he ever listen to Ellis? Really listen. "Look, I know how you feel about newspapermen. I've heard all about your run-in with the reporter at the mine, the one you quit over. But we're not all like that."

His father flinched, caught off guard.

"*I'm* not like that."

Ellis wasn't being strategic, only honest. Still, the lie in the claim pinged his conscience.

He couldn't deny the dollars he'd sprinkled here and there, making deals, trading for scoops. Truth of it was, he'd taken pride in separating himself from the vultures who'd do anything to anyone to land a story. Yet ever so steadily, that line had blurred.

"Then why in God's name," his father said coolly, "am I here bailing you out of jail?"

It wasn't a real question, just another jab. Another assumption.

Ellis was too worn, in every way, to hold back the hurt and frustration compounding inside. "You want another apology? Fine. I'm sorry for letting you down tonight, and for quitting at the plant. I'm sorry my job at the *Examiner* meant working for peanuts. I'm sorry for every goddamn time I wasn't good enough for you. Most of all, I'm sorry that when my brother died, you lost the wrong son!"

And there it was.

The unspoken had finally tumbled out.

His father stared at him wide-eyed. This time, there was no one around to ease the tension, no mother's hands to tenderly, deftly hold the family together.

Somewhere in the distance, a dog howled. Head lamps flashed as a taxicab passed.

"Get in the truck." His father's voice gave up nothing. He just turned and plodded toward the driver's side.

Ellis was shouting in his head, *That's it? That's all you're gonna say?*

The futility of it all left him bare and raw. Defeated. And so, in silence, he climbed inside. His father started the engine, anxious to leave.

He wasn't the only one.

Ellis envisioned returning to the school, retrieving his car, and clambering into bed. He'd try to forget, for even a few hours, the decisions awaiting him tomorrow.

But then he noticed the truck sat idle. Hands on the steering wheel, his father was gazing out the windshield. Across the street, moonlight streaked the courthouse.

"Pop?" Ellis managed.

For a second, he questioned if his father was breathing. When the man spoke, it was as if to himself. "A shaft collapsed at the mine."

Ellis waited for more, confounded.

"Took thirty hours to get the men out. I'd just gotten home when you fell from your bike. Broke your arm. Your mama took you to the doctor while the baby was napping. I must've drifted off, 'cause next thing I heard was your mama yelling. 'Henry's not breathing,' she was saying and holding him. And his lips were blue, and his face—" On this, his voice broke. His strong, calloused hands held a tremor.

Ellis sat in shock, as much from the story as the sight of tears in his father's eyes.

"I was twenty damn feet away. If I'd looked in on him, just once..."

The sentence dangled, the alternate outcome going unsaid.

Ellis looked out into the night, and a collage of memories whirred through his mind. They zipped and collided like fireflies in a jar. From a kid's view, he'd seen the day so differently. The past two decades, for that matter. The distancing, the gruffness. The fourth chair at the dinner table, always vacant but full. He recalled the late-night pacing that had woken him as a kid, footsteps weighted by grief—and guilt.

How on earth was Ellis to respond?

He considered his mother's words. How babies can stop breathing for no good reason. How his brother was at peace, living with the angels. His father had surely heard it all, even stowed it in the logical part of his brain. But this wasn't about logic.

On the steering wheel, his father's grip shifted. Ellis feared that this moment, a tenuous bond connecting them, would end.

"I can understand," he offered.

The assurance rang empty without specifics.

While aware his own burden could never compare, it seemed fitting to reciprocate with what he had. A dark truth that ultimately had led them here tonight, literally to this spot.

Without another thought, barring any censor, Ellis backed up to the beginning. It was a story that went beyond his summary to Lily, before his overheated engine and two boys on a porch. At the true start were his youthful aspirations for both acceptance and vanity.

His father's attention edged his way.

As Ellis moved on to the highlights of his feature and the Dillards, the commonalities he shared with his father emerged: their tales of tragedy and children and a longing to right irreversible wrongs.

When at last he'd finished, a thick quiet settled between them. For once, that silence didn't feel like judgment.

"What'll you do?" his father asked.

A real question.

"I don't know. Can't give up, though. Not till those kids are safe."

His father nodded. "You'll figure something out." There was a certainty in his voice, a glint of faith in his eyes that meant more to Ellis than perhaps was intended, but he revered it all the same.

In a typical talkie at the cinemas, this would be when the father embraced his son, or at minimum gave a squeeze to the shoulder. There was none of that here. They simply drove on toward Ellis's car. Outside the school, however, stepping down from the truck, Ellis turned to extend his hand. And his father shook it. Not just kindly. As more like an equal.

"You know where to find me," he said to Ellis, who warmed at the words, spoken like a promise.

"I do, Pop."

~

On the drive back to the Bronx, Ellis thought of his parents, his mother in particular. All these years, she'd never said a word about his father's guilt. Could be that she didn't view it as her story to tell. Maybe she was trying to protect Ellis, whose accident that fateful day was the reason they'd left the house. Or maybe, quite simply, she'd yearned to move on, telling herself that what was done was done.

Unlike the case of the Dillards.

Ellis couldn't help feeling for the Millstones' loss. Nevertheless, he'd do whatever it took to help Ruby and Calvin—in part for his father. So long as it wasn't too late, as it was for Henry, he'd find a way to reunite the family.

Geraldine yearned for the same. Ellis knew it in his heart without her having to spell it out. Lily was right about that all along.

It occurred to him to tell her so when she phoned that night, mere minutes after he'd gotten home. But given the hour—it was well after eleven—his concern shot to her son.

"Oh gosh, no," she told him. "Samuel's just fine." Her gratitude projected through her near whispering. He pictured her in the quiet of her boardinghouse. "I wouldn't have troubled you so late. It's just that I've been trying to reach you all evening."

"Sorry about that," he said. "I guess it's been a long day."

She paused. "Are you all right, Ellis?" The question brimmed with worry, but it was the comfort of her voice that muted all else.

"I'll be fine." He had no inkling if it was the truth, but at least she made him feel hopeful. "What about you, Lily? Is there something you needed?"

"Oh. Yes." She seemed to forget for a second. "I have to tell you what I've learned. It's about finding Calvin—it's good news."

After the day he'd had, Ellis could definitely use some of that now.

Something in her tone, though, said she wasn't sure of her own claim.

～

The orphanage was in Clover. It was two hours west of Hoboken. Close enough for the housekeeper to get there and back within a school day. Far enough to easily hide ties to the Millstones.

A vision of Calvin recognizing the lie of his outing—his terror and confusion of being dumped for convenience—renewed Ellis's anger, shoving out sympathy. For Sylvia and Alfred both.

Even if Alfred had been kept unaware, as the housekeeper indicated to Lily, wouldn't he have suspected something? Did he just not want to know?

At the *Tribune*, Ellis set the possibilities aside. It was nearly three on Wednesday. He needed to focus long enough to finish his piece about a stamp trader's fraudulent scheme. More than anything, it diverted him from any doubt over defying Sylvia's deal.

In an hour, he'd head out to meet Lily in Clover. Over at the *Examiner*, the instant the chief left for the day—right around four, she'd said—she would jump on the very next bus.

For Ellis, ditching another day of work wasn't all that dim-witted. It was just a matter of time before his career fully unraveled, either by Sylvia's doing or on its own. One way or another, Mr. Walker, now off meeting with Governor Roosevelt, would learn of the arrest. A permanent blot on a résumé for a reporter barely getting by.

Until then, Ellis would savor this moment, hunched over his typewriter, making calls and asking questions, surrounded by story hunters and truth seekers. Ink slingers trying to make a difference, as Ellis had wanted to do from the start.

"Got a big tip here." Dutch tossed a paper onto Ellis's desk. "Involves a cop."

Ellis bristled. He half expected the page to be a receipt for his bail from striking an officer. But it was just notes in Dutch's usual chicken scratches.

"Four cops to be exact. Dry agent says they helped twenty gangsters escape with trucks loaded with beer."

"You're right. That is a big one."

"It's yours."

Ellis was puzzled until he figured it out. A mercy scoop. His downward spiral had become that pathetically obvious.

"I appreciate it, Dutch. But really, I can't take that from you."

"Already have. When you missed yesterday's meeting—off back-alley sparring, from the looks of you—I said you were out working on the piece. Walker said he wants it by day's end. So, you sure as hell better get busy, or it'll mean my hide. These notes'll give you a good start."

Reminded of the scrape on his face, now bruised, Ellis also recalled why he couldn't make that deadline. "I wish I could, believe me. There's some personal stuff I gotta see about today. Can't guarantee when I'll be back."

Dutch had every right to think he'd lost his marbles and to say so outright. Instead, he appeared uncertain about commenting before leaning forward with a furtive look. "Reed, if you're in trouble—from playing the track, taking a loan, whatever—you can tell me. I had a brother-in-law who got in deep with a group like the Black Hand. So, if there's something going on with you, and I can help in some way…"

It was a reasonable deduction. What with Ellis's inquiry on the topic, his erratic behavior, not to mention the scuffed-up face, it definitely added up.

"It's nothing like that. Honest." Ellis wanted to divulge more, but he'd burdened enough people already.

Dutch blew out a sigh before retrieving his notes. Wisely, he walked away.

~

An hour later, Ellis quietly gathered up to leave. He'd submitted his piece on the stamp trader's racket, a half-decent article at best, and boarded the elevator. As the door closed, he caught the stink eye from Mr. Tate, a warning. Likely Ellis's last. But with Lily already en route, he couldn't turn back.

A block down from the paper, Ellis cranked the engine of his Model T. The motor barely sputtered.

"Christ. Not today." Sweat beading along his hairline, he pitched his hat into the car. He blew out a breath, then clutched the fender for leverage and tried again. The clunker coughed to life, dying a few seconds later, but it was coming around.

"Need some help, pal?" The offer came from a suited man with a hefty build. He dangled a cigarette low at his side.

"Nah, thanks. Motor's just stubborn sometimes."

"How's about we give you a ride?"

Ellis was about to decline when he caught the "we" in the question, raising his head.

"C'mon. Chariot's right over there." The man gestured to a black Packard parked two spaces back. The driver's eyes were indistinct, partially shadowed by the brim of his hat, but his face struck as familiar. Specifically the pockmarked cheeks. He was the driver who'd trailed Ellis to the school.

Ellis hadn't been paranoid after all. He tightened his hold on the crank, preparing to pull it free.

"As I was saying," the stocky one pressed, "how's about that ride?" He opened his jacket, exposing a holstered pistol. The smirk on his face was more of a dare than a threat, as if wanting Ellis to try. For the sport of it. For kicks.

Ellis surrendered his grip and came upright. He didn't know who the men were or what they wanted. But he did know one thing.

Sitting in the back seat of a Packard had undeniably more appeal than being stuffed in the trunk.

CHAPTER 34

LILY'S IMPATIENCE SWELLED with every passing minute. At the bus station in Clover, another Greyhound came and went. Passengers climbed on and off. Exhaust fumes assaulted the air.

Too restless to sit, Lily hovered beside a wooden bench and coughed into a handkerchief, waiting for the pungency to fade. Waiting for Ellis to drive up.

When she had phoned with Claire's news, he seemed worn, though as anxious as she was to bring the Dillards together. Geraldine had given up her children solely to ensure them a better life. It seemed they were getting anything but that. Geraldine would want to know this, yet Ellis had remained levelheaded, cautioning against sounding an alert until they learned more.

Sage advice. It had been two months since Calvin was left at the orphanage. What if he had already been adopted? Or, if still there, was he being mistreated as Claire had suggested?

Oh, why had she mentioned such a thing? Lily consequently spent half the night tossing about, disturbed by visions of neglected and battered children. She pictured their young, defenseless bodies, as small as Samuel's, being punished with rods, starved of food, bound to their beds.

"Ellis," she murmured, "what in the world is keeping you?"

Over the past few weeks, quite unexpectedly, he had become a person she could rely upon, someone she could trust. More than she ever should have. Her head told her this, though when she thought of him coming to her family's aid, of carrying her son from the bath, of comforting her with his arms and his words, it was near impossible to feel she had misjudged.

Either way, her window of time was narrowing, limited by the departure of the last return bus. The sun had just dipped behind the roofline of the town, an area reminiscent of Maryville. Already, most of the businesses lining the street were closing for the night.

Purse tucked under her arm, Lily marched over to the ticket clerk. "Pardon me, sir. I was hoping you could point me in the right direction."

Making her case at the orphanage without Ellis's support and testimony was going to be a challenge. Nonetheless, she would go it alone.

~

The walk stretched for more than a mile. Soreness in Lily's arches told her as much. Had she anticipated the hike, she would have worn more comfortable shoes. She just hoped the overcast sky would withhold its moisture a while longer.

Following the directions by memory, she continued past a group of children playing stickball in an empty lot. On the porch of a nearby house, an elderly man slept on his rocker. Next door, a woman was beating dust from a rug.

Lily debated on interrupting to confirm the accuracy of her path. But as she neared another road, she spotted an old brick warehouse fitting the clerk's description.

McFarland Tanning Factory was painted in white faded letters. Rows of windows dotted both levels. The orange glow of the sun blocked hints of what lay inside.

Only when she approached the front door did she find proof of the building's transformation. Over the entrance hung a sign that solidified Claire's heartbreaking tale.

WARREN COUNTY HOME FOR CHILDREN

Since the market crashed, Philly's many abandoned warehouses had become common refuges for squatters. But imagining such a place full of youngsters all alone in the world caused Lily an intake of breath.

Girding herself, she tugged twice on a dangling chain, ringing a bell. After a wait, likely shorter than it seemed, a small square in the metal door swung open, revealing a single eye.

Lily felt a sudden need for a password, as if negotiating entry into a discerning underground club. She cheerfully raised a gloved hand. "Good evening." Before she could say more, the viewing square slapped shut. She appeared to have failed the test until a low screech suggested the release of a bolt, and the door opened.

The woman had skin the color of molasses and wore a simple brown dress that hung loose on her stout frame. The stains on her apron and the frizzy locks sprouting from her headscarf denoted a long day of physical work. "You here for Mr. Lowell?"

"I've come in hopes of taking home a particular child. If Mr. Lowell is the person to speak with, then I certainly am." Lily pinned on a smile to up her chances of making it past the entry.

"Well, c'mon then." The woman waved her in and reset the bolt. Its metallic screech prickled the roots of Lily's chignon. Securing children inside for their safety was obviously a practical measure—yet equally suited for a prison.

Lily was escorted down a hall, past doorways that afforded glimpses of two classrooms with bookshelves, blackboards, and American flags. A third room appeared to be for playing, equipped with building blocks and other small toys piled near a wooden rocking horse, its mane of yarn frayed from use.

Aside from the building's faint scent of leather, the interior barely resembled a factory. In fact, for an orphanage, it seemed a rather pleasant setting.

At the fourth and final door, the guide held up a finger, a signal to wait. She poked her head into the room, her speech indecipherable from behind.

Lily caught the sounds of children somewhere in the vicinity. She strained to listen—not that she would know Calvin by ear—and battled a desire to sneak off in a search.

"Please, come in." The man's greeting turned her toward the office. "I'm Frederick Lowell, the director here." He rose from his desk, its surface eclipsed by papers and folders, much like the chief's but set in neat stacks. On the wall to the right, a corkboard even displayed scraps and notes in an organized fashion.

As Lily entered, Mr. Lowell gestured toward a pair of visitors' chairs, and the escort disappeared. "Do make yourself comfortable," he said.

She thanked him while they took their seats, and noticed a framed photograph above the window behind him. The woman in the portrait, perhaps the founder of the home, stared down with beady eyes. "I appreciate you seeing me unannounced, especially so late in the day."

"Well, I admit, we do usually meet by appointment, which should explain my rather shabby appearance."

Lily smiled and shook her head to dispel the claim. His reference to a lack of suit jacket, his sleeves rolled to the elbows, were easily offset by his smart plaid bow tie and peppered hair, kept as sleek as his pencil mustache. Except for a crooked nose from being broken at least once, he was rather handsome for his age of around sixty. "Sir, the reason I'm here today is to seek out a child."

"Yes. Mildred said as much. That's just the kind of news I look forward to hearing. Of course…I presume you and your husband have thought this well through." The ending inflection implied a need for confirmation. But it was the entirety of his statement that revealed his misconception of her intent, as well as her status. Her travel gloves, after all, concealed the absence of a ring—like the one from Clayton.

Strangely now, her single motherhood failed to spark the tiniest bit of shame.

"I'm afraid I need to clarify. You see, just yesterday I learned that the son of a friend was brought here by mistake. I'd be more than willing to present you with a long, detailed explanation if needed, but the short of it, Mr. Lowell, is that he belongs with his real mother."

The director showed no amazement at all. A signal of under-standing, Lily prayed, versus that of a common occurrence. "And which boy might that be?"

"Calvin Dillard." She suddenly realized a new name could have been forced upon him, as had been done with Ruby. "That was his birth name, rather. He was dropped off two months ago. I have a picture right here." She unclasped her purse to produce his photo from the newspaper when the direc-tor flitted his hand.

"No need for that. I'm very familiar with young Calvin."

"So, you…do have him?" Lily worked to restrain her hopes, an impossible task with Mr. Lowell's mouth curving upward.

"Yes," he said. "Well…we did. Until he was placed in a home."

The ground, solid just a moment before, opened beneath Lily. She felt herself falling through. *Why ever are you smiling?* she screamed in her head, unable to utter a word.

He reined in his expression, as if hearing her thoughts. "I assure you, he's with loving, God-fearing people. Their two sons are grown and gone on to other adventures, leaving the couple in the perfect position to raise another child."

The description brought Lily no comfort. The Millstones had sounded just as impressive until she took a closer look.

"I do recognize your friend's situation as unfortunate, of course." He shifted to a sympathetic tone. "To be quite frank, it's one that often brings unwanted children to our doorstep. While a mother's change of heart isn't unreasonable, it simply strikes too late at times."

Lily scrambled to recover her voice, hindered by resonance to her own past. "But that's not it. That isn't what happened."

He lifted a brow, a sign of intrigue. "You're saying...your friend's son was stolen without her knowing?"

"Not...exactly, no. But she was ill when she gave him up, and now... This is all a mistake." She could hear her own franticness, which only intensified as she grasped the condemning nature of her own argument. "Please, if you'll allow me to explain."

He opened his mouth to respond, but then his gaze shot to the doorway. "Yes, Mildred?"

"Sir, there's squabblin' in the dining room. You said if Freddy got to actin' up again—"

"Yes, yes. I'll handle it personally." The director was already on his feet when he returned his attention to Lily. "I do wish I could have been more helpful to your friend. Please tell her that Calvin is now in very good hands."

Lily stood up, tempted to block him from leaving. "Mr. Lowell, if you could just let me know who adopted him. Perhaps they would understand."

"Our records are strictly confidential, for the sake of the parents as much as the children. Now, if you'll excuse me—"

"Couldn't you make an exception, this one time? I'm begging you."

His lips became a firm line, his nostrils flaring in annoyance, perhaps over the delay or from having to repeat himself. There was no longer a dash of handsomeness about him. "I don't ascribe to exceptions, and I believe those of strong moral fiber should not either. As I was saying, Mildred will kindly see you out."

Short of grabbing his leg, Lily could think of no way to stop him as he whisked past her and out the door. The only thing keeping tears from pouring rivulets down her face was the shock she was still absorbing.

And the sight of the files.

On his desk.

Within reach.

"Miss?"

The address was for Lily, an ushering toward the exit. She detected urgency from Mildred. Upon returning, her boss wouldn't appreciate discovering his order unheeded.

Lily acquiesced—what else could she do?—and trailed the woman out.

But she would be back.

And somehow, she would find the information she needed.

CHAPTER 35

AS A NEWSPAPERMAN, Ellis was fully aware how often bodies were fished out of the Hudson. One of the uglier effects of Prohibition. He'd seen the photos too gruesome to publish: the bloated limbs, the tattered skin, the empty sockets.

In the back seat of a Packard now, he batted away visions of himself as a lifeless heap. It was harder to do on a wordless ride with two Mafia types up front. Neither had given hints of destination or purpose. Just patted him down before trapping him inside.

To stave off panic, Ellis remained a reporter. He observed and deduced, forging a distance from the situation.

When Sylvia had voiced her ultimatum, she didn't specify a deadline. Maybe today was the day, and her husband's buddies were tasked with ensuring the right answer. Maybe they were about to eliminate the need for an answer at all.

"Any chance of clueing me in, gentlemen? I could save us time if you told me what you wanted." It was worth another try. But the pockmarked man kept right on driving. The heftier one just puffed on his cigarette with the windows closed. Ellis suppressed a cough, relying on tolerance from the paper's daily haze.

A glance out the window said they were still in New York. The Bronx, in fact. And it dawned on Ellis that they were heading to his own apartment. Not a bad idea, if the plan were to stage an accident. A fatal slip in a bathtub, a tragic fall from a window.

At least his parked car across from the paper would serve as a telling clue.

Unless it was moved.

Ellis pushed down a swallow. The air turned thick as sludge.

Then came a jolt. A tap to the brakes slowed them just enough to cut a left into an alley, and the car rolled to a stop. Both escorts opened their doors and stepped out.

"Let's go," the driver told Ellis.

Yesterday, a guard had used the same order to prod Ellis from his cell. Being back in jail had striking new appeal.

Out of the car, he noted a door at the top of a metal staircase. He'd been here before...

"*Move.*"

Ellis was shoved from behind. His knees weakened from anticipation as he trudged up the steps. The driver, just a few feet back, was taller than Ellis had first guessed.

The stocky man remained by the car, lighting a fresh cigarette. His choice not to join them provided only minimal relief. No doubt the driver was also armed and equally comfortable pulling a trigger.

Inside, Ellis led the way into an unlit hall. The door slammed. The scene went black as pitch. Darkness closed in around him, a tunnel awaiting a hurtling train.

"Go."

Ellis plodded forward as best he could, avoiding another push that could land him on his skull. His vision was adjusting. When he reached a coat-check table that led to a draped doorway, recognition fully set in.

This was the Royal. The supper club where he'd taken his parents. Same as then, the dining room glowed beneath a large chandelier. Only this time, the place was as quiet and still as a graveyard. Ellis was glad to not find himself in a dank, abandoned warehouse, though not overjoyed.

As he continued over the club's checkered tiles, the driver stayed on his heels. Their footsteps echoed off the high ceiling. Chairs, turned upside down, were balanced on tables now bare of linens. No candles or dinnerware. No witnesses in sight. Only terror creeping in.

There was little worse, Ellis decided, than suspense from the unknown. He wheeled around and stopped. "If you're gonna take me out, get on with it. Otherwise, tell me why we're here."

The driver stared back, emotionless, before a crashing noise rang out. It traveled through the swinging door of the kitchen, on the wall to the right. A cook had dropped some pans, Ellis figured—until he heard the muffled groans, broken up by the sounds of skin hitting skin. Meat being tenderized. Someone was taking a beating.

No need to guess who'd be next.

"Ellis Reed." The voice came from behind. At the end booth, partially obscured by a white privacy curtain, a man sat snipping a cigar.

Anxiety shot through Ellis, filling every limb. Max Trevino looked no less formidable in person than he did in the papers. His neck was as thick as his shoulders, set off by an expensive, tailored suit. His black hair was slicked, fringed with gray. He had the dark eyes and bearing of a typical Sicilian.

"Have a seat, kid." Max directed him with a wave of a cigar cutter.

Ellis managed the remaining steps to reach the table. As he edged himself into the booth, the driver stood guard no more than two skips away.

"You know," Max said, "I've been familiar with your work for quite some time."

"I'm…flattered, sir."

"You shouldn't be."

Potential replies spun through Ellis's head. He opted for silence.

Max stoked his cigar with a gold lighter and exhaled an earthy cloud. "A few stories of yours caused trouble for my ventures a while back. As a businessman, I like things to run smoothly. A well-oiled machine. You understand, yeah?"

Ellis considered his old tip-offs from the Irish Mob. Several resulting articles had exposed crimes by politicians whose pockets were often padded by other competing gangs. Apparently, some of that padding came from Max.

"Hell, what am I thinking? Course you do," Max said. "After fifteen years of your old man's factory work, I bet he's taught you all about that."

The remark, flaunting his knowledge of Ellis's father, was jarring even without the noises in the background. Another punch, another groan. From a room stocked with knives.

Ellis struggled to keep his tone even. "What is it you want, Mr. Trevino?"

"This. To talk." The levity in the reply was almost convincing.

"What about?"

"Family. Importance of protecting it. I can tell we see eye to eye on this already." Max pulled several puffs from his cigar and reclined into the cushioned seat, his implied threat hanging amid the smoke. "Thing is, I hear you and another reporter—a lady friend of yours—have taken quite an interest in my sister's affairs."

His sister?

Right then, Ellis recalled something Alfred had said back at the bank. How family in New York had long been the attraction to moving out East. "You're Sylvia's brother," Ellis realized.

His editor's warning had been more about her than Alfred.

Max raised a dense black brow. "Don't play dumb, kid. I ain't got patience for people wasting my time."

The assumption was fair. Any decent reporter would have made the connection by now. Ellis had just been too busy with the Dillards, and Samuel, and yeah, time in the clink.

"I'll do my best not to."

Max studied his face, scanning for sarcasm. Ellis didn't dare flinch. "As I was saying," Max went on. "If you happened to dig up something interesting, I think we ought to discuss it. Off the record, as it were."

It was clear that little in Max's life was meant *for* the record.

"Eh, Mr. Trevino," a man called over, having emerged from the kitchen. He had to be three hundred pounds, an equal mix of fat and muscle, and was wiping his hands on a towel. Its red smears were decidedly not from tomato sauce. Ellis tried not to picture the condition of the face, or whole body, that had taken the pounding. "I think we're done in here. Need anything else?"

"Not sure yet," Max said. "How 'bout you stick around a while?"

"Happy to." The mountainous goon flicked a glance toward Ellis. "I'll just be tidying up," he said before disappearing through the swinging door. If not for more moans from the kitchen, the comment would have sounded like code for the disposal of a stiff.

A task possibly still on the agenda if Ellis wasn't careful.

Max returned his focus to the table. "So?" he prompted, picking up where they'd left off.

Ellis steadied his hands, his breathing. Any hint of dishonesty could prove detrimental. Not just to him and his parents, but even to Lily, whom he suddenly feared he might never see again. "Sir, I've got nothing but good intentions involving your family."

Though darkly quiet as he smoked, Max was listening.

Ellis kept mindful of the man's time and values and mentally scrambled to simplify the summary. "There were two kids, you

see, with a sign. But the picture I took, it was only for a feature."
He moved right along to an unplanned sale that divided a family.
No need for dates or names or any other detail that weighed
down the basics. Then he leapt to his worries over a mother,
now cured but alone, and the well-being of the children. "Your
sister too," he was quick to add.

Max had gone still. It was difficult to tell if he was glowering
or contemplating. "What *exactly* do you think you know about
her?"

If nothing else, Ellis knew this for certain: he was treading on
tenuous ground.

He took an extra moment, cautiously navigating the exchange.
He was about to reply when Max said, "Sal?"

In an instant, the driver gripped Ellis by the front collar of
his shirt. Ellis reflexively tried to resist, the pressure of the man's
knuckles tight against his throat.

"Mr. Trevino asked you a question," Sal told him.

Weaseling out with a softened, bullshit answer about Max's
sister was the most obvious move. It was Ellis's best shot at getting
out of here in one piece, literally. But his instincts—or maybe
dumb hope—said Max harbored similar concerns. That this,
more than any alleged article, was the reason for this meeting.

"I'm no expert," Ellis said, his voice strained from Sal's hold,
"but I'll share what I got."

After a pause, Max's solitary nod cued Sal to back off. Ellis
caught his breath and scraped his words together in a hurry.
While aware of the risks of being flat-out wrong, he would dare
to be candid.

Max took occasional slow puffs as Ellis spilled what he'd
gathered. He recounted the troubling observations he'd seen
and heard, the growing signs of delusion. The threats to Ellis, no
matter how depraved, would mean little in this place. So rather,
he spoke of Ruby's inherited clothes and name, of the cruel
letters and lies, of a brother secretly ripped away. He described

the many hours of punishments for hindering the resurrection of a daughter—a niece—who, in reality, was gone.

By the time Ellis finished, Max was fingering his cutter, its circular opening the size of a man's thumb. Piling on more arguments would be a gamble. There was a fine line between supplying information and dictating an opinion.

In the end, Ellis took the chance. "Quite simply, sir, I'd say you've got two choices. Your sister loses the girl...or, before long, you lose your sister."

Max's fingers slowed. The corners of his eyes tightened the slightest amount. The wait that followed brought no reassurance.

At last, he replied with finality, "A man's gotta do what's best for his family."

The ambiguity of what that meant held Ellis in place. Behind him, the squeak of a shoe indicated Sal was again moving closer. No doubt he was itching to resume one of the grimmer perks of his job.

"Tomorrow morning—eight sharp," Max stated. "You meet me at Sylvia's, and the girl goes back where she belongs. *Capeesh?*"

The unexpected plan, let alone the speed of it all, threw Ellis off. He fell wordless until Max leaned forward. "I trust you ain't got a problem with this."

Preventing another grip to the throat, Ellis answered, "N-no. Not at all, Mr. Trevino."

Max took another pull off his cigar and reclined once more. "Sal, we're finished here. Give Mr. Reed a lift back."

In stoic compliance, Sal started for the exit. Ellis hurried out of the booth to follow. This time, he'd be the one trailing behind but wishing he could charge to the front.

A few steps in, he realized he hadn't voiced his thanks. It was more of an investment than a courtesy. He turned around to find Max lost in thought, and knew not to interrupt. Particularly with pensiveness riding the man's features. The duty of telling his sister the news had to be a source of dread.

Just hopefully not enough to change Max's mind.

CHAPTER 36

LILY HAD EVERY RIGHT to be cross. Ellis was well over an hour late. And yet, when he stepped through the entry of the dimly lit pub—among the few establishments still open in town—only relief poured through her.

He appeared to feel the same. Upon spotting her, he marched straight to her table in the corner. "I'll explain," he assured her. "I'm just so glad I found you. I was afraid you'd headed home by now." He had taken a chance, traveling all this way, searching the area for her.

"Yes, well…there's a reason I stayed." She hesitated to share the news, but his expectant look pressed her on. "He's been adopted, Ellis, but I *know* we can still find him." She emphasized the last portion before catching her own volume. There were enough local patrons scattered about to be cautious.

Ellis sat across from her, his interest captured, as she caught him up and detailed her plan. "To be safe, we really ought to wait another hour. By then, the lights in the orphanage should be out for the night. The front door is heavily bolted, and other doors might be the same. But in an old building with so many windows, there simply has to be a way to sneak inside and peek at those files."

When she paused, Ellis's lack of reaction made her cringe. He had to think she was mad. What if they were caught? The director was hardly the lenient type. They could wind up before a judge, their careers and reputations destroyed no matter the verdict. Not to mention the fresh dose of gossip that would plague her family.

But they couldn't just give up. *She* couldn't.

"Ellis, if you don't want to be part of it, I'd fully—"

"I'm in." There wasn't a speck of wavering, and that confidence helped fuel her own. Still, the way he looked at her with those blue eyes nearly made her forget her purpose.

Then a noise intervened, a small relief. It took her a second to identify the growl of his stomach. A similar recollection came to her, from their time at Franklin Square.

She suppressed a smile as she slid over her bowl and spoon. "Do you *ever* remember to eat?"

He took a whiff of her remaining stew, and his mouth curved upward. "Only with you, apparently." His sigh after the third bite suggested more than one skipped meal.

As he continued to eat, Lily sought to avoid dwelling on the risks of the mission ahead. "It just occurred to me," she said, "that day in the park, you never told me the story."

He was in the midst of a swallow when he looked up, uncertain. "About a duck and…gelatin, was it?"

He half chuckled, half coughed.

"Sorry."

He cleared his throat and shook his head. "It's a silly thing. Nothing worth repeating."

"From the sound of it, I highly doubt that." She pressured him with a playful stare until he raised his spoon in a show of surrender and sat back from his stew.

"I was about ten, I guess. Wanted to go pheasant hunting with Pop, so I tried to work up the gumption to shoot a real bird. When no one was home, I took our four-ten shotgun outside, along with a carrot-and-spinach gelatin mold that Ma made for a potluck supper with some mining folks."

Lily could see where this was going. "Oh gosh. You didn't…"

"The shell was just full of tiny BBs. I didn't think a single shot could do that much damage."

"It exploded?"

"To a million bits—which wasn't such a bad thing, given its god-awful taste. Problem was, it splattered an orange-and-green mess all over our sheets hanging to dry."

She couldn't help but laugh, envisioning the scene. "Did you get in a heap of trouble for it?"

"Got a doozy of a lecture. Would've been the belt for sure, but I was so bruised from the recoil that I managed to get a mercy pass." He grinned at her. As if on cue, laughter burst from patrons across the pub, turning Ellis toward them. Inches below his hat, a terrible scrape marred his cheek. Was it a scuffle that had caused his delay?

She reached for the wound without thinking, and stopped herself when he angled back to her. "What is that from?"

Ellis went to answer, but more laughter arose. He swept a look around, seeming disconcerted by listeners within earshot. A reminder of their situation.

He tipped his head toward the exit. "Let's talk on the way."

～

A faint sprinkling dotted the windshield as they drove, the clouded sky darkening. It wasn't yet eight but looked to be ten. The stickball players were gone. The porches were vacant. All of this, Lily noted, would serve as an advantage.

Ellis parked down the road from the old tannery and shut

off the engine. Among the orphanage windows, a few upstairs glowed with lights. Those of the sleeping quarters would be the last ones out.

On her own, Lily would have been antsy with impatience. Instead, she was wholly engrossed, listening to Ellis's highlights from the past two days: the plea from Ruby, his arrest at the school, the confrontation with the Millstones, and a surprising deal with a mobster named Max.

Geraldine hadn't heard any of this yet; there hadn't been time, Ellis said. Besides, he was plainly digesting events more befitting a picture show with Pinkerton agents and spy rings than real life.

"At least Pop and I are on better footing." He offered a half smile. "We just might be living together again soon." It was a bare attempt to lighten the mood, burdened by looming consequences that could now be far worse.

Respectfully, Lily played along. "Well, Geraldine will sure be grateful to have Ruby back, especially once she's heard the full story. By then, hopefully we'll know where Calvin's gone. And if needed, goodness, I know my parents would gladly make room for the Dillards until they're settled."

Ellis nodded with another smile. He set aside his hat, and a wavy lock of his black hair fell over his temple.

For several seconds, Lily tried to leave the topic at that, but she couldn't. "Aren't you afraid of Sylvia, though? That she'll seek revenge of some kind?"

He ruminated a moment. "I guess I'll find out."

"If they're really the ones controlling your savings, could you ask that fellow—Max—about it?"

Ellis spurted a laugh. "When it comes to money, I get the feeling he'd be less sympathetic. Never mind on the heels of another favor."

Frustration kept Lily from relenting. Yes, she had given Ellis a piece of her mind when she feared the lure of materialism and flashy headlines were changing him for the worse. But to have it all stripped away was utterly unfair.

And having him help her tonight could severely compound the situation, she realized. "If you're already facing charges... Ellis, you shouldn't be here."

"And give you all the glory? Fat chance."

"I'm serious. You don't have to do this."

"Yes. I do."

"But the risks you'd be taking—"

"Aren't all that different from yours."

She could argue about his higher stakes, yet the resolve on his face said there was no point. Then he looked at her through the fuzzy grayness, his features softening. "It'll be okay. Whatever happens, we're doing the right thing."

At the gentleness of his tone—a true reflection of him, she had learned—the buffer around her heart closed in. He parted his lips as if sensing this, and over the steering wheel, his hand eased downward. The possibility that he would reach out and touch her cheek, kissing her as he once had, trapped the breath in her throat. The sensations of that moment flowed back: the feel of his fingers in her hair, of trailing down the side of her neck.

But his fingers suddenly curled under, settling on his leg.

A message, unintended or not.

She shifted toward her window. With a discreet exhale, she wiped the images from her thoughts, grateful he couldn't see them.

Would the lights in the orphanage ever turn off?

"You do realize," he said after a bit, "if we pull this off, it could make great material for your own column before long."

Aside from the chief, she hadn't discussed her offer with another soul. She turned back to Ellis. "You heard?"

He appeared just as baffled as she was. "You landed a column?"

"I thought... You sounded as if you knew."

"I didn't," he said.

"Then, how...?"

He shrugged with an amused air. "Just seen you with Nellie Bly's books about a thousand times. Always figured she'd brought you to the paper from the start."

Lily was touched by his close attention, though she wouldn't dare tell him so. "Am I that predictable?"

"Based on tonight? I'd say you're anything but that." She broke into a smile, which he sweetly mirrored, adding the charm of curved lines to his cheeks. "Anyway, congratulations. To get a slot like that from the chief, your writing must've really wowed him."

"I think it was more a matter of pestering to the point of wearing him down."

"I doubt that. The chief never had much trouble with the word 'no.'"

That much was true, and the compliment filled her with a heady sense of pride.

"So, when does the column start?"

She had no answer. As she remembered why that was, the purse on her lap gained the weight of iron. Specifically from the diamond ring inside. An anchor to reality.

"Actually...I'm not entirely sure it's going to."

"Sorry?"

"It's just that my plans might be changing."

He peered at her, a wordless prod.

The news business was a small community, a collection of professional gossipers. Ellis deserved to hear it directly from her.

"Clayton's been offered a job. It's on the national desk at the *Chicago Tribune*. He wants us to go with him. I mean, not *us*, us." She motioned back and forth between herself and Ellis, growing flustered. How ridiculous of her to clarify. "What I'm saying is, he's proposed."

Ellis's eyes went wide. "I...didn't realize..."

Good heavens. She could see him revisiting their time in the kitchen. He thought she had withheld this from him.

"It's new news," she told him. "Brand new. I've barely had a moment to process it, with the Dillards and all."

"And you're accepting?"

She didn't know yet—though she should. As planned, Clayton had given his notice at the *Examiner*, evidenced by the chief's crabbiness that would fade only with time. She had consequently spent the day steering clear of her boss unless necessary. For a vastly different reason, she had done the same with Clayton. He would want an answer soon, and she would give him one.

The right one, she hoped.

"I...think I am..."

Ellis went to speak but seemed to change course. "What about the column?"

"I suppose it would have to wait. It's really not that important." She mustered certainty as she went. "Being with Samuel, creating a family, that's what matters."

After a pointed pause, Ellis offered a pleased look. His eyes, though, said he was unconvinced.

"Please don't do that."

"Do what?"

Look at me that way. Like you understand everything about me. "What happened between us...you and me... I was emotional after Samuel's fever, and I was grateful for your help and for what you said. It truly meant so much. But I can't make another mistake, not with my son to think of. And Clayton... He's a good man, and he'll be a kind, dependable father. I couldn't ask for anything more."

Ellis just held there, taking in her words. When he leaned back in his seat, he conveyed his understanding through a wistful smile. "I'm happy for all of you. I am."

She refused to meet his eyes, determined not to falter. "Thank you."

Over the eternal stretch that followed, tension turned thick as stone. It formed with little effort, both of them experts at forging walls around them.

"It's time," he said at last and grabbed a flashlight from under his seat.

Only when he climbed out did she realize the orphanage had gone dark.

CHAPTER 37

THIS WAS THE ROOM. Aiming his flashlight through the chest-high window, Ellis confirmed they were outside the office. A pair of stacked files awaited on the desk, just as Lily had described.

The only problem: the room's lone window wouldn't budge. He shoved harder, but the lock was set.

"How about this one?" Lily whispered, already moving on.

Ellis followed and beamed his light into the neighboring room. An array of toys denoted a play area. He tried to gain entry.

No luck. On to the next.

This one was a classroom.

Same result.

Just a handful of windows remained on the first floor, at least on this side of the building. Still, the odds of finding any of them unlocked looked slim.

It was a unique precaution in a town this small.

Lily shot him a glance, as if sharing the thought. Shadows underscored the apprehension in her face. But that didn't stop her from continuing to another room, hands splayed, ready to give it a go herself.

"Hold on," he cautioned. He needed to assess it first.

Not waiting, she gave the window a shove and brightened when it rose an inch.

She was driving him batty—for more reasons than this. But he couldn't think about those now.

Fortunately, the space was vacant, another classroom resembling the first.

He stored the flashlight in his coat pocket, and they shimmied the pane upward, one side at a time, until the gap was large enough to climb through. Lily grabbed hold of the windowsill. It was too high to pull herself up, but her reluctance to ask for his help was evident.

His inclination to offer was almost as strong, in spite of any good sense. "Here, I'll give you a boost." He formed a step by lacing his fingers. Given the constraints of her work skirt, he squatted to an accommodating height.

What other options did they have?

After slipping out of her heels, she again grasped the sill. On his linked palms, she placed her foot, slick in a silk stocking, and pushed off. He averted his eyes from the length of her body, just inches from his face, as she stretched over him and into the room.

His turn to go.

He heaved himself up, wary of rattling the glass panes overhead. A low bookshelf aided his landing. Safely on the floor, he righted himself, just as his flashlight slid out.

Clunk. He swiped it up.

Breath held, they stared at the half-open door. It seemed to slowly swing wider on its own. A trick of vision at night.

Silence stretched out long enough to suggest they were in the clear.

With ragged sighs, they proceeded past orderly rows of school desks and chairs. Lily peered into the hallway before tiptoeing out. Ellis followed, still listening for signs of other movement. Three doors down, she stopped before the office—identified through the glass of the door—and gave the knob a twist. She looked at him, her worries magnified.

Locked.

Ellis wasn't as troubled. Having a father who preferred tinkering with machinery to conversation came with a few benefits.

He handed her the flashlight. At her confusion, he put a finger to his mouth to quiet her. Then he reached over her shoulder and slid two hairpins from her updo. Her auburn locks unwound, falling loose around her neck. By then, she understood and scooted aside. She trained the white beam on the door.

On one knee, Ellis inserted the pins into the knob. It was a basic one, the sole reason he ventured to try. Besides a dumb impulse to impress her.

He needed to concentrate. It had been years since he'd done this—back in his rebellious period, on a dare to pick the lock of the door separating the boys' and girls' locker rooms. He was a hero among the fellas until the shrieks broke out.

Just like then, he maneuvered now by feel, despite rising doubt that he'd forgotten how. But then a mechanism moved, sliding free, and the lock lightly clicked. He turned the knob fully, and Lily smiled. For an instant.

She crossed the room and delved straight into a stack of folders on the desk. Ellis closed the door and nabbed the second pile. It didn't take him long to finish. Most in his batch were related to utilities and permits and other regulated business.

Lily, meanwhile, fingered through records of children. She was slowing down, her attention lingering on their photographs. Notes of their circumstances were surely heartbreaking. Ellis gave her forearm a squeeze, a begrudging reminder that there wasn't time for that. Not now.

She gathered herself and increased her pace. She was almost at the bottom.

There had to be more.

An upright file cabinet drew Ellis to the corner. He tried the handles on the three drawers. A lock at the top secured them all. Was the staff really that afraid of burglars? What the devil were they trying to protect?

That was when it struck him. All these locks—on the windows, the office, the cabinets—were used because of the children. To keep *them* inside but any links to their past out of reach.

"He's not here," Lily whispered before noting Ellis's find. "Can you pick it?"

He shook his head. Even if he knew how, it was too small for the pins. "The key's gotta be here somewhere."

They quickly went to work, splitting up the room. Ellis ran his hands over surfaces in search of a hiding spot. Behind the file cabinet, atop the corkboard, above the doorframe.

"Ellis…" Lily was staring into a desk drawer. A drawer with more files. She looked up. "It's him."

He rushed to see for himself. Sure enough, in the second folder from the top, the boy's picture was stapled to a page. *Calvin*, it read. Ellis knew that round face, those cupid lips. The thick lashes and impossibly large eyes, now turned sad. There was no listed surname. Just another kid from the street, parentless and unwanted. Except that he was none of those.

They skimmed the next sheet, and the next. There were signatures, a scrawled address—

A creak made Ellis turn. Lily winced. It was the sound of metal pipes, the weathered bones of a building settling. A good reminder to wrap things up.

Lily left the top page. She stuffed the other two in her coat pocket as Ellis replaced the file. With the classroom window still open, it was best to go out the way they came.

Another peek into the hallway, a locking of the door, and they were back at the bookshelf. It would be easier to help her climb down if he was on the outside. "I'll go first," he told her. He was just raising his knee when the room lit up. A near-blinding flash.

They spun around. A colored woman stood at the doorway, hand on the light switch, eyes bulged with fright.

"It's me, it's me," Lily urged in a rasp, an attempt to prevent a scream. "From earlier. Remember?"

The woman shrank back, grasping the collar of her bathrobe, and her gaze cut to the file in Lily's hand.

Lily pulled the folder to herself, protecting it. "The little boy I came for—Calvin Dillard—I just needed to know where he went. So I could speak with the parents who adopted him. He was never supposed to be here. Mildred, you have to believe me."

Living in the building, presumably on the staff, Mildred must have known Calvin. She must have heard him speak about wanting to go home, or crying over missing his mom and sister.

But then, that probably didn't differentiate him from half the orphans in the place.

Ellis questioned if adding his two cents would help or hinder, but he had to do something. "Please, ma'am. I'm sure you work here because you care a lot about children. So many of them, I'd bet, would give anything to be back with their real family."

Mildred's eyes lowered as she loosened her hold on her robe, though only slightly.

"We can help do that if you let us." He stepped toward her without thinking, raising his hand in an appeal, and her face snapped up.

He'd ventured too close. He'd gambled wrong.

Then someone coughed. A man. Somewhere down the hall.

No one in the room moved.

A debate whirled in Mildred's eyes. Her job and duty versus questionable claims from strangers breaking the law. It wasn't much of a contest. She owed them nothing.

Ellis braced for her to flee and yell, sending an alarm to

the staff. He prepared to grab Lily, to hustle her through the window, ordering her to run.

Then Mildred flicked a hand. "Go on, get," she whispered. She was shooing them out.

Lily nodded readily. She scurried over to Ellis, who swiftly crawled out before guiding her down. Her stockinged feet had just landed when the window slid closed.

Ellis sent silent thanks to the woman behind the glass as Lily threw on her shoes. In seconds, the window went black.

Together they hurried back to the car. He started the engine in three tries and drove back toward the highway. Hands shaking from adrenaline, he glanced over to see how Lily was faring. Already she was examining the pilfered pages by flashlight.

"Briarsburg," she said. "In Sussex County. That's where Calvin went. It has to be…a half hour north?"

"About that." It took him a moment to realize she wanted to go now. "Lily, it's awfully late to make a house call." His caution wasn't about social graces. Disturbing the couple unannounced, particularly at this hour, might not be the best strategy.

Before he could say as much, she replied in earnest, "If the director notices the pages are gone in the morning, he just might beat us to the family."

Ellis considered the possibility. She was right.

But then, when wasn't she?

He reached into the back seat and rifled through his satchel. "You navigate, I'll drive," he said, handing her the map.

CHAPTER 38

SOMEWHERE ALONG THE WAY, they took a wrong turn. Two, in fact. Traversing unfamiliar highways and country roads was difficult enough in and of itself, much less on a moonless, rainy night. Add in weariness from the week, and it was no wonder Lily had misread the map. Twice.

All the backtracking was costing them more time, and civility. Her apologies for the errors had prompted assurances from Ellis, but only of the compulsory sort. From his growing aloofness, her own defenses arose. Combined, they formed an imposing third passenger. When at last they found Tilikum Road, she was more anxious than ever to reach their destination.

Car slowing, they rolled down their windows. There were fewer chances of locating the home through rain-streaked glass. The scents of mud and wet straw wafted in, as did moisture that dampened their seats and clothing. Minor grievances, given their objective.

"There's a house." Lily pointed toward lights set back from her side of the road. Could Calvin finally be this close?

"Look for the mailbox."

She strained her vision. Sprawling fields appeared to dominate the area. The irony that Calvin had landed in a place so similar to the home he'd lost was as comforting as it was cruel. "Right there." A tin postal box caught the beam of the head lamps.

Ellis stopped within reading distance and cleared his windshield with the manual wiper blade. The documents remained on Lily's lap, yet the couple's names and address were already etched into her mind.

She sighed at the painted numbers on the box. "It's not theirs."

"Just keep an eye out for the next."

He was right to sound unfazed. On the map, the road wasn't all that long. The correct house had to be here somewhere.

She resumed her focus as they drove on. The rattling of the engine was nearly lost to the pattering of rain and chirping of crickets.

Another wrong mailbox, and another. A fourth bore no markings, and the absence of lights implied that the residents had retired for the night. Ellis opted to bypass them for the time being, saying he would circle back if needed. As they continued, however, the chance that it was the right one gnawed at her.

"Could we go back to that last one now?" It likely meant waking the household, but past nine o'clock in a farming area, that was going to be a common challenge. And they simply had to present their case before the director had a chance.

Ellis gave her an assessing glance, as if to decide if she was acting on a hunch or out of impatience. Whichever the conclusion, he replied, "I'll flip around after this hill."

"Thank you."

The car sputtered up the remaining half of the incline, then coasted down. When the road went level, Ellis eased over to the side, allowing them the width to double back. As soon as they swung around, Lily spied another mailbox. Lit by the head lamps, its black letters on a white background read like a marquee.

GANTRY

"Stop," she said, and he did. The **A** was partially worn off, the **Y** obscured by rust, but there indeed was the surname. It matched the document signed by Bob and Ada Gantry. "That's them." Her pulse jittered.

Ellis leaned toward her, just enough to peer out her window.

A light was moving in the distance, being carried by someone. Then the figure disappeared into what looked to be a house.

"At least one person's awake," Lily said brightly.

Ellis agreed. But there was no racing to the finish line. He simply closed his window, cueing her to do the same, and rumbled slowly up the dirt drive. Scattered stones caused bumping and more rattling.

They parked near the barn. "Let me do the talking," he said. There was no arrogance in the statement, no note of condescension.

And it dawned on Lily that his stoicism over the course of the drive had been from contemplating his approach, as every word could be crucial.

"Are you sure?" she said. "I'd be glad to start it off if you'd like." True, her discussion with the orphanage director hadn't been fruitful—not directly so—but it had given her practice.

"I need to fix this." He sounded dutiful as he angled to face her. "They've had him only a few months. If they'll just agree to speak with Geraldine, I'm sure they'll understand. She's a caring, decent person. And she's Calvin's real mother. How in good conscience could they say no?"

"They couldn't," Lily agreed. Now she was the one who needed to instill confidence, regardless of her stirring fears. She even smiled. "I'll go with you."

He nodded, a flash of appreciation in his eyes.

Through the rain, they hustled toward the covered porch. The two-story farmhouse was light-colored and typical in structure, from what she could tell at night. Ellis didn't hesitate to knock, though the wait lasted an eternity.

Finally, the front door opened halfway. Behind the screen door, a woman held a kerosene lamp. She wore a house robe and slippers, a long braid draping her shoulder. Yellow flickered over her elongated face.

"Mrs. Gantry?" Ellis began.

"Yes?"

"Ma'am...I realize it's late to drop by—"

"Who's down there?" a gruff voice cut in, startling Lily.

In lieu of answering, Mrs. Gantry made way for her husband—presumably. He arrived barefoot in a long, plaid nightshirt that covered his hefty paunch. The back of his hair stood on end as if molded by a pillow.

Lily reflexively lowered her eyes a little.

"Well?" he barked, this time at Ellis.

"I do apologize if we woke you, sir."

"This damn well better be important. Come mornin', I got fields to tend to," he said as Mrs. Gantry set the lamp on the entry table. She receded into the background, looking timid but curious as her husband continued. "And if you're out to sell something, you can keep right on going."

"Not at all, Mr. Gantry. We've come about something else entirely."

The man slid his gaze toward Lily, who smiled amiably to no reaction before Ellis went on. "You see, we're here about a child you and your wife recently took in. A boy named Calvin. From the Warren County Home for Children."

Mr. Gantry appeared dubious. "Yeah. What about it?"

While "it" could have been in reference to the topic, Lily couldn't help balking at the idea that he was referring to Calvin.

At least the man had inadvertently confirmed the adoption. The realization sent Lily's mind wandering past the couple and into the house. Was Calvin upstairs, tucked into bed? Would he come running if she hollered his name?

She held herself back as Ellis presented the essentials of their predicament—of a child taken in error, a loving mother all alone—ending with hope for a solution, if only the couple would meet with Geraldine.

Mr. Gantry folded his arms over his nightshirt, his raised sleeve exposing a torpedo tattoo on his forearm. Surely from his time in the Great War, it suited his abrasive bearing well. "I see the problem you all got," he acknowledged. "Now this here's mine. I gave up good money for that boy. Bought him fair 'n' square."

Lily must have misheard. "Bought him?"

"That's right. Had fees for his shots and paperwork, and all that business. So, I got no interest in talking to no woman. I don't care what her story is. Boy'll be working the farm, like I got him for."

Lily made no effort to hide her disgust. No wonder his grown sons had up and left, rather than staying to help work the land. She glanced at Mrs. Gantry, who cowered with a look of shame before slinking out of sight.

"I'll pay you," Ellis said, preventing a retort from Lily.

Mr. Gantry squinted an eye. "What's that you say?"

"Whatever you spent, I'll reimburse you in full."

Laying the groundwork, that had been the plan. But that was prior to learning of Calvin's servitude.

Mr. Gantry studied Ellis through the screen. He was still leery but plainly, horrendously tempted. "That'd amount to twenty dollars."

"Done."

Ellis answered too quickly to have given it thought. The farmer appeared to catch that himself. He curled his bottom lip in a wry, calculating way. "Course, that's not including food and clothing and other troubles we gone to. Kids can be expensive, you know."

Ellis fell silent for several breaths. "How much?"

"Oh, I'd say doubling it to forty would be more in line."

It was clear from the tension in Ellis's jaw, if not the fisting of his hands, that his polite front was wearing thin. This was a human being, a child, they were bargaining over.

But if the men went to blows, Lily realized, even that option would vanish.

"Forty, you say?" Her question pulled Mr. Gantry's attention. She reduced her pace to feign thoughtfulness. "It would...be a stretch. But I think we can manage it."

"All right, then." He nodded smugly. Then he opened the screen door, holding it wide, and wiggled the fingers of his free hand. "Let's see it."

She looked to Ellis. He had told her earlier: with his account blocked, after buying gasoline for the trip, he had a mere three dollars to his name. As for Lily, she didn't have to scour her purse to know she didn't have more than five.

"We actually don't have it here," she admitted, "but I'd be delighted to get it to you straightaway." She would gladly take it out of the money she had saved at home.

"That's what I figured." Mr. Gantry huffed, concluding the negotiation—or maybe it had all been a test from the start. "Get off my property. And don't neither of you come back, or I'll sic the sheriff on ya." With that, he released the screen door. Before it could slam, Ellis grabbed on.

"Now, just wait—"

Mr. Gantry skewered him with a glare. He fed out his words through gritted teeth. "You get your paws off, or things are gonna go bad real quick."

Ellis surrendered his grip, letting the mesh return as a flimsy barrier, yet his tone gained an edge. "There's a little boy we need to think about here."

"Ada!" Mr. Gantry yelled without turning around. "Get me my shotgun."

Lily grabbed on to Ellis's arm and drew him back. "No need for that, sir. We're leaving. We're going right this minute."

Ellis resisted for an unnerving moment before thankfully giving in. "Sure," he said. "We'll go."

And they did.

Still, the farmer's gaze followed and didn't let up until the start of the engine. When the front door of the house closed, they stayed true to their word and drove away.

Though not as far, perhaps, as Mr. Gantry would have liked.

CHAPTER 39

"CAN THIS REALLY BE RIGHT?" Lily's question seeped through Ellis's thoughts and the thrumming of the rain. They were parked near the base of the Gantrys' drive to regroup and rethink. She was reviewing Calvin's papers, partially covering the flashlight to keep the car dim. "On the back here, it says adoptions take a year to finalize. That means it's not official yet. This should make it easier for Geraldine, shouldn't it?"

Distracted, Ellis was slow to reply. "I would hope so."

"Well...either way, we need to figure out a plan."

The truth was, a plan was taking shape that didn't include *we*.

"Could you hand me the map?" he asked. It was on the floorboard by her feet.

"The map? Why?"

Sensing she was going to object, he answered without fully looking at her. "I have to find a bus or train depot close by."

"Why's that?"

Their combined funds would be enough for a single ticket.

Of course, he would stay with her until morning when the next ride departed. "I'm sending you home."

She stared at him. "What are you talking about?"

"You need to get back early. You're due at the paper tomorrow."

"And you're not?"

"Lily, please. I promise I'll keep you updated." He held out his upturned hand. "Now, could you pass it over?" At her defiant stare, he reached down and snagged the map himself. He'd just spread it over the steering wheel when she snapped the light off.

Lord help him…

"You're going to do something foolish, aren't you?"

He dragged his gaze to meet hers.

"You heard Mr. Gantry up there. He'd jump at the chance to call the sheriff. If he doesn't grab his shotgun first."

"There's no need to worry. I'm not going to sneak into the house or break any other law." He saw no point in reminding her that busting into the orphanage had been her idea.

"Fine. Then, what *are* you planning to do?"

They were getting nowhere. To placate her, he'd reveal his thoughts. Just without mention of the dangers. "Since Mr. Gantry'll be working early in the fields—with Calvin, too, I figure—I could catch his wife on her own. She might be willing to help if given the chance. Maybe behind closed doors, she actually has some sway over her husband. Anyway, there's no harm in trying."

Unless…Mr. Gantry happened to come home early. Or if Ellis, as he'd done with the Millstones, was pegging Mrs. Gantry all wrong.

Lily pondered the proposal, and she nodded. A minor miracle. Ellis turned back to the map, still needing the flashlight.

"In that case," she stated, "it makes perfect sense for me to stay."

Ellis's relief dissipated as fast as it had formed.

"I guarantee she'll be more open to speaking with a woman than a man. I know I would with a husband like that."

It was impossible to counter her arguments, but he also knew the stakes. "Lily, listen."

"Where should we wait in the meantime?"

"Lily—"

"I am *not* going anywhere. Force me out of the car if you want, but I'm not leaving without that child."

She was prideful and determined and stubborn, as usual. They were traits that made him want to kiss her as much as strangle her. Another reason to send her off. He had to concentrate on the goal. Here in the dark, with only inches dividing them, it would be hard to dwell on anything but her. Rain had matted her hair and washed away her makeup, and she was still a goddamn knockout. Somehow even more so. If it weren't pouring outside, he'd take a walk to clear his senses and shake off his stupidity. She was spoken for. Practically engaged.

"Ellis, try to understand," she said after a pause. She shifted toward him, and her voice softened. "Yes, I realize it might be dangerous. But you know about my past, about Samuel…so you know why I have to see this through." Her sudden vulnerability only magnified the battle in his head. "Please, say something."

Don't marry him. The words rushed to his throat. They pooled on his tongue, ready to spill free. All he had to do was let them out.

But how could he? How could he tell her to pass up a life with Clayton Brauer? As much as Ellis wanted to disparage the guy, he couldn't. Occasional arrogance aside, Clayton would make for a worthy husband. And he could give Lily and her son the secure future they deserved.

In contrast, here was Ellis, on the brink of being penniless, jobless, and homeless. If he didn't count jail. Depending on a judge's ruling, he could be back in a concrete pen before long, rendering him useless to anyone. A valid reason for her parents to care for him even less.

And yet, in this moment, despite all that, what he feared above all was not telling her. Of spending decades like his father, festering in silence and regret.

She was waiting for a response, the rain falling harder, when something flickered in his periphery. A light near the house.

Somebody was out there.

"*Get down.*" Ellis pulled Lily by her shoulder, and they dropped low in their seats. The map fell to the floor. Had the flashlight given them away?

He imagined Mr. Gantry marching down the drive. Shells loaded, finger on the trigger.

Lily's eyes widened, questioning what he'd seen.

Ellis lowered her window for a better view. Once more, the air was black. "The light... It's gone."

It had been a mistake to park so close.

Lily dared to peek for herself. Ellis was about to start the engine, rarely an easy task, when the light reappeared. The glow of a window.

"It's from inside the barn," she said.

He'd been wrong. It hadn't come from outside. Someone earlier—Mrs. Gantry, he'd guess—had used her kerosene lamp to navigate from the barn to the house. But he hadn't seen anyone go back since.

"Something about it's odd," Lily said.

His gut told him the same. "I'd better go take a look."

She agreed, and before he could tell her to stay put, she was out of the car.

"*Lily, no,*" he rasped, unable to yell. Even if he could, some good it would do him. Bridling his frustration, he hurried through the rain and over pebbles to catch up. If she couldn't be discouraged, he'd at least stick by her side.

Without his fedora, water clouded his vision as they ascended the drive. He surveyed the house, confirming all was still and dark.

"Keep behind me," he whispered, an unbending order, as

they crept around a weathered truck. To his relief, she didn't put up a fight.

Finally at the barn, he clutched the vertical handle of the door and cautiously rolled it open a crack. Sure enough, there was a light. A flashlight beam, aimed at the rafters. His heart skittered in alarm, but not enough to back off. He inched the door farther, causing a squeak from its metal track, and the light vanished.

Confounded, he glanced back at Lily. She was anxiously hunched with their flashlight, ready to click it on when needed. In that instant, he saw himself as a kid, caught reading under the covers after bedtime.

All at once, he knew the source of the light.

He stepped into the barn, and Lily followed. The place was dry at least, but the musty air carried an animal smell, along with a chill that ran down Ellis's arms.

"Calvin?" he called out quietly. Then he closed the door and told Lily, "Turn on your light."

She did just that, and the shadows of her face underscored the horror of what they might find. They separated, plunging into a search.

Ellis wove around pieces of farm equipment. Rain from his clothing dripped onto the dirt floor. He investigated the area around creamery cans and broken stacks of hay bales. "Calvin?"

A horse nickered in reply. From a nearby stall, its black eyes glinted in the faint light. A white blaze of hair sloped from its forehead.

"Ellis, over here." Lily's urgent whisper pulled him to the only other stall in the barn. Beside her flashlight, set on the floor, was a small plate of crumbs and a Gold Shield Coffee can that reeked of urine. She was kneeling by a mounded blanket in the corner. Above the woolen fabric was a tuft of blond hair. "Calvin?" she said. "Is that you?"

Two large eyes gradually emerged. At the recognition of his small, round face, Ellis had trouble moving. Whether this was the boy's nightly spot or a severe form of punishment, the situation was sickening.

"It's all right, we're here to help you." Lily assumed a soothing maternal tone. "We'll get you out of this awful place and take you somewhere safe. I can carry you out. Would you like that?" When he didn't answer, she gently touched his shoulder. The contact sent him scrambling farther into the corner.

He didn't know her, didn't trust her.

Why in God's name would he trust anyone?

Maybe it would help, though, if he recognized Ellis.

"Hey, Calvin. Remember me?" The words sounded clogged. Ellis cleared the emotion from his throat. He summoned what cheerfulness he could. "I'm the reporter friend of your mom. And your sister too." Calvin's brow conveyed interest, but just a trace through his wariness.

For years, Ellis had reveled in collecting details, seeking importance in the smallest of things. If ever again, he needed to do that now.

He mined his memory as he moved closer, one disarming step at a time. "You know, back in the summer, I bought all those flowers from Ruby. Remember that?" He could still see the dandelions in his head, bound and wilted by the sun.

Calvin watched him intently, scrutinizing; he was, after all, the skeptical sibling.

"And you were at the apple tree, hanging on the branches." Ellis squatted beside Lily. "Your mama, she was doing the laundry. That's the day I took a picture of you on the porch for the paper…" He nearly choked on the last bit, realizing how that very photo, *his* photo, had brought the child to this.

Lily joined back in. "I'm sure this is terribly confusing. But you being here, it was all a big mistake. Just know that your real family loves you. I swear they never stopped." Her speed was increasing, a reminder that every minute in this place was a minute too long. "If you want to be with them again, you *have* to come with us. Okay, Calvin?" She tentatively reached for him, and he drew his head back as if her fingers were made of hot lead. "Calvin, please." Tears entered her voice. She turned to Ellis.

If they just grabbed him and ran, they would risk his screaming. Not to mention traumatizing him even more. He was already recoiled in his blanket, the rim of his flashlight cresting the fabric.

What else could possibly comfort him? What would Geraldine tell them to do?

She'd hummed to Samuel once, to soothe him when he was sick. It was worth a try, but Ellis had to recall the right tune.

Was it "Clementine"? No...but it was a gal's name.

Maybe "Oh! Susanna"?

Blasted. The melody echoed distantly in the hollow of his ears. He could almost catch the lyrics. About giving an answer and being half crazy...about a bicycle built for two...

It was "Daisy Bell."

"You know, Cal, I bet your mama would hum a song to make you feel better. We could sing one of her favorites, you and me. Want to try?"

Not waiting, Ellis took the liberty of alternating his humming with the verses he knew. He probably was off-key and swapped a few words, but by the time he finished, a smile teased a corner of the boy's mouth.

It was enough to give Ellis hope. "Ready to go see her?"

Calvin studied him for a long, strained moment. At last, he relented with a tiny nod, and Lily's eyes moistened as she smiled.

"I'm gonna pick you up now," Ellis said with only partial relief. "And we can all go on a car ride." With care, he put his arms around Calvin, who didn't pull away. Once the kid was in a secure hold, Ellis started to rise. But something clinked and yanked them back down.

What the hell?

Lily lifted the blanket to identify the cause. A rusted chain, bolted to the wall, was tethered to a thick leather band. A cuff that looped Calvin's ankle.

The boy was shackled.

Like a spark to gunpowder, a bolt of fury flared through Ellis. The only thing containing it was the need to get Calvin as far away from here as possible.

Lily was struggling with the binding, in a panic. "I can't get it loose."

"Tell me, buddy"—Ellis did his damnedest to sound calm— "how do they get this thing off ya?"

Calvin shrugged that he didn't know. Or if he did, he wasn't up for yammering about it.

"That's okay. We'll get creative." Ellis set him back down and joined Lily in scavenging the place for some kind of key or a cutter, anything. Then a noise came from outside, and they stopped.

Ellis would gladly take Mr. Gantry on—the wretched bastard—but he couldn't jeopardize the lives of everyone else.

Already near the door, Ellis looked out. No lights or movement that he could see. Still in the clear, for now.

He resumed the hunt until Lily called to him, "Will this do?" She indicated a tool that resembled oversized pliers, hanging among gadgets on the wall.

"Let's try it."

She reached high to pull it off a hook but sent it toppling. The handles bounced off the rail of the adjacent stall. The startled horse burst into fit of squealing and snorting. Lily tried in vain to quiet the animal as it kicked the wall with its back hooves.

Ellis raced to snatch up the tool—all the noise was going to wake the house—and returned to Calvin. The poor kid was shaking. There was no time to soothe him. Ellis tried to cut through a rusted link, to no avail.

His heart was pounding against his ribs.

Leaning down, he cupped Calvin's face to ensure the boy listened. "Don't move a muscle. You hear me?"

Calvin eked out a nod, his chin caked with dirt.

The horse had ceased kicking but was still whinnying and shifting in its stall.

Ellis laid out the chain away from Calvin. Standing with feet apart, as if splitting wood with an ax, he gripped the tool overhead with both hands and came down hard. *Clank.* The links moved but stayed intact.

"Damn it."

He laid them out again as Lily came to Calvin's side. This time, Ellis singled out a weaker-looking section. Fully rusted, it flaked between his fingers. Keeping his eyes on the target, he swung with all of his strength. *Clank.* A link broke free.

"Thank God," Lily said.

"Help me get him loose."

She hurried to unhook the chain as Ellis swooped up the bundled kid. Then she snatched the flashlight, and they all headed to the door. She opened it wide enough for them to pass through. But before slipping out, Ellis glanced toward the house. Upstairs, a light traveled past a window.

Someone was coming.

Ellis commanded in a hush, "*Run.*"

They took off in a sprint toward the car that felt a thousand miles away. Raindrops assaulted Ellis's eyes. His lungs burned. More than one stone nearly rolled his ankles, but he held Calvin snug to his chest, refusing to let him tumble to the ground. Lily never left their side.

They were almost at the car when a man's bellowing burst out. "You! Get back here!"

A gunshot cracked the air, and Ellis reflexively ducked. Lily covered her head.

"C'mon, c'mon!" Ellis told her. "Let's go!"

She opened the passenger side and jumped in, arms

outstretched for Calvin. Ellis transferred him onto her lap, the remaining chain rattling, and slammed the door. He rounded the car and got behind the wheel. The odds that the engine would come to life without several turns of the crank were slim. But with him already there in the seat, the engine still relatively warm, he gave the starter pedal a try. The motor coughed and died. But it was close.

"Ellis, he's coming!"

In the distance, the truck's head lamps were moving by the barn. Mr. Gantry's silhouette loomed at the steering wheel.

Ellis tried his starter again. A longer cough with a sputter.

"The truck stopped," she said.

It must have stalled. Ellis could hear the farmer's engine struggling just like his.

"Please, please, please," he murmured to his dear, beloved Model T. If it cooperated just this once, he'd keep it forever, restore it better than new.

He pressed the pedal again…and the car shuddered to life!

Head lamps on, Ellis opened up the throttle and tore off down the road, back the way they had come. A faint revving from behind told him not to celebrate. Hopefully, the pebbled drive would slow the truck down.

Lily whispered into Calvin's ear, rocking him, telling him everything would be all right. Ellis prayed that wasn't a lie.

He flipped the wiper to clear his view, but their breaths were fogging the glass.

Lily twisted to look back. "He's following."

In the side mirror were two pinpricks of lights, head lamps that would likely gain on them before long. Unless they figured out how to lose the guy. Found a place to hide away.

"The wrong turn we took earlier," Ellis said, remembering an option. "Where was it?"

"Which one?"

"The last one."

"It's...to the right...another half mile maybe."

"Tell me when you see it."

She lowered her window, getting ready.

Ellis swiped fog from the windshield with his coat sleeve, but the damp fabric smeared his view. *Shit.* He rolled down his window and poked his head out, squinting and blinking to watch the road ahead. Rain pelted his face. He tried not to imagine a shot to the back of his skull.

"There it is!" Lily pointed. "Down there."

He saw it. At the bottom of the hill, he swung a right. Almost immediately, he swerved into the graveled lot they'd passed on their last wrong turn. A feed store closed for the night. He came to a stop behind the building and killed the head lamps. Over his shoulder was a partial view of the main road.

Lily squeezed Ellis's hand.

Seconds stretched and thinned like endless strings of taffy. Darkness amplified every sound. The rain splashing the roof. The idle motor ticking. The blood pumping in his ears.

And the engine of the truck. Its roar gained power and momentum, louder and louder, like a rocket preparing to launch.

But Ellis, too, was prepared. He'd face the man with his fists, if nothing else. Though Ellis was no Jack Dempsey in the flesh, he'd fight till the end to keep Lily and Calvin safe.

Finally, as if in slow motion, the shadowed truck rode into sight.

First the hood...the cab...the flatbed...

Then it passed them right on by.

CHAPTER 40

DECISIONS HAD TO BE MADE: where to take Calvin, how and what to tell Geraldine, when Lily would go back to Philadelphia.

Answering the last one, as far as Lily was concerned, was the easiest. She would leave only when both children were in the safety of their mother's arms, and not a minute before. That would mean arriving late to the paper, but the chief would simply have to understand. If not, so be it. After the day she'd had, there were few challenges that would ever again make her cower.

Now settled at Ellis's apartment, she should have been exhausted, but her mind was still buzzing. She had navigated their escape, keeping them off the main roads until they crossed the state line, and spent the rest of the drive holding Calvin while periodically looking back.

Ellis had been wise to assume the duty of phoning Geraldine. Given Lily's state of mind, she'd have rambled on with far too many details. It would have been cruel to unload the full summary in a single dose. They could share more tomorrow in person when Geraldine arrived at nine, after Ruby was back in their care.

"How did she take it?" Lily inquired as Ellis hung up the phone. In the lamp's soft glow, she couldn't immediately read him.

"She's pretty shaken."

Lily nodded. Weren't they all?

He gestured toward his bedroom. "Is Calvin asleep?"

"Out like a light."

The child had been so groggy when she carried him in that they didn't trouble him with food or a bath. All of that could wait—save for the shackle. Ellis's first priority had been to remove that despicable cuff. He had carefully maneuvered with a screwdriver and pick, then flung the rusted links aside. On the boy's ankle, the red, circular mark left from the band would undoubtedly fade faster than his memory of the ordeal.

Spurred now by the target of Lily's gaze, Ellis gathered up the chain and stored it in the entry table, beside their drying coats. "Evidence," he explained awkwardly as she watched. It went without saying that, at the moment, he might not be viewed as the most reliable witness.

"I'd be glad to speak with the police myself," she offered. "The Gantrys should never be allowed to adopt again. Not ever."

"They won't. I'll make sure of it." Ellis's tone said there was no alternative. "Let's just get both kids where they belong. I'll handle the rest later."

She agreed. With such uncertainty in the days and weeks to come for Ellis, it was best to face one issue at a time. "Thank you, by the way."

"For...?"

"For not arguing about me going with you to fetch Ruby."

He smiled at her. "I figured you'd refuse to stay put, even if I told you to."

She gave it some thought and confessed, "That's true."

They both laughed a little. In the quiet that followed, a thread of remorse spiraled through her. They were on the last stretch of a marathon. In a handful of hours, she would board a train at Penn Station and they would go their separate ways.

It was a smart choice, of course.

Still the right one—despite her doubts crowding in.

"Go on, now." Ellis sent a nod toward his room. "You should catch some shut-eye."

It did feel odd to have him relegated to the davenport in his own apartment, particularly since she wouldn't be sleeping a wink. She was certain of that. Although, she imagined he wouldn't be either.

Resting beside Calvin was at least a sensible way for her to pass the time.

"Well…good night, Mr. Reed."

He smiled again. "Night, Miss Palmer."

~

Lily had guessed wrong. After she jolted awake, she realized she had fallen sleep. Beside her, Calvin's rhythmic breaths had certainly added to the comfort from Ellis's downy pillow.

How long had she dozed off? A dark gap in the curtain confirmed it was night.

Then a knocking sound reached in from the next room, and she discovered what had woken her. She pictured Mr. Gantry at the front door, rage warping his face, shotgun in his grip.

But he couldn't have known where they were.

Unless he'd managed to trail them.

She scurried off the bed, fending off waves of dizziness and terror, and peered out of the room, only to find that she wasn't alone in her suspicions.

"Is it him?" she whispered toward Ellis's back in the entry. A large kitchen knife glimmered in his hand. She risked a few steps forward for an answer. "Is it?"

He showed her his palm, an order to stay back.

More knocks reverberated with force, and Lily had a terrible notion of who else it could be. For Max, a few henchmen could solve his sister's issues in another way. Ruby's transfer could have all been a ruse.

Ellis stooped for a look through the peephole.

Breath held, Lily mentally prepared to nab Calvin. They would flee down a fire escape outside the bedroom window—if there was one. Heavens! Why hadn't she checked?

But Ellis lowered his knife and unlocked and opened the door. He spoke with the caller, blocking the person's identity, until he stepped back to welcome a familiar guest.

Lily burst into a grin. "Oh, Mrs. Dillard, it's you." In the whole of her life, Lily had never been so happy to greet anyone.

As Ellis locked the door, Geraldine scanned the room. "Where is he? I gotta see him. Where's my Calvin?" Wringing her hands, she seemed almost frantic.

A glance at the clock affirmed she was several hours early. It wasn't yet four in the morning.

Lily had to remind herself of what Geraldine, as a mother, had to be going through. She moved closer and replied quietly, "He's in the bedroom, fast asleep."

"And he's not hurt? He's all right?" Geraldine's moistened eyes pressed for the truth.

"He's fine." Or he would be, Lily hoped.

Geraldine turned to Ellis, as if in need of confirmation. But when her gaze dropped to his hand, he relinquished the knife onto the entry table. "Only a precaution."

Lily continued with Geraldine, detouring from a more daunting explanation. "It's such a lovely surprise to have you here already."

"After Mr. Reed called, I just wasn't gonna be able to wait. Doc Summers let me borrow her car, as I used to drive some… and seeing as…I'd be…" Her attention splintered, landing on a sight behind Lily.

In the bedroom doorway, Calvin stood in a grungy shirt and overalls, rubbing his eyes.

Geraldine's gasp held a quiver. She started toward him, but paused and folded onto her knees. Slowly she held out her hands, a gesture of yearning lined with fear of scaring him away. "Cal, baby...it's me. It's your mama."

He was stunned or confused. Likely both.

According to Ellis, Ruby had been aware of her mother's illness all this time. But had Calvin known as well? Did he believe his mother simply didn't want him?

Had Sylvia filled him with even more crushing lies?

Dread from such questions appeared to crease Geraldine's features. Seconds later, however, the answers became apparent, as much as needed to be, when Calvin's tentative steps soon hastened to reach his mother. He threw his arms around her neck, and Geraldine heaved a sigh. Together, they hugged and cried as she rocked him from side to side. She kissed his cheeks and hands and told him she loved him again and again.

"I love you too, Mama," he told her.

They were the first words he had uttered all night, the first words Lily ever heard him speak.

And they were perfect.

Ellis looked on with his hands in his trouser pockets. His expression reflected the sense of healing that stirred within Lily, a bond that permeated the room.

Drying her cheeks, Geraldine came to her feet, and Calvin clung to the side of her skirt. This would likely be his favorite spot for a long time to come. "Now, then," she said to Ellis, "I need to see my daughter. Where's Ruby at?"

"At the Millstones'. We'll be there at eight."

"No. I'll be going there now." Her staunchness clearly surprised Ellis as much as it did Lily.

"Mrs. Dillard," he said, "you need to trust me on this. The brother who arranged this... Let's just say he's not a guy whose orders you break on a whim. Besides, I think him being there could be a real help."

The reason for that wasn't difficult to fathom. Presuming Sylvia wasn't happy with the arrangements, Max taking the lead would ensure a smoother transfer.

"So, she expects us at eight," Geraldine said.

Lily chimed in to assure her. "Only a few hours to go."

Geraldine crossed her arms, showing a rise of agitation. "And what makes you so sure she didn't up and leave already? Haul Ruby right off with her? Way I see it, if her mind's all that troubled, I doubt she'd give any advice much weight. Now, I'm real grateful for what you both done tonight. But I'm Ruby's mother. If I gotta drive all over the city to find that house myself, and even track her down from there, I'll do it. With or without the two of you."

Lily and Ellis traded looks. The day had towed them through more loops and turns than the Cyclone on Coney Island. They hadn't had a chance to even consider disrupting Max's plan. Nor the possibility of others outright defying him.

What if Geraldine was right?

What if her daughter was long gone?

"We'll take my car," Ellis said, already grabbing their coats.

CHAPTER 41

ON THE DRIVE TO JERSEY, Ellis weighed his options against the potential costs. If the Millstones had managed to spirit Ruby away, finding her again could prove impossible. They could take on new names, a new residence, new lives. All they needed was money and the right connections. The couple had both. But offend Max Trevino, and the possibility of any help, now or later, could vanish.

And that was the best-case scenario. It wasn't hard to imagine the worst, with the visit to the Royal still vivid in Ellis's mind: the big goon from the kitchen, a bloodied towel in his hand, the punching and groaning beyond the swinging door.

"Lights are on," Geraldine announced anxiously from the back seat. They'd barely rolled to a stop in front of the house, it was true. Windows were illuminated on both floors. An odd thing given the early hour.

Calvin, nestled like a kitten in his mother's arms, rose to see for himself.

In the front seat, Lily twisted toward Geraldine. "They're

probably up early to get Ruby all ready for you." She masked the uncertainty in her voice fairly well.

Ellis tried to sound just as casual. "Why don't you all stay here? I'll go first and take a peek." Avoiding an objection, he headed right out to catch a glimpse through a window. It would be easier to do now that the rain had taken a break.

He had just climbed the steps when he spied a figure entering the parlor room.

Ellis ducked from view.

There was one voice, then a second. The glass panes muffled the conversation, but its intensity was clear. He inched himself upward.

Already dressed for the day, Sylvia was grabbing picture frames from the mantel. Alfred appeared to be pleading with her, his high forehead flushed. He was in nightclothes of plaid pants and a buttoned shirt, its collar askew.

Ellis murmured his gratitude that the couple was still there.

But then Alfred forced Sylvia to face him by holding her arms. She strove to break away, and the frames plummeted. Glass shattered against the marble floor.

"How could you?" she wailed distinctly. Pushing him off, she fell to her knees and worked to salvage the photos from the shards, slicing her fingers and yielding drips of blood. Her attempts to wipe the images seemed to make them worse. A guttural sob brought a stream of tears.

Alfred joined her on the floor, where she held a picture helplessly. He drew her in, and she let him, the photo falling free. He rubbed her back and spoke in her ear. For a moment, Ellis felt intrusive enough to back off. But with an abrupt shove, Sylvia scrambled away to stand, angling toward the window.

Ellis dropped down. From this distance in the dark, his view of Lily and Geraldine was indiscernible, but he could sense their gazes trained on his every movement, anticipating, questioning.

"Victoria!" Sylvia's summons traveled easily through the panes. "Victoria, come now! It's time to leave!"

Oh Christ.

There was no sitting back and waiting. Tracking down Max would take far too long. Ellis couldn't risk the chance of Sylvia sneaking Ruby out. The bargain was off.

He marched over to the front door and pounded with his fist. Pounded again.

The door swung open. Alfred's face sparked with relief, snuffed out by his recognition of Ellis. "What are you doing? You shouldn't be here yet."

The hell he shouldn't. "Where's Ruby?"

"Alfred," Sylvia called out, "who is it? Who's there?"

Alfred shifted into a hush. "You have to wait outside," he told Ellis. "Now, go. *Go.*" He was shutting the door, his hands and pajamas tainted with blood from the frames, when Ellis pushed forward and stopped him.

"You want me to go? Then hand Ruby over."

Sylvia appeared at the door and forced it open the rest of the way. Tears had streaked her makeup, blackening the rims of her eyes. Her gaze ricocheted from her husband to Ellis and back. "You phoned him…" She was exasperated, accusing. "You told him to come early."

"Darling, no. Don't be silly. I thought it was your brother at the door."

She shook her head, backing away, betrayal further darkening her face. The situation was on the brink of a free fall.

Ellis stepped toward her in the entryway. "Mrs. Millstone, let's just sit down and talk. Could we do that?" He needed to keep things calm, for Ruby.

But Alfred raised a hand to hold Ellis off, a signal to let him manage this. "Please, Sylvia, don't make this more difficult. We'll get through this together, the two of us."

"The two of us?" The phrase had a souring effect. She stared at him, a sudden revelation taking hold. "That's it, isn't it? It's what you've wanted all along. To get Victoria out of the way."

Alfred gaped at her, stricken. "That's absurd. How could you suggest... You don't know what you're saying."

"You told me to say it was me. That I was the one driving, because you drank too much brandy. But it wasn't me at all." Her voice sharply turned to ice. "It was you. You'd planned all of it, didn't you?"

"What? No. I wouldn't... It was an accident." Alfred grew more flustered, emotion choking his voice. "The roads were slippery. You were there. You know this. I never meant to hurt our daughter. I loved her..."

For Ellis, the staggering exchange only cemented that the Dillard kids never belonged with these people. He glanced around for Ruby, prepared to tear the house apart to find her.

Sylvia abruptly bellowed toward the stairs. "Claire!"

"Darling, listen to me." Alfred proceeded toward Sylvia, who went scuttling to the staircase, a wild animal evading a trap. Blood from her fingers dotted the white floor.

The housekeeper emerged above, already dressed in her uniform. "Ma'am?"

"Where is Victoria? I instructed you to bring her down!"

"She's collectin' her belongings. They're...not quite ready." Claire spoke with her gaze low, but it wasn't solely from being timid. Ellis recognized the effort to stall. He envisioned Ruby hiding somewhere in a corner, a closet.

Would she try to slip out a back way, venturing alone in the dark?

"You deliver her this instant, or I'll come and get her myself!" Sylvia commanded, spurring Ellis to intervene.

"Claire, you keep her right where she is." He was about to start for the stairs, hoping force wouldn't be needed to keep Sylvia back, when Ruby's small, groggy face poked out from behind the housekeeper.

"Ah, Victoria," Sylvia said. "There you are." She sighed with a smile, a disturbing switch of mood. "Come along, my dearest. We're going back to California, our real home."

Claire subtly stiffened her arm over Ruby, standing guard.

"Victoria." Sylvia was struggling against an onset of frustration. "Be a good girl now and listen to your mother."

"Ruby, it's okay," Ellis piped in. "I'm taking you to your family."

A rub to the eyes, and Ruby eased out into view. She wore a sailor dress with no shoes, her hair mussed from sleep. Slowly she began her descent, her daze lifting with her steps, her expression lightening halfway down, where she suddenly picked up speed.

Sylvia reached out to embrace her. "That's my dear girl."

But Ruby flew right past. "Mama," she cried out and sprinted into the open arms of Geraldine, now standing in the entry. Her son was scurrying in to join her, with Lily just behind.

Sylvia's arms went limp as she watched. Her red-smeared fingers dangled at her sides. Growing out of sorts, she sank onto the bottom step, shrinking into herself.

"Calvin," Lily said, trying to coax the boy away. "We need to stay outside now." She sent Ellis a look of apology, a message that she'd tried to contain him. Likely his mother too.

But what did they expect?

Then Geraldine held the hands of her children and turned to Alfred. "I got both my kids here, and I'll be taking 'em with me." She wasn't vindictive or cold, simply assertive as their rightful mother.

Alfred looked utterly lost. Only the rumble of a passing car filled the quiet as he nodded.

Claire had just made her way down to Geraldine. She handed over a small overcoat and a pair of Mary Janes. "For the lass." With a wistful smile, she bent before Ruby and gave her nose a gentle tap. "You'll mind your mam, now, won't ya?"

Ruby beamed in agreement.

When Claire shifted toward Calvin, who kept snug at his mother's side, she opened her mouth but no words came. Solemnness born of regret played over her features until the boy spoke softly. "G'bye, Miss Claire."

Claire smiled, her eyes misting over. "Goodbye, sweet lad."

Ellis had no idea how Max would feel about the change without approval, but he knew better than to stick around and find out.

"Time to go," he said.

Lily, after a kind nod to Claire, ushered the family toward the door, away from memories that hopefully one day would become a forgotten dream for each of them.

"Sylvia, no!" Alfred's order swung Ellis around. His focus cut to the staircase, now vacant, before locating Sylvia across from the parlor, at the edge of the den. She gripped a revolver with both hands. Aimed at Geraldine, it quivered in her hand.

"Darling, give me the gun," Alfred implored. "You don't need to do this."

There was a ghostly distance in Sylvia's gaze, a disconnect.

The other women clambered to protect the children in a frenzied, panicking huddle. Ellis stepped into the line of fire, though he couldn't shield them all.

"No one's taking my daughter from me," Sylvia said. No trace of anger, just matter-of-fact. Which was even more frightening.

Ellis showed his palms, a peaceable approach. "Mrs. Millstone, if you want to blame anyone, you should blame me. Not them, just me. I'm begging you."

She didn't react. She was locked in her own realm, seeing right through him.

"Mrs. Millstone," he urged, striving to break through, then came a click.

She'd cocked the hammer. Her finger hugged the trigger. Before Ellis could think, he lunged forward, reaching for the weapon. A shot exploded from the barrel, and the feel of a red-hot poker pierced his side, but he wouldn't stop. Couldn't. They were grappling on the floor, fighting for the gun. Every movement gouged him inside. The pain throbbed and spread through his body, narrowing his vision. He heard a throng of voices, a din of words. He couldn't give up, but his strength was dwindling, his limbs turning to water. The room was dimming into an endless tunnel of blackness.

The last thing he heard before his mind fell away was the blast of a second shot and a woman's bloodcurdling scream.

CHAPTER 42

OUTSIDE THE GUARDED HOSPITAL, reporters circled like hungry wolves. They wanted every detail of the shootings, including names and ages—of the children, in particular—and, of course, confirmation of links to Max Trevino. The story would soon grace many a front page.

The irony wasn't lost on Lily.

In the waiting area, on the same chair for hours—it was nearly two in the afternoon—she glanced up as a doctor appeared. He whispered to a nurse. His thick mustache was peppered like his temples and vibrated as he spoke. Lily's shoulders coiled into springs. She dreaded a look that suggested the worst. Around her, tension ratcheted from others fearing the same. The sudden quiet was deafening. But then the doctor proceeded on his way, rounding the corner.

Once more, Lily sank into her seat.

The air reeked of disinfectant, bleach, and the cigarettes of nervous smokers. Through the light haze, a man dragged a chair in her direction, shrilly scraping the tiled floor. Tiny hairs rose on the back of her neck from more than the sound. A policeman, upon learning of Lily's involvement, had warned her a detective would eventually be here to talk.

That man now sat down to face her.

"Good afternoon." He removed his brimmed hat, promoting casualness, and rested it on his lap. From his pin-striped suit and tidy haircut to his perfect white teeth, he was a recruitment poster for J. Edgar Hoover.

She didn't catch his name or anything more in his introduction—her mind was muddled from shock and fear and lack of sleep. But she could guess what information he sought.

If only she could escape—from this hospital, this moment in time. How nice it would be to leap forward by a week, a month even. The unseemly rumors would have long been buried, the puddles of blood mopped clean, the outcome of this day endured. She imagined herself then, in a secluded corner of a dim café, being interviewed by some young reporter over coffee. His fresh-faced eagerness would remind her of the person she had been when first moving to Philly, a dogged columnist in the making. Back when she believed a new start in a big city would crowd out the shame of her past. The sense of being an unworthy mother.

"What a relief," he would say, "that everything turned out fine."

For some, of course. Not all.

Then she heard "Can you tell me how it all started?" It was a standard question that blended the reporter in Lily's head with the detective before her, and she wasn't entirely certain which of them had asked.

And yet, through the lens of her mind, she suddenly viewed the past year with stunning clarity, saw the interwoven paths that had delivered each of them here. Every step a domino vital in knocking over the next.

With no small amount of regret, she nodded at him slowly, remembering as she replied. "It started with a picture."

~

For a short time then, everything but memory became a blur. The confines of the hospital drifted away. The ringing of phones and squeaking of shoes dulled to a distant hum. Lily recalled whom she was speaking to only when the detective asked a question, wanting to clarify a few points. He held a pencil over his pocket-size notepad. Its mound of flipped pages conveyed all the scrawling he had done to keep up.

In the midst of her last answer, the mustached doctor reentered the waiting area.

"Pardon me, everyone." Even without his authoritative voice, each person in the vicinity would have snapped to attention. The deliverer of either blessings or devastation, he gave away nothing in his expression. "If the family members of Ellis Reed and Geraldine Dillard would care to come forward, I have an update."

Lily sprang to her feet before realizing the designation didn't apply to her. But the children were the sole family members here. She glanced at her mother, who was watching over the little ones. Ruby, Calvin, and Samuel looked up from a Beatrix Potter book that a nurse had supplied.

When Lily had phoned the deli—after the day's terror, she was desperate to hear her family's voices—she'd repeatedly assured her father that there was no reason for anyone to come, that his comforting words were enough. Yet the moment her mother and Samuel walked in, a flood of tears and gratitude washed over Lily.

"You go on, ma'am," the detective said, rising. "I've got everything I need for now. Here's how to reach me if you think of anything more." He tore off a page from his notepad. Mindlessly Lily stuffed the information into her purse, which she then clutched to her body like armor.

Her mother waggled her fingers, urging Lily to join Ruby

and Calvin. Hand in hand, the two were plodding toward the doctor. Samuel sat and watched.

The dread in the air was palpable.

It had taken time for the hospital to reach Ellis's parents. Someone would need to relay his update once they arrived. Lily would cling to every word largely for this purpose, she told herself. Though the truth of her interest was far more personal. Her greatest concerns over Geraldine, on the other hand, resided with the children. Her reservations over what they were about to learn were clearly shared by the doctor.

"Children," he said, "I think it's best you sit back and wait while I confer with the adult here."

Straightening, Ruby wrapped her arm around her brother's shoulders. She emitted the air of a seasoned protector. "This is about our mama. We got a right to know."

The doctor looked to Lily for approval. While such an allowance was uncommon, they were hardly common kids. What was more, having lived through their father's passing, they surely grasped the gravity of the situation.

Lily submitted a nod, and the doctor proceeded.

"First off, in regard to Mr. Reed, I'm pleased to say we found no remnants of the bullet in his side region and no damage to major organs. He did suffer a fractured rib, however, and required a transfusion due to blood loss. As always, infection remains a risk. But so long as he takes good care of the stitched wounds, I expect his recovery to be a smooth one."

He stopped there, and Lily realized: Ellis was safe. He would be all right! Relief swept through her, but for just a second.

"And our mama?" Ruby asked. Her eyes alone betrayed her fears as the doctor shifted his focus in her direction.

"Unfortunately, the bullet that struck your mother's back did shatter a small but important bone. Whenever that happens, our biggest concern is the possibility of permanent damage to the spinal cord."

The potential results wrung Lily's heart. That the mother of these two young children, their sole parent in this world, could lose the use of her legs. That in a reversal of roles, the kids could be caring for Geraldine for the rest of her days.

Perhaps it had been a mistake, permitting the children to stay for this.

"So?" Ruby said. "What'd you find?" She was growing impatient, and Lily wondered how much of the medical talk the children comprehended.

"A little to the left or to the right," the doctor replied, "and we would have been in far more trouble. Your mother is a lucky woman, and a strong one too."

Calvin asked in a small voice, "She's…okay?" Ruby squeezed him closer.

"There'll be some swelling, and assisted exercises will be helpful. But yes, it's safe to say she'll be just fine."

Grins swept across the children's faces. Their glee instantly spread to Lily, and even her mother, who was gauging the outcome from her chair.

"Mr. Reed is awake now," the doctor added, "but he might be a bit groggy. Mrs. Dillard should be waking any time. A nurse can take you all to see them soon." As he walked away, Ruby wrapped Calvin in a hug, and the two hopped about like jumping beans. Despite all they had gone through, at least in this moment, they were bursting with the innocence of youth.

Then Samuel joined in, and they became a bouncing trio. Whether or not he knew what he was celebrating didn't matter a whit.

Lily hated to shush them but did so gently, being mindful of other patients, before an anxious voice came from behind.

"Lily! There you are."

Though she recognized his voice, the surprise didn't fully hit her until she saw Clayton approaching. He looked her up and down, assessing. "You're not hurt," he said with relief.

"No…I'm perfectly fine."

"Oh, thank God," he said. "The chief didn't have any details."

"The chief?"

"Your mother phoned him about you being out. I was just there packing up my desk. I jumped in my car as soon as I heard."

She was ceaselessly amazed by the support her parents gave, regardless of the effects on their lives. And now here was Clayton, another person in her life willing to look out for her, to protect her. "I feel terrible that it caused you to drive all this way. I would've assured you…if I'd known."

"Sweetheart," he said, "what in the world happened here?"

A simple question with an overwhelming answer.

All at once, she felt so very tired. Aside from a brief nap while curled up on hospital chairs, it seemed an eternity since she had truly rested. The idea of recounting the journey all over again only added to her fatigue. Even so, she owed it to Clayton to at last tell him everything.

In the background, a nurse was pushing a patient in a squeaky wooden wheelchair, fresh visitors were milling about, and Lily's mother was trying to calm the children while suppressing her own smile.

"Let's…find some place quiet," Lily said.

～

The emptiness of the stairwell amplified the silence in the stale air. A full minute had passed after Lily finished, and Clayton still stood before her, absorbing, clutching his fedora to his side.

"What I don't understand," he said finally, "is why you'd put your life in jeopardy like this. You should have told me. I would've helped."

"I know. I should have. And I was going to. The other day, I'd planned to tell you all about my column at the same time when—"

"Your column?" Confusion clouded his eyes. "Whatever are you talking about?"

She winced, her justifications crumbling into a pathetic heap. Yes, his proposal at lunch had thrown her off. But for several weeks prior, she'd had countless opportunities to go to him, and she hadn't. And not just about the Dillards.

For months, they had chatted away during car rides and over meals, both alone and with her family. Yet she never thought to tell him about the hauntings of her past, or what had long been the source of her greatest fear. She hadn't told him about her dreams of writing or even the extent of Samuel's last fever.

She could blame her defenses, upheld against any man other than her father for the sake of her son and her own scarred heart.

But that wasn't true, she realized.

Not anymore.

"Clayton, I'm sorry. There's so much more I should have shared. I honestly have no reasonable excuse."

He glanced away then, and she found herself at a loss for words. The stairwell again became unbearably quiet. "I need you to tell me, Lily," he said before meeting her gaze. "You're not coming to Chicago...are you?"

At the resignation in his voice, she strove to assure him. "I care for you so deeply, Clayton. And what you're offering is incredible, sincerely, for me *and* for Samuel—"

"That wasn't my question." He cut her off, but not in a terse way. She was meandering around the truth, and they both knew it.

As much as she didn't want to hurt him—this thoughtful, successful, dashing man who was willing to give her so much—she couldn't go on pretending. He deserved more than that. He deserved someone who would challenge him, even to a frustrating degree, to make him look at himself and others and the world in a new way. Someone who inspired him to push himself further than he ever thought capable. Someone who needed him as much as he needed her. She wanted that for Clayton.

And for herself.

At long last, to provide an answer—not only about Chicago, but about the fate of their future—she gently voiced her realization. "No...I won't be going."

He took this in, and he sighed. There was less disappointment than acceptance in his face. Perhaps he had already known it would come to this. Perhaps, from the start, they both did.

She reached into the coin pocket of her purse and retrieved his ring. She held it tight between her fingers, feeling the finality of her decision before handing it over. Wordlessly, he slid the ring beneath his overcoat and into the breast pocket of his suit.

"Clayton, please know. After all you've done for me, all the time you must feel I've wasted...I'm just so sorry..."

His brown eyes softened as he looked at her. "I'm not," he said and brushed her chin with his thumb. Then he kissed her on the cheek with a kindness she would always remember. "You take care, Lily."

A wave of emotion flowed through her as she returned his smile. "You too," she said, and she watched him walk away.

~

The question didn't need to be spoken. Curiosity over Clayton's whereabouts appeared plainly on her mother's face when Lily returned to the waiting area alone.

Getting straight to it, Lily pushed out the admission. "He's gone."

Her mother went still, comprehending the meaning.

The children were playing quietly nearby, waiting patiently to see Geraldine.

"Sit." Lily's mother gave a single pat to the chair beside her, an order Lily heeded while bracing for a lecture.

"Yes, I'm downright foolish. I know that's what you must think of me."

"What I think," her mother said, "is that you'd be foolish to do anything you're not meant to." Lily shifted to face her, not hiding her surprise. "You're our miracle baby, Lillian Harper. Your father and I have always wanted great things for your life. But nothing more than your happiness."

The words brought tears to Lily's eyes.

Her path had detoured so greatly from her parents' sensible expectations. Her subsequent shame and guilt had been her warranted load to bear. And yet, she felt the remnants of that weight disintegrating now. They dropped away like stale, insignificant crumbs.

She smiled and held her mother's hand. "Do you know how much I love you?"

"I do," her mother replied, and Lily believed her.

A mother always knew.

CHAPTER 43

THE GUN, THE KIDS, THE SHOOTINGS—the scene came back in pieces. When Ellis first awoke in a hospital bed, the images were like the Sunday funnies chopped into strips and all mixed up. He sorted most of them with a nurse's help, though he did question his grasp on reality upon seeing his parents enter the room.

After all, his scuffle at the Millstones' seemed to have just happened, making it impossible for his folks to arrive so soon. This, aside from the stone-cold fact that Jim Reed didn't go to hospitals. Ellis had known that for as long as he could remember. Granted, he only recently understood the full root of his father's aversion.

Nevertheless, here the man was, in an actual hospital. His concern over Ellis appeared to outweigh even the discomfort of his surroundings, yet it was Ellis's mother who prattled on.

"When the hospital phoned, you can only imagine what went through my head. We got here just as soon as we could."

To help shed his mental fog, Ellis pushed against the mattress to edge himself up, stopping short when a pain stabbed his side. He clenched his jaw, stifling a groan.

"Do you need a doctor?" she asked. "I can find a nurse."

"No, no, I'm fine..." He held his midsection, bound by bandages, catching his breath.

"Are you certain? Maybe you need more medicine. You did just have surgery."

"Honest, I'm okay."

"But if you're hurting—"

His father jumped in. "Oh, Myrna, let him be. He's a grown man. He knows what he needs."

Ellis sent his father an appreciative glance. Even through the grogginess, the importance of those words didn't bypass him.

His mother tsked but moved aside enough to let her husband finally chat with Ellis.

"You've had quite an eventful week," his father remarked lightly.

"It hasn't been dull." Ellis's childhood dream of writing an article that made a real impact might have come true in the strangest of ways, but with far more excitement than he counted on. "At least the kids are safe now."

"Well, like I said, I knew you'd figure something out." His father surveyed the hanging bottle of clear liquid and a tube curling its way into Ellis's arm. "Course, I wasn't expecting you to end up looking like a science experiment."

"Believe me, Pop. Neither was I."

His father chuckled, causing Ellis to do to the same until another sharp sensation needled his side.

"Gracious, Jim." His mother gave a chiding tap to her husband's arm. "You're making it worse."

As the pain subsided to a dull ache, a welcomed figure appeared just inside the doorway. A knockout, as always, by any standards that mattered. Ellis couldn't think of a better distraction.

"Hey there, Lily." He smiled, and his parents turned toward the door.

The brightness in Lily's face dimmed on a dime. "I'm sorry.

I didn't realize... I should have checked... I'll gladly wait until later."

"No, hold on," he said, not wanting her to run off. When he couldn't form the next words, his mother—the ever-keen observer and mediator—did it for him.

"It's fine timing actually. Ellis's father and I were about to check in with the doctor. And you're Lily, is that right?"

"I am. I'm...a friend. From the paper...the *Examiner*, I mean." The rarity of seeing her flustered made Ellis rather enjoy the exchange. "Please, though, don't go on my account. I could come back."

"Nonsense," his mother said. "We're in no hurry. Isn't that right, Jim?"

"No hurry at all." His father tipped Ellis a knowing look, and his mother angled back.

"If there's anything you need, love, we won't be far."

"Thanks, Ma."

After a tender pat to the crown of Ellis's head, as she'd done countless times since he was a kid, she filed out of the room with his father, leaving Lily behind.

"I didn't mean to nudge them out. I only came to hear how you're feeling."

"Like I've been run over by a roadster," he answered in truth. "But I'll make it."

She nodded, proceeding toward him. "You've heard about Geraldine?"

"Yeah. Thank God she'll be okay. I couldn't imagine..."

"I know."

There was no good reason to dwell. The Dillards would be happy, healthy, and together again, regardless of all the forces that had worked against them.

"The nurse told me Sylvia's been arrested," Ellis said as Lily settled on the chair beside him.

"For now. An officer expects there to be a deal to place her in an asylum. I suppose I shouldn't be surprised."

Lily seemed somewhat irked by this, but Ellis didn't view prison as the place for Sylvia. The woman's need for serious help had been a long time coming. And even if he shouldn't, part of him still sympathized.

"On a positive note," Lily went on, "any previous charge against you won't be an issue."

"Just like that, huh?" He hadn't considered it yet. But his bank account, too, ought to be in the clear.

"You *are* the hero of the hour."

"Right. Some hero." His banged-up body was far from that of a gallant knight—much less her dapper beau, Clayton Brauer.

"Every major paper in the city is vying for an exclusive. A detective wants to speak with you first, about the Millstones as well as the Gantrys. But after that, you'll virtually have your choice of reporters."

She was serious.

He almost laughed but caught himself, preventing another stab of pain. "Well, if I really have any pick, that's an easy one."

She scrunched her nose. "Who?"

"You."

She rolled her eyes. "That's ridiculous."

"Why?"

"Because I'm only a columnist, and barely that."

"Lily—"

"Ellis, I'm flattered. But this story is too important, and I'm far too close to it. There must be somebody else you'd trust to get it right."

As he gave it some thought, one other person did come to mind. A strong writer and a real pal: Dutch Vernon. No question, the guy wouldn't rest until he did the story justice.

"Just promise me, then," Ellis said, "that you'll tell your side too. The whole thing, beginning to end."

She still looked uncertain, and it occurred to him that this might come across as an excuse to keep her close, even as her life was moving on.

Sure, he couldn't deny wanting that. But he did have another reason. "How I see it, if my first feature brought in that many donations for the Dillards, they'll be able to fill a barge after this one. It'd definitely give the family a nice new start."

Maybe, if they were lucky, they wouldn't ever need to use Alfred's cash payment to get by, though at least they had the option.

"True," Lily said, coming around. "Of course, if you'd like, I could always leave certain elements out."

It took him a second to decode the offer, a reference to the substitution of a photo that led to a lot of good, but absent of noble intentions.

"You could," he said. "But I wouldn't want you to."

"Your editor at the *Tribune*, though—he'll be comfortable with that?"

"Probably not." Ellis smiled wryly, as career aspirations were currently the least of his worries. "But heck, there's bound to be a paper on the lookout for a highly skilled Society reporter. Or who knows? When you leave for Chicago, the chief'll need a new secretary, won't he?"

Any amusement slid from her face. An echo of their past argument, of her role as a secretary, might have pushed a sore button.

Before he could backtrack, she explained, "I won't be leaving the *Examiner*. Not for the time being. Clayton and I... We've decided to go our separate ways."

Ellis reviewed her words, hoping medication hadn't affected his hearing. Because if true, this was the sort of news he'd jump straight out of bed for—if the consequent pain wasn't sure to toss him back on his rear.

Tentative, he asked, "What about Samuel? And you two being together?"

"I've juggled our lives for this long. In one more year, he'll be of school age." She shrugged. "By then, I'll have even more savings. Especially if the column does well—"

"Which it will," he told her.

"You think so?"

"Right up there with Nellie Bly's."

Lily's mouth curved up, and he realized her stunning change of plans was in fact reality.

"Anyhow," she went on, "I was thinking we could find an apartment of our own in the city, near a park and other families. Perhaps with space for a table to hold a typewriter by a window, where we could even hang a planter box." She suddenly stopped and motioned back and forth between them. "I didn't mean *we*, we—I meant 'we' as in... Never mind." She looked away, her skin going flush.

"Lily." When she didn't turn, he reached as far as he was able, and guided her face back toward him. As their eyes held, he said, "It's a perfect plan."

A slow smile moved over her lips, which were just as perfect. Like everything about her. Then she covered his hand on her cheek, and leaning toward him, she pressed her mouth to his. The kiss was long, tender, and warm, and as she drew away, he felt genuinely thankful for every blessed mistake and pang of regret that had ever led him right here to her.

"Mommy!" The voice came only a second before Samuel sprinted into the room and over to Lily.

Her mother arrived at the doorway directly after. "Samuel Ray Palmer, I told you not to disturb them."

"But he needs my gift. To make him feel better."

Ellis assured her, "It's fine, Mrs. Palmer. Really."

With a kind look, she nodded her approval and watched Samuel place an object on the bed.

"What've you got there, you rascal?" Ellis picked it up and studied the small towel, knotted and twisted into an indistinct blob. The kid was staring expectantly, eager for Ellis's response. "This wouldn't be...a rabbit, now would it?"

Samuel nodded with zeal, highlighted by his dimples.

How? Lily mouthed to Ellis, clearly perplexed over how he managed to decipher its shape.

"It's his favorite," he reminded her, and her green eyes glimmered.

"Will he be okay, Mommy?" Samuel asked in a near whisper.

"He sure will, sugar bug." Then Lily kissed her son's forehead and slid Ellis a gentle smile. *We all will*, she seemed to say.

AUTHOR'S NOTE

(Spoilers included)

For the characters in this story, their journey started with a picture—and the same can aptly be said of my endeavor to write this book. When I first stumbled upon an old newspaper photo of four young siblings huddled on the steps of an apartment building in Chicago, their mother shielding her face from the camera, the sign in the foreground stunned me.

The image had first appeared in the *Vidette-Messenger* of Valparaiso, Indiana, in 1948 and, in a brief caption, claimed to exhibit the desperation of the  Chalifoux family. The picture troubled me so much that I bookmarked the page on my computer. (One of many odd compulsions that differentiate historical fiction writers from normal people.) As a mom myself, I kept wondering what could have possibly pushed their mother, or both parents, to that point. In the direst of times,

I could fathom perhaps having to give up my children for the sake of their well-being. But why on earth ask for money in return? Over breakfast with a writers' group, I stated that very question, meant rhetorically, yet my friend Maggie answered without missing a beat: "Because they wanted to eat."

There was such logic in her tone, and she was right to challenge my assumptions. I was judging the family through the lens of modern times, as well as by my own set of standards. My mind spun with scenarios with which I could fully empathize. Unfortunately, in the end, the purported truth behind the photograph matched none of those.

While delving into research, I discovered an article by Vanessa Renderman published in the *Times of Northwest Indiana* in 2013. It was a follow-up on the siblings who had once been the children in that haunting picture. Among the most stunning elements of their tale was this: an accusation by some family members who say the mother actually received money to stage the photograph. Looking at the sign again, I noticed how perfectly the letters were painted. They even appeared to have been embellished with reflective marks.

And that was when the premise of *Sold on a Monday* emerged, rooted in an unexpected what-if: Specifically, what if a reporter's seemingly harmless choice to stage a photo led to unintended consequences for everyone involved? Whether or not there was any deception involved in the real picture I couldn't tell you, but it did wind up going viral (to use a contemporary term). The captioned photo, much like in my story, was soon published in other newspapers throughout the country and prompted a wave of donations and offers of everything from money and jobs to homes for the kids.

Nonetheless, within two years, all the children, including a son who was born a year after the photo was taken, were given away—or, in fact, sold. One of the daughters reportedly recalled her mother selling her for bingo money and tacking on her younger brother for free, at least partly because the man her mother was dating had no interest in the children. The total price was two measly dollars. Assigned new names, the siblings were then used as forced labor on the acquiring couple's farm, where they were often hideously mistreated.

Although several decades have passed since then, I couldn't help but wish I could go back and alter those appalling events. So, while my characters are entirely fictional, it would be safe to say that the book in your hands was my attempt to give the children in the photo the loving and compassionate outcome that, in my heart, I felt they deserved.

READING GROUP GUIDE

1. Which character became your favorite? Your least favorite? How did your opinions of the major characters change throughout the story?

2. In the prologue, the unidentified narrator reflects upon "the interwoven paths that had delivered each of us here. Every step a domino essential to knocking over the next." After reading the book, do you agree with that view? Can you pinpoint a single decision in your own life that spurred a series of significant unforeseen effects?

3. At the Royal, Max Trevino makes a difficult decision regarding his sister. Do you agree with his choice? Do you believe he intended to stick with the plan he proposed? For readers of McMorris's novel *The Edge of Lost*, did your impression of Max Trevino differ while reading this book?

4. Early in the story, Lily carries a burden of shame and guilt regarding her son, due to societal norms and her own dark secret. Would you have felt the same in her shoes? Would you, or Lily, feel differently in present times?

5. Like many parents during the Great Depression, Geraldine Dillard faces a near-impossible choice when Alfred Millstone appears at her house with an offer. In her position, would you have made the same decision?

6. People deal with grief in various, sometimes extreme ways. How do you feel about the manner in which Sylvia Millstone and Ellis's father, Jim Reed, came to grips with the loss of a child? Do you sympathize with them equally? What are your thoughts on Alfred Millstone's choices and actions?

7. Throughout the story, Lily struggles to balance motherhood and work. Do you believe her career ambitions were solely for the sake of her son's future? If not, would she ever admit this to herself or another person? Have these considerations changed in today's society?

8. Lily and Ellis break several laws while on their mission to find and rescue Calvin. Do you agree or disagree with their actions? Would you have done anything differently in their situation?

9. In positive and/or negative ways, how do you think Ruby and Calvin were affected by the whole of their experiences in the story? How would these elements likely shape who they'd become as adults, or as parents themselves?

10. Where do you envision the characters soon after the story ends? How about five years from now?

For a special book-club kit with recipes and more,
visit KristinaMcMorris.com.

A CONVERSATION
WITH THE AUTHOR

Truth in journalism has certainly become a hot topic amid current events. Was this one of the major reasons you chose to write *Sold on a Monday*?

It was never my main purpose for writing the book, though I did realize early on that it was going to pertain to that subject area. There's obviously a poor decision made by Ellis, being a desperate but well-meaning reporter. And from there, the chief—along with thousands of readers throughout the country—formed their own view of what was captured in Ellis's photo. Specifically, the mother turning away from the camera was seen as evidence of her shame, and Sylvia even interpreted the picture as a sign from her late daughter.

I think it's really important to remember in today's world of viral posts, images, and sound bites that we all bring our own perceptions to the table. And that inevitably these are skewed by our past experiences or even an unconscious desire to see what we want to see. More than ever, quick judgments based on those snippets, and certainly pushing the moral line in reporting, too often can have devastating consequences to others—as Ellis learned the hard way.

When envisioning a newspaperman from the 1930s, most people likely picture a suited reporter hovering outside

a courtroom with a notepad or an oversize camera in hand. **Early in the story, why did you choose to make Ellis a more unconventional writer assigned to the Society page?**

I admit, it wasn't the first job I had in mind for him. (Sorry, Ellis!) To make his actions involving the second photo more understandable, though, there had to be a strong reason behind his desperation to hold on to his big break—something that went beyond paying the rent or achieving a promotion. I decided that him being stuck as a so-called "sob sister" would have provided that motivation. In that era, the "women's pages" were written almost invariably by women, supposedly in no small part because men were so averse to the job. So, it would have been a humiliating assignment for Ellis not only among the staff at the paper, but also with his father.

Interestingly enough, while researching for the book, I happened to learn about Clifford Wallace, the first male editor of the women's page at the *Toronto Star* and hence nicknamed "Nellie" (as in, yes, Nellie Bly). Apparently, after much begging, he was relieved of the job, which was then given to Gordon Sinclair, who did nearly everything he could to be fired or reassigned. This included limiting his work hours to only three hours a day and even clipping the majority of his material from other newspapers. Before a proofer discovered the latter, Sinclair actually managed to retain his job for more than a year!

Aside from the true accounts you've already mentioned, what are some of your other favorite pieces of history that are woven into the book?

The actual newspaper articles strewn throughout the story definitely intrigued me the most. A headline about a runaway bride reuniting with her groom made me smile, above all because it appeared as a prominent headline in a major paper. The same went for the piece about the couples caught with thousands of counterfeit banknotes stuffed in their mattresses. On the grimmer side, the slaying of Mickey Duffy, known as Prohibition's Mr. Big, is primarily fascinating for the fact that his notoriety managed to draw thousands of curious onlookers to his funeral.

As for my very favorite articles...I probably have two. One was the story about a séance held by a rumrunner's widow hoping to identify her husband's murderer, and the second was about the mythical floating nightclub known as the *Flying Dutchman*. (In my novel, I renamed it the *Lucky Seagull*.) During Prohibition, Sanford Jarrell, a reporter at the *Herald Tribune*, wrote a copyrighted lead story detailing his visit to the elusive speakeasy, complete with a map of its location and a menu of prices. The article and his follow-up pieces quickly became quite the sensation, so much so that authorities went on a determined hunt for the ship. But soon after, many of his claims began to fall apart, and when pressured with questions, Jarrell resigned with a note confessing that the whole story was a hoax. In a painful front-page admission, the paper ended up publishing an acknowledgment of the truth, admitting it had been deceived.

When it comes to bustling newsrooms, New York City quickly comes to mind, especially for a story that involves supper clubs, gambling halls, and mobsters. Was there a reason you chose Philadelphia as another setting over a city like, say, Chicago?

I actually used to live near Chicago and absolutely love that city. Since I'd already featured it in some of my other novels, though, I thought it would be fun to go with another setting. Years ago, I also lived near Philadelphia for a time, so I was already familiar with the area and its rich history. Plus, Pennsylvania's diversity of landscapes and livelihoods made it ideal for the story. Within a relatively short driving distance from all the activity of a big city, there are sprawling fields and farms, mining towns, and textile factories. And, of course, the presence there of major mobsters during the '30s added even more appeal.

What were some of the most helpful resources for your research?

Personal experience from growing up around a newsroom was probably the most helpful. As a kid, I was fortunate enough to host a children's weekly television show for an ABC affiliate station. We would shoot in the studio every Wednesday night, squeezed in between the two evening news programs. While waiting around during editing, I would hang out with the anchors, reporters, and sportscasters. But my favorite person was the meteorologist who let me move the clouds around on the weather map. (Hey, back then, this was very high-tech.) Later, while in college and exploring different career paths, I even had a summer internship in that same newsroom.

Of course, to gather more insight for the story, I relied on a combination of journalist friends, documentaries, and a stack of wonderful nonfiction books. Those I found the most valuable include *Skyline* by Gene Fowler, *City Editor* by Stanley Walker, *Nearly Everybody Read It: Snapshots of the Philadelphia Bulletin* edited by Peter Binzen, and *The Paper: The Life and Death of the New York Herald Tribune* by Richard Kluger.

ACKNOWLEDGMENTS

In all likelihood, the idea for this book would still be only a possibility scratching at my mind if it weren't for three dear friends in particular. For repeatedly insisting that I write about the photo that haunted me, I give enormous thanks to Stephanie Dray, and to Therese Walsh and Erika Robuck, whose "arm-chill-o-meters" are always my first crucial tests for gauging the potential of any story.

To Aimee Long, my incredible, hilarious, smart-aleck friend—how can I possibly thank you enough? From countless hours of brainstorming and plot fixing to trimming and tweaking every page of this book (many of which you surely have memorized), I could not have done this without you. If I weren't worried about keeping you humble, I'd add your name to the cover. At minimum, I owe you a fancy Bloody Mary and a pedicure with extra crystal gel.

Thank you to my mother, Linda Yoshida, for guiding my characters onto the right path and for listening to yet another whole book read aloud (yes, she really does this) while helping me buff and polish along the way. My heartfelt gratitude also goes to Tracy Callan and Shelley McFarland. Ladies, your unwavering support, love, and friendship truly mean the world.

To my wonderful agent, Elisabeth Weed, I offer my deepest

thanks for your insight, belief in my work, and vision of what's possible for both my characters' journeys and my own. And to my editor, the amazing Shana Drehs—your keen editing eye and enthusiasm for this story have been utterly invaluable. You are such a joy to work with. Sending huge thanks out to you and the rest of the Sourcebooks team for your tireless efforts in bringing this book to readers.

I often say that writing a novel is like composing a symphony. Similarly, the finished products are merely pages marked with ink until the musicians, or readers, bring them to life with their own experiences and interpretations. So, thank you, dear readers, for inviting my stories into your lives and homes and for venturing through those measures with me. And to the fabulous book champions out there, especially Jenny O'Regan and Andrea Katz, your encouragement and support are beyond measure.

On the research front, I have many people to thank for their time and generosity (any errors or creative liberties are mine alone): Portland police officer Sean McFarland for help on all things police and jail related; newspaper publisher and president Mark Garber for your feedback and enthusiasm; Claire Organ for, once more, ensuring the accuracy of my beloved Irish characters; Renee Rosen for crucial details about old-time newsrooms and photojournalism; Traci and Parker Wheeler for your horse expertise, sorting out my nickering, neighing, and more; Dr. Gordon Canzler for, yet again, allowing any injuries, illnesses, and "doc talk" to ring true; Ellen Marie Wiseman for being the first to bring breaker boys to my attention and for helping me to tell their stories right; and, of course, Terry Smoke and Neil Handy for such great input on Model Ts, radiators, and all that jazz. Neil, you are missed by so many.

Finally, above all, I'm grateful to my husband, Danny, and our sons, Tristan and Kiernan. Together, sweet boys, you are my rock. Your love and faith in me not only make everything in my life possible but, more important, give all of it meaning.

ABOUT THE AUTHOR

© Colleen Cahill Studios

Kristina McMorris is a *New York Times* and *USA Today* bestselling author. Inspired by true personal and historical accounts, her works of fiction have garnered more than twenty national literary awards and include five novels and two novellas. Prior to her writing career, she hosted weekly television shows since age nine and was named one of Portland's "40 Under 40" by the *Business Journal*. Kristina is a frequent guest speaker and workshop presenter and holds a bachelor of science degree in international marketing from Pepperdine University. She lives with her husband and two sons in Oregon.